Chasing The Great Gatsby
Freddie Welsh's Saga

Gene Pantalone

Foreword By Frank Stallone

Copyright © 2024
Gene Pantalone

eBook ISBN: 978-1-965192-33-7
Paperback ISBN: 978-1-965192-32-0
Hardback ISBN: 978-1-965192-34-4
LCCN Chasing The Great Gatsby: 2024917066

All Rights Reserved. Any unauthorized reprint or use of this material is strictly prohibited. No part of this book may be reproduced or transmitted in any form or by any means, electronic or mechanical, including photocopying, recording, or by any information storage and retrieval system without express written permission from the author.

All reasonable attempts have been made to verify the accuracy of the information provided in this publication. Nevertheless, the author assumes no responsibility for any errors and/or omissions.

Freddie Welsh

Contents

Show me a hero, and I'll write you a tragedy.

—F. Scott Fitzgerald

Foreword

By Frank Stallone

Frederick Hall Thomas, known to the world as Freddie Welsh, was born on March 5th, 1886, in the small town of Pontypridd, Wales. Though his name might not resonate with many today, Welsh was once a titan in the realm of boxing, his fame rivaling that of the greatest fighters of his era. Welsh's legacy is intertwined with legends such as Benny Leonard, Johnny Kilbane, Rocky Kansas, Battling Nelson, Ad Wolgast, Willie Ritchie, Johnny Dundee, and Abe Attell—all champions who shared the ring with him.

Freddie Welsh was a unique and enthralling fighter. While he was not known for his knockout power, his relentless energy, incessant flurries of punches, and impeccable defensive skills made him a spectacle to behold. He was visibly unmarked save for a telltale cauliflower ear, which stood as a testament to his adeptness in the ring.

Welsh was also a pioneer of health and wellness and a dedicated follower of the health guru Bernarr MacFadden. He was a vegetarian in an era when meat dominated the diet of most, and he envisioned a life of wellness beyond the ropes of the ring. Welsh's aspiration was to establish a health resort upon retiring, a dream he realized with the opening of Long Hill. Known for his affable and kind nature, Freddie was beloved by many. However, like many athletes, his acumen in the ring did not translate to business. The failure of Long Hill marked the beginning of a troubling decline.

Despite being a lifelong teetotaler, Welsh turned to alcohol, a change that precipitated the departure of his wife, Fanny, along with their children. This personal loss struck a devastating blow to his spirit and well-being.

In this meticulously crafted book, Gene Pantalone breathes new life into the story of Freddie Welsh, capturing the essence of a man and the vibrant, tumultuous world of early 20th-century boxing and the possibilities of how F. Scott Fitzgerald used him as his inspiration for *The Great Gatsby*. Pantalone's extraordinary attention to detail provides not just a biography of Welsh but a vivid tableau of the era he inhabited. Through these pages, the remarkable yet poignant journey of Freddie Welsh is brought into sharp focus, ensuring that his contributions to the sport and his personal struggles are remembered and appreciated anew.

This account is more than just a chronicle of Freddie Welsh's exploits. It is also a journey into the fascinating intersection of the lives of two individuals, one real and one fictional, who, in their own ways, left indelible marks on the tapestry of Twentieth-Century American culture. Welsh's interactions with F. Scott Fitzgerald, the renowned author of *The Great Gatsby*, are explored as the story delves into their relationship, unearthing the intriguing parallels between Freddie Welsh and Jay Gatsby, the enigmatic protagonist of Fitzgerald's timeless novel.

Embarking on this exploration, you will not only witness the rise of a boxing legend but also the confluence of two distinct worlds—the gritty, unforgiving arena of pugilism and the glitzy, decadent world of the Roaring Twenties. Together, these stories provide a unique lens through which you can understand the enigmatic figures that populate the pages of history and literature.

Within the pages of Fitzgerald's iconic novel, an enigmatic character named Jay Gatsby takes center stage, embodying the quintessence of the American Dream and the insurmountable desire for love and acceptance. But behind the creation of this captivating protagonist lies a lesser-known figure, Freddie Welsh, whose life and experiences, to many, served as the key inspiration for Fitzgerald's creation.

This book embarks on a captivating journey, delving deep into the facts that connect the brilliant boxer Freddie Welsh and F. Scott Fitzgerald's immortal work. Chapters begin with a quote, mostly by F. Scott Fitzgerald, paying homage to the literary genius while setting the stage for the exploration that follows. While most chapters draw upon the rich tapestry of *The Great Gatsby*, others reach into the vast depths of Fitzgerald's other literary realms, uncovering hidden parallels of inspiration.

However, this is not a book of direct references or overt connections. Rather, it invites the reader to embark on a treasure hunt of the mind, seeking the subtle threads that weave together the quotes and the text. It is through the reader's perception and observation that the true significance of these chapters unfolds—an interpretation where the quotes illuminate the text, and the text breathes life into the quotes.

Within these pages, the story of the boxer Freddie Welsh and his profound influence on F. Scott Fitzgerald's creative spirit unfolds—a tale of ambition, excess, and the ever-elusive quest for fulfillment. Prepare to embark on a literary odyssey of Freddie Welsh that continues to resonate within the pages of *The Great Gatsby* and beyond, where history and fiction converge, inviting you to traverse the realms of imagination and discover the intricate bonds between a real-life inspiration and the literary legacy that emerged from his influence.

This is a testament to the complex journey of a man who embodied the essence of resilience and the tumultuous nature of fame and fortune. As the narrative unravels the life and times of Freddie Welsh, it is hoped that you are compelled to ponder the perplexity of his existence, a remarkable tale that continues to captivate and mystify us even today.

In the annals of sports history, the name Freddie Welsh looms large as a beacon of boxing excellence. His boxing career, marked by remarkable victories and a relentless pursuit of greatness, has been celebrated and admired by pugilism enthusiasts for generations. This life story seeks to shed light on the life, struggles, and triumphs of a man whose journey through the world of boxing was nothing short of extraordinary.

In the tumultuous era of the early Twentieth Century, when the world seemed caught in the clutches of change, one man emerged from the shadows of obscurity to carve his name into the annals of history. Freddie Welsh, a name known to few but a legend to many, led a life marked by contradictions, courage, and resilience.

This book takes you on a journey through the life of Freddie Welsh, a man of paradoxes, a pugilistic virtuoso whose clenched knuckles swayed in rhythmic cadence, confounding his foes. But before the grandeur, there was a place in Wales—a coal-mining town where he came of age, where dreams were forged, and destiny beckoned.

With an audacious spirit and a yearning for more, Freddie set his sights on the promise of America. In the land of opportunity, he took on odd jobs and gradually ascended the ranks of boxing. Yet, it was the world lightweight title bout, which he won, that would forever etch his name into the annals of boxing history. But even as he basked in the glory of his triumph, dark clouds loomed on the horizon.

In the dark realm of pugilism, this narrative shall embark on a journey through the murkier underbelly of the sweet science. Here, concealed within the clandestine corners of the fight game, one encounters the sordid specters of bout-fixing and the looming figures of organized crime.

The pages that follow will take you on a journey through the life of Freddie Welsh, a man who dared to dream and reach for the stars, even when those stars seemed just beyond his grasp. It's a tale of a man who, in his pursuit of greatness, found himself entangled in the complex web of both the boxing world and the shadows that lurked just beyond the spotlight. The chronicle will delve into the life of Freddie Welsh, a legend who left an indelible mark on the world of sports and is forever remembered for his audacious spirit and unyielding determination.

Finally, in the world of literature, discussions about structure and sequence are as old as storytelling itself. Readers and scholars often ponder the significance of the order in which narratives unfold, debating whether certain chapters or segments should be rearranged or even omitted altogether. Such debates have been no less fervent in the realm of our story.

Chapter XVIII could be a subject of contention among readers and critics, and some might go so far as to argue that it disrupts the seamless flow of the narrative. It's a point that is acknowledged, and yet, it is the belief that this particular chapter remains a crucial and integral part of the tale that is wished to be told. The connection between Jay Gatsby and Freddie Welsh, as revealed in Chapter XVIII, provides a unique and compelling perspective that enriches the narrative as a whole.

A choice is offered to cater to the diverse interests of readers. For those who seek a singular focus on the world of boxing and its intrigue, you have the option to skip Chapter XVIII without losing the essence of the story. However, if you harbor a curiosity about the intricate web connecting Jay Gatsby and Freddie Welsh, you are encouraged to consider reading Chapter XVIII before delving into the opening chapters. It's the hope that this choice will enhance your reading experience and allow you to engage with the narrative in a way that resonates most deeply with your interests and curiosity.

In the end, it is you, the reader, who guides the narrative's course through your own choices. It is hoped you enjoy the journey, whether you decide to explore Chapter XVIII immediately or save it for later.

Acknowledgments

Over the great bridge, with the sunlight through the girders making a constant flicker upon the moving cars, with the city rising up across the river in white heaps and sugar lumps all built with a wish out of non-olfactory money. The city seen from the Queensboro Bridge is always the city seen for the first time, in its first wild promise of all the mystery and the beauty in the world.

— F. Scott Fitzgerald, *The Great Gatsby*

In the lower portion of the cover, an image unfurls, a photograph captured by Jack Boucher in the days of 1970. The image, now nestled within the archives of the Prints & Photographs Division at the Library of Congress, was born of a United States government program dedicated to the Historic American Engineering Record. It presents a tableau that speaks to the soul of New York: the Queensboro Bridge, a timeless sentinel stretching across the East River and Blackwell's Island, with the distant silhouette of uptown Manhattan as its steadfast companion.

Though the era it portrays is not that of our story, and the skyline may have shifted, the bridge itself stands unwavering. It is a beacon of constancy, a thread of continuity woven through the ever-changing tapestry of the city. In its enduring presence, one finds a whisper of the eternal, a reminder that amidst the flux of time and the ephemeral nature of human endeavor, there are still monuments that defy the march of years.

I would like to express my deepest gratitude to the numerous institutions and individuals who played a crucial role in the creation of this work. Their invaluable contributions and unwavering support have been instrumental in bringing this endeavor to fruition.

First and foremost, I am immensely grateful to the New Jersey Boxing Hall of Fame for bestowing upon me the honor of being inducted as a writer and historian. Also, I am indebted to the Chatham Township Historical Society and the Summit Historical Society for generously supplying me with vital material. Their commitment to preserving historical records and their willingness to share their resources have significantly enriched the content of this book. I would also like to extend my appreciation to the dedicated staff at the Library of Congress, whose diligent efforts in assisting me and guiding me toward the right sources have been immensely valuable.

Furthermore, I would like to express my gratitude to the National Library of Wales for their prompt and informative responses to my inquiries, which proved vital in the research process. I am also indebted to the University of South Carolina for granting me access to the invaluable collection of Matthew Bruccoli's emails pertaining to Freddie Welsh. These correspondences shed new light on the subject matter, and I am truly grateful for the opportunity to study them.

I am deeply thankful to the creators and maintainers of various newspaper search engines, including newspapers.com, the California Digital Newspaper Collection, loc.gov, and newspaperarchives.com. These invaluable online resources formed the backbone of my research, providing me with a wealth of historical information. Additionally, I would like to acknowledge the Smithsonian Institute, the F. Scott Fitzgerald Papers from 1897-1944 at the Princeton University Library, Buffalo & Erie County Public Library Rare Book Room, Google Newspapers, BoxRec, Cyber Boxing Zone, International Jewish Sports Hall of Fame, London Times, Brooklyn Public Library, wn.com, and Babylon Wales for their comprehensive databases and archives that proved indispensable in gathering the necessary data.

In the culmination of this literary endeavor, I am acutely aware that there may exist an unfortunate oversight—an omission of a crucial individual or organization that played an indispensable role in the realization of this creation. Nonetheless, it would be an important disservice on my part if I were to overlook the paramount force behind it all: my family. Their unwavering support, boundless encouragement, and enduring belief in me have breathed life into every aspiration I have pursued. Without their profound influence, nothing I have achieved thus far, including the existence of this book, would have been remotely conceivable. Their significance in my journey surpasses mere words, yet I endeavor to express my deepest gratitude to each and every member of my family for their immeasurable contributions.

To all the individuals and organizations mentioned above, your contributions have played an integral role in shaping the narrative of this book. I am immensely grateful for your assistance, which has made this project possible.

Introduction

The story that is Freddie Welsh casts a light on one of the most important literary creations of the Twentieth Century and concludes that Freddie Welsh was, in large part, the real Great Gatsby. Could F. Scott Fitzgerald's Jay Gatsby really have been a former champion boxer living in the township of Chatham, New Jersey? The proposed notion was first considered in the works by authors Richard Holt, who alluded to the connection in his 1990 book *Sport and the Working Class in Modern Britain,* and Andrew Gallimore in his 2006 book *Occupation: Prizefighter / The Freddie Welsh Story.* The idea that a man of such grandeur and mystique, such as Jay Gatsby, could have been modeled on a prizefighter is both intriguing and alluring. A concept that, like the fictional man himself, is both complex and elusive, leaving one to ponder its possibilities.

The preponderance of the evidence, though circumstantial, is quite abundant. It paints a picture of Freddie Welsh as the very embodiment of Fitzgerald's creation. Inevitable parallels are found between Jay Gatsby and the real-life Freddie Welsh, their common threads binding fiction and reality ever tighter. The resemblance, unmistakable and compelling, draws forth a union between the realms of make-believe and tangible existence. Such remarkable similarities serve as the manifestation of this captivating comparison.

In that illustrious novel, *The Great Gatsby,* a narrative spun through the tapestry of the Roaring Twenties,

Gatsby's former love interest, Daisy Buchanan, finds herself at the helm of his motorcar when tragedy unfurls its cruel hand, taking the life of a woman named Myrtle Wilson. A similar, though remarkably lesser-known incident dances in the shadows of history, one where Freddie Welsh, a figure of our own Jazz Age, becomes entwined in an automobile mishap that leaves a young society woman, Myrtle Wilson, by name, nursing her injuries. It's crucial to note that this incident preceded the pages of Fitzgerald's literary masterpiece.

Gentlemen of their era, Welsh and Gatsby, men of humble origins, decided to cast off the shackles of their birthright. They reinvented themselves, shedding their birth names, and set forth upon the meandering path toward wealth and prominence. The domains in which Freddie Welsh and Jay Gatsby resided, though separated by geography, bear a resemblance so vivid that it beckons imagination to merge them. Both men possessed extensive libraries, those repositories of knowledge and escape. Both reveled in the extravagant parties they hosted and their opulence. F. Scott Fitzgerald himself paid a visit to Welsh's grand estate—where the mansion and grounds where Freddie Welsh and Jay Gatsby lived are descriptively alike if one could imagine them in different locations—before embarking for Europe to conclude the tale of Gatsby and his restless quest for the unattainable.

At the tender age of sixteen, both Gatsby and Welsh left their familial hearths. Gatsby, hailing from the windswept Dakotas, emerged from a lineage of farmers. Freddie Welsh toiled in those same wheat fields before taking his first steps onto the fistic stage that would spell fortune and fame. Both roamed the Great Lakes and Minnesota regions, seeking their fortunes before wealth became their constant companion. An unrelenting fervor for self-improvement coursed through their veins, expressed in their devotion to rigorous exercise and unceasing study. World War I, a tempestuous chapter in history's annals, found both men donning the uniform of officers. Jay Gatsby was promoted to first lieutenant and then major and decorated overseas. Freddie Welsh was promoted to first lieutenant, then captain, and recommended four times to the rank of major and held many high positions of distinction in the states.

Prohibition, that mischievous epoch of clandestine revelry, cast its shadow over them both, each under the shadow of suspicion as purveyors of illicit libations. To round out the parallels, the visage of organized crime hovered near them, casting doubt upon their reputations, like specters of an era enamored with the shadowy allure of hidden dealings.

Indeed, Freddie Welsh and Jay Gatsby, two lives seemingly disparate, find themselves enmeshed in shared experiences and curious parallels, a testament to the strange symmetry of fate in the glittering tumult of the Roaring Twenties.

Freddie Welsh, also a name that once resonated through the boxing world of years past, was a man who donned the shimmering crown of the world lightweight boxing champion. In a forgotten corner of the annals of sporting history, his life unfolds as a portrait of contradictions and enigmas, a tale concealed in the sepia pages of time, little known and even less understood.

Welsh, a character of infinite complexities, was perpetually veiled in the shadows of misunderstanding, for his existence was a tumultuous dance of high-stakes adventure, where each stride forward was an invitation to fate's brutal embrace. Yet, what is endeavored to unveil here is a chronicle of one man's reckoning with the capricious whims of outrageous fortune and the treacherous abysses that accompany it, a testament to the indomitable spirit of a man painted against a vivid canvas of an era marked by extravagance and disillusionment.

Welsh, an aficionado of defensive pugilism, possessed a mastery of the sweet science that was nothing short of remarkable. His poise within the squared circle was unwavering, a tranquil oasis amidst the tempest of combat. To his adversaries, particularly those who clung to brute force and unrestrained aggression, his elusiveness proved a vexing conundrum. Eagerly, he embraced the chance to dance with a brawling foe, harboring boundless confidence in his ability to outwit and outmaneuver, even stooping to employ a few clandestine stratagems of his own.

As a tactician, Welsh was a cunning counterpuncher, a maestro in the art of feints and artful body shifts, coaxing his foes into missteps with the grace of a seasoned con artist. Yet, amidst his repertoire of skills, one particular weapon gleamed as his most important, remarkable feature—the jab. In the annals of pugilistic history, his mastery of this fundamental punch was found to have no equal. His every movement, his every nuance of rhythm, served as an elegant testament to the dance of fistic grace that was Freddie Welsh.

Welsh's most fruitful years were spent in the ruthless ring of the United States, tirelessly pursuing the coveted title of world lightweight champion, a crown that had adorned the heads of pugilistic luminaries before him such as Battling Nelson, Ad Wolgast, and Willie Ritchie. Upon returning to Europe, Freddie Welsh conquered not one but two prestigious titles—the EBU European lightweight title and the British lightweight title.

The relentless passage of time finally smiled upon Welsh, affording him the opportunity to vie for the ultimate laurels of the pugilistic realm in 1914. His adversary in this historic contest was the reigning champion, the sun-kissed son of California, Willie Ritchie.

It was a curious twist of fate that saw the battleground transplanted from American shores to the grandeur of London. Over the course of a grueling and mesmerizing encounter that stretched across twenty epic rounds, Welsh displayed his fistic prowess in a manner that transcended mere sport, ultimately prevailing in a battle of skill and will. Thus, it was with a triumphant flourish against Ritchie that he was anointed as the world's lightweight champion.

However, his victory, to some, was marked by the appearance of the involvement of organized crime figures. Amongst them, none cast a more sinister pall than the enigmatic Arnold Rothstein, forever enshrouded in the ignominy of the 1919 Black Sox scandal. But even Freddie Welsh, for all its glory and valor, could not remain unscathed by the treacherous tendrils of these sordid affairs, even hearing whispers of his fights being associated with Rothstein.

Upon his return to America, Welsh, a man of clever

insight, eschewed unnecessary risks that might see his hard-won laurels slipping through his gloved fingers. With the pragmatic approach that typified the era, he opted for bouts that bore no official decision, ensuring that his championship could only be pried from his grasp by the hand of fate or, more precisely, by a knockout blow. Though purists may have deemed this strategy less than gallant, it proved to be a lucrative gambit. In an age where cunning often outweighed pure athleticism, Welsh's decision was a masterstroke that solidified his place in the annals of pugilistic history and added to the lining of his pockets.

Welsh, a man of cunning wit, held court both within and beyond the squared circle, navigating the treacherous tides of the pugilistic business with sharpness. He possessed a talent for deftly securing the most lucrative of purses for his fistic contests, a veritable whizz in the art of the deal. Yet, an improbable spectacle unfolded in the year 1917, when Welsh engaged in his third bout with the formidable Benny Leonard.

At that juncture, Freddie had gracefully weathered thirty-one years on this earth, a time-worn existence that amounted to a decade's concession to his adversary, the venerable Leonard. It was a contest where age and the fiery spirit of youthfulness met their inevitable reckoning, as Leonard, like a wily reaper, vanquished Welsh in nine rounds to seize the coveted mantle of world lightweight champion.

As the years passed, and Freddie Welsh neared the end of his storied ring career, he sought solace on a hilltop estate, where he aspired to create a haven of health and wealth for the elite. But life, as it often does, took unpredictable turns. The man who had once been an epitome of vitality and virility found himself on a path that led to destinations unimagined.

Welsh, once the embodiment of pugilistic prowess, continued to wage battle sporadically until the twilight of 1922, yet he was but a fading specter of his former self, a poignant reminder of the fleeting brilliance that graced his bygone days in the ring, as he clung to the hope of regaining his fistic glory.

Following his relinquishment of the title, Welsh enlisted in the ranks of the army during the harrowing days of the Great War, though he never did face the crucible of combat on those blood-soaked European battlefields. Instead, he found himself amidst the mending souls and shattered bodies of Walter Reed Hospital, where his ascent from a humble private to a commanding captain bore the emblem of his remarkable character.

Upon bidding farewell to the prizefighting world, he embarked upon an altogether different odyssey, opening a gymnasium that beckoned to the aspirants of physical prowess, steering the destinies of pugilists, and holding forth upon the enigmatic doctrine of physical education. Amidst it all, Welsh's exuberance and enthusiasm brought life to the health farm he operated, a sanctuary where the weary and the worn could find reprieve from the clamor of the outside world. He found himself ensnared by the alluring allure of Bernarr MacFadden's physical gospel. Welsh devoutly embraced his precepts of exercise and wholesome living, ensconcing himself in a world of wellness and vitality.

A fervent disciple of temperance, he proudly donned

the mantle of a non-smoker and non-drinker, and he mostly spurned the consumption of meat. Yet, beneath this façade of this righteousness, a clandestine existence lay shrouded in secrecy. In the dimly lit corners of his world, he surrendered to the seductive charms of vice, relishing the forbidden fruits of smoke and spirits that he dared not reveal to the world. Such was the enigma of Freddie Welsh, the Welshman who wore his contradictions like a masquerade mask, concealing his true self beneath the veneer of virtuous living.

Welsh, who became a man of opulent means, found himself immersed in the extravagant world of high society, rubbing shoulders with the famous in the most cosmopolitan metropolises on the planet. His charisma, infamy, and impeccable etiquette allowed him to revel in a life of sheer extravagance, hobnobbing with thespians and artists alike. Yet this grandiose existence, even for those possessed of substantial wealth, proved a precarious endeavor to sustain. With Freddie's twilight as a pugilist came the waning of his fortune, the disintegration of his familial ties, and the deterioration of his well-being, all casualties of imprudent business ventures.

In the midst of eighty-six officially sanctioned fistic bouts, a mere quintet emerged victorious against him, and only once, a solitary instance, did he taste the bitter sting of defeat by stoppage; it was none other than Benny Leonard, a name whispered reverently as perhaps the finest lightweight pugilist to ever lace up the mitts. If one were to include the skirmishes of ink and paper, where only the scribes and their scrolls decided the victor, his fistic forays totaled no fewer than 168.

Esteemed scribes of the sweet science, the likes of

Nat Fleischer, found him worthy of the lofty perch at number four in the annals of all-time lightweights, while Charley Rose penned his name at number five, and Herb Goldman afforded him the honor of the ninth rank. Freddie Welsh, the luminary of the ring, found his hallowed place in the Ring Boxing Hall of Fame in the year 1960, and, in a subsequent tribute to his pugilistic prowess, the International Boxing Hall of Fame opened its venerable gates to him in 1997.

Chapter I

His dream must have seemed so close that he could hardly fail to grasp it. He did not know that it was already behind him, somewhere back in the vast obscurity beyond the city, where the dark fields of the republic rolled on under the night.

—F. Scott Fitzgerald, *The Great Gatsby*

I don't believe there ever was a champion who lived quite so full a life as myself, tasted both the bitter and the sweet, sampled more profusely both poverty and prosperity or had so intimate and wide acquaintances with all kinds, types, and classes of persons. I have studied human nature in all its moods, drank everything in the cup of life, from the dregs at the bottom to the froth at the top, and I'm glad of it all.

—Freddie Welsh[1]

In the world of pugilism, where brawn often reigns supreme, there existed a rare and remarkable figure—a boxer whose fists were as formidable as his intellect. This gentleman of the ring was no mere brute but a man of keen wit and sharp insight, whose mental agility was matched only by his physical prowess. Yet it was outside the ring where his true brilliance shone, for he was like a scholar and a philosopher, a man who could discourse on the great questions of life with the same ease that he dispatched his opponents. In him can be seen the convergence of two worlds, the sweet science of boxing and the lofty realm of the mind, a rare and captivating contrast that left one in awe.

Freddie Welsh was a boxer of legend, a true champion of the ring. His fists were like lightning, striking with power and the precision of a master craftsman. He moved with grace, dodging and weaving with fluidity, his nimble footwork and lightning-fast jabs a testament to his athletic ability. It left opponents reeling in confusion. In the ring, he was cold and unyielding, burning with a fierce intensity. As he stepped away from the arena, his demeanor softened, revealing a heart brimming with generosity and a mind teeming with intellectual competency.

Freddie was a man of contradictions, both brutal and beautiful, both scorned and admired, a paradoxical figure that confounded those who thought they had him figured out. He was a pugilistic virtuoso, a pummeling poet with fists of fury and a keen intellect. His duality was evident in every aspect of his being, an amalgamation of the vicious and the benevolent. Despite his many facets, there was a certain something that set him apart from the rest: a personality that drew people to him. Freddie was the quintessential golden boy, the very embodiment of the type of man that F. Scott Fitzgerald would have immortalized in his prose. But even as he basked in the glow of success and fame, there remained an insatiable hunger within him, a yearning for something more, as if he knew deep down that even his greatest victories could never truly fulfill him.

On one particular occasion, Freddie put down his gloves for a moment, fixated instead on the matter of a potential purchase and the opening of a health retreat—the fulfillment of his dream—tailored to serve the needs of the affluent masses. The search seemed interminable and had spanned coasts from west to east until it finally brought him to the doorstep of a palatial mansion in an idyllic town. With every penny earned from his hard-fought battles, he endeavored to make this grand property his own.

It was in the days of March 1917, near the ides, when Freddie, the champion of the lightweight pugilistic ring, made his way to Chatham Township, a pastoral haven in New Jersey. A dream, long nourished in his heart, had brought him to this tranquil setting. A dream, fueled by the words of his friend and mentor Elbert Hubbard, that had simmered in the recesses of his mind for a long time—the establishment of a sanctuary of health and wellness, a health farm retreat.

The dream of Freddie, borne from the vision of his companion Elbert Hubbard, was a glorious one indeed. His purpose was singular, and it consumed him. He was here to acquire a grand stately mansion that sprawled over an expanse of 162 acres of rolling hills and verdant valleys, a place that would become the cradle of his dreams. A place where he could breathe life into his vision.

Elbert Hubbard was unable to accompany his friend on this odyssey, a journey that Hubbard had predicted would come to pass. Freddie would have to embark on their shared aspiration alone. It was just two years prior when Hubbard himself set sail on the RMS *Lusitania*, destined for an eternal voyage. Hubbard would be swallowed by the sea along with the RMS *Lusitanian*. He and his wife were amongst the 1,198 passengers and crew who perished when a German U-boat mercilessly torpedoed her on the afternoon of May 7, 1915, just eleven miles off the southern coast of Ireland, deep in the war zone of World War I.

In the wake of his untimely departure, the Roycrofters, a movement Hubbard founded, with their masterful craftsmanship, diligently inked the pages of a book entitled *In Memorandum*. Within its bound sanctuary, a chorus of three hundred-plus souls sought solace in the eloquent artistry of words, fervently professing their affection for the man they had tragically relinquished. Amidst this heartfelt congregation, Freddie, forever burdened with the weight of loss, found solace in his own contribution to this literary requiem, a tender tribute to the departed soul he held so dear. He wrote:

"During the thirteen years I was familiar with Elbert Hubbard and his writings, I grew to love more and more the bigness, wholesomeness, kindness and courage of the man. In our strolls through the woods at East Aurora, and when he would visit me in New York City, he would relate many good stories, and he had that in his nature which enabled him to laugh when the joke was on him. He stood for everything that was clean, natural and beautiful. He lived the simple but strenuous life. He worked hard mentally, and kept himself physically fit because he understood the value of exercising the body.

"He had more working energy than any other man I ever met. He always found time for exercise and sport, whether it was hiking over the hills, wood-chopping, horseback-riding or baseball. He would discuss the boxing situation with me with the enthusiasm of a fan, and he wound up one of his last letters to me by writing, 'So here are love and blessings to all good sports, and if there is no squared circle (boxing-ring) in hell, you and I will arrange one.'

"We loved him because he loved every man, woman and child of us. If animals and birds could speak they would sing his praises, for he loved them too.

"I feel that not only have I lost a friend and The Roycrofters their leader, but the whole world lost a friend and leader when the sage of East Aurora was taken away."[2]

However, Hubbard's words were left to live on. His utterances lingered on in Freddie. Despite the passage of time, his words continued to strike a chord within him. The unique Elbert Hubbard, a deft wordsmith and purveyor of provocative wisdom, had left behind a veritable treasure trove of papers—papers that spoke of people, papers that spoke of life. One particular folder, marked with the name of "Freddie Welsh," contained a cache of notes and letters that Hubbard had penned with his own hand. Amongst the pages were banters filled with mirth and merriment, but also, there were a few missives that affirmed what only a little while before Hubbard perished, that he was advising, urging Freddie to assume the mantle of the official trainer to Mr. Overworked American.

"As for serious fighting," one of Hubbard's letters stated," I foresee that you are going to cut that out. The average fighter, when he retires, does so with a very black eye, and then he starts a saloon. You are not an average fighter because you are not an average man. You ought to be better at fifty than you are now and I believe you will be. You are a man of common sense. The plan is this—*The Fred Welsh Health Farm*."[3]

Freddie with Elbert Hubbard.

Hubbard founded Roycroft in 1895, which was in a quaint village nestled in the heart of East Aurora, New York, a town less than twenty miles outside of Buffalo. This utopia was home to a collection of skilled craftspeople and brilliant artists, collectively referred to as Roycrofters. They stood as proud ambassadors of the famed Arts and Crafts movement, their tireless efforts and steadfast beliefs inspiring an entire generation of American architects and designers. Their labors and philosophy, known as the Roycroft movement, breathed life into the burgeoning world of American architecture and design, leaving an indelible mark on the early Twentieth Century. The Roycroft movement was supposed to be illuminating the path toward a brighter tomorrow.

Harry Pollock, who was managing Freddie, wrote the following letter from New York, which referenced Roycroft:

"Sporting Editor *San Francisco Call*— Dear Sir: Freddie Welsh of Cardiff, Wales, the world's lightweight champion, is going to sail for New York on March 22. He has received a vaudeville offer of $9,000 to put in six weeks showing the paces of a 'world's champion' to an admiring public.

"Since leaving America last summer, Welsh has accomplished wonders in the fistic line. Tuned up to his old form of cleverness, speed and endurance by three months of hard work on Roycroft Farm, the home of Elbert Hubbard, the noted philosopher, at East Aurora, N. Y., Welsh returned to England, and the first shot out of the box won back his title from Matt Wells. Then he took the Australian championship away from Hughey Mehegan, who had landed in England touted as a copper riveted wonder.

"As Welsh already had Willie Ritchie's scalp tucked away in his belt, he is certainly entitled to the big three sheet toplined, 'World's Champion.'

"He has been going right down the line since the Mehegan muss and taken first money in many battles. Only last week he grabbed three victories in seven days. Friday night he beat "Young" Nipper; Monday night, Vittet, the pride of the French lightweights, and on Thursday night, Eddie Beattie, one of England's best.

"Welsh was dickering for a match with "Young Philadelphia" Jack O'Brien to take place in Liverpool the last of the month, but the club only wanted to give a purse of

$7,500 and Fred wanted that much for his end.

"O'Brien went to England a couple of weeks ago, but according to big brother Jack, expects to return to America in a month's time, and if he can make the weight and suitable inducements are offered, Welsh may meet him here later on. After Welsh finishes his vaudeville engagement, he will take a trip to the coast and look the situation over in San Francisco and Los Angeles. Yours very truly,

"HARRY POLLOK.

"Manager of Fred Welsh."[4]

Elbert Hubbard, ever the gracious host, extended multiple invitations to Freddie, who, more often than not, would accept with great pleasure. In Hubbard's esteemed eyes, Freddie was a true Roycrofter-at-large—an athlete of unmatched excellence and a gentleman of the highest order. Hubbard wrote about Freddie, "Athlete *superbus* and gentleman magnus."[5]

Freddie often contributed to Elbert Hubbard's periodical called *The Fra*, a moniker Hubbard went by, which was published by Roycroft. Freddie once wrote in *The Fra*:

"I trained at Roycroft, in the Roycroft way, and won the world's lightweight championship over Willie Ritchie."[6]

The sprawling Roycroft estate became Freddie's temporary home for weeks at a time, where he would diligently train for his upcoming bouts. Freddie would impart his expertise in exercise to the youth through long walks, handball matches, bag punching, and sparring sessions. Come nightfall, Hubbard and Freddie would engage in intellectual sparring matches that were worth their weight in gold, leaving the enraptured crowd breathless with awe. When Freddie was in town, there wasn't a soul who would dare to miss the show.

Elbert Hubbard was a master of the written word, an eloquent orator, and a shrewd businessperson of the highest order. Freddie, on the other hand, was a pugilistic virtuoso, a true artist in the violent art of boxing, whose glory was counted in the bruises and broken noses of his vanquished foes. At first glance, these two men could not be more unlike one another, and yet, appearances can often be deceiving. Beneath the surface, a profound similarity could be found, for both Hubbard and Freddie were driven by an unquenchable thirst for success, a hunger that burned deep within, a flame that, in appearance, could never be snuffed out. In the end, it was this shared passion that made them brothers, despite all their apparent differences.

Hubbard would joke, "…Freddie is the lightweight champion fighter of the world, and I am the heavyweight champion writer of the world!"[7]

The two gentlemen were kindred in spirit, united by a common love for the great outdoors. They were fervent proponents of physical vigor, preaching the importance of respect for the body and regular exercise. Both believed that a sound mind could only reside in a sound body. Together, they endeavored to establish a comprehensive regimen for wholesome living. The philosopher, Hubbard, was a sage of thirty years Freddie's senior, and both were seeking answers to the mysteries of life.

As Freddie arrived in Chatham Township, the world lay spread out before him like a vast expanse, as if the entire universe was at his feet, begging to be explored. The endless possibilities of life all awaited his arrival. The careful planning and unrelenting hard work that had propelled him to this moment were evident in every muscle of his powerful frame. With unique physical abilities that set him apart from his competitors, he had reigned supreme as the lightweight boxing champion of the world for nearly three glorious years.

During his time as champion, Freddie had amassed a fortune that would have left many a man dizzy with delight. For in those days, $300,000[8] was a sum that could buy a man a ticket to anywhere or at least give him the illusion of such a journey. But now, as Freddie gazed out, it was a given fact that his reign as boxing's lightweight king couldn't last forever. For in the ring, he was set to face a challenger he had faced before with difficulty—Benny Leonard.

Freddie Welsh, as he was known, had not always carried such a moniker. His birth name, that of Fredrick Hall Thomas, spoke of humble beginnings that would prove a stark contrast to the riches, notoriety, and esteemed companions he would acquire. It was under another name that he built his empire, that of the Welsh Wizard, a title befitting a boxing phenom who captured the hearts and adoration of fans across the land. The Wizard was a name that would resonate through the boxing circles, and Freddie would forever be remembered as the one who embodied its mystique.

Chapter II

Contemporary legends such as the 'underground pipe-line to Canada' attached themselves to him, and there was one persistent story that he didn't live in a house at all, but in a boat that looked like a house and was moved secretly up and down the Long Island shore. Just why these inventions were a source of satisfaction to James Gatz of North Dakota, isn't easy to say…

For over a year he had been beating his way along the south shore of Lake Superior as a clam digger and a salmon fisher or in any other capacity that brought him food and bed. His brown, hardening body lived naturally through the half fierce, half lazy work of the bracing days…

An instinct toward his future glory had led him, some months before, to the small Lutheran college of St. Olaf in southern Minnesota. He stayed there two weeks, dismayed at its ferocious indifference to the drums of his destiny, to destiny itself, and despising the janitor's work with which he was to pay his way through. Then he drifted back to Lake Superior, and he was still searching for something to do on the day that Dan Cody's yacht dropped anchor in the shallows along shore.

—F. Scott Fitzgerald, *The Great Gatsby*

The Welsh Wizard had etched his name in the records of fame and fortune, but the ascent to such great heights was wrought with the sweat and blood of a pugilist. The public may have been privy to the Wizard's exploits through the pages of newspapers, but they could not grasp the depth of his intellect, obscured as it was by the brutality of the old sport. The wealth that he had amassed was not the sort of inheritance that his high-society companions had been blessed with; it was a hard-earned fortune that had been battled for and won with every fiber of his being.

In Pontypridd, Wales, United Kingdom, Freddie first drew breath on the fifth of March in the year of 1886. He was not born into the lap of luxury, fortune, and acclaim was not his from birth, nor did he hail from a family of high esteem. Pontypridd was a place where the common folk were entrenched in the blue-collar grind of the coal mines and steel factories that fueled and kept the wheels of industry turning. It was a town of strivers and strugglers, a place where the simple pleasures of life were hard-won, and the pursuit of greatness seemed a distant dream.

Freddie toiled and labored to carve his own path in this world. From his youth, he was plagued with a malady that stifled his breath, and so he turned to the rigorous pursuit of physical fitness. This affliction, this hindrance, did fuel a passion within him, an insatiable desire for strength and vigor. He did not yield to his infirmity; he fought back with vigor and zeal, striding forth upon long walks and crafting a regimen of exercise and healthy eating. The passion consumed him whole, guiding him to forge a life of unyielding discipline. No obstacle could halt his ascent as he trampled his infirmities with purposeful strides. With unwavering commitment, he hardened his body into a bastion of strength sculpted by the tools of nature.

Freddie's mother, Elizabeth Thomas, born Elizabeth Hall, hailing from the town of Merthyr, her roots deeply embedded in the hospitality trade, her kinfolk proud custodians of a hotel. Alongside Elizabeth, Freddie's family included two younger siblings, a brother bearing the name Arthur Stanley and a sister named Edith Kate. Yet, a pervasive absence loomed in the shadows of their domestic household, as Freddie's father, John Thomas, found solace in a perpetually wandering path, rarely tethered to the confines of their home. In his youth, Freddie's father worked as an auctioneer, not the usual advocation for someone from Pontypridd.

Only a few months had waned since Freddie's arrival in this world when his persuasive mother managed to cajole her spouse into procuring the Bridge Inn Hotel, thus prompting a familial exodus to that establishment. Such was the life in the Welsh abode until young Freddie reached the tender age of ten, a precipice from which he gazed upon a precipitous deficit with the loss of his paternal guidance to the clutches of death.

Freddie's mother, confronted with the solitary task of administering the hotel, dispatched Edith Kate and Arthur Stanley to the comforting embrace of a distant aunt dwelling in Merthyr. Meanwhile, Freddie found himself entrusted to the guardianship of his maternal grandfather, nestled in the confines of Radyr. A year of longing and nostalgia elapsed, tugging at Freddie's youthful heartstrings, leading him on a pensive pilgrimage back to his ancestral domicile in Pontypridd. In due course, his mother entered into a marital union with Richard Williams, an innkeeper hailing from the domain of Aberdare, setting the stage for a new chapter in young Freddie's tempestuous odyssey.[1]

The family had enough money that enabled them to

secure the means to dispatch Freddie to Long Ashford, a prestigious boarding school in the vicinity of Bristol. The institution boasted a distinguished roster of graduates, including the venerable Lord Roberts [a British Victorian-era general who became one of the most successful British military commanders of his time,] the beloved "Bobs" of Tommy Atkins [a universal name which was given to British soldiers,] Dr. Grace, the famous cricketer, and a host of other luminaries. It was in this establishment that Freddie from Wales was afforded the opportunity to cultivate his intellect, a feat rarely accomplished by one of his athletic persuasion.

"While at Long Ashton, I did well in my studies and made good in athletics," said Freddie, "winning several prizes in running and swimming and proving fairly adept at rugby and cricket. All English schools teach boxing, and it was at Long Ashton that I drew on my first set of gloves and mastered the rudiments of the manly art. But I was no wonder at it, I will assure you never dreamed of becoming a professional fighter."[2]

After Long Ashton, Freddie was thrust into the tumultuous world of work. When Freddie left school at the age of fourteen, he took up work as a boilerman. Later, he worked in an iron foundry as an apprentice mechanical engineer, a place where a boy is dwarfed by the towering machinery, and the discordant din of metal-on-metal pierces a person's eardrums. Work like that is a day-after-day grind in the confines of a factory. It forges a steely resolve that can define a character for years to come.

"To begin with," Freddie said, "I am a graduate of both the Long Ashton school, near Bristol, England, and the 'College of Hard Knocks.' I took a long, hard course in the latter institution, my studies taking me all over the world."[3]

Restless and yearning for more than the drudgery that iron factory life could offer, young Freddie set his sights on North America, a land of promise and possibility. At a mere sixteen years of age, he embarked on a journey across the Atlantic in search of a better existence, driven by the elusive dream of a brighter future. He found it hard to earn money, and in a brief time, he was forced to abandon his quest and return to his familiar homeland of Wales. But the call of a New World that awaited him would not be silenced so easily. At the age of seventeen, Freddie once again embarked on a voyage Westward.

This time, he was determined to carve out a path for himself, to make a mark on the world, and to seize his slice of the Great American Dream. Little did he know that this subsequent journey would soon take a turn that would leave an indelible imprint on his existence and forever alter the trajectory of his future.

"My parents had planned to give me a university education," said Freddie, "but I nipped those plans in the bud. There was always a strain of wanderlust in me. My longing to see new lands in new scenes was insatiable. Like many other boys in the Old Country, I got the idea that the streets in America were paved with gold. I determined to seek my fortune in the New World. I had a terrible time convincing my parents of the advisability of such a venture, but with the aid of an indulgent uncle, I finally won out over them.

"My uncle gave me enough money to purchase a first-class passage to America, but my inborn Welsh frugality and economy, coupled with a spirit of adventure, made me save most of that money and come steerage."[4]

Some of Freddie's friends had seen fit to bestow upon him a few parting gifts and jewelry to use amid the unknown odyssey that lay ahead. For this voyage would be fraught with the testing of his patience and resolve. He would clutch those glittering baubles, a tangible reminder of the world he was leaving behind and of the fragile bonds that connected him to it.

Having boarded a train to Liverpool on June 29, 1904, Freddie found himself standing before the grandeur of the R.M.S. *Baltic*, a ship that was to be his vessel across the vast expanse of the Atlantic. Her immense size was awe-inspiring as she towered over the bustling docks and throngs of people clamoring to board. In the hands of Captain Edward Smith, who would later helm the tragic voyage of the R.M.S. *Titanic*, Freddie found himself with a lowly steerage ticket, which cost a meager twelve dollars in the midst of a rate war that had gripped the shipping industry. Cost aside, the value of this passage was beyond measure, for it meant the chance to start anew, to leave the Old World behind and embrace the new.

Freddie, as he took to the salty air and ventured into the promise of the land that lay beyond the horizon, soon discovered that steerage was a world of its own, quite unlike anything he had ever seen. The quarters were snug, compact, and all too crowded, with a contrasting crew of individuals who hailed from all corners of the world: Norwegians, Swedes, French, Germans, Italians, and Russians. Their tongues spilled forth in a cacophony of strange, foreign sounds that jangled one's senses and left one pining for the soothing tones of their native tongue.

It was a place where spirits could descend into a state of despondency. As he surveyed his companions on board, within the sea of unfamiliar faces, one visage stood out as unmistakably English. This gentleman, who appeared to be of similar vintage to Freddie, had fixed his gaze upon him. Without a moment's hesitation, an unspoken understanding impelled the two men to traverse the deck until they stood face-to-face and clasped hands in a gesture of camaraderie.

The young man's name was Pat Moore. The two became immediate friends. Freddie would say later in his life that outside of his wife, children, parents, and Humbert Fugazy [Fugazy, a famous boxing promoter, who would become one of Freddie's best friends that would last throughout his life,] he never thought so much of a fellow being as he did of Pat Moore.[5] Like Freddie, he was born in Wales, but as an infant, his parents took him to Australia and raised him "down under." Pat was about four years older than Freddie, and he had seen so much more life.

"Young as Pat was," Freddie said, "he had seen much of life and roughed it considerably. He had prospected for gold in Australia and South Africa and was filled with a spirit of adventure. Yet his 'Bible' used to be the *Scientific American*. He would pour over a frayed old copy of that periodical by the hour. Maybe that is why he became a successful inventor, is well off and affluent in his old hometown of Adelaide now.

"Well, Pat and I swapped boyhood confidences and ambitions. Cub *Cublike* and in the good old Anglo-Saxon way we boxed and wrestled with one another to the great amusement of the steerage passengers of other races. I told him what I knew of boxing, and he taught me wrestling. He was great at rough and tumble and had picked up many tricks in his wanderings. He taught me all of them. He was a bit older and vastly more experienced than myself, and I drank in his every word."[6]

As they arrived in the great city of New York, the pair vowed to embark on their escapades together. The next destination was to be Montreal, a place that held a special allure for Freddie, having traversed its streets on his previous journey. It was said that opportunities abounded in Canada, and Freddie had secured a letter of introduction to a man who could set them on the path to gainful employment. They hit the road for Montreal with scant funds at their disposal, eagerly in search of fresh thrills.

In their destitution, they quickly mastered the art of freighthopping. With practiced ease, they navigated the rails with a reckless abandon born of desperation. This hobo's life was hazardous, from the precarious footing on a speeding train to the real threat of violent retribution from the iron-willed authorities who patrolled the tracks. In spite of it all, they persisted, for there was something intoxicating in the freedom of the rails, a wild, untamed spirit that called to them.

"And we made our way between the two metropolises by brakebeam and blind baggage," said Freddie. "And for many, many months that was my favorite mode of travel, whenever I couldn't induce a kind-hearted brakeman or fireman to let me share caboose or tender with him.

"I'll never forget that trip to the Hudson Valley and into North Country I made with Pat Moore. It was my first glance of America, the Great New World. We drank in every scene in view."[7]

When the duo landed in Montreal, they wasted no time in finding their respective vocations. Freddie, with an air of purposefulness, chose to ply his trade as a mechanical engineer and set about his task. In the beginning, it seemed as though history would repeat itself, and Freddie's trip to North America would be nothing but a futile pursuit. The pulse of life had slowed to a dreary hum, and the horizon of possibility had grown dim. Even the most tenacious of dreamers can find themselves lost in the maze of mundanity, seeking refuge in the familiar embrace of their roots. A return to his homeland of Wales—for the second time—had seemed to be an inevitability.

It was a frivolous foray into the realm of excitement that would rescue him from his prodigal tendencies. After only two weeks, the yearning for adventure compelled them to abandon their meager occupations, which had earned them some much-needed funds. It was then that they resolved to embark on a journey headed for Buffalo to behold the grand majesty of the mighty Niagara. For Freddie, the falls were a sight to behold, a rapturous crescendo of nature's splendor. But Pat, with his travels to the far-flung frontiers of Africa, scoffed at the spectacle, declaring that it paled in comparison to the mighty Victoria Falls.

"I wouldn't believe him," said Freddie. "I've never seen anything so stupendous or awe inspiring, and I wouldn't believe there was anything more magnificent anywhere."[8]

They did not linger there long, for their adventurous spirit beckoned them further, and they set their sights on the boundless West with an insatiable thirst for new horizons. From the shores of Buffalo, they embarked upon a grand voyage through the vastness of the Great Lakes. As the boat made its way across the waters, they found themselves drawn to the company of two Norwegian ladies who were destined for Minneapolis, Minnesota, to live with their uncle. With each passing mile, they chatted amiably with their newfound companions.

"The four of us suffered quite an attack of puppy love," Freddie said, "by our mutual circumstances and conditions. We all became sweet on one another. They could only say a few words in English, and we couldn't speak Norwegian at all. Youth and love have a language all their own, however, and we got along very well together; so well, that before we said goodbye, we about planned to get hitched up as soon as we could make our fortunes. Pat and I promised to visit them in Minneapolis as soon as we could, anyway."[9]

After some gallivanting, they found themselves in Madison, Wisconsin. Freddie and Pat were Westward bound, yearning to visit the charming ladies they had stumbled upon. They embarked on a 500-mile journey from Madison to Minneapolis. The weight of their purses grew lighter with each passing mile. Again, they were reduced to vagabonds, and they hopped trains with fellow drifters. The perils of this lifestyle loomed large, for the feared Bulls, those vigilant railroad detectives with their swinging lanterns, were always looking out for their kind. Ever so vigilant, Freddie and Pat tried as best they could to evade them at every turn.

In the bleak blackness of the night, the pair of wayward wanderers huddled in the shadows of a railway car near Janesville, Wisconsin. Suddenly, as if drawn to the sinister allure of their secret mission, a fierce beam of light sliced through the darkness, casting them in its malevolent glare. The dreaded Bulls had arrived. With a quickness born of desperation, Freddie and Pat scattered in opposite directions. In a moment of reckless courage, Freddie threw a wild punch at the burly railroad cop who lunged for him, his fist connecting with a satisfying thud. The officer tumbled to the ground, dazed and bewildered, as Freddie raced off into the night with the thrill of his narrow escape.

As Freddie frantically dashed along the railroad track, a glimmer of light appeared before him, signaling the presence of another Bull with his lantern. Swiftly, Freddie diverted his course, darting off to the right and navigating his way through the rugged terrain of the woods and fields for what must have felt like an eternity. After traversing nearly half a mile, he found himself once more back upon the rails, his pursuers none the wiser.

Freddie traveled to the nearest town and waited an hour for Pat. The two had made plans to rendezvous at the post office in the closest town; a precaution should they ever become separated on their journey. They had agreed upon this spot as a fallback. After Pat failed to make an appearance, Freddie began a journey down the tracks back to Madison.

The voyage back to Madison, which Freddie had just accomplished, lasted twenty miles. He, again, waited there in front of the post office all day, but Pat never materialized. Unbeknownst to Freddie, Pat had made his way to

Jamesville. Their paths had diverged, separated by the work of the Bulls. It seemed that Freddie and Pat would never cross paths again. The memories of their lost connection faded into the background as they forged ahead.

After loitering about Madison for a couple of sunsets, Freddie found himself in a state of disillusionment. His hopes for an encounter with Pat had been rendered naught, leaving him with little to occupy his idle hours. With a restlessness born of aimlessness, he hopped aboard a freight train bound for Minneapolis, the initial destination he and Pat had set their sights upon. The journey was not without incident, for in the course of his travels, he chanced upon a fellow vagabond who spoke of having seen Pat in the company of a group of harvesters in Aberdeen, South Dakota. This tantalizing tidbit only served to stoke Freddie's desire to travel, and so he forged ahead, his determined gaze fixed upon the ever-receding horizon. Westward, he ventured, guided by its allure and his friend, Pat.

"So," Freddie said, "I changed my plans and struck out for Aberdeen, too."[10]

In the dusty wheat fields, they doled out the sums of five and seven dollars a day, complete with board, to Freddie for his labor. His days were spent working in the harvest fields of Western Canada and the Dakotas,[11] where the land stretched wide and the sun burned bright. It was there, amidst the rugged landscape of the West, that Freddie had his first fight in America. A pack of ruffians sought to strip him of his hard-earned savings, but Freddie was not one to be trifled with. With fierce determination and a swift, calculated use of his fists, he sent his assailants packing.

The Dakotas, with its vast and empty landscapes, wore on Freddie. There was no sign of Pat, the elusive friend who had led him on this futile quest, so he resolved to retreat back to the metropolis of Minneapolis.

"There was no Pat there," Freddie said, "however. Well, I put in several weeks' work in the wheat fields of the Dakotas and then I struck East again, heading for Minneapolis."[12]

As Freddie made his way back, he stumbled upon a tattered copy of a *Physical Culture* magazine, a publication bearing the name of the flamboyant bodybuilder and health crusader Bernarr MacFadden. The magazine, dog-eared and worn, exuded a sense of purpose and vigor, its pages filled with the secrets to a fitter, healthier life. Freddie's fingers trembled as he clutched the magazine; this humble acquisition could unlock a world of possibility, a world of strength and vitality beyond his wildest dreams.

With an air of reckless abandon, Freddie tore through the pages of the *Physical Culture* magazine, the holy grail of fitness fanatics everywhere. Despite the medical elite's accusations of being a quack and a sham, MacFadden's words held a certain allure to many. His steadfast defiance against the artificiality of pills and the tyranny of processed foods, accompanied by his bold assertions that rigorous physical activity, periodic abstinence, and copious quantities of milk could afford one a lifespan of a buck fifty, inspired a legion of adherents.

Freddie would consider himself an ardent follower of the great health preacher. His obsession with the firmness of flesh, the suppleness of muscle, and the alertness of health would consume him entirely. He spoke of these ideals with a fervor that bordered on the fanatic, his passion for a healthy lifestyle burning within him. Nothing was more important than the pursuit of physical perfection, and he would stop at nothing to attain it.

He beheld the opportunity of his aspirations, for MacFadden had set forth to commence a temple of physical culture in the heart of New York City. It was this desire that had been burning within Freddie—to mold the muscles of the masses and become a harbinger of physical strength. He always had a fervent desire to instruct and imbue others with the splendor of bodily perfection, so he cast aside the plans he had laid for Minneapolis and set his sights on the grandeur of the metropolis where his passion could come to fruition.

As Freddie set out for New York, he first made his way to Chicago because he got a job tending to the livestock on a stock train headed toward that city. It was a treacherous time in the Windy City, as the stockyards were besieged by a tumultuous strike amid the notorious "Chicago reign of terror." With marauding thugs and bandits running rampant, Freddie's new position promised to be fraught with peril.

Upon his arrival in Chicago, he found himself spirited away to the stockyards, where he was pressed into service as a strikebreaker. He found the rampant pillage and plunder intolerable. Besides, he was determined to make haste to New York, where he had long planned to embark upon a course in physical culture.

"They even used to hold up the hobos," Freddie said, "beating their way into Chicago. They'd drop you on the head for a $2 note as quickly as they would for a thousand."[13]

Freddie, determined to leave the restless city, found himself clutching onto the remnants that laden his pockets. These were possessions he adamantly refused to expend even when finances dwindled as if they held some promise for tomorrow or carried the echoes of yesterday. They were the items bestowed on him by that doting uncle and his Welsh friends, jewels, and trinkets that spoke of his homeland and friendships that spanned the breadth of the Atlantic. He also had the money he made during the harvest season in the wheat fields of the Dakotas. With these in tow, Freddie left Chicago in the face of uncertainty.

As another stock train brought him east, Freddie found himself deposited in Scranton, Pennsylvania, a veritable hive of Welsh miners. Rumors of a certain Jenkins Harris and his establishment where wayward sons of Wales could be staked and given work had reached Freddie's eager ears. With the light of hope in his eyes, he sought out this man and dropped in on him. Harris, believing Freddie to be penniless, took up a collection of five dollars and provided him with both sustenance and shelter. But the surprise was all Harris's when Freddie attempted to repay him for his kindness.

On the ensuing eve, Freddie set forth on a quest for a New York freight. After much searching, he sighted a poultry train aglow with a beaming luminescence. Wasting no time, he bellowed a hearty greeting into the doorway, and a gentleman, with an amiable air, invited him inside to partake in the comforts of camaraderie. The fellow was delighted to have a companion on the journey to New York City. The man, having procured a chicken, prepared a savory meal on the stove in the caboose, and they began indulging in a well-deserved respite from their wearisome travels.

As Freddie lay down, the sounds of cackling and clucking infiltrated his consciousness. It was a raucous cacophony of farm animals. Finally succumbing to sleep, he drifted off until the first rays of sunlight penetrated the train car. It was only then that Freddie emerged from his hibernation. He realized that they had already arrived at the Jersey City yards. Freddie quickly gathered his meager possessions—the valuables and a sparse collection of clothes and a humble suit of overalls—and set off in search of a haberdashery.

In Jersey City, Freddie found a shop that was open and quickly procured himself a new suit as well as some much-needed undergarments, socks, and other items. He was determined to present himself as a gentleman despite his modest circumstances.

On his journey into the city, Freddie had noticed a small inlet tucked away in the marshes along the tracks. A hidden refuge beyond the chaos of the city. He ventured back to that little cove hidden among the reeds and immersed himself in its waters, scrubbing himself clean with a determination that bordered on obsession. Emerging from the reeds, he appeared renewed, reborn.

As he changed into his new clothes, Freddie surveyed himself. The transformation was remarkable. He no longer looked like a laborer but rather a man of means. With his new appearance, which can give a man a sense of confidence, he set out into the city ready to conquer whatever obstacles lay ahead.

A ferry, slicing through the water, bore him from

Jersey City to the metropolis of his fervent imaginings. As he disembarked, he found himself drawn into conversation with a brawny Irish cop asking him where he could find cheap lodgings. The officer imparted his knowledge, pointing the way to the Mills Hotel No. 1, an establishment situated at the crossroads of Thompson and Bleecker. There, he paid a paltry sum of a quarter to secure a bed and a room.

Freddie began scouring the city for employment, all while harboring an ardent curiosity about the physical culture academy that MacFadden was going to inaugurate. It was the year of the "Panic," and the scarcity of jobs was abundantly apparent. Day after day, he wandered the streets in search of work, his weary feet carrying him from one establishment to the next. By the time he returned to his modest room at Mills Hotel No. 1, the drudgery of the day had rendered him thoroughly exhausted.

Freddie had cast a discerning eye over the crowd assembled in the hotel. The air was thick with the scent of criminality; the lowlifes, the hooligans, the fiends—they all lurked here like insidious shadows waiting to pounce. Freddie identified their ilk intimately, having run with them in the past, and he could see that the hotel was teeming with their kind. He sought out the safe in which to secure his valuables, but the overseer was nowhere to be found. Weary from his journey, Freddie opted to retreat to his room. He divested himself of his clothing and slipped beneath the sheets. He was blissfully unaware of the "suckers' trick"— the ploy by which one might tie valuables in a handkerchief and place them beneath one's pillow, a mistake he would come to rue.

As the dawn light trickled in through the window,

Freddie's head throbbed with a dull ache that pulsed with every beat of his heart. Nausea overcame him, and he stumbled to sit up, a disorienting fog clouding his thoughts. His fingers reached for the pillow, hoping to find comfort or solace in the familiar touch of his possessions. His fingers found nothing but the empty space beneath the pillow as if the world had swallowed his treasures whole.

Someone had robbed him in the night, with cunning and stealth; someone had slipped a chloroform pad under his face during the night, which made his head spin with disbelief. The weight of lost possessions can feel like a physical blow, with the absence of belongings putting an ache in a person's chest. They had taken everything, from his clothes to his shoes, leaving him with nothing but a bundle of overalls that he had clung to as if they were his only lifeline. At that moment, he was stripped bare, a hollow shell of a man with nothing to his name but the clothes on his back.

Freddie, clad in his greasy overalls, scampered down to the desk, his toes exposed to the floor. With a feverish fervor, he bellowed at the clerk, his voice carrying through the halls, proclaiming that he had been relieved of his treasures, his jewels. As the clerk gazed upon his rough, work-worn hands and his tattered attire, a boisterous chuckle escaped his lips, "Jewelry?"[14] he queried with a smirk, hardly able to contain his amusement.

The sole source of contentment for Freddie lay in the pity of the clerk, coupled with the promise of employment. His upbringing had instilled within him the precept that labor was noble. Freddie's parents had taught him "that all work was honorable and the biggest coward in the world was the man or woman who was afraid of work." He took the job.

"In Wales I had been taught that anything worth doing at all was worth doing well," Freddie said. "Menial as was that first job I secured in New York; I took care of to do it well."[15]

He found himself in the dingy recesses of the hotel, surrounded by the discarded remnants of people, literally. As he moved from room to room, his job seemed simple: cleaning the cuspidors. It sounded so regal, yet it wasn't. But he soldiered on, even the most menial of tasks was necessary if he hoped to make his way in this world. So, he cleaned with his rag and bucket, which was a symbol of the resilience that had carried him this far.

"Yes, Siree!" Freddie said. "They made me Cuspidor General of Mills Hotel No. 1. And for my most valuable and highly trained services I was paid the large and magnificent sum of $5 per week."[16]

Only three days had passed since Freddie first began his work tending to the cuspidors. A job so lowly that even the heartiest of men would falter. Yet, Freddie had persisted where others had wilted. He had watched as each worker came and went, a revolving door of faces that blurred into one another. Until the night bath attendant, a man whose presence Freddie barely registered, submitted his resignation. The position was offered to Freddie not out of merit but by virtue of his right of seniority, he was told. A reward for his service, however brief it may have been.

The employment prospect may not have boasted a glamorous façade, yet for Freddie; it represented a much-needed departure from the menial task of purging cuspidors.

It also granted him the freedom to venture out into the daylight hours and scour the city for better opportunities. But it was still the year of the "Panic," when the economy lay in shambles, and livelihoods were lost at a staggering pace. Freddie, like many others, treaded over endless stretches of New York's avenues in search of a means to provide for himself.

Freddie perused the advertisements in the newspapers with scrupulous attention, his eyes scanning every inch of the printed page with a keen and watchful gaze as he sifted through the columns of typeface a sudden glimmer of hope sparked within him as if, by some miracle, he chanced upon an advertisement that set his spirits soaring.[17] Freddie recalled the ad that had caught his eye, the words leaping off the page like a revelation from the heavens:

"Wanted.—Alert, Intelligent, courteous, clean, neat appearing young man to assist gentlemen instructor in downtown gymnasium. One who can box preferred. Apply at 9 a. m. Dr. Joseph P. Knipe, Franklin Street."[18]

The position was a veritable dream. It was the very reason that brought Freddie to the grand city of New York in the first place, having perused an article in the *Physical Culture* periodical detailing MacFadden's intent to establish a physical culture institution in the metropolis. Such an opportunity was the pinnacle of his aspirations, a means by which to accrue enough funds to enroll in the program and ultimately fulfill his destiny as a physical culture instructor.

When Freddie emerged from the steamy depths of the baths at the crack of dawn, he wasted no time in sprucing himself up as best he could with the meager selection of clothes at his disposal. His only dress options consisted of a grimy set of overalls, but even so, he was determined to put his best foot forward as he set out for Dr. Knipe's gymnasium. Though the advertisement stated that the doors would not open until nine, Freddie was shrewd enough to recognize the value of being punctual, and so he strode forth with a sense of purpose, ready to seize whatever opportunities lay ahead.

From the moment Freddie arrived at the interview, as early as he made it there, he found himself swallowed up by a sea of men, an absolute army of would-be employees. They extended all the way into the stairwell. The gymnasium, perched high on the third floor, was awash with candidates, both nice-looking and impeccably mannered. It seemed as if the odds were stacked against Freddie, with so many ahead of him in the queue, each vying for the same position. Despite the seemingly insurmountable odds, Freddie refused to be disheartened. The world was full of surprises, and anything was possible for those with a dream and a little luck on their side.

In an instant, a spark of ingenuity alighted within him. Through the windowpane, he glimpsed a wagon bearing the moniker of a plumbing enterprise, and an idea materialized in his mind. Without hesitation, he propelled himself forward, determined to penetrate the gang congregating on the staircase. With assertive elbows and persistent shoves, he pressed onward and upward, interjecting with a plausible excuse that he was a plumber summoned to remedy a pernicious leak. Such chicanery propelled him to the forefront of the queue, depositing him on the threshold of Dr. Knipe's gymnasium.

"It was an hour before Dr. Knipe put in an appearance," said Freddie. "All the while I was afraid some of the mob of applicants would get wind to my hoax and throw me down the stairs. I was only a slip of a lad and some of the rest of 'em were big, powerful fellows who could break me in two."[19]

At long last, Dr. Knipe made his grand entrance, a towering figure, sturdy and robust, standing at a lofty six feet. His athleticism was unmistakable, a testament to his prior triumphs as an amateur heavyweight boxing champion. Swiftly producing a key from his pocket, he deftly inserted it into the lock, unlocked the door, and swung it open. Freddie started to push his way into the open room.

"Hold on!" said Dr. Knipe. "What do you want?"

In Dr. Knipe, Freddie heard the timbre of a man's voice, a melody from the Emerald Isle. This was a man of his own ilk, and perhaps, just maybe, he would lend a willing ear to Freddie's pleas. Perhaps this was the break he had been waiting for, the chance to prove himself in a world that had not always been kind.

"His rich North of Ireland brogue," Freddie said, "a hint of the Old Country, gave me hope. Here's one of my own kin, I thought to myself. He'll listen to me."

"I'm the plumber," Freddie answered.

"You're on the wrong floor, my man," Dr. Knipe replied.

"No. I'm not, doctor," Freddie replied, "begging your pardon. There's a leak in there. If you will let me in, I will show it to you. Just keep that mob back for a minute, that's all"

Dr. Knipe's face betrayed a quizzical expression as he pulled the door shut on the remaining individuals and pivoted toward Freddie with a gruff demeanor. His inquiry cut through the tense atmosphere, demanding answers.

"What's your game?" Dr. Knipe commanded. "What's the big idea?"[20]

Freddie launched into a rapid-fire speech as if his life depended on it. He had to pull out all the stops to win the favor of Dr. Knipe, and so he artfully played upon their shared ancestry from the Old Country. In vivid detail, Freddie recounted the unfortunate plight that had befallen him and how he had been forced to pass himself off as a common plumber just to gain access to the doctor's privileged inner circle. With aspiration, he spoke of his lofty dreams to become a physical culture teacher and how the audacious ploy he had just pulled off proved beyond a shadow of a doubt that he was alert and intelligent, precisely the qualities called for in the job advertisement. Freddie implored Dr. Knipe to grant him a chance to demonstrate his abilities, and the next time, he would show up clean and neat, vowing to prove beyond any doubt that he was the man for the job.

"I like your nerve!" said Dr. Knipe after Freddie was finished.

"Stand aside, here," he added as an afterthought. "If I don't find someone in the line that I like better than you, why I'll hire you."[21]

Freddie stood poised, watching with keen interest as

Dr. Knipe sifted through the masses of hopefuls, each vying for the coveted spot. The process seemed interminable as Dr. Knipe meticulously assessed the skills of each applicant before finally selecting four others to join Freddie. Dr. Knipe summoned the chosen quintet to the gymnasium. As they entered, Dr. Knipe pulled down two sets of boxing gloves from the wall. One set he tossed to a tall, skinny looking man while the other he flung toward Freddie, saying:

"Put these on. I want to see which one of you fellows is the best boxer."[22]

In those days of youth and adventure, boxing was a trifle to Freddie, a sport he had only dabbled in during his time at the Long Ashton school and in the friendly brawls with his vagabond companion, Pat Moore. The nuances and intricacies of the sweet science, those delicate moves, and strategies, were foreign to him. Despite his ignorance, Freddie possessed a vigor and vitality that belied his years, and a physique honed by the rigors of rambling across America and Canada. Hardened and rugged, he was a force to be reckoned with, a young man who could strike with force. But such power was nothing without the refinement that would come with time and training, and Freddie had yet to taste true pugilistic glory.

Dr. Knipe had Freddie box a formidable adversary in the ring, a man who knew how to throw a punch with precision. One could tell from the first exchange that his opponent was not one to be taken lightly. His only hope was to land a decisive blow, a knockout punch that would send his opponent reeling. Freddie bided his time, patiently waiting for the opportunity to present itself. And when it finally did, he struck with ferocity, his fist connecting with a resounding crack against the unsuspecting jaw of his opponent. It was a moment of triumph, a sweet taste of victory, as Freddie's rival sank to the deck and lingered long after he had been hit.

Dr. Knipe hurled a brimming pail of water upon him, jolting him from his stupor. His body writhed in spastic convulsions, his mind still veiled in the shadows of oblivion, when he muttered something unintelligible to most, "why in hell doesn't that plumber fix the leak? The water is pouring all over me!"[23]

After observing the fistic abilities of a duo of contenders, Dr. Knipe commanded Freddie to lace up his gloves again and face the subsequent adversary. This strapping, bull-necked brute bore the visage of a wrestler, lumbering about with leaden feet. Freddie made easy work of him, deftly outmaneuvering his lumbering foe. Employing every ounce of skill and science at his disposal, Freddie fought with a conviction that suggested a fighter destined for greatness. His pugilistic proficiency proved enough to vanquish the competition and land him the job. Dr. Knipe advised Freddie to don some respectable garb and assured him that, should he appear presentable enough, he would secure the position.

Freddie's new job title would be assistant instructor. He had hoped to be the next boxing instructor at Dr. Knipe's gymnasium since he put in a good showing, but Dr. Knipe had other plans. As he donned his new suit, a sartorial splendor he had crafted through a combination of his meager salary of $4 per week and the sly selling of pawn tickets procured from his fellow patrons at the Mills Hotel, he knew not what Dr. Knipe had in store for him.

As Freddie made his way back to the gymnasium, he was met with a most unexpected request. Dr. Knipe didn't have a glove or a ring in mind for Freddie. He wished for him to don the role of an advertising man, a purveyor of promotional wares, and distribute cards advertising the gym. Freddie was taken aback, for he had not expected such a task, but he accepted the challenge.

The cards that Freddie was to distribute were adorned with a quotation from Shakespeare, which he noticed right away because he had a familiarity with the Bard. Being well-read, he knew well the quotation from Shakespeare:

"The wise for cure on exercise depend."[24]

Freddie set forth into the streets, his cards in hand and his head held high. He distributed them with self-confidence. Although he may not be boxing, if he did well, it could lead to a greater position.

Freddie had been entrusted with a solemn mission: to disseminate the cards throughout the vicinity's various buildings and ensnare an unsuspecting passersby into partaking in a health course at Dr. Knipe's gymnasium. He assigned Freddie a territory consisting of towering loft buildings. As Freddie scoured the labyrinthine interiors for potential clients, he soon discovered that his efforts would bear little fruit. The denizens of these dwellings were a breed apart; their minds fixated on matters of commerce and trade, their bodies resigned to the sedentary rigors of the office. The gymnasium held little appeal for these strivers of the urban jungle. Freddie was left to the futility of his enterprise amid the noise of clattering typewriters and ringing telephones.

As Freddie strolled his way downtown along the bustling streets of Manhattan, he drifted by the elusive Wall Street man—that illustrious figure whose very name was synonymous with power and wealth.

"It's the Wall Street man," Freddie said, "the businessman who is most interested in this health culture system, I reasoned. I'm going down to Wall Street and lower Broadway and see what I can do."[25]

So, he made his way toward the heart of the financial district. As he walked down the street, his gaze fell upon the stately edifice of the New York Life Insurance building. This was where his quest would begin. For if there was one thing that the Wall Street man valued above all else, it was surely his own life and health. And what better way to secure that than with the aid of the health culture system?

Freddie crossed the threshold of the grand building, his eyes scanning the crowds for any sign of his elusive quarry. The air was thick with the heady scent of ambition, making it apparent that he was in the right place. It was time to get to work. He decided that places like these were good hunting grounds.

"So," Freddie said, "for two days I combed the New York Life building, leaving a card in each office on every floor. If you don't think that is some job, try it. See how long it takes you."[26]

Freddie had been expelled from the building on numerous occasions, but he persisted in his efforts to return and continue his canvassing. After a brief period of distributing cards, Dr. Knipe summoned Freddie to his office. He inquired whether Freddie had been disseminating the cards as instructed. Freddie replied with a measure of dishonesty, telling him that he had indeed carried out his orders, though he knew that this was true only in part. He had not been disposing of the cards in a trash receptacle like the majority of his peers, nor had he been dutifully covering the region assigned to him. As Freddie recounted his actions, Dr. Knipe regarded him with a look of perplexity and posed a probing question:

"That's funny; well, never mind. Keep on working."[27]

As Freddie made his return that afternoon, Dr. Knipe once more interrogated him about the cards. He seemed to suspect that Freddie was engaging in some sort of deceitful activity, perhaps even discarding the cards altogether. Fearing he had lost the trust of his employer, Freddie made a candid admission: he had ventured beyond his designated territory and divulged that he had been laboring away in the great building of the New York Life insurance company.

"Ah, that explains it!" Dr. Knipe exclaimed. "Why, I've got six patrons in two days from the building, and I couldn't understand what brought them here."

"Now you'll give me the job of boxing instructor, won't you?" Freddie pleaded.

"No, Freddie," Dr. Knipe declared. "you're worth more to be delivering these cards. Keep it up."[28]

Freddie persisted in his labor for another week and then approached his superior, imparting to him his intention to depart. Freddie expounded upon his yearning to become a physical culture instructor and conveyed his conviction that he would indeed procure such a vocation, be it under the auspices of his present employer or another. Upon being presented with the ultimatum for Freddie's impending resignation, Dr. Knipe assigned him the role of an instructor within the gymnasium and concurrently augmented his compensation to a sum of $5 per week.

Freddie immersed himself in the manly arts of boxing, grappling, and handball and helmed the discerning clientele of Dr. Knipe's gymnasium. Among the distinguished gents who frequented the establishment were those whose pugilistic prowess surpassed Freddie's own, from whom he gleaned an abundance of knowledge. However, it was Humbert Fugazy, son of the illustrious Luigi Fugazy, a respected Italian-American banker, who became Freddie's trusted confidant, mentor, and lifelong friend. Having grown up in the ring, Humbert had sparred with some fine boxers of his day. His expertise was boundless, and his experience even more so. It was under his sage tutelage that Freddie honed the finer points of the sweet science, and thanks to Humbert, Freddie's skills dramatically flourished.

Freddie's coffers swelled with the spoils of his salary and the generosity of his patrons in the form of tips. With his newfound prosperity came the chance for a change of scenery. The Mills Hotel was a place of the past, for he had his sights set on the charm of Greenwich Village. He procured for himself a modest apartment on Ninth Street. The sum of $1.25 per week was all it took to secure his spot in this vibrant community, where art and culture intermingled. Freddie left behind the drab and the dull, embracing the pulsing beat of life in the Village.

Chapter III

James Gatz—that was really, or at least legally, his name. He had changed it at the age of seventeen and at the specific moment that witnessed the beginning of his career…

So he invented just the sort of Jay Gatsby that a seventeen-year-old boy would be likely to invent, and to this conception he was faithful to the end.

—F. Scott Fitzgerald, *The Great Gatsby*

During the era when Freddie made his home in the city, the noble art of boxing was prohibited by the law in the great state of New York. However, in the labyrinthine tangle of legal jargon, one could always discover a crack or crevice to exploit. Such was the case with Dr. Knipe, who discovered a loophole in the law, and like many, he seized upon the opportunity. The law did permit certain performances to be held within the pugilistic trade. These performances, known as membership shows, were open only to a select few, and it was within these constraints that Dr. Knipe staged his clandestine boxing bouts. The cost of admission was ten dollars per head, but for those willing to part with such a sum, the thrills of a good old-fashioned boxing match were well worth the price of admission.

One evening, Dr. Knipe was saddled with a problem because his prized boxing performers had failed to show up, leaving him stranded with a clamorous audience who demanded their entertainment fix. With their cries for action ringing in his ears, the beleaguered host found himself in a predicament of dire straits. And in his desperation, he sought out Freddie, hoping that he would somehow salvage the situation.

"What will I do, Freddie?" Dr. Knipe queried. "What will I do? There isn't a boxer here. Won't you help me out? You've got to go on with Johnny Mazzier. You and Johnny can give them a regular fight if you want to. Won't you help me, Freddie? Won't you help me?"[1]

Freddie vowed to lend a hand, for his livelihood hung in the balance. Should he refuse, his job could slip away. Donning his boxing attire, he slipped on his gloves in preparation for what Freddie called his inaugural bout as a professional. The ring was a foreign land to Freddie, whose pugilistic training had thus far been confined to the confines of Dr. Knipe's boxing room or the sprawling mat of the open gymnasium. The ring was an installation reserved only for the pugnacious pageantry of fight nights.

Freddie strode into the ring and took a seat on the stool. Across from him, his opponent sat in his corner, a rough-and-tumble Italian with a fierce punch, a fair amount of speed, and a shrewd mind. This fighter was no stranger to the game, having spent many a day as an instructor and rubber at Dr. Knipe's gym. Mazzier's second, Jack Frugazzi, stood beside him, a sturdy countryman. And the referee, Dan Daly, was none other than Mazzier's dear pal and roommate.

"What a hell of a chance I've got against that combination!" remarked Freddie to himself.[2]

As Freddie took in these details, he had to silently reflect on the task at hand. For it was not just a matter of physical prowess but a game of strategy and intellect, of outmaneuvering and outwitting the opponent at every turn. And with that, Freddie had to be sharp and focused, for there was no room for error in this dangerous dance.

Obstacles were simply a challenge for Freddie to conquer. If he didn't take down this fellow with absolute authority, he would undoubtedly endure a drubbing himself. Freddie was unflinching in his resolve, determined to emerge victorious. Though his nerves were frazzled, as soon as the bell tolled, all of his anxiety dissipated into the air, and he focused single-mindedly on the task at hand. With a swift and decisive blow, he sent his opponent reeling to the mat, vanquished in the face of Freddie's raw determination. In that moment, he had emerged victorious in his inaugural bout.

As the day was salvaged and the grateful patrons exchanged words amongst themselves, a most peculiar happening took place. In a display of solidarity, five of the fight nights' patrons each dug deep into their pockets, parting ways with a singular greenback. For the feat and in honor of Freddie's formidable performance, they presented him with a grand sum of five dollars. These modest contributions may have seemed meager to some, but to the recipient, they held a priceless value. Though Dr. Knipe declared there was not an abundance of wealth in the house, he expressed his profound gratitude for Freddie's selfless service.

"Being a Welshman," Freddie said, "many persons think that I broke into the game in England. That is wrong. I was only a schoolboy when I left the Old Country, and the only boxing I did there was during my school days at Long Ashton. Boxing is a part of the curriculum of every English school. The manly art is part of the training of every educated Englishman. It was in America, New York City, that I broke into the fistic game."[3]

The pugilistic display did not catapult Freddie into the glory of the ring. His fervent desire to disseminate the principles of physical culture apparently remained steadfastly at the forefront of his consciousness. Only after a considerable number of months had elapsed did he finally come to the decision to embrace it as his vocation.

After working for months at the establishment of Dr. Knipe, Freddie found himself transfixed by the allure of MacFadden, that figure of great renown in the realm of physical culture who had just opened his new establishment. He strove fervently so that he might one day attain the same level of mastery that he gazed upon MacFadden's new academy situated at the intersection of Eighteenth Street and Sixth Avenue. The sum of ten dollars per week, encompassing both wage and gratuities, was all that Freddie could muster in his present occupation—insufficient to fund the enrollment fee demanded by MacFadden.

Despite his deficiency of funds, Freddie decided to take a chance on the recently established enterprise. He managed to secure a spot by the graciousness of MacFadden, who paid him a humble sum of one dollar a day to serve as a boxing instructor's assistant. MacFadden also extended the privilege of allowing him to sleep on the gymnasium mat. It was in this most unconventional of lodgings that Freddie found himself sleeping more peacefully than he had in a long time. The mat was no less than a sanctuary.

Finally, Freddie was poised to fulfill his most fervent

aspiration—to ascend to the position of a physical culture instructor. With great diligence and unwavering focus, he immersed himself in his studies, proudly becoming a quick-witted apprentice. This realm was his true calling, the direction in which his innate talents and knowledge inevitably converged. The laborious toil and unceasing study, far from being a burden, served as an enjoyable recreation, a cherished pastime, for Freddie had found his true vocation.

As Freddie journeyed toward the ever-elusive destination, his wandering heart stumbled upon a most enchanting sight. A vision of feminine grace and beauty embodied in the form of a woman. A woman who captured his attention and beguiled his senses. Enamored, he became as he longed to know her better and discover the mysteries that lay hidden beneath her intoxicating charm. Life was gifting him this unexpected treasure on his journey.

"While a student at MacFadden's," Freddie said, "I became acquainted with one of the female instructors. Our acquaintance ripened into friendship and blossomed into love. Despite opposite racial strains and religions—she was a Jewess—we are married. I have never regretted it. Practically everything I have I owe to my wife. She had and has a splendid business instinct, something never I shall possess, and she has been as wonderful a business partner as she has been wife and mother."[4]

The woman who Freddie met went by the name of Fanny Weston, though her true roots lay in the distant land of Jewish Russia. Her given name was Brahna Weinstein, but like so many others of her kind, she had found it necessary to shed her old identity in order to carve out a new life in the land of opportunity. Freddie knew her only as Fanny, and he was captivated by her.

Freddie and Fanny.

After graduating from MacFadden's school, Freddie commenced the arduous task of establishing a loyal following of his own. The endeavor was not one that yielded fruit without the sweat of one's brow. Freddie's name did not carry the weight of eminence within the profession, which was already inundated with an excess of practitioners. Nonetheless, with the aid of his friend, Humbert Fugazy, and other associates, Freddie was able to corral a small number of businessmen. The great many of these fellows were consumed with an infatuation for the sweet science rather than the broader realm of physical refinement to which

Freddie had pledged himself. The work failed to yield enough money, so he began his search for gainful employment, eventually stumbling upon a gentleman who shared his passion.

He perused the ads of the newspaper, his eyes scanning the print until they alighted upon an advertisement calling for an athletic instructor in the employ of one Bill Brown. He made his way to the gymnasium, where he was met with a throng of hopefuls vying for the same post. The proprietor decreed that the contenders engage in fisticuffs for the opening, a curious method of selection, but Freddie had done this before vying for Dr. Knipe's employment. Undeterred, Freddie faced a burly adversary of brawn and bulk, and emerged victorious with the reward of the position laundering the sweat-soaked clothes of the establishment's athletes at a salary of $15 a week.[5]

"Bill Brown," Freddie said, "who now has his famous Brown's Pine Hill Health Farm up on the Hudson, about the greatest place of its kind in the world, then ran Brown's gymnasium on Twenty-third street, near Sixth Avenue. Bill was kind enough to let me bring my boxing patrons to his gym for instruction, only charging me the nominal fee of $1.25 per week rental."[6]

For a fleeting moment, business had been booming, but it soon began to ebb away. Freddie now desperate, needed to secure a new position. He took to haunting the city's eateries, working as a busboy and waiter in a series of nameless diners and cafes, hoping to find some solace in the hustle of the daily grind. Then, he started employment at the St. Regis, where he served as a humble bellhop, carrying the baggage of the wealthy and powerful. It was there, amidst the opulence and glamour of the St. Regis, that he chanced upon an advertisement for an assistant boxing instructor at Gerhardt's gymnasium, housed in the Berkeley Lyceum on Forty-fourth Street.

Freddie responded to the ad and fixed a meeting. By his side was Fanny, the woman who had captured his affections. As they arrived at the appointed destination, Freddie left Fanny waiting below as he ascended the steps and rapped upon the door. A strapping man, hailing from Elizabeth, New Jersey, answered his knock. He was Jack Clifford, a boxer of Italian descent who had made a name for himself in the ring, now gainfully employed as a boxing instructor.

Jack Clifford discovered from Freddie that he held ties with Humbert Fugazy, and it was then that he opened up. The two conversed for an extensive period, and Jack shared with Freddie that the position didn't yield much in terms of financial compensation, but what Freddie ought to do was venture into the boxing arena. Jack revealed that he managed to secure a match every two weeks, or thereabouts, and every time he stepped into the ring, he amassed anywhere between $150 to $300 per fight.

At the time, that was big money for Freddie. Jack Clifford also told him that a certain Mr. Dalton, an entrepreneur who ran a swimming school downstairs, was in need of a tutor. The position promised to pay well, and its hours would not interfere with Freddie's boxing aspirations. A fortunate situation in favor of Freddie, for he was an excellent swimmer, and the job was tailor-made for his skillset.

With his unrelenting pursuit of success, Freddie found himself at a crossroads. His passion for boxing was growing and burning bright, yet the need to earn money gnawed at him incessantly. The possibilities this job held with it were great, for he could be the master of his own future. It would give him a once-in-a-lifetime chance, and he wasn't one to squander such an opportunity. He could be standing at the precipice of greatness, with his fists primed for the ring while his body ready for the waters to pay the way.

As Freddie descended the staircase, his mind was awhirl with a feverish ambition, the likes of which he had never known before. The notion of amassing such wealth had been but a distant, fanciful dream, yet now, as he stood on the cusp of greatness, he felt as though he could almost reach out and grasp it, as he later stated, "So, I started down the stairs with the new ambition in my head of becoming a professional fighter."[7]

Fanny awaited him below. With breathless fervor, Freddie launched into a rhapsodic tale of his newfound aspiration to become a fighter, conjuring a vision of unparalleled success and riches beyond measure. As he waxed lyrically, Fanny remained silent, her gaze piercing and unyielding. At last, with a steely determination that allowed no argument, she spoke.

"Did you get the job?"

Freddie, with a cavalier air, seemed to pay no heed to the query at hand and instead continued expounding to Fanny his grandiose plans for reaping a fortune from the brutal sport of prizefighting. The air was thick with tension as they held their positions, Freddie with a continuance of an explanation of his scheme, and Fanny with a quiet resolve. Despite this, Fanny remained steadfast in her questioning, pointedly repeating her inquiry as if it were a drumbeat to which Freddie stubbornly refused to march.

"Did you get the job?"

Freddie relayed to Fanny that the position was not one of considerable pay, and he chose not to pursue it. Temporarily casting aside his lofty ambitions, now shattered in reality, he offered up hope to ease her disappointment, disclosing a prospective opportunity as a swimming instructor for which he would seek employment.

"Alright, Fred," Fanny said. "Get a job and then we will think this fighting question over. The main thing is to get a job."[8]

As Freddie walked into the office for the job as a swimming instructor, the room had the weight of his competition. Half a dozen other applicants, each angling for the position, were ready to stake their claim to the coveted position. Several of them had won medals and prizes attesting to their swimming proficiency. He wouldn't be able to match them stroke for stroke, but he refused to let his spirits sink; his wit, more than anything else, would help him get the job.

As Freddie sat in the office, his eyes were drawn to the photographs adorning the walls. They depicted the legendary Captain Davis Dalton, whose feats in the water were nothing short of extraordinary. The clippings spoke of his triumphs and his teachings, a legacy that had left an indelible mark on the swimming world.

This could be his chance to shine, for the man who would be interviewing him would be the son of the great Davis Dalton. This could make him stand out amongst the other applicants; a chance to impress the son with his knowledge of his father's exploits and teachings could put him ahead of the other applicants.

In the annals of swimming achievement, Captain Davis Dalton holds a place of distinction that few dare to aspire to. It was the year of 1890 when Captain Dalton set out to conquer the great English Channel fifteen years after its initial triumph. But the twenty-three-hour arduous feat was met with skepticism and disbelief. The *Times* and the *Daily Mail* cast doubt on it, refusing to concede his achievement.

But for Captain Dalton, the skepticism of the Channel swim was met with another triumph that awaited him. With fearless determination and unflinching courage, he set out from the peeling boards of Ravenhall's Pavilion, near the old iron pier of Coney Island, early one morning, his sights fixed on the distant shores of Sandy Hook, New Jersey. A boat followed him to Sandy Hook. For two long days, he battled the churning currents, his unwavering spirit undaunted by the perils that beset him; he completed the task.

His mastery of the aquatic arts was not only unmatched but also immortalized in his book, *How to Swim*, which still remains in the halls of learning today. A veritable paragon of lifesaving, Dalton boasted a record that surpassed even the most seasoned of lifeguards. It was said that he had rescued a staggering 278 souls from the jaws of death of the waters.

As fate would have it, even the mighty Dalton could not evade the siren song of the sea. In the year 1899, off the coast of Hog Island, Far Rockaway, New York, Dalton met his untimely demise. The cause of his tragic end was the merciless stroke, which claimed him as its own. As the ocean's salty embrace enveloped him, a champion of the sea was lost, who had given his all to save others.[9]

Freddie arose and surveyed the framed depictions adorning the walls. He consumed every morsel of knowledge in them, becoming intimately familiar with every last detail chronicled about Captain Davis Dalton, searing his accomplishments into his memory. When the appointed hour for his interview arrived, he took to the task with fervor, armed with his newfound wisdom. He captivated Captain Dalton's son, who was taken aback by the breadth and depth of Freddie's knowledge. He continued to wax poetic about the captain's feats until his interviewer, overwhelmed with admiration, halted his discourse and granted the position of swimming instructor to him for the sum of twelve dollars per week.

The pay was rather handsome for the time, and with the addition of overtime, one could earn a sum of $25. After only a few days of laboring, an intriguing opportunity presented itself—a vacancy for a feminine swimming instructor. He confessed to Dalton he was too modest and bashful to plunge into the aqueous depths alongside the ladies. Instead, he proposed that Fanny, his girlfriend, would be an indispensable ally and an ideal candidate for the position. Freddie's endorsement ultimately secured Fanny's employment.

Freddie recounted how the role of swimming

instructor was the inaugural post that graced his pockets with ample coin. Yet, he was not able to linger in this coveted position for long. The constant immersion in water, the temperature of which hovered at a balmy ninety degrees, took its toll on his well-being. He withered away, shedding twenty pounds in the process.

"My career in the prize ring dates from my giving up the swimming instructor's job at Dalton's," said Freddie. "All the while, however, I unconsciously, a great part of the time, and consciously and intelligently, later on, was paving my way for successful entry into the prize ring."[10]

After Freddie quit his job, he indulged in a well-deserved respite for a week. Soon enough, his appetite for excitement and a quick buck resurfaced. He reached out to Bill Brown and implored him for a preliminary bout at his club. To Freddie's delight, Brown acquiesced to his request without much argument. The fight was set—a six-round clash of fists between Freddie and Young Peterson. And in return, Freddie was rewarded just five dollars. But the thrill of the fight and the lure of the ring were enough to satiate Freddie's restless spirit, if only for the time being. For in the world of boxing, glory, and riches could be achieved by those who dared to step into the ring and take fate by the throat.

"It was Bill Brown who gave me my ring name of Freddie Welsh," Freddie said. "As you know, my right name is Frederick Hall Thomas. Up to my bout with Peterson at Brown's, I never had known any other."[11]

As the hour of battle drew near, Bill Brown asked Freddie if he would fight under his real name. Freddie replied he'd rather not. He didn't want his family to know that he had taken up fighting until achieving a true mastery of the art. Freddie fought that day under a pseudonym; his true identity shrouded in mystery as he battled his way to glory. Maybe someday, he could shed his mask and reveal himself to the world as the champion he was destined to be.

"Alright, Fred," Bill Brown answered in his usually crisp, brusque manner, "I'll give you a name. You're from Wales, aren't you?"[12]

Before words could escape Freddie's lips, Bill Brown's hand shot up with a flourish as though he were announcing the arrival of the heavyweight champion of the world. In that moment, he was a spectacle, a showman, a master of ceremonies. Before anyone could interject, he bellowed out his declaration, his voice carrying across the room like a clarion call. His words hung in the air at that moment, there was no doubt that Bill Brown was the center of attention, the star of the show, the main attraction. As for the question at hand, it was almost forgotten in the wake of Bill Brown's performance. With his grand gestures, he bellowed out a bold proclamation.

"In this corner," roared Brown, "Young Peterson! Over here, Freddie Welsh! Let 'er go!"

"That's how Bill Brown turned Frederick Hall Thomas into Freddie Welsh, the fighter,"[13] Freddie said.

Freddie and Young Peterson found themselves embroiled in a fierce bout. With such ferocity of their tussle, it caught the attention of Billy Elmer, the proprietor of the local gymnasium and fight club. Impressed by the display of grit and determination shown by these young pugilists,

Elmer saw fit to bestow upon them the honor of a return match to be held at his establishment. Freddie and Young Peterson eagerly embraced the challenge, for in the ring, boxers are acutely aware of the potential glory that beckons.

Dan Hickey, once a sparring partner and trainer of the great heavyweight champion Bob Fitzsimmons, who refereed the fight for Bill Brown, told Freddie that Philadelphia was the right place for a beginner to make a fortune in the ring. With that information, Hickey handed Freddie a letter of introduction addressed to Diamond Lou Bailey, the proprietor of the Broadway Club in the City of Brotherly Love. With a letter in hand, this was Freddie's chance to make it big in the brutal world of boxing. But Fanny, his sweetheart, remained rooted in New York City; he would have to leave her behind. Freddie set his sights on Philadelphia, where there existed visions of glory and riches.

In the midst of the streets of Philadelphia, Freddie found himself grappling with the rigors of the fight game. Even with the hope that a letter of recommendation could provide, his ascent up the ranks proved to be a formidable task, as Bailey was slow to provide him with a ring contest. In the interim, he navigated the city streets, peddling pins and knickknacks and taking up the post of janitor. He then landed a job as a pulley exercise demonstrator in Gimbels Department Store. Days stretched into weeks and weeks into months, as Freddie found himself languishing in obscurity, with the possibility of a career in the fight game eluding his grasp.

Before the year 1905 was out, Freddie and Fanny became man and wife, surreptitiously uniting in the heart of New York City. The news was not to be disseminated to the world at large but only to those in the innermost circle of familial bonds. Fanny, ever resourceful, declared that the shroud of secrecy was necessary to shield her husband's burgeoning pugilistic aspirations from prying eyes. The seeds of their clandestine union were sown.

For eight long years, their sacred vows remained concealed, an obscured affair that bore witness to Fanny's steadfast devotion to her beloved Freddie. As his renown grew in magnitude, and they were spotted together on occasion, they affected the facade of siblings, a ruse so convincing that even their closest confidants were tricked.

As the years trickled by, the veneer of their disguise became ever more polished. The whispers and rumors of their relationship would become but a faint murmur in the background of the brutal boxing world. To the unsuspecting masses, they appeared to be just siblings as they had circulated, bound by blood but not by passion. Fanny was often regaled as the Welsh Rose, a moniker that belied her true origins and a designation that amused the couple to no end because of her not being of Welsh origin. It served to throw off any scent of suspicion.

Beneath the veneer of their well-crafted charade, the two reveled in a private joke. Fanny would whip up sumptuous meals for her "brother" before each bout, even as their true identities lay concealed. The humor of it all was not lost on them, and they shared many a quiet chuckle, savoring the delicious wit of their sham.

After much anticipation, Diamond Lou Bailey arranged for Freddie to face off against the formidable Young Williams at the Broadway Club on December twenty-first, 1905 [this is recognized as Freddie's first professional fight in the official records]. As reported in the *Philadelphia Item*, Freddie was billed as Fred Thomas. The crowd was abuzz with excitement as the two fighters entered the ring, and Freddie wasted no time in proving his worth. With a flurry of fists, in the third round, he delivered a decisive blow that knocked out Young Williams.

Since Young Williams had quite a reputation in Philadelphia, word of Freddie's victory spread through the city's fight circles, and his reputation began to grow. He soon found himself in high demand, receiving offers for several other bouts. With his newfound success, he was appointed as the chief boxing instructor at Jack Clancy's Physical Culture School located at the corner of Thirteenth and Chestnut Streets. His victory over Young Williams would become the start of an illustrious career that would make him a big-time boxing attraction.

When the devastating earthquake rumbled through the streets of San Francisco on that April day in 1906, Jack Clancy found himself packing his bags and bidding farewell to Philadelphia. His parents were living in California, caught up in the chaos, and he could not bear the thought of leaving them to face the aftermath alone.

Before he departed, Jack decided that he would sell his percentage in the gym to Freddie, who took on the responsibility of running the physical culture school. Just because Freddie was a new owner, it did not mean that his dreams of being a fighter had faded away. He was determined to make a name for himself in the ring, to show the world what he was made of. While the baton of ownership had passed hands, Freddie's dreams of pugilistic glory remained steadfast.

On July 13, 1906, Freddie, a relatively unknown pugilist with a fierce determination, had his first headliner bout when he stepped into the ring at the National Athletic Club of Philadelphia to face off against the formidable Young Erne. The city's pride, Erne, had a countrywide reputation that preceded him, while Freddie was but a novice, an overwhelming underdog in the eyes of the crowd.

Freddie stunned his opponent, delivering a conclusive blow that sent Erne reeling. When the final bell rang, it was Freddie who emerged victorious in a newspaper decision that was given in the *Philadelphia Item*. Freddie's triumph that day was more than just a win in a boxing match. It was a turning point in his career, a moment that propelled him from obscurity into the top flight of the lightweights in the city. From that night on in Philadelphia, he would be known not as a mere fighter.

It was not until two weeks had passed that Freddie would have an opportunity to allow his name to resonate on a national scale. The occasion was his match on the twenty-seventh of July. The man just vanquished by Freddie, Young Erne, was due to enter the ring with Hock Keyes, a sensational young Australian fighter who had held the lightweight titles in Australia and New Zealand. Dayton, Ohio, had been the chosen battleground for a grueling twenty-round bout between these two battlers.

Erne's manager, Billy McCarney, had a falling out with his charge in the week leading up to the bout. Erne, refusing to take to the ring under such strained circumstances, left McCarney in a lurch. McCarney, however, was not one to be deterred so easily. In his hour of need, McCarney made an unlikely pilgrimage to Freddie's newly acquired gymnasium, where he implored the young fighter to fill Erne's void against the formidable Keyes. Notwithstanding the paltry five days afforded for preparation, Freddie accepted the offer, embarking on the adventure and the risk he was taking.

The pugilistic affair looming before him would go a long way in determining if he truly was the rising star he seemed or merely a fleeting spark that would soon be snuffed out. The sport of boxing had proven to be the undoing of many a hopeful youth, so for Freddie, the stakes at hand were high. His future hung in the balance; it would be swaying precariously with each jab and hook that his opponent threw his way. It was a battle not only against his adversary but against the doubts and uncertainties that plague one from within. Victory would cement his place as an up-and-comer, while defeat would consign him to the ranks of the forgotten, a simple footnote in the annals of boxing history.

In the heat of battle, Freddie unleashed a fury upon Keyes that left him reeling, downed twice in the sixteenth and twice more in the seventeenth round. With a final, decisive blow in the seventeenth, the bout was stopped, a resounding victory for the young up-and-comer. This triumph was only the beginning for Freddie. As news of his stunning win spread, promoters from far and wide came knocking at his door, eager to sign him on as their newest prized fighter. In the world of lightweight boxing, Freddie was now one of the hottest commodities of them all.

Freddie's boxing skills were growing and would become recognized worldwide, making him one of the greatest defensive fighters ever. With his pale and lean frame, he was a beguiling enigma both in and out of the ring. A master of the left jab and an adept scrapper, capable of spoiling his opponents' every move with cunning finesse. His skillful and elegant style could send hearts soaring, yet he was not above frustrating his audience with artful fouls and a general air of cynicism, all executed with consummate skill. Freddie was truly a fascinating conundrum, a paradox that left the boxing world in awe and wonder.

The vivacious and sagacious mind residing within Freddie's head always seemed to buzz with tumultuous thoughts at constant odds with itself. One could easily envision Freddie as capricious, growing wearisome of mundane pursuits that failed to pique his intellect. Freddie professed to be abstemious, a devout vegetarian, and an abstainer from tobacco. And for the most part, he held true to his convictions. He held his physique in high esteem long before the catchphrase "keeping fit" became in vogue. Nevertheless, Freddie was not averse to indulging in a succulent chop or imbibing a fine glass of claret and found pleasure in drawing puffs from the tantalizing Turkish cigarettes that tortured his lungs.[14]

Freddie possessed an astute awareness of the currency his name held, and he strove to preserve its pristine allure with unyielding resolve. He comprehended the potency of the media apparatus, its formidable power to shape narratives and manipulate reality, and deftly wielded it to his advantage, adeptly shrouding the veritable aspects of his existence. Fanny, his clandestine spouse, who remained veiled from the prying eyes of the press, divulged that her enigmatic husband was an individual of an exceedingly delicate disposition—an attribute that may well have spurred his inclination to safeguard the sanctity of his private affairs.

Freddie, the puzzling figure, remained an elusive subject of speculation among the people. One would question whether he espoused the zealous tenets of vegetarianism or succumbed to the intoxicating allure of carnivorous indulgence. Would he, in the sanctity of his solitude, raise a glass to the liquid mirth that flowed abundantly, or did he shun the seductive embrace of alcohol altogether? The whispers lingered, evoking a haze of uncertainty—did Freddie, the embodiment of contradictions, surrender to the whimsical rituals of tobacco's slow-burning waltz or find solace in unadulterated air? Certainly, a haze of mysteries enshrouded Freddie, enveloping him in a perpetual veil of enigma.

The inexorable march of time possesses an uncanny propensity to unveil the artifice of deception and lay bare the authenticity that lies concealed beneath. However, even when veracity is exposed, impassioned adherents of a cherished creed can remain obstinately blind to the most glaring truths, stubbornly averse to acknowledging the irrefutable reality that lies glaringly before them.

No matter the veil that draped Freddie's personal affairs, his pugilistic prowess danced upon the public stage, inviting scrutiny and yielding judgments. The prevailing verdict, in its decree, hailed his fistic aptitude as nothing short of extraordinary.

In 1965, Mel Beers penned a quaint piece on Freddie—an article that graced the pages of the defunct

Boxing International magazine. Beer's musings on the pugilistic craft's most pivotal punch:

"The left jab, properly used, is a thing of beauty in motion. It is boxing's basic punch and those who mastered it usually went on to become world champions or leading contenders. Billy Conn and Willie Pep mastered the jab. So did Abe Attell, Packey McFarland, and Benny Leonard. Tommy Loughran was another who built his boxing wizardry around a jab that shot straight and true to any part of the opponent's anatomy.

"Who had the best left jab of all? It is impossible to say, but after plowing through piles of yellowed newspaper clippings and talking to scores of experts with long memories, the name of Freddie Welsh comes up more than any of the others."[15]

A man of formidable defense, a master of the art of guarding his chin. His craftiness in the ring was unmatched; his gloves were a shield of steel, and his defenses were sharp as a razor's edge. Even four years hence, Willie Ritchie, the man dethroned by Freddie's fists, could not deny the artistry he had witnessed that day, stating:

"Welsh was a great defensive fighter … Welsh fought typically slugger fashion, all covered up, coming in with his head down, bent over forward … He had his gloves in front of his face, and you couldn't score cleanly with the gloves there."[16]

Freddie in a boxing pose.

In 1906, Freddie fought his way across America, his reputation ever-growing. It was not long thereafter that he resolved to embark on a return journey to the grandeur of the

United Kingdom, and by 1907, he was back in his country of origin. With grandiose style, he indulged in the most opulent of ocean liners, luxuriating in the finest of cabins, his expenditures tenfold what he had once shelled out for a modest berth in the bowels of a vessel on his voyage across the Atlantic to America.

Upon arriving in London, he basked in the splendor of the most opulent of accommodations, staying in the finest of luxury suites. How far it was from the unassuming life of Frederick Hall Thomas—a testament to the dizzying heights to which one may ascend through wealth, fame, and fortune.

While in London, one of the first people he met was an old schoolmate from the Long Ashton School, who didn't know about his boxing adventures. The weight of this revelation left his old-time friend in a state of disbelief, struggling to comprehend the transformation that had taken place—that the famed boxer, Freddie Welsh, was none other than his dear old schoolmate, Fred Thomas.

Freddie was now earning himself a string of victories and boxing titles on both sides of the Atlantic, traveling back and forth between the United States and Great Britain. As Freddie embarked on his boxing pursuits, Fanny was his steadfast companion most of the time, accompanying him on some of his transatlantic voyages while remaining rooted in their home for others. The transience of their lives and the excitement of their adventures seemed to never cease enthralling those around them, leaving many to wonder what marvels the future had in store for them.

Through it all, Freddie remained true to himself, a man who recognized the value of hard work, determination, and the enduring bonds of friendship. Life became a never-ending adventure, a wild ride that took him to the heights of fame and fortune. His eyes fixed firmly on the prize as he continued to pave his way toward greatness—for he was a man with ambition, still driven by an unyielding determination to succeed at any cost.

Freddie, having climbed to the success of a prominent boxer, found himself basking in a life of opulence and extravagance, an existence diametrically opposed to the bleak days of his humble beginnings in America. No longer known as the hobo Fredrick Hall Thomas but now heralded as Freddie Welsh, the boxing luminary, he traversed the breadth of America, ensconced in luxurious Pullman cars, and cloistered in the privacy of his own compartment.

Back in the States in 1908, Freddie's laughter could be heard through the train car as he gazed out the window at the familiar scenery passing by. Memories of his past journeys filled him, each one a colorful story in its own right. Sometimes, he'd catch a glimpse of a familiar face among the wandering vagabonds that still roamed the rails.

One frigid winter's day, Freddie set out to make the trip to Schlitz Park in Milwaukee. He was to face off against Charlie Neary on the last day of January 1908. The idea had taken hold of him to travel as a hobo, to experience the raw, unfiltered grit of life on the road once again. The cruel bite of the thermometer and Fanny conspired against him. The chill was so fierce Freddie relented and stayed in the refuge of the warm embrace of a Pullman car. The match with Neary, both men fighting with all their might, ended in a draw. Neary retired after this bout, per the *Tacoma Daily News*.

As Freddie made his way back home again on a grand arrival in Great Britain in the year 1909, an impressive spectacle greeted him in the streets of Cardiff and the surrounding valleys. For Wales was in the midst of a glorious era for pugilism, its golden age, where the sweet science reigned supreme over all other pursuits.

It was August 23, 1909, when Freddie claimed a major victory. With the grace and skill of a true champion, he defeated Henri Piet for the coveted EBU European lightweight title. The Grand Pavilion in Mountain Ash, Wales, bore witness to this remarkable achievement. Freddie's triumphs did not end there. Less than three months had passed when he once again rose to the occasion and claimed another title. This time, it was the British lightweight championship that Freddie secured, defeating Johnny Summers at the National Sporting Club in Covent Garden, London, on November 8, 1909.

In the twelfth month of 1910, Freddie found himself pitted against the one they called Jim Driscoll, a fellow Welshman who was more adored in Wales than Freddie, in a momentous clash of fists that would be remembered through the ages. The sheer magnitude of this affair was felt throughout the entire land as if the heavens themselves had conspired to make it so. At the time, it was one of the biggest sporting events staged in Wales. It was a dirty, scrappy bout by both men. In the end, it was Freddie who emerged the victor, though by no clean nor elegant means, for his adversary had been disqualified in the tenth round for a most unsportsmanlike headbutt.

"I can't say that I ever worried much about what people thought or said of me," said Freddie.

"I like to be liked and have often wished that I could be as much loved as Jim Driscoll, say, but I have never been able to bow down to rules and regulations."[17]

With each triumph, Freddie's celebrity swelled, a tale woven of ambition and daring, a saga fit for the grandest of stages. However, with the possibility of every approaching loss, doubt inevitably could creep in and would question his actual mettle and skill. In this endless dance of glory and uncertainty, Freddie lived his life a hero one day, a mortal the next, forever chasing the elusive dream of greatness.

Freddie, a man of swift fists and quicker wit, had held the British lightweight title until on the twenty-seventh of February in the year 1911 when the title slipped from his grasp. The National Sporting Club, Covent Garden, London, stood witness to Freddie's defeat at the hands of Matt Wells by decision. Not only seizing the British lightweight title, but Wells also laid claim to Freddie's coveted EBU European lightweight title.

Freddie, ever the master of outward appearances, presented the press with a carefully crafted explanation for his defeat in the boxing match against Wells. It was a tale spun with calculated finesse, one that hinted at the tumultuous journey leading up to that fateful encounter. In the weeks preceding the bout, Freddie, who must have been cognizant of the formidable challenge that awaited him, yielded to the counsel of his companions, who implored him to partake in the hearty sustenance of meat. They fervently insisted that such a course of action would bestow upon him the fortitude and vitality required to prevail in the ring.

"I foolishly followed this advice," said Freddie. "What was the result? I was slow on my feet, my brain seemed frozen, and my hands and arms were like lead. I could not move quickly. I was unable to think quickly, and my boxing suffered because my arms and hands were as slow as my feet and brains. Meat made me a sluggard…"[18]

Undaunted, Freddie took to the road and rebounded with a fierce determination. He traveled back to the United States and emerged without a loss from his next nine bouts over twenty months fighting across North America and one back in Great Britain. He fought bouts in New Amsterdam, San Francisco, Vernon, Winnipeg, Buffalo, Columbus, and Liverpool.

In one of those planned fights, fortune finally favored him with the long-awaited opportunity: a chance to face off against the reigning world lightweight champion, Ad Wolgast. The stage was set for a grand spectacle in San Francisco, scheduled precisely on Thanksgiving Day in the year 1911. Yet, as fate would have it, the eve of the match witnessed Wolgast succumbing to appendicitis, a cruel twist that led to the abrupt cancellation of the anticipated showdown.

But as swiftly as adversity struck, destiny unveiled a new path. A replacement swiftly stepped into the limelight, and so it was that Freddie found himself poised to engage in combat with the formidable Willie Ritchie on that Thanksgiving Day. Such was the capriciousness of destiny, where setbacks and substitutions intertwine, shaping the narratives of champions and challengers alike.

Freddie, with an air of audacious grace, readily

embraced the amended trajectory. He proclaimed, in the void left by the ailing lightweight champion, his intent to ascend the ring and defend Wolgast's coveted lightweight title for him.

"There is no one that has any better right than I have to defend this title and I will do it," Freddie declared. "When Wolgast is fully recovered I will then meet him for the honor."[19]

Freddie's declaration resonated deeply among the aficionados of pugilism, an audience keenly attuned to the nuances of honor and merit. There was no trace of conceit in his words; rather, they carried the weight of undeniable veracity, a testament recognized by those immersed in the intricacies of the prizefighting world.

"But how about the $2,500 forfeit Wolgast put up to meet you?" he was asked. "Do you intend to claim it?"[20]

Scorn gleamed in Freddie's eyes as he spoke a solitary word, "No."[21] With nary a pause, he spun on his heels, retracing his steps to the quiet refuge of his training quarters. The weight of his refusal was a silent testament to his resolve.

It was a tough, fierce twenty-round fight against Willie Ritchie, but Freddie was awarded the decision. After the eight bouts in North America, Freddie came back to Great Britain to win a bout at Liverpool Stadium, Pudsey Street, Liverpool, setting him up for a return match against Matt Wells.

On November 11, 1912, amidst the grandeur of the National Sporting Club in Covent Garden, London, Freddie reclaimed his titles as the British lightweight and EBU

European lightweight champion with a triumph over the formidable Matt Wells. The glories of his victories were but a prelude to his ultimate goal, a prize of the highest order in the pugilistic realm—the world title. He would seek the highest ring honor possible for a man of his poundage, lightweight at 135 pounds.

To achieve this feat, Freddie would embark on a tumultuous journey, traversing the vast Atlantic on countless occasions, pitting himself against an array of formidable foes in twenty-seven arduous battles, including wins against great fighters such as Johnny Dundee, Mexican Joe Rivers, and Joe Mandot. This epic quest would consume the next twenty months of his life as he relentlessly pursued his dream of claiming the world title and cementing his legacy as a true champion of the ring.

Chapter IV

'Meyer Wolfsheim? No, he's a gambler.' Gatsby hesitated, then added coolly: 'He's the man who fixed the World's Series back in 1919.' 'Fixed the World's Series?' I repeated.

The idea staggered me. I remembered of course that the World's Series had been fixed in 1919 but if I had thought of it at all I would have thought of it as a thing that merely happened, the end of some inevitable chain. It never occurred to me that one man could start to play with the faith of fifty million people—with the single-mindedness of a burglar blowing a safe.

—F. Scott Fitzgerald, *The Great Gatsby*

This isn't just an epigram—life is much more successfully looked at from a single window, after all.

—F. Scott Fitzgerald, *The Great Gatsby*

Meyer Wolfsheim, the man who fixed the World Series back in 1919, was obviously based on gambler Arnold Rothstein, whom Fitzgerald had met in unknown circumstances.[1]

—Matthew Bruccoli, preeminent F. Scott Fitzgerald scholar

"I Will Be Alone"

That was his complaint, not his actual problem. Arnold Rothstein was incapable of love that is, of loving any human being. He loved money. He loved power. He loved the good life, the bright lights of Times Square, the thrill of fixing a World Series or a championship prizefight, the warm glow of knowing you were smarter than the next fellow—and his knowing it, too.[2]

—David Pietrusza, Arnold Rothstein Biographer

Freddie's original desire to establish a physical culture academy persisted as a dream that glimmered with an ethereal quality. However, the prospect of grasping the world boxing championship loomed, a tantalizing prize that beckoned with an alluring call. Such a feat, however, was no mere trifle, for the reigning champion, Willie Ritchie, a native of San Francisco, remained adamant in his resolve to shun any contenders and had no intention of giving him an opportunity.

In the autumn of 1912, on November 28, in his hometown of San Francisco, Ritchie had faced off against the reigning lightweight champion, Ad Wolgast, the man Freddie was to fight for the title before Wolgast had to withdraw because of appendicitis. The Ritchie-Wolgast bout was fraught with tension and intensity. Wolgast succumbed to the unsportsmanlike conduct of low blows, and the title was ceded to the victorious Ritchie. After winning the title, Ritchie stepped into the ring five times during his tenure as lightweight king and graced the canvas in a number of exhibition bouts.

Freddie, with his fists and fortitude, had fought valiantly to arrive at this precipice, but to secure a chance at the coveted title demanded an even greater struggle, a grueling climb up the steep incline of public opinion. Pouring his fortune into the pages of newspapers, he stoked the flames of public demand, beseeching the people to rally behind him and demand a shot at the championship.

In 1914, Ritchie declared that he would take on the formidable Freddie in a bout for the handsome sum of fifty thousand dollars. No soul of sound mind and ample means would be willing to furnish him with such a princely sum. However, the nation of Great Britain was in dire need of a return of their cherished boxing title, which had been absent from their shores for a considerable length of time.

Enter Freddie's manager, the enterprising Harry Pollock, who hustled relentlessly to procure the necessary financial backing for the fight, eventually securing a guarantee of forty thousand dollars. There was, of course, a catch: neither fighter was allowed to engage in any other matches prior to the bout. Ritchie, though initially agreeable to these terms, made the disastrous error of reneging on his pledge. With no official document to bind them, Ritchie's error in judgment proved to be a monumental misstep.

On the twenty-sixth of May, Ritchie found himself in a non-title bout with Charley White in Milwaukee. White unleashed a merciless pounding from the beginning. According to the newspapers, Ritchie resembled San Francisco after the great fire. Despite the fight being a non-decision affair, the verdict was unanimous among the press, who quickly bestowed the laurels upon White.

On the day before Ritchie's downfall, May 25, Freddie entered the ring with Joe Mandot in New Orleans with a better outcome. Displaying his nimble feet and skilled fists, Freddie nearly dealt a crushing blow to his opponent, sending him down to the canvas. Though Mandot managed to weather the storm and survive the ten rounds, it was clear that Freddie emerged victorious.

This all in spite of Freddie going into battle with less than proper preparation the day before, for he had indulged in the delights of New Orleans with his brother, Arthur Stanley Thomas, who went by his middle name. They passed the hours before the fight, basking in the glow of afternoon baseball games and reveling in the late-night rhythms of the city. Freddie, a master of the dance floor, let his feet guide him through the night in a tango, even with the task ahead.

The two bouts had bestowed upon Freddie's crew a powerful leverage over Ritchie. Harry Pollock, with Freddie's nod, dispatched a telegram to Ritchie, apprising him that the organizers had nixed their encounter and now aimed to pit Freddie against Charlie White, which wasn't truthful. The move paid off handsomely when Ritchie wired back, urging them not to scrap the match until he conferred with them. The day that followed, Ritchie acceded to the bout with Freddie, but at a reduced rate of $25,000 guaranteed, and added an audacious concession—the fight would be on Freddie's home soil in Great Britain.

On the ninth of June, in New York City, Ritchie affixed his signature to a preliminary document for the impending fight. Freddie, however, was nowhere to be found, and Pollock signed in his stead. The next day, Ritchie embarked on his maiden voyage to England aboard the *Aquitania*. By happenstance, Harry Pollock, too, was aboard the vessel, but Freddie and his brother Stanley set sail across the Atlantic on the *Imperator* shortly after.

As the voyage wore on, Freddie received word that his wife had given birth to their first child. A girl, they had named her Elizabeth, after Freddie's mother, though they intended to call her Betty. Soon enough, his beloved wife and newborn daughter would cross the Atlantic to join him in England once they were deemed fit for the journey.

In a brief amount of time, Freddie rendezvoused with Ritchie in London's Piccadilly Hotel to thrash out the particulars of their bout. Ritchie acceded to tip the scales at the English limit for a lightweight, at nine stone, nine pounds, which was the lightweight limit of 135 pounds. The astounding concessions that the reigning lightweight champion, Ritchie, granted gave Freddie a distinct advantage. Surprising all, he opted for the leading English referee, Eugene Corri, instead of an American official. In the absence of judges, Eugene Corri would single-handedly determine the victor, barring a knockout. Furthermore, Freddie had the home-field advantage. Though he was more American than Welsh by now, to many, he was still a Welshman's progeny, and the audience would firmly be in favor of their countryman.

In a spectacle even more astounding than the concessions bestowed by Ritchie came at the hand of Arnold Rothstein, a man known for his penchant for manipulating sporting events to his financial advantage.[3] The fight between Ritchie and Freddie was funded in no small part by Rothstein's immense guarantee,[4] a necessary weight to anchor the match. Whispers and murmurs abounded that the match was a mere pawn in Rothstein's game of corruption. A grand manipulation that meant the fight was preordained to end in a predetermined result.

"Arnold Rothstein backed his manager and to guarantee me twenty-five thousand," Ritchie said years later, "the gangster who was murdered. He put up the money in a New York bank in my name subject to my fulfilling my contract. They made me an offer of $25,000 for the match in London, and traveling expenses, so I accepted it."[5]

Rothstein, a notorious gambler, possessed connections to the underworld. He was rumored to have amassed colossal sums of wealth by placing bets on guaranteed outcomes—outcomes that he himself rigged. His most infamous manipulations were still in the making. The 1919 baseball World Series was allegedly fixed by the gangster Arnold Rothstein, but his true passion was manipulating horse racing and boxing events. His purported cohort in crime was Abe Attell, the former featherweight champion who Freddie had vanquished in 1908. Attell, it was said, served as Rothstein's errand boy and was believed to have played a prominent role in several of the scams.

Abe Attell and Freddie Welsh.

Abe Attell had come to know Freddie through the bitter sting of defeat, a shared experience that bred an admiration between the two. It was a bond, born of sweat and blood, forged in the crucible of the ring. Attell, when probed for the secret to vanquishing Freddie, possessed the ultimate utterance on the artistry that defined Freddie when he said:

"How do you beat Freddie Welsh? If you can lay a glove on that guy five times in twenty rounds, let alone beat him, you'll get the verdict, sure! If you don't want to be made to look like a sucker, take my advice: go away and train. Train good and hard. Then sprain *yer* ankle the night before the fight."[6]

Joe Humphries, who had taken up the mantle as guardian of Freddie's fistic endeavors for some of his early fights, ventured forth with a tale of his own engagement with these fighters. Through his recollection, Joe beckoned the listener to behold the fragile fragility of glory and camaraderie in a realm governed by the relentless pursuit of victory.

"Welsh was brought to me by Abe Attell," Humphries recalled, "who had been outpointed by Freddie, and Abe insisted he was the cleverest man in the world with his fists. Welsh, at that time, was a featherweight and had no manager, so I took hold of him for several of his matches before he went to England and won the title from Ritchie. As a blocker of punches and judge of distance, I think Welsh was the nearest thing to Young Griffo, the boxing game has ever seen. In the matter of timing and boxing intelligence, he was Joe Gans, but without that master's punch.

"That fact that Welsh was able to outpoint Attell in fifteen rounds, and also in the same year hold Packy McFarland to a draw, is a tip off as to the greatness of Freddie's boxing skill."[7]

Rothstein, a man of great fortunes and even greater mysteries had been known to amass anywhere from $100,000 to $800,000 in winnings in a single event. But it was the inexplicable windfalls that left cities buzzing—tales of a single horse race where he raked in an astounding $1,350,000[8] and a $125,000 wager on Gene Tunney, a prized fighter and dear friend to Abe Attell, at four-to-one odds in his heavyweight title bout against the formidable Jack the "Manassas Mauler" Dempsey. The fight took place on September 23, 1926, at Sesquicentennial Stadium in Philadelphia, where a record 120,757 fans gathered and paid a staggering $1.8 million to witness the historic spectacle. [The hot-ticket Willard-Dempsey fight had drawn just 20,000 fans and a $450,000 gate.]

The oddsmakers had placed their odds heavily in favor of Dempsey as if he were a surefire thing. On the day of the fight, two of the most notorious men in the city, Abe Attell and Arnold Rothstein, were in attendance. Dempsey's ever-vigilant bodyguard, Mike Trent, handed him his customary small glass of olive oil to ease his stomach, but this time, it proved to be of little use. After drinking it, Dempsey was wracked with severe pain in his gut.[9] Tunney won every single round of the match, seizing the coveted heavyweight title from Dempsey's grasp. As for Rothstein, he walked away with a sum of $500,000 lining his pockets.

In the wake of the bout, whispers of a scheme permeated the air. Fingers were pointed every which way. The court of public opinion doled out accusations, implicating Arnold Rothstein, Abe Attell, Gene Tunney, Billy Gibson [Tunney's manager,] and even the fight's promoter, Tex Rickard, in their speculations.

In the roiling aftermath of the pugilistic match between Dempsey and his opponent, even the luminary of journalism, Ring Lardner, could not abide by the outcome and harbored a deep-seated animosity toward the now-former champion. Lardner's ire, as it were, was fueled by a personal motive, for he had risked five hundred dollars on the favored pugilist at a two-to-one ratio and now entertained misgivings about the fairness of the triumph. Cognizant of the perils of defamation, Lardner refrained from any overt public castigation and, instead, confided his vexation in a letter to his friend F. Scott Fitzgerald and his better half.

"The thing was a very well done fake," he wrote to Scott and Zelda Fitzgerald in France, a few weeks after the fight, "which lots of us would like to say in print, but you know what newspapers are where possible libel suits are concerned. As usual, I did my heavy thinking too late; otherwise I would have bet the other way."[10]

Tunney, a man who was near unbeatable during his fight career, had seen but a single defeat in his sixty-seven skirmishes within the professional ring. The notion that he could be tangled in such dubious affairs was met with nothing but a scoff from the new heavyweight champion. Tex Rickard, too, rebuffed the idea with similar disdain. A day arrived when Rickard was caught in the throes of indignation, perched atop a chair fashioned from the horns of cattle. From the confines of his Madison Square Garden office, the fight promoter ruminated on the matter at hand and the potential involvement of Rothstein.

"…I play percentages," said Rickard, "but I'm not a sure-thing gambler like Arnold Rothstein. That ain't gambling, and it ain't adventure. I'm the kind of a gambler who gambles, and don't look to a 'fix' to win. You know something? Rothstein is going to get *hisself* killed.

"…You don't need inside information down where I come from. A real gambler like me, a feller who likes it like some fellers love booze or women, and not just because it's a marked-card deal or a fix, well, we got hunches, and we play 'em. I knew all the time up in Alaska I'd never get shot. Me? I play percentage, but no fixing.

"It's my guess that Rothstein will be shot before the year is out. He's been askin' for it. They tell me he's been mighty slow lately makin' good on some big losses in the floatin' card games."[11]

Rickard's prophecy was destined to come to fruition. In the year 1928, Rothstein was found lifeless, felled by the force of a gunshot, a bitter end to a life fraught with peril. It was said that his death was the result of unpaid debts accrued from a series of high-stakes card games.

On the seventh of July in the year nineteen fourteen, Freddie engaged in a bout with Willie Ritchie at the Olympia in Kensington, London. The stakes were high, for the world lightweight championship title was on the line. About ten thousand individuals, who paid a modest sum of five shillings to a whopping ten pounds and two shillings for a seat, bore witness to this epic clash of the pugilistic titans. In the sport of boxing, where fortunes are won and lost in the blink of an eye, only one man would emerge victorious, basking in the glory of triumph, while the other would have to endure the bitter sting of defeat.

With a slick of sticking plaster masking his left eye from a training incident, Freddie made his way through the ropes.[12] The Reverend Father Bounder, a man of the cloth from Saint Michael's Anglican church and the master of ceremonies, took the stage to introduce the contenders. Ritchie came out strong, throwing stiff right-hand punches, and all were well aware of Ritchie's devastating punching power, especially his thunderous right hand, but Freddie, a cunning defender, continually slipped away, taking the sting out of those blows. Freddie proved to be a master of evasion, bobbing and weaving, blocking, and sidestepping with ease, using the ring to his advantage. His opponent was left perplexed at every turn. Freddie's cunning was on full display as he deftly wielded his left hand, inflicting most of the damage with that one punch. The referee was forced to intervene time and again as Freddie relentlessly tied up Ritchie, leaving him little room to maneuver.

As the final bell tolled, the fate of the bout lay in the hands of the arbiter, for neither combatant had dealt a decisive blow in the grueling twenty rounds. Freddie, his left eye ravaged, his nose in a state of disrepair, and his lips lacerated, had weathered a storm of blows from Ritchie, who bore the marks of Freddie's unrelenting left hand. Ritchie's lips were oozing blood, and his right eye was swollen from the relentless barrage of Freddie's hooks. It fell to Eugene Corri, the man in the middle, to declare a winner, and he did so in Freddie's favor.

The admirers of Freddie, perched ringside, were seized with a rapturous frenzy as the verdict of victory was proclaimed. In a spontaneous display of merriment, they hoisted the jubilant Freddie onto their shoulders and paraded him to his dressing room. In stark contrast, Ritchie, appearing vanquished and despondent, retreated to his own quarters, where no revelry awaited him. Initially, he was disinclined to engage in conversation with anyone, but eventually, he yielded to their requests.

"I do not intend to make a holler," said Ritchie, "but I do think the worst I should have got was a draw. Welsh was holding all the time, and I was doing the fighting. Therefore, I think the decision was not fair to me."[13]

In the throes of title bouts, where the fates of pugilistic warriors hang in the balance, a clandestine code silently presides: the advantage tips toward the reigning champion. It is within this unwritten law that Willie Ritchie found his discontentment unbound as he decried the breach of this sacred principle at the hands of referee Eugene Corri. In the dramatic result of Ritchie's championship clash with Freddie, Corri, embodying the role of sole arbiter, awarded Freddie the coveted title by the narrowest of margins, a solitary point. With each round etched into the scorecard as an even stalemate, save for a singular exception, the course of destiny shifted, stirring a tempestuous tempest within Ritchie's soul.[14]

"There has always been an unwritten law that unless a champion is beaten by a good margin," Ritchie said years later, "he gets a draw. That's more or less an accepted conditions in boxing, but of course, in this case it was overlooked. Most referees wouldn't take the title away from a man on a very close score. They'd give him a draw so he wouldn't lose the title. I felt shock. I felt hurt. I felt that I've been tricked. But I said nothing because who wants to be a sore loser, even if he hasn't lost?... So I felt that I had pointed him easily."[15]

The printed word carried a tale of triumph, emblazoned in bold letters across the front page: "Winning a World's Championship on Carrots, Peas and Spring Water." And yet another headline proclaimed, "Fred Welsh, Lightweight Champion of England Finds That a Meatless Diet Increases Endurance." The victorious Freddie himself attributed his success to his newfound love for vegetables, proclaiming with conviction, "Vegetables did it!" The *Los Angeles Times*, ever eager to label and classify, dubbed him a fruitarian, the vegetarian philosopher phenom.[16]

Freddie and his cohort's jubilation was not universal. Arnold Rothstein's purported hand in the triumph cast a lingering shadow over the outcome. Though no concrete evidence implicated Rothstein in the victory, the grapevine propagated the notion with such convincing tenacity that no pugilist hailing from America would defend his championship on British soil for almost thirteen years following the bout. The widespread faith in the rumor was largely due the presence of but a single name, that of Arnold Rothstein.[17]

After the fight, Richie found himself confronted with a curious predicament when his much-anticipated sum of $25,000 graced the streets of New York. This fortune was not entirely entrusted into his eager hands, at least that was the conjecture by some, for there existed a provision that dictated a portion of it was under the watchful gaze of Billy Gibson, who managed Benny Leonard. Whispers of this arrangement echoed through the city, reaching even the seasoned ears of Bat Masterson, that sage connoisseur of all matters pugilistic. It was Masterson who, with his aged wisdom, confirmed the venture, revealing that the funds had been gathered and delivered into Gibson's unyielding grasp.

Ritchie found himself once more in the sprawling

embrace of New York City, where, as Masterson had proclaimed, the elusive promise of monetary fortune failed to materialize. The disillusioned Californian, with misguided hopes in tow, returned to his home, anticipating the overdue settlement would inevitably grace his pockets. The anticipated windfall remained elusive and left his pockets barren, devoid of the promised balance that had cruelly eluded him.

"The inner circle further alleges," wrote Bat Masterson, "that it was to settle the deficit that Leonard was allowed to meet Ritchie and run second. The money Ritchie was to get out of the bout, along with the prestige a point victory would give him, would more than make up for the shortage in the $25,000 he was to receive from the battle with Welsh.

"Not only that, but another meeting between the men was arranged to come off later in the East somewhere. That is the story exactly as we got it, and, if it is true, it would indicate that the Leonard-Ritchie affair was another one of those things. The story, while not exactly a confession or squawk, is nonetheless plausible and will in time leak out, if true. Somebody connected with the affair will be sure to talk about it after a while."[18]

While the authenticity of Bat Masterson's conjectures remained shrouded in mystery, the outcome of the pugilistic duels bore witness to their own tale. In the initial clash, held in California, fortune favored Ritchie over Leonard as the spoils of victory fell into his hands. The journalistic arbiters, oscillating between impartiality and bias, proclaimed the verdict a draw, albeit inclining toward a modest triumph for Ritchie, as underscored by the *San*

Francisco Chronicle. Reiterating a similar sentiment, the *San Francisco Examiner* also cast its favor upon Ritchie. Two months later, in New Jersey, a twist of fate brought Leonard to triumph over Ritchie, his dominance proclaimed through a resounding technical knockout.

"It isn't wonderful that boxing is popular," wrote journalist Louis Dougher in response to Masterson's assertions. "It is more than wonderful that it still lives."[19]

In the wake of the Ritchie-Welsh title fight, Freddie's stature was cast in a dubious light, and the crowd he ran with for years to come only added to the skepticism.[20] The doubt casts a deeper shade when one considers that Freddie participated in many newspaper fights while holding the lightweight boxing title, which meant the only way an opponent could wrest the title away from him was to knock him out. Nevertheless, Freddie would always be fast not to attribute his triumph to chance or extraneous aid—no, it was the sweat of his brow and the cunning of his strategy that secured the victory. Brains over brawn, always.

"I've had my pockets full of rabbit feet," Freddie said a couple of years later, "four-leaf clovers, and such like, but they all go on strike when I get them. If it were raining rubies and diamonds, I would catch cramps in both hands. When they were handing out horseshoes, somebody made a mistake and gave me the left hind shoe of a mule."[21]

"The road to the championship is not an easy one," Freddie would say, "but I for one, found it worthwhile. I lived on the dregs of life for five years here in America before I found my proper sphere. Yet, I regret nothing. I have looked on life in all of its varying moods and phases. It has given me an understanding of human nature and a feeling for my fellow man, which no university curriculum can hope to teach or instill."[22]

With the world title annexed and the adoration of fans ringing in his ears, Freddie was a man on a mission. He stepped into the ring with a fierce determination, fighting not once, not twice, but twenty-one times over the course of the following year. And yet, amidst the chaos of the boxing world, there was one thing that grounded him—the love of his wife, Fanny.

In the midst of his boxing fervor, Freddie and Fanny welcomed their second child into the world—a baby boy born in the days of 1915. They named him Freddie Jr., a tribute to the father who had worked so tirelessly to provide for his family.

As the summer sun beat down, Freddie hung up his gloves for a time, choosing to savor the sweetness of life with his loved ones. Together, they journeyed to the warm embrace of Venice, California, where they frolicked in the sun and basked in the beauty of the land.

Freddie and Fanny owned considerable properties in Venice, and it was looked after in Fanny's capable hands that ensured the place was a sanctuary. They resided in a little cottage situated on Florence Avenue in the town of Venice. Within those walls, an idyllic domesticity reigned supreme. Fanny, the matriarch, presided over the household affairs, and Freddie didn't interfere. Rarely did the topic of boxing permeate the serene atmosphere of this domicile, for the reigning lightweight champion found his greatest joy in frolicking with his children, Betty and Freddie, Jr.

Fanny was not just a housewife; she was a trusted confidante of Freddie in all financial matters. Not a single coin was spent without first seeking her counsel and never was a penny invested against her sound judgment. In Venice, Freddie and Fanny were inseparable, two souls entwined in a world of their own. As the dawn broke over the town each day, they would plunge into the cool embrace of the ocean while their infants were tended to by a watchful nurse on the beach.

"Prize fighting as a business is alright for my husband," Fanny said, "but it will not do for our boy.

"I have other ambitions for him. He is now but seven months old and by the time he develops into a fine large boy, Freddie will be out of the game and prize fighting will have run out of the family.

"Little Freddie, when he grows up to be a man, will devote his time to elevating the men of the world....

"No woman ever had a better husband than have I and a better father never was heard of. I do not object to Freddie's vocation and have never done anything to discourage him.

"It is his business and as a business we both regard it. There is not a quarrelsome hair in his dear head; no wife ever had a more affectionate husband, and no children a kindlier and better father than Freddie.

"He is only a great big boy around the home. The neighbors regard him with surprise and the children are always after him for a romp. The ring is alright for him, but it will never be for little Freddie."[23]

Freddie, in perfect accord with his wife, could not

bring himself to entertain the notion of his beloved son following in his own fisticuffs-laden footsteps and embracing the brutal sport of boxing. Freddie had suffered and bled in the ring and tasted the metallic tang of blood in his mouth and endured the cruel punishment doled out by his merciless opponents. Such a fate was not fit for his offspring, for his precious flesh and blood.

"I don't want my boy to go through what I went through," said Freddie later. "Yet if I myself was to start life anew, I don't know but that I would choose the same course that I did pursue."

"I have looked upon life and found it good," said Freddie. "Maybe that's because I'm still a young man. Youth, health, strength—the view is always cheerful from those windows."[24]

For three blissful months, Freddie had put aside the thrill of the ring, content to soak up the love and warmth of his family. And though the call of the boxing world would soon come again, he relished this time of respite, cherishing each moment with those he held dear.

Freddie, Fanny, Betty, and Freddie, Jr., in Venice, California.

Chapter V

Their house was even more elaborate than I expected, a cheerful red and white Georgian Colonial mansion overlooking the bay. The lawn started at the beach and ran toward the front door for a quarter of a mile, jumping over sun-dials and brick walks and burning gardens—finally when it reached the house drifting up the side in bright vines as though from the momentum of its run. The front was broken by a line of French windows, glowing now with reflected gold, and wide open to the warm windy afternoon, and Tom Buchanan in riding clothes was standing with his legs apart on the front porch.

—F. Scott Fitzgerald, *The Great Gatsby*

Amidst the glitz, glamour, and brutality of the boxing world, Freddie stood out as a curious anomaly. His triumph in claiming the lightweight title was only the beginning of his intrigue. Rather than carousing at the clubs, he preferred to immerse himself in the pages of a book. He wasn't just an ordinary scholarly person—Freddie was a pugilist with a brain, a brain box with a punch, as he would proclaim to all who would listen. His dapper appearance and striking features only served to augment his fanbase, particularly with the fairer sex. Though he had been wed to Fanny since 1905 and had already fathered two children with her, he saw no harm in exploiting his charm to draw in the crowds. And draw them in he did, for Freddie's championship belt proved to be the gateway to a veritable goldmine.

Freddie, now a fighter of great renown, engaged in countless newspaper battles, a commonplace spectacle in his time. Victory was never guaranteed, for the verdicts of such contests were left to the whims of ink-stained scribes. Only by way of knockout could Freddie truly be dethroned, and though he suffered numerous defeats in the court of public opinion, his championship belt remained firmly clasped around his waist. Such contests were, however, a fountain of wealth and fame, and he remained the champion of the people.

After the crown had been won, Freddie took to the ring a staggering fifty-one times between the sweltering summer days of July 7, 1914, and the blooming spring of May 1, 1917. This included wins over great fighters such as Benny Leonard, Battling Nelson, Johnny Kilbane, Rocky Kansas, Charley White twice, and Ad Wolgast twice. Though the sun had risen and set on seventeen scraps in the year 1915 and twenty-two in the following year, only a paltry pair were deemed official for the grand prize of the illustrious title of lightweight champion, both of which were claimed with ease by Freddie in 1916.

The perturbing truth of Freddie's perilous flirtation with relinquishing his boxing crown on a mere couple of occasions weighed heavily upon the vigilant eyes of the press. Their insatiable appetite yearned for a spectacle, an enthralling contest where his coveted title would hang in the balance, instead of the bouts that posed little peril to his celebrated reign.

A newspaper, with a voice akin to the collective conscience of the masses, captured the unspoken sentiments of the multitudes. It dared to give expression to the whispers that hovered in the halls of societal consciousness. As ink flowed from its righteous quill onto the pristine canvas of newsprint, it crafted a verse that resonated deep within the hearts of its readers. The resonant voice embodied the unvoiced reflections.

"Take Freddy Welsh the world's champion lightweight for an illustration," the paper printed. "He is a wonderful boxer, especially for ten rounds, but he refuses to engage in championship matches over what is considered a necessary distance—twenty rounds—without getting a fortune to risk his title. He demands $25,000 for his end for a match with Ritchie and $15,000 for a match with White, a bout of twenty rounds, besides other concessions, which is simply exorbitant. Just because Ritchie demanded unreasonable terms for a match when Welsh won the title is no reason why the Welshman should follow in the same path.

"Welsh will have to defend his title in a real match or lose his power as a drawing card in this country. Freddy is a splendid little gentleman, but even that does not give him the right to demand such unreasonable terms. Ritchie was just as bad when he was champion, and so were many of the others before him, but a dozen wrongs do not make one right. The same state of affairs exists among champions in other classes, and it is about time a halt is called."[1]

Freddie had discovered years ago that boxing was a skill at which he excelled. His nimble footwork and quick fists proved to be his golden ticket to glory. The lightweight championship, once a lofty aspiration, had now become his glittering reality. Yet, behind his pugilistic pursuits lay a greater ambition—the coveted ownership of a health farm that he and Elbert Hubbard had long fancied. While the boxing title had brought him riches, fame, and hobnobbing with the opulent and powerful, it was only a stepping stone toward his ultimate goal. With single-minded determination, Freddie now set his sights on fulfilling his true dream.

Freddie had it all laid out before him—or so it was believed. With meticulous planning, sweat, and unique physical abilities, he ascended to the pinnacle of success. The lightweight boxing championship of the world, once his ultimate goal, had been his for nearly three glorious years. A fortune amassed in that time would ensure a comfortable existence for him, his wife Fanny, daughter Betty, and son Freddie Jr. Freddie was not content to simply bask in the spoils of his triumphs.

When the inevitably of the ring would be fading into the past, Freddie did not intend to spend the remainder of his life in idleness. Instead, he had mapped out a new path, one that he believed would bring him even greater renown and fortune than his days in the ring. He would realize his dream of constructing a health farm.

For years on end, Freddie scoured the expanse of America in search of the idyllic spot to birth his health farm. He crisscrossed the land in tireless pursuit, never wavering from his mission. Finally, near the ides in the days of March 1917, he chanced upon a gem in the quaint municipality of Chatham Township in New Jersey. It appeared filled with endless possibilities, for he had stumbled upon his destiny.

Freddie's fancy fixated on a property of palatial proportion, a veritable mansion sitting upon 162 acres perched high atop a hill at Johnson's Gap. He would name it the Long Hill Health Farm, but to many, it remained the house on the hill. Long Hill described the hilly terrain along River Road that extended for miles into neighboring communities. The mansion occupied the entire hilltop. From its exalted vantage point, the estate commanded a sweeping vista in every direction of the Passaic Valley, its reach extending for miles in all directions, an unrivaled splendor to behold.

The white mansion that perched on the land was a manor with wings that unfurled forward like open arms. The roofs and gables were of a vivid rich red hue,[2] creating a blaze against a brilliant blue sky that could be seen for miles on a cloudless day, a beacon amidst the sea of greenery. During the summertime, the beaming golden sunshine would enkindle the gentle green slopes, embraced by basin-like valleys that enfolded the land.

Beneath the grand, sprawling estate and wide-reaching mansion, the emerald lawn cascaded down to the roadway below, its green glittering carpet stretching far and wide. A lofty windmill, fashioned from a sturdy steel framework, lay concealed behind an overgrowth of ivy and a tangle of woodbine that rose up and clung to its peak. To the left of the structure stood a colossal barn with a ruby rooftop. Beyond the barn, the cow yard, pig pen, and poultry run sprawled out in rustic harmony, and further still, the orchards and hay fields danced in the gentle breeze.

Atop the lengthy and gradual incline, the mansion's immediate surroundings were bare of trees and lacking in shrubbery, allowing it to be seen from the roadside. The incline was flanked on both sides by an abundance of trees, particularly fruit trees, and shrubbery, that rose up to the property's zenith, whereupon they angled to form a perpendicular line with the house. Additional shrubbery embellished the front of the dwelling. A handful of steps leading to a path with a solitary shrub to its right awaited a passersby from the road. The path snaked to the right and left, meandering up the property's left side through the trees and shrubbery until it reached the mansion. The adjacent acreage encompassed a vast expanse of fields and woodland.

The mansion possessed a peculiar charm, one that seemed to breathe with a life of its own, as if cursed by some malevolent force. Dubbed the Pelletreau mansion, it bore witness to a series of misfortunes that plagued its previous dwellers. Commissioned by a wealthy real estate mogul, V. F. Pelletreau, the grand edifice was intended as a summer getaway, fashioned to his every whim and fancy.

Sadly, fate proved unkind to Pelletreau, who met his untimely demise in Morristown, New Jersey, after a fatal horse-riding mishap when thrown from his mount and killed instantly. The property, years later, now alleviated of its patron, was left in the hands of a New York merchant by the name of George E. Duncan, who took up residence in the house, only to meet his end unexpectedly in the city, mere months before Freddie's interest was piqued.

Freddie paid no mind to the ill portents that clung to the abode; Freddie pressed on with unflinching determination. This was his fated path. He would conquer the ominous presence and mold it to his will, for he was a man of unyielding resolve, determined to succeed and make a life within those walls.

"For nearly ten years," Freddie said, "I have had this

idea in mind. For more than three years, I have been looking for a place to strike my fancy. I wanted one that would both be a good place for my wife and two 'kiddies' to live on and at the same time serve as a training camp. This deal was closed five days ago. Within the next ten days, I intend to take over the title and this spring I expect to have the training farm in first class condition."

''The house there," Freddie continued, "is one of the finest I have ever seen … I intend to have a fine golf course. There will also be tennis, horseback riding, and various other forms of sport to drive away worry from the mind of the tired businessman…."[3]

Freddie, in his wisdom, chose the property partly for its convenience to the folks of New York. The estate lay twenty-nine miles from the great city. Eighty trains traversed the distance between New York and the neighboring town of Summit on a daily basis, allowing a swift and easy journey of forty-five minutes, which would surely entice those seeking Freddie's services. As part of his grand plan for a health farm business, Freddie was to establish offices in the illustrious Commodore Hotel in New York.

In that domain of opulence where the estate resided, the well-to-do were aplenty. Country estates owned by the affluent were strewn across the terrain, serving as summer abodes for their privileged denizens. The town adjacent to Chatham Township, Summit, was a veritable paradise for the wealthy, who flocked there to bask in the tranquil pleasures of country life. The Blackburn resort, which was later called the Grand Summit Hotel, was erected in 1868 and swiftly became a beloved haven for those seeking refuge from the city's sweltering heat.

Just prior to acquiring the estate, Freddie's pal William C. Lyons, the United States senator from Colorado, hailing fresh from a New York sojourn with Freddie, was mighty impressed with the place. Lyons was a man who owned every room he stepped in, a man of few words—well, a few thousand, perhaps. No one labeled him as "Bill Cyclone" and "Wild Bill" Lyons on account of his meekness. Senator Lyons was a rip-snortin', two-gun man who held a pearl-handled pistol[4] and counted Jack Dempsey, the future heavyweight champion of the world, among his cronies. His fame as a boxing timekeeper was known from coast to coast.

"This stuff about Welsh retiring in July is all off now," said Lyons in his high decibel, ear-piercing voice, "I had a personal talk with the champion, and he says he will meet all comers for five more years. He is in excellent shape now and is putting the kayo on his sparring partners each day."[5]

On the day of April 3, 1917, Julio J. Julio and Lester S. Duncan, son of George E. Duncan, affixed their signatures to a document relinquishing their claims to the ownership of the property that Freddie sought. It was a dream made manifest, a cherished ambition finally fulfilled.

Chapter VI

The victor belongs to the spoils.

—F. Scott Fitzgerald, *The Beautiful and Damned*

At this life's juncture, Freddie paused on his health farm, dwelling in Long Island, his days filled with fervently training in the town of Douglaston, Long Island, for an upcoming battle. Soon, Freddie was to face his greatest challenge yet as he prepared to defend his title against Benny the "Ghetto Wizard" Leonard. This was to be no unpretentious sparring match but a clash of titans that would test the limits of their endurance and skill. The true measure of a champion lay not in the easy victories but in the fierce battles that, in the past, had tested Freddie's mettle and left him triumphant in the end.

Leonard spoke of Freddie in grand terms, proclaiming him to be among the cleverest and most formidable defensive boxers to have graced this earth. What lay ahead for Leonard was far from a simple task, for he had traversed this path before.

In the past, when Leonard would return home after a fight, he would find his father reading the Torah.

"Did you win?" the parent would invariably ask.

Benny would say, "I licked him in one round," or two rounds, as the case may be.

But there came a night when Benny's report wasn't so satisfactory.

"Well, did you win?"

"No."

The father closed the Torah.

"What happened?"

"Why, it was a draw." [Newspaper decisions, first fight went to Freddie, second to Benny Leonard.]

"But your face—it is terrible! Tell me how it happened."

"Well, this Freddie Welsh is better than any of the men I ever fought before. Every time I tried to hit him, he was out somewhere else, and he hit me oftener than all of the other fighters I have ever fought."[1]

Freddie and Benny Leonard in the ring before one of their two bouts in 1916.

On the twenty-eighth of May, in the year nineteen-seventeen, the Manhattan Athletic Club would bear witness to a bout of epic proportions. It would be a battle between two battle-tested pugnacious warriors. Freddie, with his glory days fast receding into the horizon, was poised to engage in a fiery skirmish against Benny Leonard, his counterpart in every way. This was not the first time these two had crossed paths. In fact, this was their third meeting. Freddie retained his title after the previous two bouts because even though the official record shows that Leonard outpointed Freddie in one of the contests—Leonard maintained he outpointed Freddie in both fights—he failed to knock him out. Leonard had to deal Freddie a knockout blow if he wished to snatch the lightweight title from his grasp.

Weeks before the bout, Leonard was acutely aware of the looming fact. It weighed heavily on him like a sullen cloud, casting an ominous shadow over his every thought. The trouble was everyone felt the need to impress upon him what he already knew, exacerbating his anxiety to the point of exhaustion. The mental strain proved to be his greatest nemesis, a formidable adversary that threatened to derail him at every turn. In the crucial moments of the most significant fight of his life, he found himself beset by nervousness and trepidation. Though he emerged unscathed physically, the battle waged within would be harder than any he had ever fought in the ring.

"The mental strain made it hard for me," Leonard said. "I had beaten Welsh twice in no-decision contests but had been unable to reach his jaw with a knockout punch. When we were matched for our third scrap, the thought that I must knock out one of the greatest defensive fighters that ever lived, preyed on my mind constantly. Billy Gibson [Leonard's manager] continually reminded me that I must win inside the limit for he said it would probably be the last crack I would get at the champion. When I went out for a walk my friends told me to flatten Welsh. My trainer, George Engel, demonstrated punches with which I must knock out Freddie."[2]

On the night of the bout, the atmosphere was charged with tension. Leonard, rooted in his dressing room, was besieged by a discordance of voices, each one imploring him to vanquish his opponent with a decisive blow. "You must knock him out—You've got to knock him out,"[3] The incessant exhortations had taken their toll on Leonard, who was now on unsteady legs as he made his way to the ring. The weight of expectations hung heavy upon him, threatening to crush his spirit before the fight even began.

"For weeks," Leonard said, "I heard nothing but 'knock him out.' When I finally walked into the ring for the contest, my knees were banging together, not due to fear of Welsh, but because I was afraid I wouldn't get an opportunity to land a punch that would rob Freddie of his senses and title. Sitting in the corner before the gong rang, Gibson and Engel whispered to me. 'You must stop him. You must.'"[4]

"The bell finally sounded and with the words," Leonard said. "'knock him out' ringing in my ears I started to fight."[5]

"Welsh was strong," Leonard said. "He was in wonderful shape and boxed defensively as never before. I tried to get him to open up, but he wouldn't. It was just a case of jabbing and then falling into a clinch. My, how I try to reach his jaw with a right-hand smash. It was impossible."[6]

Eventually, the youthful Leonard, twenty-one summers old, would set an untamed pace, relentlessly targeting Freddie's lean physique with a ferocity unmatched. Benny's fists, swift and unyielding, found their mark with deadly precision, assaulting the ribs and midsection of the thirty-one-year-old champion with a fury that knew no bounds. In an attempt to shatter Freddie's unshakable confidence, the agile challenger brazenly extended his chin, tempting his opponent with an open target. Rarely had Freddie misjudged his tactics, but he was now ensnared by the quick and clever mind of his opponent.

"Finally, after two or three rounds," Leonard said, "I started to direct my punches to the body. I soaked him with rights and lefts to the midriff, and all the time I could hear 'Knock him out—You've got to knock him out.' Beginning with the fifth round, I could feel Welsh's holding tactics begin to slacken, and I knew he was weakening."[7]

It was in the fourth round that Leonard landed a crushing blow, a slashing right counter that would become his trademark, leaving Freddie's head recoiling and his knees buckling from the sheer force of the strike. For a few harrowing moments, Freddie found himself unable to stand on his own two feet, but his ring savvy soon kicked in as he bluffed and hustled his way out of the predicament.

"Then," said Leonard, "Gibson and Engel reminded me that I already had outpointed Welsh in two previous ten-round bouts, and, if I didn't knock him out before the finish of this match, I probably never would get another opportunity to win the title.

"I wanted that championship. I craved it. Every boxer is anxious to become a title holder. And as Gibson's and Engel's pleadings for me to score a knockout became greater and greater, my frantic efforts became harder and harder."[8]

"In the eighth round," said Leonard, "Welsh was greatly fatigued. The bell found him tired and worn."[9]

"For eight rounds I tried hard to land a finishing punch but couldn't," Leonard said. "Welsh absolutely refused to lead, and although I was outpointing him, I could see visions of Freddie walking from the ring, beaten but still champion."[10]

In all actuality, the veteran pugilist was simply stalling the inevitable, as all great and proud champions are liable to do. Deep down, he must have known that his time had come, just as the equally intuitive Leonard surely recognized that this was his moment to shine.

"Then the ninth," said Leonard. "After Referee Kid McPartland had dragged us out of several clinches and I had backed Fred into a corner, I felt sure of the championship."[11]

With a quickness born of pure instinct, Leonard surged forward at the onset of the ninth round, delivering a crushing right that sliced straight through Freddie's defenses. And yet, for all that, Freddie's stubborn pride refused to let him stay down for even a moment, as he leaped back up to his feet without accepting a count or so much as a second thought, only to charge headlong into a merciless hailstorm of blows.

"Poor Freddie!" Leonard said. "He was all in. I was

wishing for a towel to come from his corner. But the sign of defeat made no appearance, and I waded in, punching my hardest with both hands. The finish came when Welsh was unable to hold up his guard any longer."[12]

"The ninth of that bout probably the most dramatic in boxing history," Leonard continued. "With Welsh in some manner holding himself up with his elbows on the top rope, I was punching him as if he were a bag when Referee Kid McPartland touched me on the shoulder and sent me to my corner.

"Game to the end, Welsh extricated himself from the corner, staggered toward the center of the ring with his right hand raised as if to swing it, and then reeled and tottered toward the ropes. He half dove out of the ring, falling limply over the second rope. He was 'dead' out."[13]

Following the pugilistic encounter, Referee Kid McPartland rendered his appraisal of the tumultuous ninth and ultimate round. The raucous bout had unfolded with fervor, every punch bearing the weight of fate in the hallowed ring. As the crowd's crescendo of roars and gasps filled the air, McPartland stood as the arbiter of destiny, his eyes keenly surveying the sweat-soaked combatants who battled for both honor and triumph. In this fistic symphony of blood and courage, he wielded the power to decide the fate of gladiators, their fates dancing on the edge of his deft judgment. Amidst the fervid heartbeat of the sporting arena, McPartland's words descended upon the expectant ears, concluding a saga that would linger in the annals of pugilistic lore.

"In the ninth round," the referee, Kid McPartland

said, "which proved to be the final one, he was in pretty bad shape…. Leonard started a terrific attack which Welsh could not stave off, and finally a series of heavy punches sent Freddie sagging down toward the floor. As he went down, he grabbed the upper rope in his glove hand and thus kept himself from going down. I will never forget the set smile that was on his face as he hung there, a helpless mark for the finishing smashes of the oncoming Leonard. Of course, I could not let Benny strike his man in that condition.

"'That's enough, Benny,' I said, motioning him away.

"As Leonard stepped back, I turned toward Welsh, and he was still on his feet with the ring rope still clutched in his hand. It took all my strength to pry loose those fingers and no sooner were they loosened then Welsh staggered around still trying bravely to keep his feet until suddenly he pitched back into the ropes and hung there out, but still refusing to go to the floor."[14]

"Since that contest," Leonard said, "my nerves never have failed me, and I never since have suffered such a mental strain."[15]

"I was happy but felt sad," Leonard continued. "I, Benny Leonard, have become the lightweight champion, but I felt sorry for the grittiest gloveman that ever lived. He was game, was Freddie Welsh, gritty to the finish."[16]

Freddie, who had held the world lightweight title for coming on three years, suffered a crushing defeat at the hands of Benny Leonard in the ninth round, succumbing to a technical knockout. Three times Freddie met the unforgiving canvas in that fateful final round. Leonard, gracious in victory, offered Freddie a chance to reclaim his title in a rematch. Freddie, unyielding in his pride, protested that he hadn't even received a one-count in that decisive ninth round and thus believed the championship to still be his. However, he had been savagely beaten, and the referee, Kid McPartland, saw it all unfold in a different light.

"There never was a championship decided without a man getting a count," Freddie said immediately after the fight. "I received no count tonight and consider my title in no way affected by what happened. Though I was in a bad shape, nine seconds rest would have done me a lot of good, and I certainly would have come back.

"I was not given the opportunity the rules call for, and hence I cannot see how Leonard can claim the title. For his victory over me I have nothing but praise for my opponent. I still insist, however, that I would have been able to continue had the rules been lived up to and I had been given the privilege of a count."[17]

Upon being told what Freddie had said, Leornard countered with, "That's all Bosh! He did not receive a count because he did not stay down for one until he was gone, and it was all over. My first right in the ninth knocked Fred silly. If the veteran had not lost his head, he would never have got up so quickly as he did. He would have stayed down and taken the benefit of the count.

"Freddie was out off his feet after that solid right that first dropped him. It was instinct and not fighting sense that brought him up so quickly. When McPartland did step in, Fred was gone for good. He could not stand on his feet and fell through the ropes. He would not have come to for an hour if his seconds had not picked him up and worked over him.

"I am sorry for Freddie; honest, I am. Of course, I'm glad I won. Look what it means to me and my family, but I would rather have taken the title from almost anyone than Freddie."[18]

The lightweight crown, once firmly held by Freddie's hand, had slipped away into the abyss. With his dreams of pugilistic glory shattered, he retreated to his newly-acquired estate in New Jersey, determined to resurrect his fading aspirations. Armed with a wealth of riches, he vowed to amplify its magnificence beyond measure, making it even more lavish and opulent.

Chapter VII

On a chance we tried an important-looking door, and walked into a high Gothic library, panelled with carved English oak, and probably transported complete from some ruin overseas....

"The books?" He nodded. "Absolutely real—have pages and everything. I thought they'd be a nice durable cardboard. Matter of fact, they're absolutely real. Pages and—Here! Lemme show you."

—F. Scott Fitzgerald, *The Great Gatsby*

Freddie, with his wife Fanny, daughter Betty, and son Freddie Jr. in tow, could have easily succumbed to a life of leisure, buoyed by his carefully crafted wealth. But Freddie was not one to linger in the shadows of his past glories, for with the finality of ropes, stages, and cheering galleries, idleness was not an option. Freddie had set his sights on a new pursuit, one that would elevate him beyond the fisticuffs that were fading away. He would build a health farm, a concept that was all the rage in his era. And it was the late Elbert Hubbard, that sage purveyor of life advice, who had urged Freddie to take on this endeavor. For Freddie, the health farm was not just a means of financial gain but a chance to bask in the limelight once more and to reap the rewards of recognition and fame. With this new venture, Freddie envisioned a future of even greater notoriety and riches.

Less than a month in the wake of relinquishing his title, Freddie found himself settled in Chatham Township, New Jersey, as the thorough refurbishing of his estate unfolded. It was during this time that news reached him: the Bamberger Cadet Corps, hailing from Newark, was in the area. This group, seventy-five strong, had taken a vested interest in setting up camp along the serene banks of the meandering Passaic River, a mere stone's throw from Freddie's stately domain. Intrigued by their military presence, Freddie felt an irresistible compulsion to seek them out, extending a gracious invitation to camp within the confines of his orchard.

A luncheon came to pass, meticulously orchestrated by Freddie himself in a style befitting a disciplined military regiment, all beneath the sheltering canopy of his trees. Eager to showcase their prowess, the cadets rendered a dazzling exhibition drill upon the expanse of Freddie's estate.

Not long after Freddie's return to his estate, the distinguished Senator Bill Lyons found himself in receipt of a letter from Bertha Weston Schaefer, who was the sister of Freddie's wife, Fanny, and was working as Freddie's secretary. In the letter, Bertha talked about Freddie's flourishing foray into the realm of healthful living, nestled amidst the environs of a New Jersey health farm.

The letter detailed Fanny's newfound domesticity, toiling away on the farmstead and even doing her own laundering and everything else. Bertha further elaborated on the culinary abilities of Fanny, who whipped up the most delectable preserves. Bertha told him that some obliging chap had bestowed upon Freddie a quartet of the wildest, most adorable pheasants one ever did see, and the farm also boasted a flock of snowy white turkeys, whose exuberant gobbling could be heard across the idyllic countryside from the back porch.

In the letter, Bertha divulged the happenings of their estate. Feathered friends roamed the backyard, from clucking chickens to quacking ducks. Freddie had just wrapped up the construction of his handball court and was now embarking on the installation of a luxurious swimming pool. Bertha boasted that her dear Freddie was transforming portly New York businessmen into skinny figures. Bertha also said her sister, Fanny, was a girl who liked to dance and have a good time, and it must be awfully lonely for her at times sitting out on the back steps.

Finally, in the letter, Bertha thought that maybe they could get Bat Masterson to come over from New York because Billy Lyons was telling her that he was getting awfully old and grouchy and that all he does now is sit in his office. Masterson's boss kept running in and out of the office and telling Masterson what to write about. He would only make suggestions, but if you were disinclined to write the way he wanted, he'd explain that two heads were better than one. Bertha said he may have been right at that, but it all depended on the kind of heads.[1]

The mansion on the estate already boasted more than thirty rooms adorned with the most exquisite hardwoods known to man. Many of the rooms featured a substantial fireplace, warming their inhabitants with an inviting glow. The walls were canvases of dozens of hand-painted hunting scenes, while hand-carvings imported from Italy dotted the rooms.

The tri-level structure mansion had dual two-story wings, perfectly angled toward the road and surrounded by sprawling porches. The windows were draped with vertical striped awnings, providing shade and shelter from the sun's rays. According to the *Lewiston Daily Sun*, the farm cost $70,000. Freddie, being Freddie, made renovations to his abode and surrounding estate, elevating the grand total to a staggering $150,000—an amount equivalent to his entire life savings and an additional mortgage of $35,000.

Freddie had spared no expense in decking out his estate with every imaginable contrivance to put a man into shape. Freddie, being quite the ambitious sort, went ahead and constructed a fitness emporium, including exercise chambers, tiled shower baths, and massage parlors. He transformed the interior with a kitchen of the latest invention.

His crowning achievement was an illustrious library. One was enveloped in a milieu of sophistication and cultivation, as Freddie's library boasted a value that was inestimable, and his knowledge of the classics was on par with that of a learned professor. The library displayed a ceiling of oak beams, and the room was embellished with opulent mahogany furnishings, plush leather armchairs, and bookcases stretching along the walls, lined with his treasured books. The furniture was cast in partial shade in the wake of the majestic luminescence that emanated from the cathedral light of the great stained-glass chandelier, fashioned in the form of a regal crown.

A fervent reader, Freddie had stocked the shelves with volumes of literary greats, their artistry embossed on sumptuous bindings. Works by luminaries such as Oscar

Wilde, Eugène Brieux, Robert Louis Stevenson, William Shakespeare, Leo Tolstoy, Ralph Waldo Emerson, Bernard Shaw, O. Henry, Mark Twain, and many other acclaimed writers adorned the shelves. Some of these were exclusive editions inked with the author's own hand.

Upstairs, the wings had been transformed into airy sleeping apartments for those who wished to breathe in the crisp air, with full casement windows adorning three sides. A myriad of bedrooms, a dozen to be exact, catered to the whims and fancies of various tenants. Simplicity and cleanliness were the guiding principles of many of these chambers, resembling the austere quarters of uncomplicatedness.

Freddie said of the bedrooms, "These are not supposed to be living rooms; I want the guests here to cheer up, be natural, stay downstairs or outdoors, and keep with the bunch. These are not worry rooms. These are sleeping rooms!"[2]

Yet, with all the necessities in place, nothing was superficial. It was Freddie who added a touch of grandeur to all the rooms throughout the dwelling, embellishing them with a piano, a billiard table, and even a reception hall, not to mention the generous expanse of lawn, perfect for languorous pursuits between dinner and the hour of the hammock.

He completely revamped the estate's landscape, adding a golf course, an al fresco squash and handball court made of cement, pristine tennis lawns, and a swimming pool that stretched an impressive seventy-five feet and was fed by a never-ending spring. This swimming facility was situated in a grove of ivory-white birches and was nothing short of a marvel. One could not help but recall the wise words of his bygone friend Elbert Hubbard, "Blessed is that man who has found his work!"[3]

What Freddie could not build on the sprawling estate, he filled with a flock of pristine white turkeys, accompanied by radiant golden pheasants—the ones Bertha mentioned in her letter to Lyons— and his cherished companions, the Welsh terriers. The estate was dotted with majestic Kentucky saddlehorses, inviting the guests to take a ride while a plethora of other fauna filled the spaces, completing the idyllic scenery.

The grand estate of Freddie, oh, how it dazzled the senses. It was to serve as a haven for the weary, a place where the businessmen and professionals who found themselves trapped in the humdrum of routine or chaos could come and learn the art of proper living. Nestled high up in the hills, the air was a wonder to behold, pure and crisp, a veritable elixir for the soul. Every breath was a rejuvenation; every inhale filling the lungs with a vitality born of the mingling of oxygen and the blood's iron. You felt yourself a part of the cosmos, a minuscule fragment of the vast universe. The recipe for wellness was simple yet potent: wholesome food, untainted water, and moderate exercise. These three components were the magic trifecta for one's health.

As June swept in on a warm breeze, Freddie, ever the savvy entrepreneur, made a bold move. With the ink still wet on the property deed, he extended an offer of sixty acres to the mayor of the nearby town of Summit. His intention was clear: to create an aviation field for the pilots of the burgeoning airplane age, as well as to cultivate a general garden of exquisite beauty.

Freddie's ambition knew no bounds. With this gambit, Freddie positioned himself as a true visionary, a man ahead of his time. For while others saw only a humble farm, Freddie saw limitless potential. And with each passing day, his dream grew ever closer to reality.

On a summer's day in 1917, the Long Hill Health Farm was unveiled with much grandeur and ceremony. The well-to-do and elite of society were invited to partake in the festivities, including a bevy of famous personalities. Amongst the throngs of guests, the infamous Bat Masterson made an appearance, regaling onlookers with his description of the farm as a "session magnificent house high on a hill, like an acropolis."[4] It was a sight to behold, with its opulent decor and stunning views that seemed to stretch out to the horizon.

In the annals of the Wild West, Bat Masterson's name was writ large, his exploits as a gunfighter and lawman still the stuff of legend. He was also known as a United States marshal, army scout, and gambler. But it was in the latter days of his storied life that he found himself in the metropolis of New York City, where he forged a new path as a boxing promoter and sports columnist for the *New York Morning Telegraph*.

In the midst of the Yuletide season of 1915, Bat received a gift from his friend Freddie that would adorn his person. A Waltham pocket watch of exquisite craftsmanship, with a fourteen-karat gold octagonal case encircled by a delicate silver filigree. Freddie had the inside back cover engraved with the inscription "To Bat Masterson from Freddie Welsh XMAS 1915."[5] The watch was a sight to behold and its value beyond measure.

The bestowment, in itself, was nothing out of the ordinary. Freddie had a proclivity for presenting lavish offerings to his famed, affluent, and influential friends. They served as a gesture of gratitude, signifying both the prosperity he had amassed and the kindness he harbored toward his acquaintances. Bat Masterson, the man who had faced down some of the most fearsome gunslingers of the West, came to cherish a gift from a dear friend, a token of their enduring bond.

On this opening day of the health farm, a new chapter in the saga of luxury and wellness was born. With the resplendent Long Hill Health Farm as the backdrop, the sky was the limit, and possibilities were endless. For in this wondrous place, one could forget their troubles and immerse themselves in a world of indulgence, relaxation, and absolute serenity.

Felix Shay visited the health farm and described it in a published work, *A Little Journey to the Fred Welsh Health Farm*, circa 1917. Shay was a writer, adventurer, and mutual friend with Freddie's departed Elbert Hubbard, for whom Shay was the biographer. He said what Freddie had built represented an investment upwards of $100,000 of earned money from boxing. Nothing was slighted. All in all, he believed that it was the best-equipped place for the purpose of a health farm in America. Felix Shay said the purpose was to instruct those who are open to conviction, by precept and example, in the conservation of the most precious of all resources—health!

Freddie, his wife, Fanny, their two children, Betty and Freddie Jr., and Auntie Pattie, were all there to greet Felix Shay. There was much friendly talk among them. Shay remarked that it was a pleasant little family.

"Felix," Freddie said, "I have searched this country from New York to California for a place that would seem like home to the man who opened the front door—and this is my choice!"

"The man who built this house and furnished it," Felix Shay said, "whoever he was, did it for someone he loved. I know that. The furniture was perfection, and in excellent taste; much of it built regardless of expense, and many of the rooms were furnished in the natural woods to match—walnut, Birdseye maple, and mahogany. There was scarcely any paper, only silk tapestry. The billiard room, large enough for a men's club, had side walls and benches with red Morocco leather. There was an elegance, a restfulness, of blended tones and colors, of harmonious woods, and rugs, and murals, that pervaded the entire place and created an extraordinary atmosphere of comfort and cheerfulness, which as Freddie says, makes it 'seem like home!'"[6]

Shay, with his vernacular, so aptly described the grandeur that Freddie had erected. He wrote:

"Last week I saw a dream made real. I saw the Fred Welsh health farm. I spent a day with Freddie…. Freddie is interested, interesting, sympathetic. He knows his business. He's an instinctive teacher. No man can place himself in Freddie Welsh's charge for two weeks or so, and not come away much better for the experience.

"Summit, New Jersey, twenty miles outside New York City, on the Lackawanna Railroad, is a high point in the Blue Ridge chain, and is called the Mountain City. Long Hill towers over Summit. On the very top, the pinnacle, of Long Hill, looking for ways to the distant horizon, rest Freddie's establishment....

"Freddie Welsh is a real sportsman, which is not the same as a 'Sport.'"[7]

As Shay and Freddie ambled across the fields, they traversed the terrain from the bountiful orchard to the humble chicken coop, from the trickling spring house to the sturdy box stalls, and from the blooming gardens to the frigid icehouse. Astonishingly to Shay, throughout the span of two hours, Freddie never once spoke of fighters or fights. Shay, taken aback by this unexpected turn of events, was struck by the remarkable exuberance of his hospitable companion, finding him to be one of the most captivating acquaintances he had ever made.

As Freddie and Shay traversed the fields, Freddie gestured grandly to his bountiful orchards, which had already yielded barrels upon barrels of the sweetest apples the countryside had ever seen, which was impressive since the neighborhood yield was light, failing to deliver even a fraction of Freddie's grand harvest. The earth beneath their feet seemed to brim with life, for in one particularly fruitful patch, two hundred bushels of potatoes had been coaxed from the soil.

And yet, these were but mere tokens of Freddie's grandeur, for he had in his possession a chestnut saddle horse with a reputation for speed that stirred the blood because he was supposed to have had a time record. Further still, Freddie bade Shay follow him to the spring-fed swimming pool, where a brace of wild ducks waddled, which some admirer had shipped in. But the ultimate glory of Freddie's empire was surely his grand library, brimming with authors of every stripe, their pages aglow with the wisdom of the ages. As they engaged in a lively debate over the merits of each book, Shay found himself quite taken with Freddie's intellect. Shay enjoyed the cerebral sparring.

"Freddie's not the typical pugilist," Shay said. "No, nothing like that."[8]

As Shay trudged toward Summit to catch the train to New York City, something caused him to halt his advance. He cast his gaze backward toward the lofty white mansion perched atop the hill like a regal monarch overseeing its kingdom. The edifice exuded an air of aristocracy and refinement, a dazzling spectacle that drew Shay in with an irresistible allure. Mesmerized by the splendor of the mansion, he couldn't help but wonder for a moment. He was torn between the allure of the unknown and the necessity of his journey, but in the end, he shook off his contemplation and turned toward his destination, leaving it behind as a fading memory, but said to himself, "There's an enterprise that will succeed."[9]

Freddie's mansion, the house on the hill.

Section of the driveway.

View from the top of the lawn.

Section of the porch.

Outdoor squash and handball court.

Dining room.

The grand library.

Billiard room.

Chapter VIII

I had been actually invited. A chauffeur in a uniform of robin's egg blue crossed my lawn early that Saturday morning with a surprisingly formal note from his employer—the honor would be entirely Gatsby's, it said, if I would attend his 'little party' that night. He had seen me several times and had intended to call on me long before but a peculiar combination of circumstances had prevented it— signed Jay Gatsby in a majestic hand.

—F. Scott Fitzgerald, *The Great Gatsby*

The only building in sight was a small block of yellow brick sitting on the edge of the waste land, a sort of compact Main Street ministering to it and contiguous to absolutely nothing. One of the three shops it contained was for rent and another was an all-night restaurant approached by a trail of ashes; the third was a garage—Repairs. GEORGE B. WILSON. Cars Bought and Sold—and I followed Tom inside.

—F. Scott Fitzgerald, *The Great Gatsby*

In the flush of ambition, Freddie penned his latest venture with fervent penmanship, a testament to his zeal for the art of advertisement. With a flourish, he etched his words onto the page, for in this world of cutthroat competition, only the boldest and most daring could hope to succeed. With each stroke of his pen, he was one step closer to his destiny— a destiny that would be shaped by the power of his will.

Freddie, to draw customers, wrote of his new endeavor:

"The rush, hurry and worry of American life wears men out. Many are old while yet young. They break down. These break downs are called by many fancy and scientific names, but a correct diagnosis is not a cure.

"Health that is lost must be regained by *Natural* Methods. Nature is best.

"The man who finds himself in a bad way, must resolve—and the sooner the better! —to go back to the Beginning and get a Fresh Start!

"Primarily, he has three things to accomplish:

"(a)He must restore his physical body to health.

"(b)He must throw off the old habits of neglect and carelessness, and achieve a new way to live.

"(c)He must learn to *enjoy* getting and keeping in A 1 condition.

"That's it—a clean start! A new set of healthful habits! An appreciation of the joys of right living! I believe a few weeks spent with me at my Health Farm will accomplish much toward the that end for you! I have given years of patients study to Health Culture. I have worked out my theories under 'test' conditions.

"I know what can be accomplished!

"You are regarded as an individual, examined as an individual, and your course of treatment plan for your individual needs.

"I am a believer in no particular 'ism.'

"I have no *cure-all*.

"I believe in a well-proportioned, well-balanced diet. But I do not specialize on all vegetables, all milk, or two thin slices of toast and a cup of tea.

"A diet must perform a different service for different men; therefore, the diet must often be *different*.

"I believe in baths; all according to schedule, based on the patient's condition. There is a complete equipment here of Shower and Needle Baths, of Sprays and Sitz and Tub Baths, and a large Swimming Pool. But I would not shock a Nervous Man with a cold shower, or make a weak man weaker with a Hot Tub.

"There's a moderate middle-method, an understanding, healthful method, that I like better. I believe in Exercise. I have built a new gymnasium for that purpose. But I call it the '*Exercise Room*', and I have no desire to invite a man in the forties or fifties to attempt gymnastic 'stuns.'

"No man will be asked to tax himself behind his strength. Rather he will be urged not to! I have a knowledge of Anatomy; At the Nervous System and its ailments; of the Digestive Tract and its disarrangement, and kindred subjects; Along with how to take on and take off weight.

"More, too; I have initiative. I generally know what to do and I am not afraid to do it. Nevertheless, I see to it that a skilled Physician is in attendance, to advise and to cooperate with me.

"I believe in the psychological effect, the quieting effect, of a beautiful, well-ordered home on a person who is neither quite well or very sick. Therefore I have made my place as unlike an 'Institution' as possible.

"The guests are members of the family and live as we live—that's all! Because I like pure

"Because I like *Pure Food*, I produce most of the vegetables, fruits, foul, eggs, milk, butter, etc., that we serve on our table, and then I see to it that they are improved in the cooking!

"Because I like to walk over Open Country, I own 162 of the most interesting acres you will find anywhere in America—Hills and Valleys, Large Trees and Small, Gardens and Cornfields, Meadows, Swimming Pool, Horsebacking, Hunting and Fishing. If you like to Chop Wood, well, there's the Ax!

"May I finish this personal message to you by saying that I would esteem it a privilege to show you around my Health Farm whenever most convenient for you, and to walk with you over the hills and through the thickets, and along the soft earth back-roads!"[1]

Freddie, with all his grandiose ambitions, proudly proclaimed the rates for his prestigious health farm. For three weeks, the sum of $180 was to be expected, with an additional charge of $60 per additional week per person. These fees were inclusive of room and board, as well as access to the health course, luxurious baths, and all other privileges one might expect while residing on his estate. Freddie seemed to revel in the magnificence of his enterprise and longed for the world to bask in the glory of his splendid creation.

Freddie, a soul destined for perpetual misfortune on the treacherous roads of existence, would display an unfortunate lack of skill behind the wheel of an automobile, perpetually plagued by a series of accidents. One of the first of these ill-fated encounters took place in the hazy realm of May, in the year 1918 when his hapless vehicle met its demise. On that occasion, an automotive congregation, with Freddie as its host, narrowly evaded the clutches of grave injury as calamity struck near the bend at the foot of Springfield Avenue in the western part of the town of Summit. Accompanying Freddie on this ill-omened journey were G. M. L. Brown and Doctor Barnby, a patron of his curative sanctuary.

Together, they traversed the roads that led from Summit, ascending the interminable hill as the midnight hour cast its dark cloak upon them. Chance conspired against their progress, for it was at the base of that arduous incline that a twist of fortune manifested. Without warning, a rim detached itself from the monstrosity of machinery, delivering their vessel into the hands of a cruel destiny. The vehicle careened towards a steadfast tree, a sentinel guarding the southern periphery of the thoroughfare, and executed a disorienting impact upon them. The passengers, jettisoned from their precarious sanctuary, mercifully emerged without bodily harm, though their fragile psyches could not evade the clutches of shock. As if this were not enough, the twisted remains of their automotive misadventure ignited with a sudden ferocity, flames lapping at the remnants of their ill-fated voyage. A call for salvation was promptly dispatched, summoning the stalwart chemical truck of the engine company, whose expertise and valor doused the fire that threatened to consume the remains of Freddie's ill-fated vehicular contraption.

In the realm of enterprises, Freddie embarked upon

yet another ambitious venture—the genesis of an automobile dealership. August of 1918 bore witness to the birth of his brainchild, christened the Freddie Welsh Auto Company, which had been in operation as an unincorporated enterprise. Nestled amidst the confines of Summit, a neighboring township, at Summit Avenue, this establishment found its footing with Arthur W. Prevost assuming the mantle of its president and William Siebert adorning the title of secretary. This enterprise functioned as an agency representing the Ford Motor Company.

Freddie, with his characteristic eye for opportunity, strategically positioned his showroom for the revolutionary Ford motorcars at 57 Summit Avenue. A testament to his ambition and keen sense of aesthetics, the building exuded an air of sophistication with its sturdy brick construction. Not one to rest on his laurels, Freddie further solidified his presence in the automobile world by placing his garage at the neighboring 49 Summit Avenue,[2] its brick façade mirroring its companion. These structures, adorned with the majesty of brick construction, stood as a testament to his unwavering determination and unwavering belief in the boundless possibilities of the age.

Prevost, a fellow son of Great Britain, amalgamated his interests into Feddie's automobile enterprise, encompassing a taxicab establishment and a garage, thus giving creation to the corporation. However, fortune dealt a cruel hand as mere days transpired after the confluence of his endeavors, for he was abruptly ensnared by the clutches of illness, which manifested itself as a simple cold and high fever, but in a brief time, he found himself succumbing to its remorseless grip on the day after he welcomed his thirty-third year of existence.

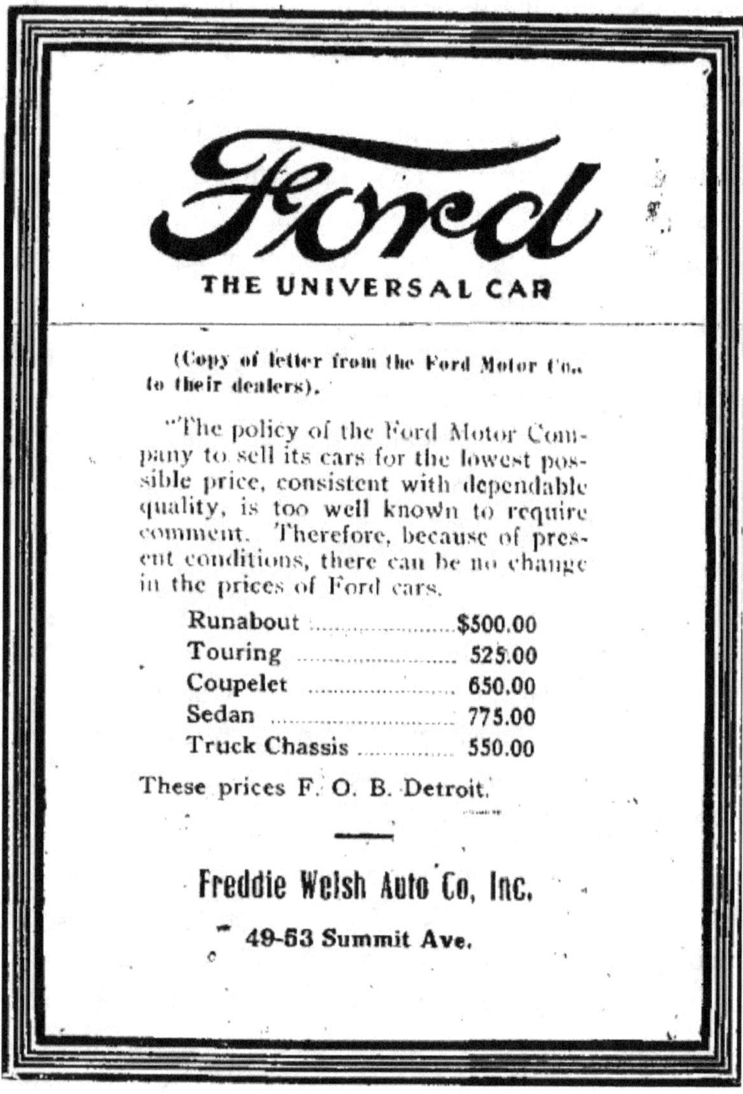

The Freddie Welsh Auto Company.

Freddie started concerning himself with the war

effort in 1918. He found himself seized with a patriotic fervor, and in February, he journeyed to Trenton, New Jersey, to make his voice heard in the halls of power. Before the assembly of the House Welfare Committee, Freddie spoke with a conviction born of his unwavering faith in the righteousness of his cause. He made the case for a bill that would harness the power of the pugilistic arts to whip soldiers into shape.

For Freddie, boxing was not merely a sport but a crucible in which men were forged into warriors. He argued that the rigors of the ring would toughen the soldiers' bodies and minds, preparing them for the rigors of battle. Not only that, but he maintained that boxing would instill in the men a sense of moral fortitude, a code of honor and ethics that would serve them well on the field of war.

Freddie's involvement in advocating for the use of boxing in the war effort wasn't unusual. Boxing was a popular sport during that time, and many believed that it could be used as a way to train and discipline soldiers. By arguing that boxing could improve soldiers' mental, physical, and moral standing, Freddie was tapping into the idea that sports and physical training could have a positive impact on character development. This idea was not unique to boxing, as other sports, such as football and track and field, were also used to train soldiers during wartime.

On the first of June, in the year nineteen hundred and eighteen, Freddie hosted a conference and party at his estate. The evening's theme, as decreed by the host, was physical efficiency. With the shadow of the Great War casting its pall over all, the gathering quickly turned into a military spectacle. Nearly 200 accepted Freddie's invitation that he had extended to esteemed guests, including congressmen, journalists, and other luminaries. They arrived in droves, whether by automobile or on their own two feet. It was by far a mostly pro-war assembly, fervently championing the cause of battle and conquest.

The distinguished attendees hailed from diverse backgrounds, with the likes of the financier and statesman Everett Colby, who was once a schoolmate of John D. Rockefeller. The honorable councilman and learned barrister, Edward G. Pringle, was also in attendance. And there, too, was the renowned innovator, scientist, and wordsmith, Hudson Maxim, whom Thomas Edison himself regarded as "the most versatile man in America."[3] Maxim, a titan of his era, although now largely forgotten, was no less celebrated than Edison in his prime. The inventive genius was a master of explosives, and his patents and discoveries were widely recognized and extensively employed by the United States Government during the tumultuous World War I, a cause Maxim staunchly championed.

In the year 1894, at his New Jersey powder works, Maxim found himself immersed in an audacious pursuit. Within his laboratory, he delved into the intricate mysteries of a novel fulminate compound, a potent concoction that teetered on the precipice of peril. Even though deemed one of the foremost experts in the perilous art of explosions was no ordinary distinction, he nonetheless was guided by a minuscule lapse of attention with a catastrophic consequence that came forth as an explosion occurred, mercilessly snatching away his left hand, leaving only a truncated wrist.

Hudson Maxim, left, with Thomas Edison at his laboratory in West Orange, New Jersey.

That Saturday afternoon, the ideal climate prevailed for the much-awaited excursion. The sultry sun, after a trinity of chilly, humid days, evoked all the innate beauty of the countryside. In the estimation of one journalist, it was the ideal of a locale, a peerless panorama of magnificent splendor that inscribed itself indelibly upon his consciousness.

Freddie, the gracious host, led his entourage through the sprawling estate grounds, showcasing the splendor that lay before them. Amidst the lush greenery, some found respite under the shade of the towering trees, engaging in a discourse on the latest war, agricultural produce, and the soaring cost of living. Others were drawn to the glimmering oasis of the outdoor swimming pool, relishing in its opulence. While some indulged in the state-of-the-art gymnasium, all reveled in the lavishness of the get-together.

For Freddie, nothing but the finest was worthy of his esteemed guests.

It was upon the stroke of five o'clock when the orations commenced. The Reverend Cornelius J. McInerney, the assistant rector of the nearby Saint Teresa's Church in neighboring Summit, presided over the gathering, adroitly assuming the mantle of master of ceremonies. He then proceeded to present to the audience the guest of honor, who stirred the fervor of the audience. The man, Hudson Maxim, a name that reverberated throughout the crowd, was the undisputed star of the hour, as his mere presence elicited an uproarious applause from the masses.

Maxim, with his commanding presence, addressed the pressing matter that lay heavy on the minds of all in attendance: the victorious culmination of the war. He opined that had the United States taken proactive measures, the war could have been averted. He lamented on the havoc wreaked by the tenets of passivism, which had drained the world of its vitality, costing a price in blood and treasure that surpassed the combined cost of all wars fought to date—a statement that resounded with thunderous applause.

He could not bring them tidings of triumph but urged them to confront the reality, for it was only by acknowledging it that they could wholeheartedly devote themselves to the war effort. He warned them that the situation on the Western Front was dire, much more dire than they had imagined. But there was hope, he said, if only they could hold the line till July, then the Germans would be vanquished, and they could launch a counteroffensive to push them back.

"We got into the war too late," Maxim said. "We didn't have the proper training. We were as amateurs, stacking up against Freddie Welsh."[4]

Maxim beheld the promise in the airplane and professed unwavering faith in the government's lavish outlay of one billion dollars for these winged wonders.[5] He owned up to the blunders that had transpired but refused to be daunted by the past. He extolled the urgency of grooming competent officers and pronounced with conviction that the German nation had long mastered the art of molding battle-ready officers. He proclaimed that the colossal coffers emptied for the sake of these flying contraptions had not been squandered in vain and stated, "…and it is going to tell for something. Our machines will soon be darkening the skies of northern France. Then we will make trouble behind the line. We are going to have flying machines faster than we can find ships to carry them—25,000, perhaps 50,000 of them." His closing sentence was, "If the Huns win this war, the world will not be a safe place in which to live. We will be living in bondage."[6]

Former Senator Everett Colby talked for ten minutes with tales of his journey to the battlefront. In a voice that carried the weight of a man who had witnessed the horrors of war, he spoke of the indomitable spirit of the American soldier, their unflinching bravery in the face of untold hardships, and their unwavering loyalty to their cause. Quoting General Pershing, he proclaimed that these brave warriors were the finest bunch of men in the world. He paid homage to the Boy Scouts of England, drawing a comparison to the stalwart American Scouts who shared the same unbreakable bond of loyalty. The former senator assured the crowd that he had firsthand knowledge of the fighting quality of the American soldier, and he was convinced that they would make them proud in the heat of battle.

Councilman Edward G. Pringle, a New York lawyer, caused quite a stir when he said, "We ought to stop scrapping among ourselves and go for it."[7]

After the orations had subsided, a squad of soldiers hailing from Port Newark marched forth onto the lawn, their weapons poised in disciplined unison. The sharp rat-tat-tat of a fife and drum corps kept time with their synchronized steps, infusing the air with an infectious spirit of patriotic fervor. Soon thereafter, the assemblage of guests began to amble about the pastures of the farm, taking in the picturesque scenery for about a half-hour.

Freddie donned the gloves, exchanging blows with two guests for multiple rounds under the watchful eye of a referee. His opponents were in impeccable form, but the former lightweight champion demonstrated that he had retained much of his fistic ability, for the ring was his stage. As this spectacle unfolded, the mayor made his grand entrance, espousing his belief that his idea of preparation was having men of the Freddie Welsh type.

Amidst a sun-dappled afternoon, the gathering indulged in the delights of a barbecue as the sweet scent of apple trees wafted through the air under which they were served. As the sun began to dip, it marked the end of a most enjoyable afternoon.

Not long after the revelry had subsided, Freddie, consumed by his eagerness to convert his land into an airplane hub, tendered a slice of his vast real estate in the month of August to the government for deployment as an aviation field or for any other purpose they deemed fit, as he had done previously with the mayor. Though his generous proposal was declined, it served as a testament to Freddie's unwavering loyalty to the cause of the war.

Among the throngs of guests that had gathered throughout the years was Robert Ripley of the publication *Ripley's Believe It or Not*. He and Freddie, both men of means and influence, had formed a bond of brotherhood, united in their fervent pursuit of physical perfection and their admiration for the teachings of Bernarr MacFadden.

Ripley, a man of great ambition and vigor, was enamored with the sport of boxing. He had spent the better part of his adult years in the company of the nation's most renowned athletes. He first discovered his passion for the sweet science in the city of San Francisco. He would frequent the New York Athletic Club. On occasion, he would even step into the ring with his heroes, Jack Dempsey and George Carpentier, who were regular fixtures at the club.

In June 1918, Bertha wrote another letter, this time to Marion T. Salazar of the *San Francisco Call*:

"Dear Mr. Salazar: Just a few lines lest his many friends in California may have forgotten that there is such a person as Freddie Welsh.

"Freddie is still a full-fledged Jerseyite in his health farm looks finer than ever. Freddie very seldom goes to town; he is a very busy young man, and I, his private secretary, am a very busy young lady.

"Wish you had been here to see Freddie's babies

selling war saving stamps. They were dressed in khaki costumes, and in their wee voices they could be heard in the crowd, 'Buy a bond from my daddy! Buy a baby bond!' Freddie altogether sold $10,000 worth of bonds.

"Would like to have you see the ex-champion in his overalls. He has twelve men working for him and he is the 'majordomo.' He has sown the land to grain and potatoes, and what comes therefrom will help Uncle Sam. Harry Pollock sends regards to all his California friends. Please also give our regards to Tim McGrath."[8]

Chapter IX

"I accepted a commission as first lieutenant when it began. In the Argonne Forest I took two machine-gun detachments so far forward that there was a half mile gap on either side of us where the infantry couldn't advance. We stayed there two days and two nights, a hundred and thirty men with sixteen Lewis guns, and when the infantry came up at last they found the insignia of three German divisions among the piles of dead. I was promoted to be a major and every Allied government gave me a decoration—even Montenegro, little Montenegro down on the Adriatic Sea."

—F. Scott Fitzgerald, *The Great Gatsby*

In September of 1918, Freddie's farm was doing well. He had enough patrons to keep the place going at capacity at all times. It was showing thousands of dollars of profit a year. In the twilight of that year, Freddie, driven by his boundless ambition, proceeded to file articles of incorporation, an elaborate proclamation of his grand vision, at the county clerk's office. With resolute determination, he sought to transform his fledgling enterprise into the esteemed New York and New Jersey Health Corporation, its regal office established within Chatham Township. The incorporation came to fruition with a sum of one hundred thousand dollars, a considerable fortune. A thoughtful balance was struck, as seventy-five thousand dollars were designated as preferred stock, while the remaining portion took the form of common stock. The incorporators were

William H. Turner and Lefferts A. McClellan, with four shares each, and John V. Sweeney, with two shares.[1] Yet, amidst these intricate arrangements, the press, ever fond of simplicity, clung tenaciously to the original name—in fact, references to the New York and New Jersey Health Corporation cannot be found after this transaction—depicting Freddie as the sole proprietor of this promising empire.

However, Freddie was going to give it all up. World War I continued, and he wanted to put his own efforts toward winning the war. He decided he would enroll in the United States Army even if it meant shutting down his health farm business, which he would do. He went to Washington, DC, seeking a commission. However, they only offered him a position of private stationed at the medical barracks at the Capitol. As such, he was obliged to do kitchen duty and other such duties commanded by the humblest private. He entered the army under his birth name, Frederick Hall Thomas.

"I thought you had a commission," Freddie was asked.

"You can see by my uniform," Freddie replied, "that I'm nothing but a buck private. Of course, I'm going to try my best to fight my way to the front ranks just as I did in the boxing game. I passed my physical examination 100% perfect, despite my long service in the boxing game, and I am going to try hard to win a commission. I hope that it won't be long before I'm over in France, helping the allies to whip the Germans.

"I was glad to find that I was in such splendid trim and maybe after the war is over, I'll try to get another chance at the lightweight championship, but for the present I'm going to devote every second towards helping to beat the enemy."[2]

On the autumnal eve of September 24, 1918, a momentous occasion unfolded as Freddie, a British subject turned United States soldier, embarked upon the treasured privilege of casting his inaugural vote upon the shores of America. This land, which had swiftly embraced him into the embrace of its armed forces, now extended the mantle of citizenship upon his stalwart shoulders. With his newfound loyalty and patriotism, Freddie penned his name upon the sacred parchment of democracy, electing to bestow his fervent support upon Mayor Franklin in his pursuit of congressional ascension. Such was the manifestation of his growing voyage into the intricacies of the American political scene, where his voice, once confined by the sea's vast expanse, now resonated through the corridors of this noble republic.

Freddie's enlistment into the ranks beckoned forth a yearning for foreign lands, an ardent plea for overseas duty. The army, in its regard to keeping him in the States, held him back, tethering him to the grounds of Walter Reed Hospital in Washington. A bastion of medical expertise, this institution stood as the veritable linchpin of the nation's army hospitals during the harrowing war.

It didn't take long for Freddie to get his commission. Transitory was his tenure as a humble private; mere months elapsed before the grace of higher echelons bestowed upon him the rank of first lieutenant, elevating his stature in the regimented structure of the military. The army continued to station First Lieutenant Frederick Hall Thomas—his ring name absent in the army—at Walter Reed Hospital in the Sanitary Corps, where he was charged with reclamation work and exercise for wounded soldiers returning from France.

Within the halls of Walter Reed, Freddie's prodigious expertise in the realm of physical culture and the art of health building emerged, casting an enchanting allure upon the discerning eyes of the Surgeon General's office. With great readiness, his knowledge of corrective and remedial exercises captivated their attention, affirming his place amidst the pantheon of renowned healers at the hospital.

Hype Iago, a luminary in the world of journalism, crafted evocative prose that captured the singular artistry of Freddie's innovative methods in mending the shattered bodies of war-torn soldiers:

"Welsh startled the learned doctors with some of his feats of reclaiming at Walter Reed Hospital in Washington…One in particular was an individual triumph.

"A young aviator had been brought down behind his own lines. He had been horribly burned about the legs with flying gasoline as he cracked down.

"In the end he was bedridden. The burned muscles had contracted so that his left leg was drawn up until it almost touched his knee. The doctor said that he would never walk again and advised amputation. Welsh always fought that decision, no matter how desperate the case. He asked permission to treat the fellow. He began with a painstakingly series of kneading and massaging. He worked faithfully on those distorted muscles until he found them becoming pliable under his expert fingers. He got his man up on crutches. Then he fashioned a sort of long barred spur for the patient's shoe. It extended from his heel, straight out and into a socket at the end of this bar, he placed a lead shot, four times the size of a baseball.

"This was done in order to create and maintain a gradual and constant bearing down pressure on the contracted leg. Inch by inch, the leg came down toward the floor. Many long weeks did Welsh watch that experiment, carefully adjusting the ball so that each day would find it properly balanced for a further effort toward getting the flyer's foot to the floor. Welch was certain that the muscles had not been destroyed by the burning. The doctor shook their heads.

"His heart beat fast the day that an adjustment of the weight brought the man's toe within half an inch of the floor. Before night, it had touched the floor. Welch and his patient kept the secret to themselves. They wanted their little joke on the doctors. They kept on patiently with their experiment.

"Then one day, Welsh contrived to have all the doctors and the nurses meet in the big room where the patient's law. Welsh walked to the door and opened it and in walked the aviator, slowly, carefully as a child learning to walk but walking!

"It was the first time that anyone had known that army doctors had a hip hip hoorah in their systems. They turned them loose in chorus with the fellows on the cots. Welsh, with his great confidence in nature, had shown them something they said was impossible."[3]

One journalist, J. V. Fitz Gerald, was taken by

Freddie's modesty, writing, "Freddie Welsh, former lightweight champion, has been made a lieutenant in the Medical Corps. He had been stationed at Walter Reed Hospital, where he was assigned after he joined the colors as a private without proclaiming to the world that he had enlisted. Boxers in the service in a capacity other than that of boxing instructors are not numerous. None of them, so far as we know, is a commissioned officer in the army. Welsh showed the stuff of which he is made when he enlisted. The bars he has gained represent a deserved reward for work well done."[4]

It was true; reliability abounds in the statement that among the constellation of pugilists who chose to join the noble ranks of the armed forces during the relentless tempest of war, Freddie, in all likelihood, emerged as the solitary figure worthy of the distinction of an officer. A certain truth prevails, for no historical annals bear witness to the anointment of a commissioned officer in the list of professional boxers who had joined the military.

It was not soon after his rank was raised to captain, and he was promoted to Director-In-Chief of the Physical Educational Department of Therapeutic and Corrective Exercises. Freddie's siblings also believed in the war effort. His brother, Stanley, became a lieutenant in the British Navy, and his sister, Edith Kate, did Belgian relief work.

Captain Fredrick Hall Thomas.

Even those working with Freddie in the army were unaware of his pugilistic past. He wanted to be known for his current vocation—soldier. A boxer, Corporal Joe Chip, worked under Freddie. In a letter, Chip wrote that Freddie was a "peach of a captain" and "his captain had told him he could get a furlough if he was offered any big bouts."

"His name is Fred Hall Thomas," wrote Joe Chip,

"and he is a fine officer. He knows all about boxing and is a real enthusiast."[5]

To Chip's amazement, the recipient of the letter wrote back, telling Chip that his captain was the former world lightweight champion.

It was in February 1919 when Freddie, stationed at Walter Reed, sought the company of his pal Jack Dempsey. The pugilist, set to face Jess Willard for the coveted heavyweight crown in just five months' time, was implored by Freddie to grace the wounded soldiers with his presence and lend his weight to the inauguration of a new gymnasium. The young men in uniform, their bodies broken and their spirits flagging, yearned for a reprieve from the tedium of hospital life, and what better way to lift their morale than with the spectacle of a true heavyweight champion contender in action? Dempsey, along with his manager Jack "Doc" Kearns, answered the call to bring a glimmer of hope to those who had sacrificed so much for their country.

"…surest thing you know," responded both Jack Dempsey and Jack Kearns, "will be showing in Washington next week and we'll find time to sandwich in an exhibition for the wounded men and be glad to do it."[6]

When Jack Dempsey arrived, Freddie was the first to emerge and greet him. Freddie, the mastermind behind the gathering, had corralled a troupe of boxers and Vaudevillians, all eager to bask in the glow of the main event. Yet, it was Jack who would reign supreme, the star attraction. In the center of the ring, Jack sparred with boxer Terry Keller.

Freddie would see Jack Dempsey again when he

journeyed to Toledo, Ohio, the land where the heavyweight championship was to unfold on American Independence Day. His friend Jack Dempsey was set to face Jess Willard, a battle that had the nation's attention upon it. Freddie was now a man of the written word, there to capture the bout's essence and detail it in ink for a paper in Washington, DC. It was an army paper destined to reach the eyes of the wounded soldiers, their spirits in need of upliftment. Freddie's endeavors didn't end there, for he had managed to obtain from the maestro of boxing promotion, Tex Rickard, a promise for the reel of the fight film. A masterful move, for Freddie would tour the army hospitals, carrying with him the glorious moments of the bout, lighting up the faces of the men who had fought for their country.

Freddie had tipped his hat to Jack Dempsey as the victor in the ring. He spoke with a wisdom that suggested a knowledge of boxing that surpassed the common fan.

"I saw both the big fellows Saturday," said Freddie, "and if there is a man in the world who has a chance to lick Willard, Dempsey is the man. Of course, Willard may not be the beaten, but I say there's no one alive who can beat him if Dempsey doesn't."[7]

Along with the fervor of the fight, a certain animosity stirred within the smaller Dempsey, who stood tall at six feet and one inch, his weight tipping the scales at 187 pounds. His indignation had been aroused by Willard's disparaging remarks, spoken with the ease of a man confident in his own prowess.

"This will be the easiest fight of my career,"[8] stated the bigger six-foot, six inch, and 235-pound Willard.

The heavyweight champion had proclaimed his intention to return the coveted title belt to the white race, a feat he had achieved once before when he vanquished Jack Johnson in 1915. Dempsey's heritage was as diverse as the American landscape itself, comprising a fusion of Irish, Cherokee, and a Jewish maternal great-great-grandmother.

Willard's pre-fight words were like a match to gasoline, igniting a fury within Dempsey that would result in a battle so brutal it would become legendary. From the first round, Dempsey pounced upon Willard with unrelenting force. A half-minute into the bout, a crushing left from Dempsey shattered Willard's jaw into countless fragments and sent him sprawling onto the canvas. The punishment did not stop there—Dempsey continued to knock Willard down an additional six times in that same round, displaying a raw, animalistic power.

Incredibly, the skirmish endured until the inception of the fourth round, at which point Willard proved himself unable to emerge from his corner. As Dempsey was adorned with the laurels of victory and went on to valiantly defend his championship for a full half-dozen years, the elder vanquished Willard quietly retreated from the ring and never again graced its canvas, save for the occasional exhibition.

The shattered jaw was but a token of the savagery Willard had endured in the ring. When the fight was over, the physicians' discerning eyes revealed other afflictions—a broken cheekbone, caved-in by Dempsey's unrelenting blows, shattered ribs, and irreparable hearing loss. One witness described seeing half a dozen of Willard's teeth spew from his mouth in a rainbow of bloody mist during the first round.

With the cessation of World War I, the war to end all wars, an event that had transpired already on the eleventh day of November in the year nineteen-hundred and eighteen, one can grasp an inkling of Freddie's worth within his particular vocation during the harrowing conflict. Such insight can be gleaned from the circumstance that he, with a mere twenty-four officers, emerged as a chosen few, retained for the arduous task of reconstructive labor after the dissolution of the Sanitary Corps, composed of many thousands. Freddie, earnestly seeking release from his obligations, submitted his application for discharge alongside the twenty-three other supplications, only to witness their return from the echelons of authority, marked with red ink denoting their "Indispensable Services." Consequently, Freddie found himself absent from the opportunity to reunite with his family and embrace the solace of his health retreat until a subsequent date. The signing of the armistice that sealed the chapter on the First World War also curtailed his ascent to the rank of major, a position he had been recommended for on four occasions.[9]

Freddie, content in his soldierly pursuits, found himself increasingly removed from his pugilistic past. In October 1919, trouble brewed between the onetime champion boxer and his former handler, Harry Pollock. Matters quickly deteriorated into a scuffle, leaving Pollock hospitalized and Freddie facing an accusation in the court of law. Pollock's legal representative alleged that Freddie had savagely bitten off a considerable portion of his client's right ear, further muddying the already murky waters of their tumultuous relationship.

In the corridors of justice, under the watchful gaze of

Magistrate Alexander Brough, a somber affair unfolded within the walls of West Side Court, New York. It was here that Freddie, a figure caught in the web of legal scrutiny, found himself standing in the defendant's shoes. The complainant, Harry Pollock, his presence missing, languished in the confines of the Polyclinic Hospital, wrestling with the agony of a lacerated ear. With a weighty deliberation, Freddie's fate teetered on the precipice as the judge ordered him detained on a formidable bail sum of one thousand dollars.

The tale, as recounted by Detectives Fitzgerald and Brady, hailing from the West Forty-seventh Street Station, who arrested Freddie upon Pollock's complaint, unveiled a disconcerting chronicle according to Pollock. It began amidst the backdrop of a restaurant nestled at the juncture of Fiftieth Street and Broadway. Here, in the heat of an altercation, Freddie unleashed an act of savagery, sinking his teeth into Pollock's right ear, rending it in halves.

The defense, led by the attorney John C. Dyer of 51 Chamber Street, presented a tale of circumstance to challenge the prevailing narrative. Dyer asserted that on a Saturday night, his client, Freddie, found himself shadowed by the relentless presence of Pollock within the confines of the same establishment. Unyielding in his pursuit of annoyance, Pollock's actions pushed the boundaries of civility, and it was Freddie who stood as the harbinger of restraint, imploring Pollock to quell his intrusive advances. The counsel proclaimed, Pollock obstinately ignored this sage counsel, provoking a tempestuous response from Freddie, whose forceful blow propelled Pollock toward a broken bottle, its shattered fragments severing the flesh of his ear.

Freddie explained to the court that the accusations against him were entirely unfounded. He vehemently denied the biting of Pollock's ear and stated that the mishap was simply a regrettable consequence of a scuffle that had occurred. In his testimony, he made it clear that the broken bottle on the floor was the true culprit for the injury inflicted upon his former manager's ear.

"Your honor, do I look as if I would bite a man's ear?" he asked the magistrate.

"You certainly do not,"[10] the magistrate replied.

Magistrate Alexander Brough did decree that Freddie shall make an appearance for trial in the week to come.

Returning to court, decked out in his captain's finery, Freddie came forth to again refute Pollock's accusations the week ensuing. A police officer in attendance relayed that Harry Pollock, for the third time, was a no-show, reneging on his intent to levy charges. Consequently, the magistrate in charge summarily dismissed the case. Following the proceedings, Freddie proclaimed his departure from pugilism, vowing never to set foot in the ring again.[11]

Chapter X

I don't want to repeat my innocence. I want the pleasure of losing it again.

—F. Scott Fitzgerald, *This Side of Paradise*

In just a span of five months, Freddie's once steadfast declaration began to wane. The sweet science, boxing that he once swore off slowly crept back into his heart. It was as if the sport had cast a spell on him, seducing him with its allure and hypnotizing him with its promise of glory reborn.

As his thirty-fourth birthday approached on the fifth of March 1920, Freddie could not shake off the feeling that his boxing career was far from over. The army, which he was set to be discharged from, was now an afterthought. Like many retired boxers, the ring was calling his name. Similar to countless boxers his age who had been relegated to the pugilistic scrap pile, Freddie would make a comeback, seeking to regain his lightweight title. It had been about three years since Freddie's last fight when he lost the title to Benny Leonard. The excitement from the roar of the crowd, the bright lights illuminating the ring, and the exhilaration that it brings had been missing. Freddie, longing for a past completed with the promise fulfilled, would take to the ring again.

"When I lost the title to Benny Leonard," said Freddie, " I was promised the first chance at him over the 20-round route by Billy Gibson, and as Benny has met no one ever the long route the promise still holds good.

"As soon as I get out of the army—I expect to receive my discharge the first of next week—I will go after a rematch with the champion. I think I have a good chance to regain the title, and I hope I get my chance this year. I don't believe I should be expected to fight my way through the ranks to get a crack at the title that once was mine. I've been through all that. If I fail to get Leonard into a ring, I will do little professional boxing and devote my time to my health farm at Summit, New Jersey.

"I understand Jimmy Coffroth is seeking a suitable opponent for Leonard in a 20-round bout at Tia Juana. He need look no further. And if he wants me, I will be ready anytime."[1]

The army discharged Freddie with the rank of captain in the middle days of March of 1920 from the Fox Hills Base Hospital in Staten Island, where he had been reassigned. He returned to the sprawling estate of his Long Hill Health Farm.

Though the health farm had basked in early triumph, tumultuous times lay ahead. Freddie's lavish parties, though undeniably grandiose, exacted a steep monetary toll. His military endeavors had led to the farm's faltering sense of purpose. Unlike the early days, the outflow of funds was far surpassing any inflow. Freddie was left to grapple with the harsh realization that his financial standing was in dire straits.

In addition to his financial woes, he found himself possessed of a nagging restlessness, a thirst for action that he could not quell. That was why he had decided that a return to the ring, that great stage of his former triumphs, might prove the answer to his troubles, the means by which he could regain his eroding wealth and success. Despite having been away from the ring for more than three long years, he resolved to pursue his comeback with a fierce determination, to fight with all his might to return to his former glory.

As May unfurled, Freddie found himself once again entrenched in the grueling routine of training. His once-immaculate gloves lay buried in dust, but the fire of his past glory still flickered. The future, elusive as ever, remained shrouded in the mists of uncertainty. Though he still basked in the adulation of his fans and the camaraderie of high society, the absence of the coveted championship belt dulled their enthusiasm. It seemed as if only the golden memories of his past triumphs could light up the path ahead.

It appeared he yearned for a chance to reclaim what was rightfully his. The glimmering prize that had once shone bright in his grasp was now snatched away by the cunning hands of his adversary. The glory and adulation that now enveloped the one who had stripped him of his crown appeared to gnaw at him day and night. A promise had been made, a vow to give him a shot at redemption, but could he trust Benny Leonard to keep his word? And even if he did, did the world still thirst for a battle between the two after a long and winding hiatus? It was a gamble, a roll of the dice, but he had to take it for his honor, for his legacy, for his own soul.

As Freddie set out on his comeback crusade, his trusted Welsh Terrier trotted by his side, loyal as ever, during jogs. A novel addition had joined their ranks—a most curious creature. Josephine, a young black bear cub, had been bestowed upon Freddie by an ardent admirer eager to elevate his profile. Elevate it; she did, for soon, the boxing world was abuzz with talk of the charismatic bear. But it wasn't just the fans who were enamored with Josephine—Freddie's children, Betty and Freddie Jr., were utterly charmed by her as well. In fact, the bear was as obedient as any well-trained pooch and would respond to her name with the same eagerness as his Welsh Terrier.

Josephine was an instant boon to Freddie's publicity maneuvers, a veritable gem in his bag of tricks. Though Freddie may have lost his touch in some respects, he still knew how to enthrall the public with his flashy stunts. Together, he and Josephine even crafted a short film featuring the bear and the erstwhile champion. To make sure the media got wind of it, Freddie extended an invitation to journalists for a photo op with him and his furry co-star.

He even partook in a grand spectacle at the local Fireman's Carnival, where he dared to face off against the formidable adversary that was the fearsome bear. Freddie, ever the audacious showman, reveled in the spotlight, spinning tales of the wild and dangerous art of bearbaiting. To him, the challenge of outwitting a lumbering beast was far more formidable than the fisticuffs of any good boxers. The ink-stained victims of the press, always eager for a sensational yarn, fell for his daring narrative, blazoning his exploits across the pages of their dailies. Freddie reveled at the attention, relishing the chance to bask in the adulation of the masses.

"While the bruin isn't as finished a boxer as Georges Carpentier," printed one paper, "or as hard a hitter as Jack Dempsey, the ex-lightweight champion finds that a round or two of slugging with the newcomer is highly exciting."[2]

As Freddie readied himself for his grand return to the ring, the young black bear, barely a year old, had passed on to the great beyond. Yet even in death, the bear's story lingered on, so potent and powerful that it seemed to defy the laws of time. For though the bear had departed this world in the throes of July's scorching heat, the press continued to speak of her come October as if she still roamed the wilds of Freddie's health farm.

Freddie at his health farm with Josephine the black bear.

"The most versatile man in America" found his way once again to Freddie's home at the health farm, as the year 1920 unraveled its days. Descending from his abode in the confines of Hopatcong, New Jersey, Hudson Maxim graced the premises with a subdued grandeur, far less ostentatious than his earlier sojourn amidst the fervor of the Great War, now conquered. The presence of the Bray Pictures Corporation, serving as a visual chronicler of Maxim's reunion with Freddie, accompanied him on this occasion, ensuring that no fragment of their encounter would slip into the oblivion of time.

The principal scene of the motion picture unfurled as Maxim ventured forth, embarking on a journey that led him to the presence of Captain Freddie Welsh. The rendezvous was set amidst the verdant expanse of the health farm, where the grandeur of the old country manor stood resolute. Within those walls, Freddie had orchestrated a metamorphic oasis, an assembly wherein fractured souls sought solace and resuscitation. With unwavering determination, Freddie had erected a sanctuary of bodily redemption where the infirm could be mended and rejuvenated upon the grounds they traversed.

Freddie found himself thrust into the limelight, demonstrating with fervent gestures the intricate maneuvers required to vanquish the insidious Bay window effect that had seized Maxim's belly, which wasn't missed by the attention under the scrutinizing gaze of the camera. Freddie materialized, leading Maxim into the mansion's inner sanctum, their reappearance revealing an exquisite transformation as they emerged, togged in boxing attire. The two warriors converged, their paths intertwining in a spirited conflict.

It was not the maiden occasion where Maxim and Freddie partook in fisticuffs, for their hands had danced prior. It was some time in the past, at the esteemed Roycroft Inn, owned by their mutual friend, the late Elbert Hubbard, in East Aurora, where their friendship's bond found itself tested amidst the pugilistic fervor. In that space, their pugnacious spirits entwined, unleashing a lively round that left an indelible mark on their souls. The clashing of fists bestowed upon them a newfound admiration, forging a mutual respect that endured throughout their lives.

Some thirty-five years prior, before the unfortunate occurrence causing the loss of Maxim's left hand, he had delved into the art of pugilism with an ardent zeal, seeking tutelage from some of the most esteemed boxing teachers that the nation could offer. A custom-made contrivance, fashioned meticulously, endowed him with an artificial appendage adroitly sheathed in a glove, enabling him to exhibit a formidable presence before the motion picture camera. With candor, he humbly acknowledged Freddie was far and away the most scientific and liveliest proposition he had ever put up against with the gloves.[3]

Autographed photo of Freddie to his friend Hudson Maxim.

By the days of September, in the year 1920, a significant acquisition had transpired in the life of Freddie's kin. His brother, Stanley, had procured an estate adjoining the health farm. Stanley, who had navigated the tempestuous seas as a captain of vessels for the last fifteen years, now contemplated relinquishing his maritime vocation. Rumor had it that he would soon assume a distinguished post amidst the docks of New York, tending to the affairs of the Kerr Steamship Company as a superintendent. Stanley eventually diverted his course and ventured into the realm of automobile commerce along with his brother, a dealer of motorcars in Summit. Stanley's life further unfurled as he and his spouse rejoiced in the birth of their son at Overlook Hospital in Summit, whose arrival promptly stirred his uncle's heart, unabashedly proclaiming him to be the harbinger of a pugilistic dynasty, destined to assume the coveted mantle of the heavyweight championship.

The allure of a health club for the city's elite was a notion that entranced Freddie. He would soon discover the businessmen of the metropolis were not so inclined toward the pursuit of physical fitness. They flocked to the health farm, not for the sake of their own well-being but for the chance to rub shoulders with the celebrities that frequented the place. The question that must have plagued Freddie was whether these men of wealth and influence graced his establishment with their presence for his ideal or if they truly held no regard for the importance of exercise. The dilemma would be succinctly summed up by one man when Freddie threw one of his lavish parties.

At the time, Freddie's place was buzzing with excitement, a hive of energy pulsing with the presence of the wealthy and influential. Amidst the festivities, a single guest would prove to be the harbinger of Freddie's destiny and the fate of the heath farm. Jack Dempsey, the undisputed heavyweight champion of the world, his words of discourse with the attendees foretold of ominous events to come.

"Go on and box," Freddie said to one of his guests. "Jack won't hurt you."[4]

The man was strong, sound, and peppy.

"If Dempsey will promise?" said the man.

After Dempsey gave his promise, the man, a mere guest in this grand spectacle, climbed into the ring where Dempsey awaited him. They got down to it. After only a minute of battle, the guest was left completely spent, unable to continue. Freddie, the shrewd ringmaster, must have known the man would not last and had already prepared a second guest, gloves at the ready, for an inevitable repeat of the first man's effort.

"Go on and finish the three minutes," Freddie said.

It seemed like a cinch to the second man. Dempsey was merely evading his first adversary, barely requiring the opponent to lift his gloves or shift about the ring. The replacement man confidently hopped over the ropes, yet within as little as ninety-seven seconds, he was staggering back to his corner, his arms aching, unable to lift his hands or even catch his breath. He managed to endure for a bit longer, yet even without Dempsey striking a single blow, the two men were unable to endure the three minutes of the round.

"Don't you fellows ever take any exercise?" asked Dempsey in amazement.

They did not partake in any physical pursuits. Instead, they climbed up and down the subway steps as part of their daily routine or leisurely perused the shop windows during the bustling buying season. Though they appeared to be in as good physical condition as any nine businessmen out of ten, a farm boy, with just a sliver of common sense, could have easily bested either of them in a scuffle if he could just evade a single strike.

The onlookers couldn't help but be amused, but Dempsey was not. He struggled to understand. His face crinkled in comical lines as he attempted to piece it together. Eventually, one of the onlookers had to explain.

"Most businessmen are like that,"[5] he said apologetically.

Dempsey, with a look of disappointment etched upon his face, simply gave a slight shake of his head. The gesture spoke volumes, conveying a sense of disillusionment with his fellow man's unwillingness to at least attempt to work on their physical well-being.

The health farm wilted under the oppressive weight of financial distress, yet there was a glimmer of hope that shone amidst the dreariness. Freddie, the onetime champion pugilist, had built for himself an enviable reputation in the ring, and boxers flocked to his health farm to hone their skills. The Long Hill Health Farm was sought not for its restorative virtues, as Freddie had envisaged, but for its sparring facilities. Despite his best efforts to revamp the health farm into a sanctuary of wellness, Freddie was reluctant to turn away those who wished to wield gloves within its premises.

In the month of September, a gentleman made his way to Freddie's health farm, whose arrival would send a stir through his establishment. This man was no ordinary being but rather a boxing sensation of international renown, his fists wielded with the precision of a master craftsman. His appeal to women was no less a formidable force, a magnetism that could only be matched by his striking visage. To add to his impressive credentials, he had even gallantly served his country as a hero of the Great War.

He was hailed as a hero of World War I aviation and adored on both sides of the Atlantic. The French bestowed upon him their highest military honors, the *Croix de Guerre* and the *Médaille Militaire*, but it was his talent and charisma that won the hearts of the people. He was a man of many charms, possessing the good looks that bewitched women, earning him the moniker of Gorgeous Georges in the press. His ring name, The Orchid Man, was a curious choice for a boxer, but it suited him well, for he was a man of elegance and refinement.

Georges Carpentier, a dapper Frenchman of renown, was a pugilist of repute who graced the Long Hill Health Farm. Carpentier, the European heavyweight champion, was also the last person to hold the world white heavyweight championship, an accolade created in the wake of Jack Johnson's conquest of the world heavyweight title in 1908, the first black man to do so by defeating Tommy Burns. The title was discarded as soon as Johnson lost his grip on the championship.

He strode onto the premises with a purpose, a mission to vie for the coveted world light heavyweight championship. But this was not his maiden voyage to the New World, for on the thirteenth of March in the year nineteen hundred and twenty, the fighter embarked upon the

French steamship *La Savoie*, accompanied by his bride, Georgette Elsasser.

It was a honeymoon, to be sure, his previous trip to America, but it was also a matter of business, for Carpentier was under the purview of the fight promoter Jack Curley. From May the third until July the seventeenth, with an option for a further five weeks, he was honored and cheered, traveling throughout the States, delivering one exhibition match after another. The Frenchman's matrimonial interlude was transformed into a golden and most lucrative opportunity that endeared him to the American people.

For his current trip, Jack Curley, the representative of Carpentier in America, was not the manager of the Frenchman, as that role was occupied by Francois Descamps. Prior to departing for the Levinsky light heavyweight title bout across the ocean, Descamps uttered a statement that resonated with the spirit of the Frenchman.

"Georges will begin immediately to condition himself for the Levinsky bout," Descamps said. "He will work at Freddie Welsh's farm in Summit, New Jersey, and will live a short distance away from the farm. Georges prefers the simple life to the big city hotels. Besides, he will be surrounded by a homelike atmosphere, for Marcel Thomas's sister is the hostess and will provide the cooking to which Georges is accustomed. With us will be Thomas, Charley Ledoux, and Gus Wilson, making our own little family."[6]

Although he came to America to fight for the light heavyweight championship, as Carpentier sailed across the Atlantic, leaving behind his wife and young child, his attention was fixed on a singular obsession: a chance to challenge the reigning heavyweight champion of the ring, Jack the giant killer, otherwise known as the mighty Jack Dempsey. The mere thought of a showdown between the two titans had reverberated across the land, with predictions of the biggest purse in boxing history.

On September 13, 1920, Carpentier's ship, the *La Lorraine*, pulled into the energetic port of America. As he disembarked amidst a sea of waving banners proclaiming "*Vive* Carpentier," the Frenchman basked in the adulation of the cheering crowds. With his manager, Descamps, acting as interpreter, Carpentier addressed the throngs, setting the stage for his impending clash with Battling Levinsky for the coveted world light heavyweight championship. After some exchanges, he stated through Descamps:

"They tell me that Levinsky is one of the hardest men in the ring today. But should I care. That makes it all the better for me; that's just why I'm going to fight him. Like you Americans say, 'The harder they come, the harder they fall to the surface.'

"I was really qualified to meet Dempsey right after I knocked out Joe Beckett of England. The people here ridiculed me, though. They said the fight was one-sided; that Beckett wouldn't have had a chance against anyone even slower than I. That's why I'm going to take on Levinsky first."[7]

With a solemn sense of purpose, Carpentier eschewed the trappings of fame and fortune that had brought him to the shores of America. He made his way not to the offices of Jack Curley, his American impresario, but instead to the remote retreat in the wilds of Chatham Township, New Jersey. It was there, amidst the bucolic beauty of Freddie's Long Hill Health Farm, that he would prepare himself for the bout. With unwavering determination, he trained day and night, honing his body and mind for the fateful clash with Levinsky, set to take place on the twelfth of October at the Westside Ballpark in Jersey City, New Jersey.

On Carpentier's maiden voyage to America, the masses anticipated the pugilist to lace up his gloves and square off in more fisticuffs then he did, but his contract indicated that his talents were solely reserved for the silver screen, leaving boxing enthusiasts disheartened. This time, however, Carpentier arrived with a belligerent intent, ready to take on his challenger. His luggage consisted of fourteen trunks brimming with his lavish attire, a marked improvement from his previous transatlantic voyage that required an armada of forty. Clearly, the respite he took in a villa outside of Paris had done wonders for his constitution, as he appeared in robust form. Carpentier confided that he was weary of the tedious formalities that accompanied his presence in New York. He was all about the pugilistic arts this time, and his intentions were exemplified by his sojourn to Freddie's health farm to train.

Carpentier, in his ire, did not mince words when speaking of the American press and their condemnation of his previous refusal to engage in many fisticuffs. His determination, now firmly in place, to devote himself wholly to the sweet science could not be questioned. He made it plain that his dalliance with the silver screen would be suspended until a certain bout with Jack Dempsey, the heavyweight champion, took place, which he proclaimed with no hint of modesty would come to pass only after he had secured the light heavyweight championship.

Carpentier arrived with an entourage of sparring partners in tow, each one a pugilistic force to be reckoned with. Among them was the French welterweight champion, Marcel Thomas, and Joe Blumfeld, the featherweight from England. And then there was Joe Jeanette, the heavyweight whose glory days may have been behind him but whose experience and expertise were invaluable to Carpentier's training. Even Freddie himself stepped into the ring to lend a helping hand.[8] Together, these formidable fighters pushed Carpentier to the limits of his endurance, building his speed and agility with each punishing blow.

Jeanette, hailing from New Jersey, possessed formidable ability in the realm of fisticuffs during his prime. His victory over Carpentier in Paris on March 22, 1914, after fifteen rounds of thunderous pugilism, elevated him to the upper echelons of the heavyweight division. Jeanette's superior skills, and because he was black, prevented him from ever contending for the most coveted prize in boxing. The crown jewel of boxing history was reserved for the "Galveston Giant" –Jack Johnson, leaving Jeanette to defend his position as the colored heavyweight title holder, a title relinquished by Johnson when he ascended to the throne. Jeanette and Johnson had engaged in ten bouts that saw the resilient Jeanette tasting defeat twice, emerging victorious once via foul after a meager two rounds, settling for two draws and five no-decisions.

One night, the Elks Club, nestled in the neighboring town of Summit, invited the illustrious Carpentier. Accompanied by his trusted ally, Joe Jeanette, the duo graced the stage and sparred. The crowd, though scant in numbers, was rapt with attention as the pugilists sparred.

Joe Jeanette with Georges Carpentier at the Summit Elks Club.

Despite his protestations to the contrary, Carpentier found himself drawn to the bright lights and frenetic energy of New York City. Taking a brief respite from his training regimen at Freddie's health farm, the French pugilist made his way to the International Sporting Club (ISC) for a luncheon held in his honor. Accompanied by Freddie, Carpentier was greeted with thunderous applause that echoed throughout the grand hall, a tribute to his rising star in the world of boxing.

The luminaries of the city's sporting and political circles had gathered to pay homage to their esteemed guest, Carpentier, including the likes of William Fox, the toastmaster of the event, and Senator James J. Walker, the father of the law legalizing boxing in New York. Also present were the likes of Gabriel Delvaux, editor in chief for the Franco-American Gazette; Robert Leconte, representative of the French government; Charles H. Ebbets, the Brooklyn Baseball Club president; Alfred L. Marilley, ISC attorney; Tex O'Rourke, ISC matchmaker; promoter Jack Curley; Walter Hooke and Edward Ditmars, Boxing Commission members; M. Ribaute, who greeted Carpentier on the La Lorraine; W. A. Gavin, ISC managing director; Benny Leonard, world lightweight champion; and many other prominent people of boxing. Amidst this sea of glittering personalities, Carpentier made a stirring speech, his words resonating with all who were present and cementing his status as a true champion of the ring.

"I came here a stranger last March and was pleased with the reception which greeted me," Carpentier said. "I returned yesterday and was amazed to experience the same reception, the same crowds again as if I had never been here. It makes me feel that I am welcome, and I will try to deserve all that has been done for me. I was censured for my activities while here before, but, in explanation, I will remind you I am a professorial man. I must make money, and I had moving picture and circus contracts. The bout I wanted was not available.

"This time it is different," Carpentier added. "I have come here to fight and expect to engage in several bouts and possible arrange for a bout with Dempsey. No matter what the outcome of my fights, whether I win or lose, I hope they are all proper and that the public is pleased. If I lose against Levinsky, I will have no excuse to offer. I am in the best condition and will let the public judge my work as a fighter. Therefore, I say if I do not win, I won't cry.

"When I face Dempsey, it will be the same. I have no fear of him, and, like every other fighter, am confident of myself. What terrors has he to make anyone afraid of him? He is but human; he has two hands and two feet like myself, so that he is only natural. When I meet him, it will be the same as with any other boxer. I will hope and strive for victory."[9]

After the midday meal, Carpentier retraced his steps back to the Long Hill Health Farm, resuming his rigorous regimen. On the day of the match, both contenders issued statements, each with their own brand of bravado.

"I realize that I am under the inspection of a jury of fight fans who know boxing from early childhood. I invite inspection. I am ready. I will win," Carpentier said.

"I am in shape," Levinsky said. "When I am at my best no man in the world can beat me. We'll see whether this marvelous idol, Carpentier, isn't made of brittle clay. I'm going to knock him over."[10]

Carpentier, at the age of twenty-six, made quick

work of his opponent, Levinsky, who was two years his senior. The young fighter was in complete control of the bout from the beginning. And in the fourth round, Carpentier unleashed a fierce left, followed by two rights, which left Levinsky dazed and confused. The crowd was on its feet, cheering wildly, as Levinsky hit the canvas, unable to rise to his feet. Carpentier, the picture of a true champion, along with Levinsky's handlers, lifted the fallen warrior and carried him to his corner. With that victory, Carpentier secured his place in history as the new light heavyweight champion of the world.

Carpentier, in winning the bout, had seized the much-coveted opportunity for the heavyweight championship of the world. It was on November 5, 1920, in New York City, that a contract was signed by the champions, Dempsey and Carpentier, along with their respective managers, Kearns and Descamps. The flamboyant Tex Rickard, alongside the other promoters Brady and Cochran, were also present at the signing. The stakeholder, Edgren, lent his presence as well. A princely sum of $300,000 was assured to Dempsey, while Carpentier received a not inconsiderable $200,000. And not to forget the movie rights, of which each received twenty-five percent. The promoters had also posted $50,000 as a forfeiture for each fighter. With the ink drying on the parchment, Carpentier bid adieu to the bustling city, sailing for his beloved France the next day. It was on November thirteenth when he finally arrived home, a hero of the people.

Carpentier had taken flight, leaving Freddie with a handful of paltry pugilists to train amidst the backdrop of his health farm. Freddie had ascended to the mantle of hosting a big-name fighter, reigning over his own kingdom. Now gone, the throngs no longer flocked to witness the fisticuffs as they had during Carpentier's tenure when he contended for the luminous light heavyweight crown and seemed destined for the distinguished position of top heavyweight challenger. Freddie remained merely a former champion, stripped of his title for over three years.

On the twenty-eighth day of December, in the year nineteen hundred and twenty, Freddie, the pugilist of great renown, did make his return to the ring after a lengthy hiatus of three years and seven months. The venue for his comeback was in Newark, New Jersey. Standing opposite him was a fighter hailing from the streets of Boston, one Willie Green. Possessing a record of seven wins, five losses, and seven draws, Green proved to be no match for the skilled and seasoned Freddie, who outclassed his adversary despite showing little of his old form. After four rounds of a scheduled twelve-round bout, Green, his body battered and bruised, refused to answer the bell for the fifth. The victory, by way of technical knockout, belonged to Freddie, a fitting reward for his triumphant return to the sweet science.

James J. Corbett, former champion of the world in the heavyweight division, spoke out that young Green—who appeared more like the worst fighter that ever stepped into a ring—was no match for Freddie. Corbett extolled the sheer potency of Freddie's punches, which he described as phantom-like and had grown infinitely more potent with time. However, not many shared Corbett's lofty estimation of the seasoned pugilist.

In days gone by, a battle featuring Freddie would stir up the inkwells of journalists and send them scribbling away with frenzied vigor. Such was the norm for this pugilistic wonder, whose every move was scrutinized and chronicled with great zeal. Times had changed, and the once-celebrated fighter now found himself relegated to a meager two-paragraph snippet tucked away in the recesses of a sports page. The headline, though present, was but a feeble echo of the resounding praise that once accompanied his every triumph. The *Oakland Tribune* demonstrated this with the headline:

"Freddie Welsh Stops An Unknown Boxer."[11]

If Freddie was to catch the eye of Benny Leonard's team once more, with a rematch for the lightweight crown to be given, then he'd have to bring forth more than what he had shown in this match. No number of past pledges could sway their decision, for the present was all that mattered now. The pugilistic stage was not one for the faint-hearted or the timid, and if he wanted to bask in the glory of victory once more, he'd have to step up his game and show them what he was made of.

Freddie would have none of it. Like Corbett, he was pleased with his performance. At thirty-five years of age, he refused to succumb to the defeatist attitude that had felled many a man before him. With a resolute spirit and unwavering confidence, Freddie boldly declared his intention to rise above the naysayers and emerge victorious. Determine he was to rise again, for Freddie was not one to be counted out.

"Maybe it will be the same with me and maybe it won't." declared Freddie. "Anyway, I have gone back into the ring warfare confident that I am a better man now than I was before I lost my championship. My fight the other night was the first I have waged in more than three years. But I think that my showing was enough to increase the hope that I can take my place once again with the leading lightweights.

"On that night in May 1917, when Benny Leonard dethroned me, he told me he would give me a return battle. For some months afterward, I attempted to have Leonard make good on this promise, without result. Just about then we became seriously involved in the European warfare and I gave up all thought of fighting and got into the uniform.

"My long service in the American army put me into the best condition of my life. After I got back into 'civvies', I continued to work for improved condition. Most of the months since then have been spent outdoors rebuilding. Gradually I reached the point where my muscles became as hard as nails, where my endurance powers were better than they have been at any time in ten years and where I felt that I had a stiffer punch than ever before."

"Victory in that first fight has enthused me," Freddie continued. "My showing was all that I had hoped for. I realize that a man at thirty-five who is attempting a comeback can't take on one or two easy fights and then jump right in against the tough ones. He has to work his way gradually the same as does a youngster. My program calls for talks taking on three or four fighters of the Green type and working along easily until I have reached the point where Benny Leonard alone stands in my way of regaining the title.

"Leonard repeatedly has said that he would give me another fight. I don't see why he shouldn't. I gave him three cracks at me while I was lightweight champion, and it is only fair that he should give me at least one return bout if I make good in my comeback. If he does, it is my hope that I will have worked myself back to such condition that I can whip him. Leonard isn't unbeatable, and I hope to be the man to prove it."[12]

Freddie was a man on a mission, a quest to attain what the masses deemed implausible: the restoration of his championship status at an age deemed unfit for pugilistic triumph. Freddie was no ordinary fighter; his cerebral proficiency had always set him apart from the rest. Perhaps, with his revitalized physical form and nimble mind, he would surpass the obstacles that stood between him and his coveted title—a feat that many had dared to undertake but few had succeeded. The comeback was his to achieve, and Freddie was determined to seize it with all his might.

Chapter XI

"I found out what your 'drug stores' were." He turned to us and spoke rapidly. "He and this Wolfsheim bought up a lot of side-street drug stores here and in Chicago and sold grain alcohol over the counter. That's one of his little stunts. I picked him for a bootlegger the first time I saw him and I wasn't far wrong."

—F. Scott Fitzgerald, *The Great Gatsby*

The year 1921 ushered Freddie further away from his modest origins in Pontypridd, Wales. He gravitated closer to the affluent, prominent, influential, and well-heeled. In that year, Freddie eagerly anticipated the arrival of his most renowned patron, who also happened to be what he considered a close confidante. This figure was known throughout the world as a veritable colossus of the ring. The heavyweight champion, Jack Dempsey, would soon be under Freddie's watchful eye as he prepared to face off against Georges Carpentier, the reigning world light heavyweight champion and heavyweight champion of Europe. It was Carpentier who had previously trained at Freddie's health farm when he clinched the light heavyweight title, and now the two champions would collide in a bout of epic proportions.

As Dempsey made plans to make his way to Freddie's health farm, it was said he was coming for the thrill of the forbidden, the lure of the illicit. It was this that drew him to this particular destination. Friendship, of course, was a possible façade, a thin veil to cover his true intentions. For Dempsey, there may have been only one reason to visit Freddie's health farm, and that was to partake in the potent potables that were being brewed there.

It was a darker purpose that lurked in the shadows of the minds that drew some to the health farm. This was the era of the Roaring Twenties, a time when Prohibition reigned supreme, when whispers of illicit brews could be heard on every corner. But for those who knew where to look, there were still ways to satisfy one's thirst. And Freddie's health farm was one such place, a veritable oasis in the desert of sobriety. It was a not-so-well-kept secret that the land held a secret stash of the finest home-brewed ciders and beers, fermented to perfection in the privacy of the farm. And Dempsey, like so many others, couldn't resist the temptation to indulge in these forbidden delights.

The authorities were always on the lookout for those who dared to flout the law, and the consequences of getting caught were dire indeed. But for Dempsey, the risk was worth the reward. He grasped that once he set foot on Freddie's property, he would be transported to a world of pleasure and excess, a world that was hidden from the prying eyes of the law, ready to embrace the illicit pleasures that awaited him there.

Roger Kahn, in his Dempsey biography *A Flame of Pure Fire: Jack Dempsey and the Roaring '20s*, wrote:

"Kearns set up Dempsey's first camp in Summit, New Jersey, on property owned by a former lightweight champion, Freddie Welsh. The big attraction was cheap booze: Welsh home brewed excellent cider and beer."[1]

Tex Rickard, the promoter, had put forth the challenge to the boxing world. Come July 2, 1921, the event would unfold and be remembered for ages to come. The fight of the century, that's how Rickard pitched it, and he envisioned it as the inaugural sporting occasion with a gate of a million dollars. It was a fisticuffs bout the globe pined for, and Rickard's actions showed he was cognizant of this truth.

On January twenty-first, in the year nineteen hundred and twenty-one, a momentous transaction occurred that would forever alter the course of the upcoming historic fight. Tex Rickard, that shrewd impresario of the sweet science, seized control of Cochran and Brady's stake in the upcoming bout with a flick of his pen. He had the foresight to fork over a sum of sixty-six thousand and six hundred and sixty-six dollars, bringing his total forfeiture money to one hundred thousand dollars,[2] cementing his status as the undisputed sole promoter of the event. For Rickard appeared to understand, as he had gleaned from his earliest forays into the world of boxing, that the business of fight promotion required ample reserves of capital if one were to reap the rewards of the fisticuffs.

Rickard's ambitious adventure couldn't have taken place without the help of one man. Tex Richard's moneyman, the cunning and resourceful Mike Jacobs, proved himself a master of the game. With his sharp wit and quick tongue, Jacobs orchestrated a financial coup. In just eight short hours, he summoned forth a staggering sum of $100,000 in cash, enabling Rickard to seize complete control of the much-anticipated Jack Dempsey-Georges Carpentier world heavyweight championship.

Their partnership had its genesis in 1904 at the Gans-Nelson fight, Rickard's inaugural foray into the fight game. Jacobs, then a young man, had already shown an uncanny knack for raising funds for prizefights, and Rickard recognized his prodigious talent. He helped Rickard become active throughout the New York area where Jacobs lived. Together, they swept through the New York scene, forging an empire that spanned decades. Their origins were as disparate as their styles: Rickard, a son of the heartland, and Jacobs, born and raised in New York City.

Rickard received a telegraph that Carpentier would set sail for New York come May. Descamps, Carpenter's manager, telegraphed that the pugilist, along with his sparring entourage and other parties of the heavyweight fray, would be traversing the Atlantic aboard the Steamship *Savoie*. As per the communiqué, Carpentier was in the pink of physical fitness, and only time stood between him and the fight of his life.

In the month of March, a stir of excitement swept across the land as the much-anticipated Dempsey-Carpentier bout drew near. And in the midst of the fervor, a certain distinguished gentleman, the United States Senator Bill "Cyclone" Lyons, graced a sports journalist with his presence and talked about his dear friend, the reigning heavyweight champion of the world, Jack Dempsey. The senator, a sports enthusiast of great repute and no stranger to the boxing ring, often served as timekeeper for the pugilistic endeavors of both Freddie and Jack, his fellow son of Colorado.

The senator was bedecked in a green hat and a debonair pair of spats, accompanied by seventeen of his walking canes. The one he held dearest was a Patagonian sword cane, a triumph of fine craftsmanship. A pocket watch joined his display of gifts, a platinum split-second watch of a Christmas past, bequeathed by Dempsey, worth a grand. A horological masterpiece, the dial was adorned with miniature photographic portraits of Dempsey, Lyons, and Kearns, encircled by a plethora of diamonds. At the watch's rim, alternating rubies, sapphires, and diamonds contributed to its patriotic motif. Six more stones lent hues to the back of the case, which bore a diminutive photographic vignette of Dempsey in pugilistic posture. It contained the enameled text of "To a True Friend, My Pal, Sen. Bill Lyons, From Wm. Harrison (Jack) Dempsey, Heavyweight Champion of the World, Christmas 1920."

The senator possessed yet another timepiece bestowed upon him by Freddie himself. This particular chronometer was an Elgin 15-jewel pocket watch crafted from white gold bedecked with a dazzling array of sixty-four emeralds, resplendent in their green and blue opulence. The watch's visage bore photographic representations of Lyons and Freddie donning their military uniforms, harkening back to their valiant exploits in the Great War [the photo may have been added at a later date, as the watch had a date of 1916, and Freddie didn't enter the army until 1918]. On the reverse side, a tinted full-color portrait of Freddie was emblazoned, adorned in his finest boxing attire, alongside an inscription etched in the left corner, "To Senator Bill Lyons Always 100 Per Cent," and the right side with "From Freddie Welsh Lightweight Champion of the World."[3] The top and bottom were engraved with the date October 3rd, 1916.

Senator Lyons and Jack Dempsey

With the duo of timekeepers in tow, the senator reckoned he was destined to have a good time wherever he went. The senator professed that Freddie was dead set on making a glorious return to the ring among the lightweights. Lyons, for his part, held steadfast in his conviction that Freddie had the goods to trounce all but the mightiest of pugilists and rake in a pretty penny while doing so. He also held the view that there wasn't a chance Freddie would ever be mingling with Benny Leonard again.

Lyons declared that Dempsey was currently swaying through the grand vaudeville circuits, his presence a sensation in each city he visited. The champion would grace Winnipeg with his presence, followed by Victoria the following week, and then on to Spokane, where the masses eagerly awaited his arrival. Dempsey and his formidable "act" were set to arrive in San Francisco the next month. As for the senator, he was en route to Spokane to rendezvous with Dempsey, eager to witness the champion firsthand.

The senator, with a certain air of authority and charisma, extended his astute observations on the upcoming Dempsey-Carpentier match. The scribes and sportswriters hung on to his every word, for in this world of high stakes and fierce competition, knowledge was power, and the senator had it in spades.

"Dempsey and Carpentier," said Lyons, "will scrap on July 2, as announced, and the bout will take place in New Jersey. And as sure as they meet, Dempsey will beat Carpentier as fast or faster than any other heavyweight he has ever met. In condition—right—something he wasn't for Brennan but will be for Carpentier. Dempsey will take Carpentier, Willard, Fulton, and any one other heavyweight you can name in the same ring, one after another, and knock them all out. I'm not kidding you, either.

"I'm going to join Dempsey in Spokane and come back here with him. The champion is doing light training all the time and will be ready to start active work for Carpentier as soon as his vaudeville tour is over.

"You can say what you want about Tex Rickard showing these two big guys in the title bout. He isn't doing it because he wants to. He's doing it because he has to. Jack Kearns has him tied up so tight he just has to put the bout on.

He is contemplating building a great arena in Jersey. At present, he is undecided how large the place will be. To my way of thinking there can be no limit to the crowd the fight will draw, and Rickard knows this."[4]

It was the spring of 1921, and the great Jack Dempsey had returned to the city of New York. Fresh from his vaudeville circuit engagements, the heavyweight champion of the world had come to New York to commence his preparation for the most anticipated bout of the season—his showdown with Georges Carpentier in the state of New Jersey. Dempsey declared that he tipped the scales at 191 pounds, and with that, he said he would make his way to Freddie's health farm, where he planned to spend the next few weeks amidst the rolling hills.

He made scant allusion to preparing for the impending clash, which was some months hence. Dempsey said he would play golf and take long walks, ride horseback and try his hand at handball. And, of course, there would be a bit of baseball—for what is springtime in America without a good game of ball? He seemed to grasp that the fight with Carpentier would be a battle for the ages, but he was ready; he was hungry, and he was the champ. He was home.

Upon returning East, Dempsey made his first stop at the luxurious Belmont Hotel in New York City. In his company were Freddie and Dempsey's manager, Jack Kearns, a slim and stylish fellow who had once been a pugilist himself but quickly learned that his nose was better suited for smelling roses than taking punches. As they settled in, a buzz of excitement filled the air as Damon Runyon and a group of other reporters made their way into the apartment. Dempsey was once again the talk of the town, and all eyes were on him as he regaled his guests with tales of his travels and triumphs.

Dempsey was decked out in a slick ensemble, draped in a green suit that exuded a certain swanky aura. Perched upon a windowsill that towered over the bustling metropolis below, Jno, Dempsey's cheeky monkey companion, was basking in the panoramic view. However, their tranquil moment was shattered by the irruption of a pack of pressmen, causing Jno to abandon his lofty perch and lunge toward the intruders with a brazen leap, landing squarely on their unsuspecting shoulders.

"Ain't that a cute monk?" asked Dempsey. "Wild Jno Reilly gave him to me for a present."[5]

Wild Jno Reilly, known far and wide as the Duke of Ninety-sixth Street and for whom the monkey was named, was a curious fellow, shrouded in mystery and draped in a certain degree of unsavory reputation. His love for the sweet science was legendary, having attended more prizefights than any man alive, according to many scribes. But it wasn't his passion for pugilism that made him an enigma, but the endless stream of questionable schemes and shadowy dealings that seemed to surround him. As one bold journalist once remarked:

"Reilly is recognized in every city from coast to coast where the fight game flourishes. The columns of feature stuff that have been written on Wild Jno in New York, by writers from Damon Runyon to Bat Masterson on down, would fill a small size library. There hasn't been an important fight in years that Reilly has not attended.

"Many and sundry attempts have so far failed to

'make' Reilley's 'racket.' It is generally conceded that he took $30,000 out of Toledo at the time of the Dempsey-Willard scrap. It is further reported that during the week previous to the Criqui-Kilbane fight in New York, he sold the rights to Harding's world court for a neat sum...."[6]

Another newspaper made mention of the notorious Wild Jno, with the words leaping off the page:

"Well, Wild Jno, is in town, and when I find this out some days ago before the rodeo fights, I rushed right down to the police department and tell them to lock up everything which is valuable around their premises because Wild Jno is here. They say who is Wild Jno? And we can take care of our own valuables without locking them up, but I say no, if you do not know who Wild Jno is, you know nothing about it! Wild Jno, I tell them, is the kind of a baby which will blow into this man's town and sell section 36 back to the Standard Oil after he is here about three days. He is likely as not to come down here, I tell them, and take the beats away from your best cops. He is the guy which Jesse James thought he was, I say to them, and do you not be careful you will be missing a city hall some fine morning and will find that Wild Jno has sold it to some sheepherder. You will look fine, I told them, without any city hall over your heads and nothing but the basement to tell for it. Lock up everything you have got, I say, and publish it from 'Dan to Beersheba' (scripture, I think) that Wild Jno Reilly is in town."[7]

As Dempsey began to speak, Jno, the cheeky simian, grew restless with the monotony of the press conference. A sudden spark ignited within the primate's tiny frame upon hearing the commanding timbre of the heavyweight champion's voice. Without a moment's hesitation, Jno pounced upon Dempsey, his beady eyes fixed on the glimmering watchchain that hung from the fighter's waistcoat. Dempsey had no time to react before the monkey was grabbing for the chain from his person.

"He don't like this green suit I've got on," said Dempsey as Jno scrambled back to his windowsill. "He's friendly with everybody but me, and it's all on account of this suit."[8]

As Damon Runyon laid his keen eyes upon the suit, his admiration for the simian wit swelled. In a fleeting moment, he had glimpsed a brilliance in the primate's distaste of the attire, with a newfound respect for the monkey's intellect.

Dempsey, with a flourish, unveiled his hand, a wound that told the story of a scuffle with the mischievous monkey. The creature, with its uncontainable nature, had sunk its teeth into his flesh, leaving a mark.

"He bit me there last night," Dempsey said. "I guess I'll have to throw the suit away."[9]

In the spacious chamber, a wardrobe trunk lay ajar, its once-pristine contents strewn haphazardly across the floor. Amidst the tangle of fabric and finery, a particular piece caught the eye of Runyon, who proclaimed it a sartorial abomination of the highest order. A white overcoat it was, blindingly immaculate in its snowy hue, a flagrant affront to the refined sensibilities of the room's occupants. Such an egregious display of fashion gaffe, Runyon opined, ought to be prohibited by law.

"We're moving out this afternoon," said Dempsey. "Going out to Freddie Welsh's to start training tomorrow."[10]

Freddie strolled into the chamber, accompanied by Joe Benjamin, Dempsey's sparring partner hailing from the Golden State who had sparred with the revered Benny Leonard and was now under the tutelage of Kearns. Jack Kearns himself then made his grand entrance, his authoritative presence permeating the atmosphere. And then, in a sudden flurry of motion, Jno Reilly, the man, materialized in the room, compelling Jno, affectionately known as the monkey, his simian instincts taking hold, to promptly leap upon his human namesake.

Next, Arthur O'Connell, the manager of the Belmont Hotel, swept into the room. In an instant, the gathering took on the appearance of a small convention. Jno, the restless soul that he was, bounded from head to head, searching for the perfect match. None of the guests quite fit the bill, leaving him to languish in his perpetual discontent.

"I start light work the first thing in the morning," said Dempsey. "My training partners will commence coming into camp right away. Kearns has got quite a bunch of them and he's still looking for more.

"Well, come on, men—bring the monk!"[11]

Off they walked toward the elevator, Wild Jno Reilly clutching Jno the monkey close to his chest, nestled cozily beneath his coat, now seeming content. Out of the elevator, Freddie took the lead, ushering the group toward the automobile that would chauffeur them down to his haven of health in New Jersey.

Dempsey arrives at Freddie's health farm and is greeted by
Freddie and his children, Betty and Freddie, Jr.

Jack Dempsey and first wife, Maxine Gates [1916-1919,]
Freddie, Fanny.

Dempsey, the man of the hour, announced with a swagger that come May Day, he would settle upon a regular training camp and plunge into the daily grind of wrestling, boxing, and other rigorous exercises to prepare for the championship bout. The location of said camp was yet to be decided, but several options were under his scrutiny.

Soon after his arrival in New York City, the fighter had secured for himself a top-of-the-line automobile, a purchase that he was quick to boast of. It seemed to Dempsey that the roads between New York City and Freddie's health farm were quite the spectacle, and he declared himself thoroughly content with them.

In the spring of 1921, all eyes turned toward Freddie's Long Hill Health Farm, for Jack Dempsey had made his way there. The press and their flashing cameras descended upon the premises, hungry for a story to regale the masses. Not a soul was there to bear witness to Freddie's own return to the ring, for something far greater was afoot.

The air was rife with anticipation, for it was to be a battle for the ages—the heavyweight championship with Jack Dempsey pitted against the likes of Georges Carpentier.

At Freddie's health farm, Dempsey, the great champion, was not alone in his grandeur; the vernal season had arrived, a splendid and welcome guest. The fertile land was now adorned with a profusion of buds and blossoms, painting the days with their vivid hues. Spring had donned her most exquisite attire in every living thing, flaunting an array of emerald greens, oranges, yellows, scarlets, pinks, and purples. Even the browns of winter were transformed into golden shades by the warm and brilliant sunshine. The apple and peach trees, with their delicate pink and white petals, were vying for attention, while trailing arbutus adorned the sun-kissed hillsides, and the dogwoods, with their burgeoning blooms, announced the arrival of spring in the valley below. The air was alive with the melodious chirping of bluebirds and robins from the leafy thickets and treetops. It was a languid warmth and a gentle caress that embraced everything around.

Dempsey possessed the sort of talent that could have raked in four to five hundred dollars a day simply by charging a fee to those eager to catch a glimpse of his training regimen. While residing at Freddie's health farm, the man discouraged any such money-making scheme. He was loath to indulge in such an ostentatious display, content to rest, to delight in the tranquil tranquility of the countryside.

However, Dempsey, in his characteristic fashion, exhibited no aversion to the notion of selling away the exclusive rights to Pathe, the creator of newsreels, for the captivating depiction of his everyday exploits at Freddie's establishment, all in preparation for his forthcoming epochal encounter. Bound by the stipulations of this binding agreement, Dempsey found himself precluded from participating in any form of motion picture posing, whether for the benefit of a motion picture enterprise or an individual, throughout the duration of his portrayed rigorous training regimen leading up to the day of his much-anticipated clash with Carpentier.

Under the auspices of Pathe, the distributing of a brief one-reel news piece entitled "A Day with Jack Dempsey," offering a cinematic chronicle that documented the pugilistic champion's daily routine, commencing from the moment he emerged from his slumberous sleep in the early morn, traversing through the exhaustive drills and exercises that occupied his waking hours, and including a riveting two-round sparring session with his companion, Freddie.

During his stay at Freddie's health farm, Dempsey found himself with an abundance of leisure time, which he spent gallivanting about with the press and engaging in leisurely pursuits. However, despite his tough-guy image, Dempsey harbored a deep-seated fondness for children. Every day, he received a veritable torrent of letters, but it was those composed in the bold, rounded hands of young children that he truly cherished. As it so happened, Freddie shared Dempsey's soft spot for the little ones and had even installed swings on his property for his own offspring—the sprightly Betty, now six years of age, and her younger brother, Freddie Jr., a boy of five. The children of the surrounding countryside flocked to the estate, lured by the promise of ice cream, and could often be seen rolling down the front lawn with the likes of Dempsey and Freddie alongside his own youngsters.

On a bright afternoon, the hillside of Freddie's health farm was a spectacle of sport and style. Dempsey was garbed in a handsome ensemble of dress shoes, pants, shirt, tie, and vest, as was Freddie. The young ones of Freddie's were also attired in their Sunday best, making for a scene of refined elegance. Dempsey and Freddie paused their training to engage in a playful exhibition of boxing. Freddie Jr. had on his gloves and was eager to test his mettle against the great fighter. Freddie took on the role of the referee and called the match. Dempsey, ever the showman, knelt on his right knee to be at eye level with the young challenger. With his typical bobbing and weaving, Dempsey let Freddie Jr. land a solid hit on his head. Dempsey, in jest, went down for the count while Freddie Sr. counted him out as Freddie Jr. joined in on the referee's tally. It was a moment of pure sport and amusement, set against the backdrop of the rolling hills and blue sky.

Jack Dempsey boxing with Freddie, Jr., while Betty looks on.

L-R, Betty, Freddie, Jr, Jack Dempsey, Freddie at the health farm.

Dempsey was all too eager to indulge the insatiable thirst of the press hounds that descended upon Freddie's health farm every day to catch a glimpse of the champ. No request was too outlandish, no feat too daring for Dempsey as he basked in the flashing lights of the feverish paparazzi, their eager faces illuminated by the flash of cameras as they clicked away with relentless abandon. Even the famed manager, nearly as famous as Dempsey, Jack Kearns, quivered with trepidation at the reckless abandon of his charge as he put his life on the line to satiate the voracious appetites of the yelping press pack.

Early in his stay, the media hoards arrived by way of the Summit railway station from New York, where they chartered tin lizzies to traverse the remaining distance to Freddie's health farm. They arrived rattling and rolling their way through the town of New Providence and clattering across the bridge that spanned the Passaic River, the tie linking Freddie's rural Chatham Township. Disembarking at their destination, the scribes huffed and puffed their way up the elongated knoll to Freddie's expansive white manor. There, they were ushered by the champion's handler, Jack Kearns.

"Come on down and hunt him up," Kearns said. "Jack will be mighty glad to see you. He's down around the barn somewhere. I think, for I saw him heading that way with the kids a few minutes ago."[12]

As they descended the sprawling lawn of the estate, the green expanse seemed to stretch out before them endlessly under the sun's warm embrace. Their feet traversed the lush carpet of grass until they came upon the imposing sight of the towering windmill cloaked in a shroud of ivy and woodbine. Undeterred, they continued their journey, treading more until they arrived at a point where they saw the sprawling, red-roofed barn that loomed ahead, its size and grandeur almost overwhelming. Beyond it lay the vast expanse of orchards and young, golden fields of hay awash in the radiance of the sun. As they approached the barn, a discord of sound assailed them, the frenzied squeals of animals mixing with the ecstatic cries of children. Amidst the pandemonium, a resonant baritone voice reverberated, commanding attention.

"Whoa, Maggie, whoa there, steady old girl, or you'll get your neck deep in mud."

"What's up, I wonder?" Kearns said, with a quickening pace, uttering his words into the frenzied air, and in pursuit, the press corps trailed behind him, hungry for a morsel of news.

"What the devil can he be up to now?"[13]

In a sudden and startling turn of events, they found themselves abruptly halted by the crude confines of the pig pen. And there, amidst the chaotic clutter of a swine, perched atop a large sow, was none other than Jack Dempsey himself, straddling the creature like a seasoned jockey, his hunched back a testament to his formidable strength. Gripping tightly onto the porker's ears as if they were reins, the heavyweight champion of the universe sat proudly in the center of the pen.

Dempsey, in his usual flair for adventure, had earlier darted into the pigpen with the intent of snatching up a pair of squealing porkers, much to the chagrin of their irate mother. With each snap of her formidable jaws, Dempsey deftly sidestepped her fury, his quick feet nimbly evading her menacing tusks.

Now, Kearns, watching what was unfolding, his nerves alight with apprehension, watched on with a worried and excited state, anticipating what would happen as the champion, now dismounted, narrowly avoided the relentless advances of the mother sow, whose sharp tusks threatened to tear him limb from limb. Unmindful of the danger, Dempsey climbed upon the back of one plucky mother pig again and rode her round and round the narrow pen, his wild ride evoking a careless and carefree spirit that knew no bounds.[14]

The sow's screeching cries rang through the air, a shrill and piercing sound that bespoke her utter terror and dismay. Dempsey, his triumphant laughter booming amidst the chaos, still astride her form, reveling in his dominance over the creature. Meanwhile, high atop the pen, young Betty Welsh and her brother Freddie watched with excitement. Freddie, Jr., with dreams of following in his father's footsteps and becoming a lightweight champion, had already earned the nickname "Champ."[15] Together, the siblings shrilled instructions, alternately directing their advice to both man and beast alike.

"Hold tight, hold tight," shrieked Betty.

"Buck him off, Maggie; buck him off," shrilled the boy, a speaking voice that pierced the air, echoing with the same inflections as his distinguished father, Freddie, Sr.

"Whoa there, whoa there, old rose!" Dempsey yelled.

"Whe-e-e-e. whe-e-e-e, whø-e-e-e," shrilled the sow with a frantic fervor as she careened about the pen, heedlessly scattering her tiny brood of pink and white piggies hither and thither.

Her shrill cries resonated through the air, piercing and urgent, as she raced in wild circles, a whirlwind of chaos amidst the serene stillness of the farmyard. The frantic sow, the scampering piglets, and the frenzied dance of life and motion, all set against the backdrop of the tranquil countryside, picture-perfect in its beauty and its madness.

"Whe-e-e-e. whe-e-e-e, whe-e-e-e," cries of her progeny resounded, like their mother, reverberating through the countryside for miles.

In the midst of it, the champion suddenly espied journalists and the manager as they leaned against each other, laughing till tears ran down their faces.

"Huh?!" Dempsey grinningly snickered. "Just in time for the show. I told Betty and Freddie I was the greatest bronco buster alive, and they brought me down here and made me prove it. And I'll tell the world I'm some rider."[16]

The champion descended from his lofty steed and approached the swarm of reporters with a certain air of triumph. However, in that precise moment, a wee piglet, still quivering with fear and careening recklessly around the pen, darted right between Dempsey's legs. He valiantly attempted to sidestep the darting swine, yet alas, his efforts were for naught. The pugilist stumbled and tumbled, not onto the canvas, but into the muck, to the unbridled glee of Freddie's children, whose joyful screams were heard throughout the countryside, threatening to rupture their tender vocal cords.

"Haw, haw, haw," roared Kearns with glee.

Waving his hand, he started counting the champion out.

"One, two, three," Kearns yelled.

"Four, five, six,"[17] awkwardly grunted Dempsey in return.

Dempsey then grasped a handful of mud in his big, brown paw, and without a moment's hesitation, he took aim and, with unerring precision, hit the unsuspecting Kearns right in the eye.

It was then the champion's turn to laugh as he watched his manager trying to separate his face from the layer of wet Jersey clay. At that moment, the champion assumed the role of the jester, relishing in the spectacle of his manager's futile efforts to remove the wet layer of Jersey clay from his face. His laughter rang out with the exuberance befitting a pugilistic champion, a booming bellow that bespoke the might of a warrior who had vanquished all challengers.

Dempsey, a man of vigor and vitality, was not one to abide by the confines of the gymnasium or the indoors. Such locales were alien to his nature and disposition. It was the perfection of Freddie's estate that truly spoke to him—where the cerulean sky served as the ceiling and the scorching sun acted as a balm to unknot his muscles, allowing for a proper physical response. Even the right frame of mind eluded Dempsey in the throes of training in the heart of a bustling metropolis—as was the case in one of his last bouts. He needed to be out in the open, far from the reach of his companions and the hustle and bustle of civilization.

As they ascended the hill toward the grand mansion, the press remarked something of that nature to him, and it caught his attention. The champion strolled along with a sense of confidence while the little golden-haired Betty clinging to his hand and the rosy-cheeked Freddie Jr. darting ahead in excitement.

"Yes," he agreed, "you're right, dead right. I made a big mistake in training the way I did for Brennan. I burned myself out—had no zip and pep left in me. That was proved by the abnormal blood pressure, pulse, and respiration that doctor's examination showed when I weighed in on the afternoon of the bout. Why I was so nervous, grouchy, and worn out I didn't know myself."[18]

"Remember the story you wrote about six months after the Willard fight?" said Kearns. "You said you didn't believe Jack ever again would be quite the ring wonder he was when he fought Willard; that all the gymnasium training in the world would not give him the battle edge he received by the string of hard belts leading up to the big scrap in Toledo.

"I got a bit sore at that yard then—thought you didn't know what you were talking about. But I can see that you were partly right, now. I believe Jack can be whipped into just as great shape as he was for Willard; but he will have to have some of the real fights you were telling about. He's going to get them, too. No more ping-pong tactics—no, siree. There will be no light sparring and gentle cuffing around. When Jack starts training for Carpentier, I'm going to have Kid Norfolk, Jim Darcy, and one or two other huskies around who can both give and take. And I'm going to see that Jack gets plenty of mauling and roughing it. That's the only way to give him his old edge."[19]

Dempsey was not yet in the throes of his rigorous

training for the Carpentier brawl, for that would have been a fool's errand. He had just finished a contractual stint of seven weeks, a period rife with bouts staged in one-night stands and hasty jaunts across the nation. Undoubtedly, such a venture had the potential to debilitate his vigor. His stage performance required him to engage in boxing for no less than ten rounds every sunup. His eating and slumber schedule were askew, and his lifestyle was thoroughly disrupted, with every passing eventuality jeopardizing his routine, which was crucial for a man of his profession. Above all, what the boxer craved was a couple of weeks' respite and leisure before embarking on his preparatory groundwork. This was exactly what he was pursuing at Freddie's health farm, and once his arduous training commenced, he intended to shift to an alternative location.

Kearns said, "His boy is just playing around over in Jersey."[20]

Dempsey, a man of great athleticism and vitality, was not one for idleness or indolence. He was game for a round of pinochle, a game of chance played with cards, or for the hurling of nickels at a line, where skill and precision were paramount. He would even run a foot race or engage in an impromptu experiment with a new headlock, applied with precision and force, on the snout of a massive swine. He would engage in a multitude of activities yet refrain from talking about fighting or arduous labor. However, what Jack Dempsey called rest and recreation would be hard training for the ordinary man. To Dempsey, rest and recreation were but a different kind of toil.

In the lazy, languid countryside of the health farm, his mornings were instilled with a certain sense of leisurely riches. Rising early as part of his daily routine, often before the sun itself had stretched its rays across the pastures, he would slip into his white flannels and white shirt. On occasion, he would venture forth to the barn, where the cows lay heavy with milk, and lend his hands to the labor of milking—a humble task, but one he undertook with a certain grace as if it were but another facet of his duties.

"Gee, I get lots of fun with the milking," laughed Dempsey as he commented upon it. "It's fun now, but I used to call it work. You know, I was born and raised on the farm and acted as chambermaid for the bossies for many years."[21]

Dempsey, the fabled fighter, would tend to the fields with a rustic pitchfork and tend to the grass with a mechanical reel lawnmower. Such humble tasks were a mere facade, a publicity ploy to hone his image for the masses who seemed to favor his adversary, the dashing Frenchman Carpentier, even in the heart of America. Dempsey still endured withering criticism from those who viewed him as a shirker, a craven draft dodger, while Carpentier basked in the glory of his storied wartime heroism.

Through it all, Freddie, a veteran of the army, never wavered in his staunch support for the embattled Dempsey, serving as a loyal defender against the slings and arrows of outrageous detractors. The crafty promoter Tex Rickard saw a golden opportunity to weave his magic, pitting the dashing Frenchman as the hero against the rugged Dempsey, the villain. He had no idea the magnitude of the event that would unfold. Rickard's shrewd sense of showmanship proved prophetic, for the spectacle that ensued would surpass all expectations, the magnitude of which reverberated throughout history.

On an idyllic afternoon, the press corps found themselves in the company of Dempsey and his affable companion, Freddie. In a moment of levity, the burly champ couldn't resist lacing up his gloves and engaging in boxing three rounds with Joe Benjamin, a worthy sparring partner. It was not all horseplay and pugnacity for the boxer, as he found solace in performing manual labor around the farm, he laughingly explained, "now that I don't have to do it."[22]

Just before dinner, the search was on for Jno, the monkey who had gone missing. The hunt led to the back of the barn, where a stack of cordwood lay. With a glint in his eye, Dempsey seized a saw and pointed to another, challenging one of the newspaper writers to a duel of sawing ability.

"Come on, now," said Dempsey, "and will have a sawing match. I've heard you were a lumberjack once. You're fat and soft as a baby now, and I'll bet you I can saw two sticks while you are sawing one."

"This isn't a whipsaw," the journalist replied, "but I, too, was raised on a farm, and sawing firewood was a part of my chores. I'll take you up."[23]

Wonders of wonders, the scribe bested the champion. Dempsey remained unaware, but the word jockey had spied on the lumber he had chosen—oak, gnarled and unyielding, with fibers coursing like veins of steel. It was the most difficult timber in the world to sever. The scribe had cunningly selected a log of cedar—heftier and more impressive in appearance than Dempsey's choice but nearly as malleable as cardboard. There are tricks to every trade.

"Jack's, a light eater," Kearns remarked during a

conversation that afternoon. "Fruit and an egg or so in the morning, a little roast beef or something at noon, more the same at night."[24]

As the media disembarked from their sumptuous feast that evening, prepared by Fanny, Freddie's missus and an adept nutritionist who knew precisely what culinary delights a pugilist in preparation should partake in, the scribes pondered with intrigue as to what sort of chap Kearns would deem a "heavy eater."

On that good day, the champion had but a meager meal to sate his hunger pangs—a mere two plates of broth, accompanied by a pound and a half of delectable, rare tenderloin, six baked potatoes, and generous helpings of spinach, string beans, and eggplant. In addition, he indulged in a salad of crisp lettuce and ripe tomatoes and a heaping plate of ice cream—a treat he shared, on the sly, with young Betty and Freddie, Jr., taking care not to draw their mother's attention. To wash down his feast, the champion downed three large goblets of thick, creamy milk, still warm from the daily day's milking of the dairy cows.

"That was a pleasant little appetizer," smiled the champion as the table was cleared. "Many man would feel inclined to call it a real square meal."[25]

As the evening fell upon them, Dempsey and his companions lounged lazily on the piazza in the gathering twilight, a friend of his strumming idly on a ukulele. Soon, a tune floated into the air, and someone began to hum the familiar melody of "Mammy." Before long, the entire group had joined in, their voices blending together in perfect harmony. Fanny's rich contralto mingled with Freddie's tenor and Dempsey's deep baritone, and even Kearns and Benjamin, along with some of the other guests, added their voices to the mix. Finally, as the night drew to a close, they sang "The End of a Perfect Day," the perfect ending to a perfect evening.

"Huh," gently remarked Freddie as he took out his watch, "Reckon it is the end of a perfect day."

"Whew," he exclaimed, "It's six minutes past ten. Time for all hands to hit the hay. Ten o'clock is 'lights out' in this shack. Come on fellows. Shake a leg. Early to bed and early to rise makes a man healthy, wealthy, and wise."[26]

JACK DEMPSEY,

At Freddy Welsh's farm, Summit, N. J. Jack stops long enough in his labors preparing for the big battle with Carpentier to caress a pair of pigs and incidentally satisfy the "hungry" camera man.

Jack Dempsey at Freddie's farm in 1921.

In the crisp air of April twenty-fifth, Dempsey was sweating it out at Freddie's training grounds, honing his muscles and mind for the upcoming bout. Meanwhile, Tex Rickard, the mastermind of the ring, proclaimed that Jersey City would be the site of the bout on July 2nd. He set his sights on Doyle's Thirty Acres, a patch of soil known as Montgomery Oval that was once home to the Eastern League baseball team. There was one problem with the choice: the ground was bare, empty of any stadium to host the monumental event. And Tex, with his usual style, had to wave his wand and conjure up a colosseum in just over two months, a daunting task.

"I have just made this selection," Rickard said. "I like this site from the very first, before a time there was certain difficulties in the way that it appeared insurmountable. These difficulties were overcome through the assistance of prominent men in New Jersey, and the deal was closed today."[27]

The locale possessed an air of accessibility that was unrivaled amongst sports locations in the area. One could reach it with ease, a mere jaunt from the Grove Street station of the Hudson Tubes and the Jersey City terminals of the ferries. Its proximity to several wide boulevards facilitated the heavy flow of automobiles and provided ample parking spaces. Additionally, a Pennsylvania rail spur, with the capacity to accommodate no less than 240 Pullman cars, was but three blocks away.

On the eve of the announcement, Dempsey was putting in a spirited day, gallivanting about like a carefree young buck. As relayed by Freddie, the chap had taken a grand liking to lawn tennis and could oft be found perfecting his strokes on the courts of Freddie's health farm. He played through several arduous sets, lost in the thrill of competition. Handball, too, had a pull on Dempsey, and for a full hour, he pummeled the rubber orb with all his might, reveling in the sheer physicality of the game. Such were the joys of leisure, and Dempsey was relishing every moment of it.

The news had it that Freddie and Benny Leonard were scheduled to cross gloves for the lightweight crown in the same arena where Dempsey-Carpentier would fight. It was to take place the day before the big match between the two heavyweights. Though the match was still up in the air, its prospect was bright. When Leonard snatched the title from Freddie, Billy Gibson, the manager of the new champion, gave his word to offer Freddie a chance to regain his lost glory. Leonard, being the man of honor that he was, reiterated the promise. Yet, despite Gibson's two attempts to set up the match, it was always thwarted by some unforeseen circumstance. But Gibson always stated he was willing to live up to his promise.[28]

Dempsey declared from Freddie's health farm that he would shift his training grounds to the sandy shores of Atlantic City, New Jersey, prior to the big fight. The scribe Henry Farrell paid a visit to the farm to revel in the company of Jack Dempsey in the waning days of April.

"I'm just resting, eating, and having a good time," Dempsey told Farrell.

Farrell said that Dempsey would rise early and take a leisurely jog through the hills, returning with an insatiable hunger that could demolish a platter of ham and eggs and a few quarts of fresh milk. By the strike of nine, the champ could be seen on the road alongside his sparring companions, Freddie, Joe Benjamin, and Teddy Hayes. Jimmy Darcey, a middleweight from the West Coast, was also in the camp to duke it out with Dempsey in sparring sessions. On the day Farrell was there, they strolled by a stream, where the champ worked on his back, snatching frogs from the water to rattle his pet monkey, Jno, when he returned to the mansion.

After sating himself with breakfast, Dempsey whiled away his time reading the news or engaging in a game of handball or tennis. On other days, he'd hoist his golf bag and make his way to the nearby Baltusrol golf course, where he had already established himself as a firm favorite among the golfing crowd. Dempsey held a warm relationship with George Low, the golf professional at Baltusrol, and they could be seen playing a round or two either morning or afternoon, sometimes both, for Dempsey had developed a keen affection for the ancient Scottish pastime. The champ's adoration for his swings and putts had begun to rival that of his jabs and hooks.

As the afternoon wore on, his eyes lit up with the succulent tenderloin steak that awaited him, along with a generous supply of milk and tea to soothe his parched throat. The noon hour passed by in a blur of culinary indulgence, leaving him content and satisfied. But the day had only just begun, and he eagerly awaited the afternoon's festivities. A game of pinochle, a few rounds of nickel tossing, and a raucous wrestling match in the front yard with his merry band of companions all served to further whet his appetite. After that, he retired to his chambers for a well-deserved rest, knowing that a sumptuous dinner awaited him on the other side of slumber.

"I'm not going to do any work until we get to Atlantic City training camp,"[29] Dempsey stated.

"I'm feeling as good as I ever did, and I can get in shape with six weeks work. I over trained for Bill Brennan, and I'm not going to make the same mistake this time."[30]

"Yes, I have been dancing a little bit, and I went up to a midnight show last week with Babe Ruth. I know I was criticized for doing it, but a fellow's got to have a little amusement once in a while."[31]

Farrell divulged that Dempsey had taken up the gentler pastimes of tennis and handball, no doubt, in an effort to expand his athletic ability beyond the ring. Dempsey had also ventured into the world of billiards, perhaps seeking to find the same satisfaction in sinking a ball with a cue as he did with a well-placed punch. He soon discovered the two were not alike.

"I tried pocket billiards," Dempsey said, "but I was the fish for the whole settlement. Joe Benjamin got rich on me, so I quit."[32]

As the champ remained immersed in his leisurely pursuits at Freddie's health farm, Tex Rickard and Jack Kearns toiled tirelessly to arrange the perfect venues for boxing and training. Rickard himself journeyed to the location of the title fight, Boyle's Thirty Acres, in Jersey City. With less than two months before the fight, he declared the scene to resemble a lumberyard. There were stacks of timber piled haphazardly about the barren earth. Though several trainloads of lumber had been delivered with the utmost haste, waiting to be assembled into a majestic arena, the grading work had not yet been completed.

Rickard was unperturbed by the fact that a referee had yet to be selected for the impending bout. To him, the matter was of little consequence, and he gave it scant consideration. According to the terms of the contract, the principals were responsible for appointing an arbiter, and Rickard expressed confidence that the ample pool of competent referees in New Jersey would render any potential issue moot.

When journalist Farrell had asked Dempsey about the yet-to-be-arranged details of the Carpentier bout a few days before, Dempsey said, "I don't care, Doc (Kearns) will take care of those things."[33]

When asked if he cared who refereed the fight, Dempsey replied, "As long as he knows how to count."[34]

It was April the thirtieth, and journalist Sparrow McGann was off to Freddie's health farm to see the champ. He aimed to witness Dempsey's training regimen in those bucolic Jersey hills but found himself idling away three hours until the champ finally arrived when he blew in with his big motor car. Dempsey, who'd been absent for more than a day, bolted through his meal when he sat down at the dinner table, chowing down on the wholesome food that Freddie had provided. It was then that McGann, ever the talkative type, struck up a conversation.

"Jack, I came up here to see you training. The paper said you were hard at work training."

Dempsey laughed.

"The papers have to say something. It makes better reading to have me training. No, I haven't started it yet, except a little hike every morning."

"When are you going to begin?"

"Monday, a couple of my sparring partners will come up and then I will begin to get down to business."

"You look pretty fat now. I don't think you ought to go too hard with the bout two months away."

"You are right. I don't want to go stale. What I'll do will be to work and then at different spells lay off; that is until a month before the fight. Fact is I've been putting on a little weight up here. I weigh about 200 now."

"Now, about Tuesday," Dempsey replied after McGann asked when he will start. "I'll go down to Atlantic City, where I will have permanent quarters. This is the finest country here that ever was made, but I like the sea air for training. When I get really in training, I want my meals exactly on the minute. If I don't get them, I get peevish. Also, there will be better facilities for working, bigger ring, and so forth."

"Then you don't mind working before crowds?" McGann asked.

"No, I don't care. I like to have my friends see me workout. The only thing is that a few days before I fight, I begin to get on edge. You know how it is—a fellow is worried about the battle and is getting his mind in a tough fighting mood. Just about that time if some friend butts in on you, why, you're apt to hand him one before you think."

"That is apt to lose you some friends."

"Well," smiled Dempsey, "if they are real friends, they will respect your feelings and not bother you. And if they do bother you and get a quick comeback, they'll understand just why it happened. That is, they will if they are the sort of pals that amount to anything."

"You look as though you had kept yourself in good condition."

"Well, I have. That is, I don't think I will have to do more than three weeks of real rugged training. I never have had to before. The only reason I'm going to begin work on Monday is to give myself something to do. I hate to be idle. That's the reason I went into the vaudeville show, just to pay expenses and keep busy."

"Did you like the show business?"

"No. You appear three or four times a day, punch the bag, spar, and do a monologue. I get darn sick of it. Still, it was something to do. They tell me Bill Brennan enjoyed acting. But I guess he didn't have many lines."

"What do you think of Brennan?"

"He's a little dandy, fine kid," Dempsey laughed. "Last Christmas he got out some Christmas cards showing himself standing with arms folded while I was in a doctor's office having my ear sewn up because of that wallop he gave me in that fight of ours. But at that, I think he looked worse than I did after that scrap. I could have gone twenty-five rounds that night easy, the way I felt."

"The fight with Carpentier ought to be a good one."

Dempsey's big white teeth gleamed through his grin.

"There will be time enough to think about that fight."[35]

At that moment, someone started to dance as a merry melody burst forth from the phonograph stationed in the hallway, beckoning all to abandon their repose and join the merriment. In the blink of an eye, Dempsey sprang from his seat and seized Jimmy Chapin, Freddie's trusty farmhand, as a dance partner and gave an exhibition of the art of shimmying.

Freddie, poised for his second comeback return to the ring, felt as if fate had swung in his favor. With the taste of victory still lingering from his previous bout, he spoke with an air of confidence and self-assurance. Freddie grasped that if he measured up to the standards he had set for himself, he would accept the bout being arranged against his conqueror, Benny Leonard. The bout was still set to take place on the first of July, on the grounds of Boyle's Acres, just one day prior to the highly anticipated Dempsey-Carpentier match. For Freddie, this fight would be more than just a chance at redemption. It was a chance to prove to the world that he was more than just another has-been.

Freddie was on the comeback trail, a desperate journey fueled by desire and need. His coffers were becoming bare, and his fistic fortunes were in peril. He, too, was training, but for a different purpose: to prove that he still had some fight left in him. Freddie took to the ring for his second comeback fight with no one else but his friend, health farm resident, and heavyweight champion of the world, Jack Dempsey, refereeing. Freddie's opponent was Young Willie Jackson, a veteran of the ring with a record of 75-32-12.

On May 3, 1921, in Summit, New Jersey, at the Elks Club under the auspices of the American Legion, Freddie's fists did the talking before a scant crowd of about one hundred. The bout was scheduled for ten rounds, and in the third round, Jackson found himself counting the seconds as he struggled to get back on his feet after taking counts of eight and nine. But Freddie was not one to be underestimated, and in the eighth round, he delivered a knock-out punch that sent Jackson tumbling to the mat. The victory was Freddie's. His last two opponents were not exactly of the first-class variety, but they served their purpose, providing a necessary tune-up for Freddie, the once-great pugilist whose boxing skills had faded.

Dempsey was not one to procrastinate until his purported trip to Atlantic City despite what he had stated. He commenced his rigorous training regimen at Freddie's health farm. May fourth saw the arrival of two more sparring partners, namely the middleweight Alex Trambidas and welterweight Steve Latzo. With not a moment to waste, Dempsey set them to work, honing his skills and sharpening his senses.

As dawn illuminated the skies, Dempsey emerged from his slumber, his attention already focused on the grueling day ahead, which represented a typical training day. Training was his daily bread, and he treated it with the utmost reverence, never missing a beat. The routine was familiar, comforting even, as he readied himself for the roadwork that lay ahead. Trambidas, Latzo, and Joe Benjamin accompanied him. As they set off, the wind howled around them, a reminder of the challenges that lay ahead. Undeterred, the quartet pushed on, their strides a blur covering four miles of jogging, racing, and hiking as they dashed toward their goal. Even as the day wore on and the weather grew more challenging, Dempsey never lost his focus, even as his infrequent horseback riding was curtailed. For Dempsey, nothing could dim his burning passion for the fight, and he remained steadfast, unwavering, and resolute.

In the afternoon, Dempsey delved into a strenuous hour and a half of work. With dogged determination, he summoned the pulleys, pummeled the bag, danced with his shadow, skipped rope, and executed floor calisthenics with effortless grace. But that was just the prelude to the main event: sparring. Benjamin stepped into the ring with Dempsey, his gloves at the ready, and the two went at it with a frenzied pace. Trambidas and Latzo followed suit, each taking turns in the ring with the champ. Throughout the sparring, Dempsey remained composed and collected, urging his partners to come at him with all their might—to rush, push, pull, maul, and attempt an attack. Such was the heart of a true fighter, always pushing the limits and striving for greatness.

Pete Latzo had barely scratched the surface of his pugilistic career, with a record that hardly dazzled the boxing world with nineteen victories against seven defeats. Yet, it was in those early days that fate had conspired to bring him into the orbit of one Freddie, a master of the sweet science. Under Freddie's tutelage, Pete honed his skills, and in time, his mastery of the craft became approaching perfect. Pete often spoke of Freddie with reverence, for Freddie was the only one who had believed in him besides his trainer, Al Thomas. Freddie had imparted upon him a wealth of knowledge that would prove invaluable in his crowning moment. In 1926, Pete Latzo defeated the formidable Mickey Walker, known as the Toy Bulldog, for his tenacity to seize the welterweight championship. As he prepared for his first defense against Willie Harmon, Pete declared with steely resolve:

"I'm going back to my old pal's place—to Freddie Welsh—where I really got my first start. I owe it to him, and it's there I'm going to train for all fights in this vicinity."[36]

For Pete, there was nothing quite like receiving a compliment, especially from Freddie—back when he was but a nobody of the ring. It was a time of simpler pleasures when men of sport were measured by their fists and the size of their hearts. Freddie's words had been like a beacon of hope in the darkness, a glimmer of recognition for Pete's talent and tenacity. He had held onto that compliment like a cherished possession, polishing it with each victory and using it as fuel for the battles yet to come. It was a small thing, a single gesture of kindness, but for Pete, it had meant everything.

As the day drew to a close, Dempsey professed his adoration for automobiles, and when the opportunity presented itself, he readily agreed to accompany Freddie on a jaunt through the countryside to Morristown. But it wasn't just a jaunt, as Freddie had another match. The pugilistic pair, along with a duo of companions, set out on their journey.

Freddie, in the midst of his comeback attempt, had yet another bout scheduled against the inexperienced Tommy "Kid" Murphy. Once again, Dempsey was called upon to officiate the fight. Freddie unleashed a barrage of merciless blows upon his hapless opponent's body. With merely two minutes elapsed in the second round of the scheduled ten, Murphy's corner was compelled to throw in the towel. Freddie secured a technical knockout against his lesser-skilled adversary, marking his second such triumph within a twenty-four-hour span, having vanquished Willie

Jackson the night before.

Jack Kearns had yet to grace Freddie's health farm with a return of his presence. The man was holed up at the Belmont Hotel, nestled in the heart of Manhattan's midtown. Rumors circulated that he would not return until the following day. When he did, Kearns would undoubtedly be focused on finalizing plans for the champion's training on the velodrome in Atlantic City. The negotiations for this location had been ongoing ever since it was announced that the battle would take place at Boyle's Thirty Acres in Jersey City. Recent reports from New Jersey's resort city hinted that the arrangements had been open-endedly settled. The site promised to provide every convenience and luxury for the champion's training period. As for Freddie's health farm, it would be left without a significant attraction, with Dempsey expected to make his way to Atlantic City the following day.

Dempsey had wrapped up his initial stint at Freddie's health farm by the fourth of May. In the course of his stay, he had achieved precisely what he had set out to do. The air, so richly endowed with freshness, had been inhaled in abundance; his frame had amassed a notable amount of bulk, liberated his tense muscles, and he reached a state of preparedness that would equip him to undertake the Herculean task that lay ahead of him—the Carpentier bout.

The following day, with the freshness of May still clinging to the air, Dempsey did shift his training from the tranquil confines of Chatham Township to the buzzing hive of Atlantic City. Meanwhile, on the seventh of May, Carpentier, with his sights set on the shores of the United States, set sail from the port of Le Harve aboard the

Steamship *Savoie*. Before he departed, with a cool confidence that could not be swayed, he proclaimed that regardless of who was to claim the championship title in Jersey City, the bout would not persist beyond the fourth round.

As Carpentier bade his farewell to France, he resolved to train at Freddie's health farm, where he had achieved victory in the Levinsky brawl. He soon discovered that Dempsey had already secured the coveted spot, having beat him to the punch. Without a clue that the venue for Dempsey had shifted to Atlantic City, Carpentier altered his intended course. On May sixteenth, upon landing on American soil, he settled on Manhasset, Long Island, where he would prep for the impending match. A telegram dispatched on April sixteenth to Joe Jeanette, his trusted chief sparring partner, and advisor, requested him to reprise his role, given their successful collaboration at Freddie's health farm for the Levinsky bout.

Freddie had observed Dempsey with utmost attention before he departed from his estate and proclaimed with great conviction that the champion was now exquisitely primed, stating:

"Dempsey has laid a good foundation for his future work in preparation for the fight. He has a lot of excess weight to work on, and if he delays hard work till a month before the battle, there is no danger of him going stale, as he did previous to the fight with Brennan. To me, Dempsey looks to be in rugged health, and care in his training should send him into the ring in excellent condition."[37]

An inescapable inquiry lingered, permeating the

opinions of those who held a vested interest in the fate of Jack Dempsey. The pugilist's sojourn to Atlantic City, that haven of gaiety and extravagance, loomed ominously. Would the celebrated fighter succumb to the temptations that awaited him amidst the glitz and glamour of the bustling resort, or would he prove himself immune to its seductive allure? Such was the quandary of his supporters and detractors alike as they awaited the outcome of Dempsey's upcoming excursion to the fabled land of sun, sand, and sin.

"Wise move," wrote journalist Henry Farrell when he came to Freddie's. "The night songs of the owls will be better for him than the rumble of the elevated."

"He'll never get into condition there," Farrell wrote when he planned to depart for Atlantic City. "The bright lights'll get him."[38]

It wasn't the sheer indulgence of Atlantic City that the Synod of the Reformed Church found at odds with their righteous sensibilities but the unbecoming spectacle of boxing and the unsavory throngs it threatened to attract. They were unequivocally opposed to the Carpentier-Dempsey pugilistic affair. The Jersey City Chamber of Commerce, in rebutting their objection, sent this reply:

"The legislature of our state has declared that boxing is a legitimate amusement enterprise, and from a business standpoint the Chamber of Commerce can see no difference between the establishment in the city of a baseball club, a moving picture theater or a boxing arena. The Chamber of Commerce would certainly be doing less than its duty had it neglected to secure for Jersey City a legitimate business enterprise capable of producing more than $1,000,000 revenue for the people of our city."[39]

In response to the clergymen's accusation that the impending brawl would attract a ruffian crowd to Jersey City, the esteemed Chamber of Commerce was swift to retort. With a proud air and measured tone, they declared that the match was nothing short of a high society affair. The ringside seats had been exclusively reserved for the likes of His Royal Highness the Prince of Wales, Edward, the American financier J. P. Morgan, the American philanthropist Miss Ann Morgan, American steel magnate Charles M. Schwab, the renowned playwright David Belasco, the former governor of Vermont Charles W. Gates, and other such distinguished personages. The city's elite relished the prospect of witnessing a spectacle fit for kings and queens.

As the duo of principals diligently honed their skills, Tex Rickard was busily constructing a stadium of epic proportions. On the twenty-eighth day of June, just eight weeks since the initial whirring of the steam shovel's excavation, the grand structure stood in all its glory. Never before had such a magnificent boxing arena been erected, a testament to Rickard's unwavering ambition. The sheer scale of the project required the employment of five hundred skilled carpenters and four hundred laborers, who labored tirelessly to create a masterpiece. Over three hundred thousand square feet of space emerged from the amazing sum of 2,250,000 feet of pine and spruce lumber, which was fastened with a staggering sixty tons of steel nails.

The arena was a marvel to behold, a magnificent structure with an octagonal shape that rose thirty-four feet above the ground. Constructed by J.W. Edwards, brother of the governor of New Jersey. But its grandeur came with a price, a hefty sum of two hundred and fifty thousand dollars, twice the original estimate, but such was the price of greatness. A masterwork of engineering, it could house over ninety thousand spectators within its walls, and all would be clamoring for a glimpse of the main event. The last rows of seats were perched precariously over three hundred and twelve feet away from the center ring as if in a lofty perch, but even from there, the spectacle would be a sight to witness.

They erected a wooden chamber beneath the bleachers, specially crafted to house the radio broadcast. Major J. Andrew White would commandeer the radiophone, while H. L. Walker manned the control panel. This was the first time a sporting event was to be broadcast over the radio, a newfangled technology of mass communication. Telephone lines, together with a makeshift radio transmitter, courtesy of the Radio Corporation of America, were fitted at the Delaware, Lackawanna, and Western Railway terminal, situated in the heart of Hoboken, New Jersey. The signal would voyage across the Atlantic from steamship to steamship until it reached Europe. Amongst those who would be receiving the broadcast was Carpentier's wife, Georgette; her ear would be closely attuned to the telephone's every vibration. The mastermind behind this undertaking, promoter Rickard, sought to disseminate the appeal of this pugilistic contest to every corner of the world.

The sale of the coveted tickets commenced on May thirteenth, offering a sumptuous range of prices. The ringside box seats fetched a sizeable sum of fifty dollars, while the modest accommodations in the distant corners could be obtained for a mere five dollars and fifty cents. The crowds thronged in, snatching up tickets in a frenzy, until there was not a single seat left to be had. The mastermind behind the event, Rickard, lamented his lack of foresight, ruefully opining that he ought to have doubled the prices.

The sweet anticipation for the clash of the pugilistic titans, Freddie and Benny Leonard, soared high in the air the day before the Dempsey-Carpentier melee. Fortune had other plans, and the two formidable fighters never graced the ring together. It was a cruel blow for Freddie, whose heart yearned for the rousing cheers of the masses, as he missed his chance to revel under the bright lights of a grand boxing spectacle.

The second of July had arrived, and with it, an overcast sky and the stifling humidity of midsummer that hung heavy over the event. The fight dubbed the Battle of the Century, was the talk of the town. Though the official count put the attendance at 80,103, with 2,000 ladies present, the stands, with their seating capacity of more than 90,000, were filled to capacity, teeming with eager enthusiasts. As if that weren't enough, 300,000 more tuned in to listen to the live broadcast of the bout, marking the first time in history that such an event had ever been aired on the radio waves. With receipts totaling $1,789,238,[40] it was a momentous occasion that marked the birth of the million-dollar gate in the world of sport.

Dempsey, the darling of the odds-makers, stood at two to one. The raucous crowd, with a fervor that could only be mustered on American soil, cheered on the Frenchman, Carpentier. The ring is a lonely place, and Dempsey's might was too much for his opponent. At precisely 3:27 that afternoon, sixty-six seconds into the fourth round, Carpentier tasted the canvas. He lay there, helpless, his consciousness a fleeting memory, as Referee Harry Ertle put an end to the pummeling. The curtains drew to a close on a spectacle of titanic proportions. The truth was inescapable: the fight had not lived up to its grandeur, but the event did.

Jack Dempsey, left, Georges Carpentier, right, before a huge crowd in Jersey City.

Jack Dempsey watches as Georges Carpentier lay on the canvas.

Chapter XII

Twenty miles from the city a pair of enormous eggs, identical in contour and separated only by a courtesy bay, jut out into the most domesticated body of salt water in the Western Hemisphere, the great wet barnyard of Long Island Sound.

—F. Scott Fitzgerald, *The Great Gatsby*

East Egg condescending to West Egg, and carefully on guard against its spectroscopic gayety.

—F. Scott Fitzgerald, *The Great Gatsby*

Fitzgerald set his masterpiece in the fictional bayside villages of West Egg and East Egg, which seem to geographically correlate to the real-life communities of Great Neck (West Egg) and Port Washington (East Egg). The towns match the author's description of the twin peninsulas as "a pair of enormous eggs" that "jut out into… the great wet barnyard of Long Island Sound" about 20 miles from Manhattan."

—David Ozanich, film producer and writer, *The Great Gatsby's Gold Coast*[1]

As the dust settled on Dempsey's departure, Freddie's health farm continued to draw in elite boxers. The first to arrive was the formidable Bob Martin, a heavyweight with a fierce reputation, set to face off against Frank Moran at the Boxing Drome in the Bronx. With many still in town from the Dempsey bout, the Martin-Moran fight was sure to draw a crowd, with many speculating it would be a better fight than the Dempsey-Carpentier bout. Among those at the health farm was Gunboat Smith, fresh off a loss to Martin in his second to last career fight, now acting as Martin's chief sparring partner. Smith had a brilliant career, having faced off against a dozen different Boxing Hall of Famers a total of twenty-three times, including the likes of all-time greats Jack Dempsey, Harry Greb, Sam Langford, and Georges Carpentier. Despite Smith's presence, Freddie found himself going three rounds with Martin every day. Martin was convinced that he was the only true contender for Dempsey's crown.

Bob Martin, an ex-doughboy of the military, had won more ring battles by the knockout route than any other man who had worn the heavyweight crown. Those who were going to attend the fight at the Boxing Drome in the Bronx were abuzz with excitement, and special boxes were being erected for the many notables who were coming to New York to see the American Expeditionary Forces (A.E.F.) champion face off against Moran. Major General Robert Lee Bullard and his staff had already accepted their invitations, and even General Pershing had plans to attend. The *New York Times* reported this bout was an exciting slugfest as Martin emerged victorious, delivering a knock-out blow in the seventh round on July 12, 1921.

Jack Britton, the three-time welterweight champion, was the next to descend upon Freddie's pastoral training grounds to sharpen his skills. He was to face off against the formidable Mickey Walker, a man who had held both welterweight and middleweight titles in his storied career and would use Freddie's farm to train for other fights. The twelve-round bout was to be contested at the Armory in Newark, New Jersey. And on the eighteenth of July, the two men would enter the ring, their fates to be decided in a thrilling draw.

Freddie, with his eyes set on redemption, was training at his health farm for his continued comeback after he was denied an encounter with Benny Leonard at the site of the Dempsey-Carpentier bout. Determined to reclaim the glory that still lingered in him, he set his sights north of the border, where his next bout would take place in the city of Calgary. On the eighteenth of August, he stepped into the ring, facing off against Bert Forbes of Vancouver. The two men engaged in a fierce battle, but it was clear that Freddie's cunning and skill were too much for Forbes to handle. As the final bell rang, the judges declared Freddie the victor in a ten-round decision.

As the year 1921 drew to a close and December cast its icy grip upon the land, Freddie shuttered his health farm for the winter. A year that had brought many notables in the world of boxing to his health farm, granting him the fame and adulation once held as champion, now came to a close. He would make his new home in the prestigious Bayside, Long Island, a haven for the wealthy elite of Long Island's glittering "Gold Coast."

With Freddie's appearance, it seemed the Long Island resorts would once again become the epitome of sophistication for the sporting gentlemen of the era. Boxers, in succession, kept coming to his facility to train. In years gone by, the legendary former heavyweight champion, James Corbett, used to train at a roadhouse on the outskirts of Flushing before ultimately finding solace in the seclusion of his own barn in the picturesque Bayside.

At Bayside, Freddie had outfitted his property with a new gym and equipment to put a man into shape for a boxing bout as he drifted further and further toward his old sport of boxing. His first tenant, who he would train, would be future world lightweight champion Rocky Kansas. The young fighter was to fight Benny Leonard for the lightweight championship, and Freddie himself, was scheduled to fight on the undercard. The excitement of the impending bout was palpable in the air as Freddie worked tirelessly to prepare his charge for the ultimate test of strength and skill.

On February 10, 1922, the grand Madison Square Garden played host to a bitter disappointment for one Rocky Kansas. As the bell rang for the final round, it was clear that the unanimous decision would not be in his favor. A single knockdown by Leonard occurred in the eleventh round when Kansas hit the canvas with a thud. Freddie's match was to transpire in the same manner as the one he was slated to engage in against Benny Leonard on the eve of the Dempsey-Carpentier bout—it did not take place.

The next boxer to grace Freddie's Bayside residence was twenty-three-year-old Oakland Jimmy Duffy, a man from the West Coast unknown in the East. He was set to face off against Lew Tendler, a fighter considered by many to be one of the greatest lightweight and welterweight boxers to never win a world title. The shrewd Jack Kearns, who took an interest in Duffy, and Duffy's manager, Dan McKettrick, had decided to host a grand "show off" party at Freddie's residence in order to introduce the West Coast invader to the elite of the East Coast boxing scene.

As the party reached its pinnacle, Freddie stepped into the ring with Duffy to test his mettle. He conceded that while he may have a fighting chance, Tendler would prove a formidable challenge for the West Coast pugilist. Freddie was the last of four boxers to get into the ring with Duffy. Phil Kaplan, Johnny Martin, and Pete Hopin, a welterweight from Belgium, also gave Duffy a try.

On February 24, 1922, Duffy fought Tendler at Madison Square Garden. Because there were too many people fighting under the name Jimmy Duffy, he was forced to fight under his real name, Hymie Gold. During the fight, in the heat of battle, Duffy refused to fight further after claiming he was fouled. The referee, unfazed, disagreed and declared Tendler the victor in an eighth-round technical knockout.

Before the Duffy bout, Freddie made his way to Madison Square Garden on February 17, 1922, for the much-anticipated battle between Jack Britton and Dave Shade. As the fight progressed, Freddie watched as something seemed off about Britton. Despite the mixed decision draw, which meant that Britton retained his welterweight title, he appeared to be a shadow of his former self in the ring. Freddie took notice. He called him a pathetic figure over the distance of the fight.

"It's sad to see a veteran slipping as Britton is slipping," said Freddie. "I thought Jack would be able to hold his own with the California boy, but there is no question about it. He is on the toboggan and going at a great clip—

toward oblivion. I know just how he feels. He thinks he is as good as ever, but his actions speak louder than words. During the first part of the bout, I could see Jack trying to keep away. I knew then he was simply stalling. His fire has died down and the first hard puncher that hangs one on his chin is going to walk away with the title."[2]

Freddie continued to say the trouble with these veterans is their brain tells them they are alright, but the muscles refuse to stand up under the gaff. He said Britton will realize he is going—when he is gone.

At the time of Freddie's statement, Britton was thirty-six years old. Freddie, still making a comeback in the ring of his own, was days away from his thirty-sixth birthday. Britton would keep fighting until age forty-four with seventy-four more bouts.

Chapter XIII

"I wouldn't ask too much of her," I ventured. "You can't repeat the past."

"Can't repeat the past?" he cried incredulously. "Why of course you can!"

He looked around him wildly, as if the past were lurking here in the shadow of his house, just out of reach of his hand.

"I'm going to fix everything just the way it was before," he said, nodding determinedly. "She'll see."

He talked a lot about the past and I gathered that he wanted to recover something, some idea of himself perhaps, that had gone into loving Daisy. His life had been confused and disordered since then, but if he could once return to a certain starting place and go over it all slowly, he could find out what that thing was…

—F. Scott Fitzgerald, *The Great Gatsby*

The man responsible for crafting the sports headlines of the day slipped his story on the New York telegraph in the evening hours. As the sun set on the bustling streets of New York, he wove a tale of triumph and defeat, capturing the essence of the athletic endeavor in words.

"How the Mighty Have Fallen."[1]

The tale was one of a man who had once basked in the radiant glory of the boxing world, a man who had held the coveted title of world's lightweight champion. It recounted how the emergence of an inexperienced fighter, rising from the shadows, had dealt the crushing blows that shattered his reign of dominance and sent him spiraling into a pit of despair.

It was the tale of a man who, like so many before him, had reached the point of no return, where the weight of his mistakes had finally caught up to him. The man in question was none other than Freddie, who had met his downfall. The assailant, a man known only by the moniker of Archie Walker, had dealt the fateful blow.

On April fifteenth, 1922, Freddie's comeback in the ring came to a bitter end. The once-great boxer, who had risen to fame, was defeated by the young upstart Archie Walker. Though Walker's record was meager, with only three wins and one loss to his name, he proved to be a formidable opponent for Freddie. The ten-round match ended in a decision, and it was clear to all who watched that Freddie's comeback had been a failure. With a career record of seventy-four wins, five losses, and seven draws, Freddie was forced to retire for a second time, his dreams of reclaiming his former glory forever dashed.

The mighty had indeed fallen when an unknown contender could emerge to vanquish a man of Freddie's once great caliber. It was a stunning achievement of this young Walker, who had made the combat so decisively one-sided. The judges and referee had no choice but to award him the decision. While Freddie was fortunate enough to weather out the ten scheduled rounds, his glory days were now nothing more than a distant memory.

They once hailed him as "great," but now his last

fight was nothing more than a lamentable memory. A "has been," they said, and that he should throw away his gloves forever and return to his Jersey farm, leaving the brutal business of boxing behind. They hoped he would find contentment in the glory that still reflected from his past. One can never truly judge how long a fighter should remain in the game, save by the results they produce. Some seem to possess an age limit, while others do not. But with Freddie, the statistics spoke for themselves—ample proof that he had had more than enough of the ring. Seventeen years in the business, several more than nature allows for the average fighting man.

As the embers of passion and energy flickered and died, it was time for hm to retire from the ring. It was the natural order of things for the old to step aside and allow the young to take the reins. But even as he hung up his gloves, the feverish thrill of battle still coursed through his veins. The fight, it seems, is never truly over.

Not many newspapers had a kind word for Freddie's comeback disaster. With the title "They're All the Same!"[2] one newspaper that was emblematic of many others and particularly harsh wrote:

"Freddie Welsh, former lightweight champion of the world, doesn't seem to have any more sense than the rest of the old time once was champions. We note that he took a ten-round licking the other day at the hands of an amateur. These old shells never know when they are through. A special section in an old lady's home ought to be set apart for them."[3]

By September 1922, the golden glimmer of Freddie's

wealth had also continued to fade. The gleaming automobiles that once lined the driveway of his Long Hill Health Farm were slowly disappearing, and the lavish parties that had once played host to senators, congressmen, famous scientists, sports figures, and other celebrities, too, had become but a distant memory. As the leaves began to turn and the days grew shorter, Freddie found himself turning to the pages of the *New York Times*, placing desperate ads in hopes of finding a way to save his faltering finances.

"SUMMIT—$10,000 cash buys magnificent 150-acre hilltop estate (hour Manhattan); modern mansion, farm, swimming pool, gymnasium; other features; liberal mortgage; sacrifice; quick action. Telephone morning, Freddie Welsh, Columbus 2905."[4]

The grand property purchased and meticulously restored by his own hand now sat before him, ready to be relinquished at a fraction of the cost it had incurred upon him.

Chapter XIV

Never confuse a single defeat with a final defeat.

—F. Scott Fitzgerald

Why shouldn't I go crazy? My father is a moron and my mother is a neurotic, half insane with pathological nervous worry. Between them they haven't and never have had the brains of Calvin Coolidge.[1]

—F. Scott Fitzgerald, letter to Maxwell Perkins.

Amidst the rolling hills and verdant pastures of the Freddie Welsh Health Farm, a dream lay shattered. Freddie had poured his heart, his soul, and his life savings into this venture, only to see it crumble before his eyes. Despite the promise of wealth and success that seemed to linger just beyond his grasp, the health farm remained unsold, its value unchanging in the eyes of potential buyers.

Freddie ignored the changes that were sweeping through the world of boxing. He had seen the massive financial windfall that came from the legendary match between Georges Carpentier and Jack Dempsey, both of whom had sought the rolling hills of the Long Hill Health Farm as their training ground. As more and more boxers flocked to these fertile fields to prepare for their battles, Freddie refused to abandon his vision. He continued to promote the health benefits of his establishment to the wealthy business elite, never losing sight of the potential that lay just within his reach but refusing to see the obvious that it was the boxers who sought out his establishment.

In addition to the financial burden of the health farm, Freddie was also burdened by a lease of his Bayside, New York home.[2] So, on January 30, 1923, a golf and country club was poised to sign a lease with Freddie for the Long Hill Health Farm property, its rolling hills a perfect fit for their golf course.

As January gave way to February's frigid embrace, Freddie found himself drawn to a voyage back to the shores of Great Britain. His yearning for home had been awakened, and he resolved to embark on this journey. Accompanying him on this transatlantic odyssey were his brother, Stanley, his ever-loyal friend and boxing promoter Humbert Fugazy, and Jack Sharkey, a bantamweight of renown. Their vessel of passage, the S. S. *Baltic*, carried them across the Atlantic, and on the twenty-sixth of February in the year 1923, they set foot upon the grounds of Liverpool.

Once, in his heyday, Freddie would have been met by throngs of adoring admirers upon his ship's disembarkation, a symphony of applause and fanfare. This time, a chilling absence greeted him—a void where the echoes of his past glory should have resounded. A local newspaper, in its stark prose, proclaimed that America could no longer provide him with a living, leaving him to confront the stark reality of his diminished stature.

In the midst of his stay in Great Britain, Freddie found himself captivated by the prospect of arranging pugilistic exhibition encounters, but such ambitions were met with little success. The once fervent promoters, his own countrymen, seemed to have forsaken their interest in his pugnacious pursuits. Freddie seemed to still yearn for the cheers and adulation that had once been his throughout the arena. He stayed in the British Isles for a span of two months, his days largely consumed in the enchanting embrace of Wales, where he embarked on familial reunions that offered solace to his wearied soul. He then departed on the S.S. *Majestic*, steering his course back toward the vast expanse of America, a realm brimming with both hope and uncertainty.

Freddie and Humbert Fugazy returning to
America in March 1923 aboard the S.S. *Majestic*.

When Freddie returned to America in late March of 1923, and the golf and country club deal from January thirtieth remained undone, whispers swirled about the impending actions of the legendary golfer Walter Hagen. It was reported that the ace golfer, fresh from his world tour with the talented Joe Kirkwood, was said to be putting his wealth to practical use. The two had performed with such artistry on golf courses all around the world, captivating audiences with their trick shots and dazzling displays, which were then featured in news reels for all to see. And now, it was whispered, the British Open champion had set his sights on acquiring Freddie's health farm with the intention of crafting a golfer's paradise, a place where one could bask in the beauty of the sport and revel in its luxurious lifestyle.[3]

In the vibrant era of the Roaring Twenties, Hagen was a shining star among the constellation of sports legends: Babe Ruth, Ty Cobb, Walter Johnson, the gridiron giant Red Grange, pugilists Jack Dempsey and Gene Tunney, and the incomparable golfer Bobby Jones. With his larger-than-life presence and irrepressible spirit, he was more akin to Babe Ruth in personality than any other sports hero of the day. It is said that he paved the way as the first professional athlete to earn a million dollars in his golfing career, cementing his place in the annals of sports history.[4]

Walter Hagen, a legendary figure in the realm of American golf, cast a grand shadow in the first half of the Twentieth Century with his formidable prowess on the green. His mastery on the course was unmatched, securing him a place among the greats with his impressive tally of eleven professional majors, trailing only the legendary Jack

Nicklaus and the prodigious Tiger Woods. Dubbed the "father of professional golf," Hagen brought a level of prestige, publicity, and wealth to the sport with his booming presence, lucrative endorsements, and grandiose prize money. He remains, to this day, a paragon of golfing greatness, revered as one of the greatest golfers to have ever played the game.[5]

The rolling hills and verdant fields of the farm, it was written, were the epitome of the ideal golfing terrain, reminiscent of the rolling hills and serene countryside of England. The grand and stately mansion at the heart of the estate would make the perfect clubhouse with ample space to accommodate the construction of an eighteen-hole course. Hagen, the visionary behind this project, envisioned a blending of his passion for golf with Freddie's innovative health farm concept, offering the weary businessman the chance to recharge both body and spirit through the practice of this honored and timeless sport.

The transaction for the creation of a world-renowned golf course was but a fleeting illusion that collapsed. The harsh reality of the health farm's past all but guaranteed the inevitable failure of yet another scheme. And so, it was with the would-be entrepreneur, Walter Hagen, that aspirations dissipated into nothingness. Just another venture lost in the web of the health farm's financial instability.

Despite the storm clouds of financial ruin looming overhead, Freddie remained steadfast in his commitment to acts of kindness and charity. In June of 1923, he took on the mantle of referee at an exhibition boxing match held at the grand Bernards Inn in the picturesque town of Bernardsville, New Jersey. The night was a spectacular affair, with five hundred patrons gathered under the auspices of the Intercounty Baseball League to witness the six-bout card. The funds raised from the event were earmarked for the cause of the hiring of official umpires for the upcoming baseball season. Amidst the chaos of the boxing ring, Robert Waite and Jarvis Badgley, two musical talents from Freddie's neighboring town of New Providence, lent their voices to the occasion with songs and piano solos, making the evening one to remember.

In the summer of 1923, Freddie confided in Willie Ratner, a reporter for the *Newark Evening News* and a close acquaintance, that he planned to rejoin the army and would receive a commission as captain. He needed a trusted friend to manage his health farm in his absence, and so he turned to Madame Hranoush Sidky Bey, a friend with a reliable hand. Two cherished photographs, given by Freddie to Madame Bey, proved the strength of their friendship. One showed Freddie with his wife, son, and daughter, inscribed with, "To Hranoush, With every beautiful wish from the Welsh family." The other depicted Freddie in his boxing gear, inscribed with, "To Mrs. S. Bey, With every good wish, Sincerely, Freddie Welsh."

Freddie approached Madame Bey with a proposition to oversee the day-to-day operations of the health farm. The following morning, Ratner received an invite from Madame Bey, who also was a friend. She requested his presence as she had something of utmost importance to impart. Upon arrival at her home, Madame Bey revealed that Freddie had extended an invitation to her to take charge of the health farm, with the added liberty to board boxers. The offer was a generous one, as Freddie had expressed no expectations from her, and she would be in charge until his return from military service.

Madame Bey was a woman of elegant refinement and grace. She graced the capital city of Washington, DC, with her presence during her husband's tenure as a Turkish diplomat. Fluent in seven languages, including English, Armenian, French, German, Greek, Italian, and Spanish, she was a woman of remarkable intellect and culture. She was fortunate enough to have the President and First Lady count her as a dear friend. Tragically, she bore witness to the assassination of President William McKinley, standing only a few feet away when the fatal bullet struck, forever marking her memory.

After departing the diplomatic scene, her successful rug business with her husband, however, fell victim to a poor business decision, leaving her with nothing but memories. Little did she know, when Freddie approached her, that she would soon be drawn into the world of boxing, a realm of which she had previously known nothing.

Madame Bey, burdened by her own financial difficulties, made her way to Freddie's health farm, eager to accept his proposition—she lived only one mile down the road. With Willie Ratner at her side, offering counsel and reassurance, she agreed to Freddie's terms, provided he would grant her the ability to host boxers, which Ratner had advised her to do. It was a moment of uncertainty; Madame Bey comprehended nothing of the sport of boxing but agreed and stepped into a world unfamiliar to her.

"Give it to me, and I'll make it go," Madame Bey told Freddie.

Freddie's own lack of success in making the establishment flourish was a source of disappointment, as he had so confidently believed grandeur would occur. With skepticism, Freddie declared that she would never succeed.

"He told me I couldn't make a go of it but gave me the keys," Madame Bey said, "and I took over bag and baggage."[6]

On the next day, Madame Bey and her spouse, Sidky Bey, traversed a journey of a mile, leaving behind their unpretentious home for the grandeur of Freddie's mansion atop the hill. They extended an invitation to their dear friend and business associate, Ehsan Karadag, to join them in their adventure.

After he handed over the operations of his health farm, Freddie found himself shrouded in a new uniform, donned with the title of Captain Thomas in the United States Reserve Corps. The announcement was made through the army headquarters on the last day of July. He set off for Camp Devens in Massachusetts, where, as a member of the athletic staff, he was tasked with molding the bodies and minds of roughly two thousand young New Englanders in the Citizens' Military Training Camp. It was a grand undertaking, and Freddie basked in the golden glow of this newfound responsibility.

President Calvin Coolidge's son, John, was a private at Camp Devens, where Freddie kept him occupied with varied activities at the Citizens' Military Training Camp. The newspapers depicted Freddie teaching the young Coolidge some of the finer points of the boxing game, for which he became learned of the techniques of the boxing.[7]

President Calvin Coolidge's son, John, and Freddie.

As Freddie passed his days at Camp Devens, Madame Bey was creating a destination that lured the world's fiercest boxers. With an open heart and a warm kitchen, she welcomed each fighter, beginning with world middleweight champion Johnny Wilson. By autumn's arrival, the Long Hill Health Farm was teeming with eleven of the sport's finest, including Joe Lynch, hailing from the streets of New York City as bantamweight champion, and other notables such as Paul Berlenbach, Carl Duane, Bud Gorman, Sid Terris, Pancho Villa, Charley White, and the notorious Battling Siki.

Amidst the throngs of pugilists that arrived at Freddie's health farm under the auspices of Madame Bey, Siki was one who shone with a particularly radiant aura—not for his prowess in the ring, but for the distinctive flair that surrounded his being. The "Singular Senegalese," as they called him being from Senegal, Siki was a figure of controversy in the boxing establishment, who drew the eyes of the world with his flamboyant lifestyle. His notoriety was such that he was numbered amongst the four or five most celebrated black men of the era,[8] and his arrival in the City of Lights was an event that could halt the pulse of Paris for a full hour.[9]

"He was a wild guy," journalist Willie Ratner recalled, "not a bad guy but wild. Used to walk around with wild animals, a lion, or tiger on a leash."[10]

In the golden light of Parisian fame, the flamboyant Battling Siki emerged as a true champion. With a swift and stunning blow, he toppled the beloved French hero Georges Carpentier, claiming the coveted world light heavyweight title. This historic moment marked the first time a Muslim and African had claimed a world boxing championship, elevating Siki to a status of legend in the sporting world. The glory of his victory resounded throughout the city, to the dismay of many, but a testament to his raw talent and indomitable spirit.

Journalist Willie Ratner remembered with vivid

clarity the moment when Freddie received word that Battling Siki had taken up residence at his health farm. Fury raged within Freddie, his wrath boiling over.

Freddie made his feelings known. Johnny Wilson and his boxing companions, including Battling Siki, were gathered at the Long Hill Health Farm. As they were relaxing, the shrill sound of the telephone pierced the tranquil atmosphere. Freddie was on the other end, his voice charged with fervor as he spoke with Madame Bey. His words were filled with the fire of his anger, a testament to the depth of his convictions.

"Get that Siki out of my place immediately," Freddie told her, "or you've got to go. I won't have that fellow there. He'll ruin my reputation."[11]

There were whispers among the masses that Freddie was envious of the success of the business, a feat he had been unable to attain. Madame Bey was consumed by uncertainty as to how to handle the situation. Johnny Wilson was the first to offer his thoughts. The others soon followed suit, each offering their own words of encouragement. The message was clear: Siki was not an embarrassment. He was a fighter to be respected, a champion in his own right.

"If you put Siki out, I will go,"[12] Wilson told her.

Bey was unperturbed by Siki, affirming that he conducted himself with the utmost decorum whenever in her company. Her fighters, all eleven of them, were in full agreement, providing her with a steadfast alliance.

"Where you go, we'll go,"[13] the boxers told her.

And so, she embarked upon her new venture. The crisp autumn air of the Northeast rustled the leaves as she led her family of boxers down the road to her secluded home. With Madame Bey's departure, Freddie had his health farm back, but a new chapter in her story began.

Madame Bey had stumbled upon the elusive solution that had eluded Freddie all this time. It was not the grandiose idea of a wellness retreat that would bring him closer to his aspirations but rather the craft that he had been trained in—boxing. Freddie remained blind to the glimmer of hope that lay before him, oblivious to the signs that pointed to his inevitable triumph. The past and present had conspired to reveal the way to him, but Freddie remained obstinate, unable to grasp the obvious path to his own dream.

Madame Bey's boxing camp was destined for greatness, a shining inspiration of the sweet science that would bask in the glory of legendary status. A glory that would attract the finest pugilists of the day. No less than fourteen titans of the ring, who had claimed the crown of heavyweight champion, and a veritable horde of legends, with a total of eighty enshrined in the International Boxing Hall of Fame would grace her camp. The camp would last from 1923 to 1969.[14]

Chapter XV

Then came the war, old sport. It was a great relief, and I tried very hard to die, but I seemed to bear an enchanted life.

—F. Scott Fitzgerald, *The Great Gatsby*

Life starts all over again when it gets crisp in the fall.

—F. Scott Fitzgerald, The Great Gatsby

With Madame Bey gone, Freddie, still in the army but on leave, returned to his Long Hill Health Farm in December 1923. Still in financial straits, things were looking up. All in that month, despite his continued financial struggles, a glimmer of hope could be seen on the horizon. With the arrival of navy wrestlers and boxers, determined to secure their place in the navy championships, a vice admiral of the United States Navy, army dignitaries, a budding young boxer with limitless potential, a champion bicyclist, and the steadfast presence of his friend and heavyweight champion Jack Dempsey, there seemed to be a sense of renewal in the face of adversity.

Perhaps Freddie had glimpsed the route toward the perpetuation of his aspiration, all thanks to the triumph of Madame Bey. Only time could bear witness to whether he had truly seized the glaringly apparent opportunity presented before him.

The throngs of visitors who streamed onto Freddie's health farm were reminiscent of the early bygone days.

Many visitors hoping to participate in the gatherings of the famous flocked to the grounds, leaving Freddie in a quandary—no longer was the question of attendance a concern, but rather how to accommodate the sheer numbers that arrived. The great many guests proved to be overwhelming, forcing Freddie to turn many away, leaving him with no choice but to hang a sign declaring that the health farm could hold no more.

Upon Dempsey's arrival in the chill of December 1923, his fists had been idle, and his calendar was devoid of any matches. Instead, he had come seeking solace and leisure in the form of light training while his trusted manager, Jack Kearns, and his shrewd promoter, Tex Rickard, plotted the course of his future in the boxing ring.

Dempsey, still the heavyweight champion of the world, had shone brightly in the ring since the last time he had graced Freddie's health farm with his presence when he prepared for the Carpentier bout, after which he had laid dormant for two years. In two successful title defenses, he had conquered his opponents, displaying his toughness in the ring.

He made those two triumphant title defenses after the long layoff. First, he had defeated Tommy Gibbons by a decision in Shelby, Montana, and then he fought Luis Firpo of Argentina in a slugfest. The Firpo match took place at the Polo Grounds, New York that captivated over 80,000 fans and garnered a gate of a staggering $1,250,000, second only to boxing's first million-dollar gate. Firpo was sent down to the canvas seven times in the first round, but to everyone's amazement, he caught Dempsey with a surprise right, sending him flying through the ropes. Dempsey, dazed but not defeated, clambered back into the ring at the count of nine, determined to survive the round.

As the bell rang for the second round, Dempsey stood tall with his opponent before him. With determination, he unleashed a barrage of blows upon the challenger, sending Firpo tumbling to the ground time and time again. Firpo would not yield easily, rising each time. But soon, it became clear that this would be the final round. He sent Firpo crashing to the floor for the eleventh and final time, unable to rise from the canvas. It was a moment of triumph, a testament to the might and skill of this great champion. It would be remembered as one of the most intense and unforgettable heavyweight battles in the annals of boxing history.

Like agile cat or puma, Jack Dempsey, the Manassas mauler, shinned up a tree at Freddie Welsh's health farm at Summit, New Jersey, and turned good fellow to birds by presenting them with a Christmas feed?

Jack Dempsey at Freddie's health farm in December 1923.

While Dempsey stayed at the Long Hill Health Farm, the air was thick with the sound of gloves hitting leather and the grunts of men grappling in the ring. Sixteen pugilists from the United States Navy had gathered there, along with ten wrestlers, all with eyes fixed upon the prize of the navy titles to be fought for at Madison Square Garden on December eighteenth. The navy candidates training at the farm were from the Brooklyn Navy Yard and Philadelphia. The road to the finals had been a grueling one, with elimination bouts to determine which of the sailors would represent their assigned ships. Freddie, with his practiced eye and experienced hand, oversaw the training of the eight boxing classes, from the small flyweights to the towering heavyweights.

"It is a pleasure to work with these boys after mingling with the professional boxers," Freddie said. "They take such a keen interest in their preparations."[1]

Dempsey gazed with admiration upon the nautical men as they honed their skills, wishing for but a moment to cast aside his attire and join them in their athletic pursuits. A tinge of regret washed over him as he realized his pressing schedule left no room for such an escapade.

Freddie had the privilege of entertaining Vice Admiral Newton A. McCully of the United States Navy, a man of great distinction and valor, who came to watch his navy men. A veteran of two of the greatest conflicts in American history, the Spanish–American War and World War I, the Vice Admiral had been honored with the coveted Navy Distinguished Service Medal, a testament to his bravery and unwavering devotion to duty. The presence of such a remarkable figure added a touch of grandeur to the gathering.

The gathering of young navy men at the farm was each with aspirations of glory and distinction. Though rivalries simmered just beneath the surface, the candidates trained together with a singular focus, undeterred by distinctions of class or race. Freddie, with a keen eye for order and discipline, presided over their daily routine, sculpting each man into a tool of strength and skill.

Freddie was a strict taskmaster who would rouse his charges from slumber promptly at the crack of dawn.

Without delay, be it drenched in the rain or basked in sunshine, they embarked upon their morning jog, arriving back at the mansion for a much-needed rubdown by 8:30. By the time the clock struck ten, they had satiated their hunger with a hearty breakfast.

After breakfast, Freddie took the outfit out for a hike, which ended up being a journey of exploration, traversing the rolling hills for an hour from eleven to twelve. As the sun reached its zenith, they paused for respite, basking in the serenity of nature until two. Then, with renewed vigor, the two divisions undertook their afternoon exercises, the Philadelphia boys sweating and straining from two to three while the Brooklyn candidates strained and perspired from three to four. As the day waned, the men sat down to a sumptuous feast at the stroke of five before retiring to their beds at ten, exhausted from the day's labors.

In the aftermath of the departure of the naval pugilists and grapplers, the health farm saw the arrival of Young Stribling, also known as the Georgia Flash, who rose as the shining star of Georgia. He was endearingly referred to as W.L. by his doting parents, the moniker a nod to his initials.

William Lawrence Stribling had recently entered his nineteenth year of existence, one day prior to his arrival at Freddie's sprawling health farm that December. With his charming brown tresses, piercing blue-eyed gaze, and chiseled features, this youthful boxer was a prodigy in the art of fisticuffs, a talent honed by his parents, who served as his coach and manager. His future, charted by his mother in particular, was to be one of greatness within the boxing ring.

His quick reflexes and sharp mind made him the perfect performer, and not an ounce of extra flesh marred his chiseled form and muscles that rippled beneath his skin, which were perfectly suited for the art of combat. He was a vision of physical grace and agility, moving with a fluidity that spoke to his lineage. From a family of performers, they performed under the name of "The Four Novelty Grahams," a troupe consisting of father, mother, and two sons, one being W.L. They were renowned for their death-defying feats in the circus ring. As their careers progressed, they took to the vaudeville stage, thrilling audiences with their awe-inspiring acts.

He entered Freddie's establishment with a determined gait, ready to face Dave Rosenberg in a New Year's Day showdown. Despite his tender years, Stribling was a seasoned pugilist, having stepped into the ring for his first professional bout at the age of sixteen. With sixty-seven victories, three defeats, and thirteen draws under his belt before arriving at Freddie's, he had already accomplished more than most boxers could hope for in a lifetime. Little did he know, his long and illustrious career had only just begun, a career that would see him rack up a staggering 291 bouts with 223 wins, thirteen losses, and fourteen draws, with thirty-nine additional battles fought in newspaper fights. He fought with a ferocity unmatched, facing fifty-five opponents in a single year and knocking out a record-breaking 129 opponents in his career, a feat only surpassed by Archie Moore.

Young Stribling was filled with a sense of eager longing to train with his hero, the great Jack Dempsey. But his hopes were dashed when Freddie had to inform Stribling that Dempsey was not there at the time. Freddie broke the news to him that Dempsey was away in the city for the holiday. Despite the absence of his idol, he stepped into the ring with Freddie, determined to prove his worth.

After two rounds of sparring, it was evident that Stribling was a formidable opponent with a lightning-fast left hand and agile footwork that allowed him to sidestep and duck punches with ease. Even in close quarters, he was a master of defense, his gloves guarding him from any incoming blows.

Mrs. Stribling, Young Stribling's mother, was thirty-five years old and looked more like Stribling's sister, not his mother. She was enamored by the picturesque landscape of the rolling Jersey hills. The stone walls and charming farmhouses, reminiscent of a quaint English countryside, elicited a sense of longing within her. As she gazed upon the vast fields, she couldn't help but envision the limitless opportunities for sporting adventures, be it gliding on ice skates, teeing off on the greens, serving aces on the court, trekking across the countryside on foot, or galloping through the hills on horseback.

She was captivated by the rough-around-the-edges charm of Freddie's place. Freddie and his boxing companions would soon be savoring the flavors of her southern home cooking, and she hoped that it would bring a taste of comfort to their rugged lives.

Freddie, ever the showman, presented the Striblings with a wheelbarrow for a publicity photograph. The image captured showed Young Stribling straining under the weight of his parents, Ma and Pa Stribling, as they were whimsically dubbed by the press. The scene was a testament to the bond of a family, captured in a moment.

As Freddie stated, Dempsey made his way back to the countryside of Jersey prior to Stribling's match. He boarded the train from the bustling city when a young woman caught sight of him. After some time, she finally mustered up the bravery to approach the great heavyweight champion. To her delight, he proved to be an amiable conversationalist, eagerly engaging in a prolonged discourse with her. Despite his standing as the revered idol of the boxing world, Dempsey was always gracious in his dealings with everyday people, imparting a warmth and charm that endeared him to many.

As Dempsey returned to the health farm, he mingled with both the prominent and obscure alike. One such notable to grace Freddie's sprawling estate was Alf Goulett, a bicycle champion of world renown in an era when the sport held the collective gaze of the public. Dempsey and Goulett had been dear friends for many a year since their days residing in the city of Salt Lake.

On one occasion, as the day waned at Freddie's health farm, the three champions had gathered—Dempsey, Freddie, and Goulett. As they amused each other with tales of their conquests, suddenly, Dempsey shocked his audience by revealing a hidden aspect of his past. He confessed that he, too, had once dreamed of being a racing cyclist, but thankfully, he had seen the light before it was too late.

As Dempsey made ready to depart from Freddie's sprawling estate, he took a moment to indulge the eager young fighter, Stribling. The champion was struck by the boy's eagerness and with a nod of approval, granted him the chance to spar. The youthful Stribling proved himself a formidable opponent, impressing even the great Dempsey with his raw talent and skills. It was clear that the boy did not disappoint the reigning heavyweight champion, leaving an indelible impression upon Dempsey's rugged exterior.

The reporters had flocked to Freddie's, eager to catch a glimpse of the rising star in the boxing world. Among them were W. C. Vreeland and Mike Callaghan, two seasoned journalists from the *Brooklyn Daily Eagle*. Vreeland, when asked to comment on the young fighter's mother, deferred to his colleague Callaghan, giving the man who was capable of spinning a tale worth reading.

Mike Callaghan, with a sense of eagerness, approached Ma Stribling as he prepared to delve into the depths of Ma Stribling's beliefs. Mike Callaghan asked Ma Stribling:

"Would W. L. fight a colored boxer in order to reach the light heavyweight championship?"[2]

With the mere mention of the query, the demeanor of the pugilist's matriarch underwent a profound shift. The once radiant and youthful grin that graced her visage was replaced by a steadfast and resolute expression, aging her features with the weight of purpose. The once cheerful appearance was now taut with an unwavering determination.

"What? My boy fight a black man? NEVER! We all don't need prominence or money that bad. Do you think he ought to?"[3]

With a sense of disbelief and wonder, Mike Callaghan took pen to paper, scribing his thoughts onto his column later that day:

"The question showed a Yankee trait unexpected in a Georgian and we were momentarily embarrassed…

"The lady is so different—er—so world embracing an' everything."[4]

The conversation continued.

"Oh, no—er—y-yes," the reporters answered, somewhat inanely.

"Shucks! That doesn't make any difference. None whatever to me," said Mrs. Stribling. "We all down yonder know more than you do about some things, that's all. We folks don't hate the black people. Why, my boys love their 'black mammy,' but they are not going to fight black men. Never, no time. No, Sir!"

"Do you ever encounter an attitude in other women of distance because of your active interest in your boy's fights?" The reporters asked.

"Well, now, that's an odd one," she replied quickly. "Why, say I, there are some silly women that would scorn a mother's activity in her boy's success—in any honest endeavor. I'm glad to say I never met them. Don't jump to the conclusion that my boys are rowdies; they are show folks—performers. Both my boys are very active in school athletics and social events of our town.

"W. L., his daddy, Herbie, and I are in perfect harmony, always in our plans. W. L. will graduate this coming spring from the Lanier high school and then he will go to college."

"What does W. L. intend to prepare for?"

"He is going to be a doctor. I want him to be a champion in that, too. He knows more about his body right now than some doctors could tell him."

"Did W. L. cause you any annoyance by promiscuous scrapping when he started school?"

"Not once. You see, he was trained in boxing by his daddy. Ever since, he could talk, and he was always confident that he could take care of himself. W. L. wouldn't strike a person in anger, no how. Why, he doesn't even get downright angry in the ring."

"Wouldn't that fact be considered a drawback, inasmuch as it might mean lack of vindictiveness or aggression?"

Mrs. Stribling laughed at that.

"My goodness, that's a queer notion!" she chuckled. "I was an acrobat. Do you-all think I had to work up a grudge against the elephants before I could turn a somersault over them? As I see it, skillful boxing is an acrobatic stunt requiring cool calculation, strength, and control, instead of just an ambition to do bodily harm to the other fellow. In fact, W. L. has some of the warmest friends among the men he defeated."

"Does he like Mike McTigue?"

"Well, he doesn't dislike him. We felt bad about the wrong impression Mr. McTigue seemed to have taken away with him regarding the attitude of the crown toward him. He doesn't know Georgia. Schoolboy admirers of W. L. made most of the noise, and if Mr. McTigue had stayed long enough to see the real people down there, he would have saved himself much good nature ridicule."

"Do you attend the fights W. L. has?"

"Attend. 'em? I should say I do! I have a seat right back of his daddy. His daddy is his second, but W. L. always looks right over daddy's head at me. I always talk to him in his fights, and he pays attention to what I advise him, too."

"Wouldn't your instructions to W. L. be overheard by his opponent also?"

"Let the other fellow listen. He won't know what we are talking about because we all talk pidgin Spanish. We learned it in Cuba while we were there with a circus two summers."

"Are you competent to give W. L. directions in boxing?"

"I don't interfere with his boxing. His daddy looks after that. I encourage him. We have a lot of fun out of it. For instance, in his fight with McTigue, W. L. looked over Mac's shoulder and said: 'Mom, do you remember that funny stunt I pulled on pa when we were boxing in the gym? I did it just like this!' And he gave McTigue a right smart uppercut that made that Irishman see stars."

"What would you do if W. L. should be knocked out?"

"I'd just sit right where I was until he was counted out, but you bet I'd go to him then."

"Are you sure you could remain cool while he was lying unconscious on the floor?"

"I don't say I'd be indifferent to such a situation, but I hope I have enough sense to realize the possibilities in this business. I told you already that we are acrobats. Perhaps you don't know that falls and tumbles in our profession carry a

K. O. worse than boxing. Both my boys have been knocked out by falls more than once when they were learning the show business. You must not think I lack motherly solicitude. Nothing like that. Necessity made me practical, that's all."

"Would a knockout discourage W. L. in his ambition to be champion?"

"Not at all. Didn't Jack Dempsey get knocked out while he was trying? It did him good, and W. L. would learn by it, too, if he was unlucky enough to get it."

"I suppose you know that Dave Rosenberg is very tough in the ring?"

"I'm surely glad he's tough 'cause in the ring with W. L. is sure no place for a tender fellow. I think it best now to let my boy's work speak for itself. It isn't long now until New Year's afternoon. While New York fans are feeling sorry for W. L., you all put down a little wager on him, and you all will have what I wishes you—a happy New Year."[5]

On the first of January 1924, in a dazzling display of athleticism and perseverance, Stribling emerged victorious against Rosenberg in their light heavyweight showdown held at the First Regiment Armory in Newark, New Jersey. Despite being cast as the underdog, Stribling proved himself a formidable opponent, clinching the twelve-round decision with near-unanimous wins in every round. This triumphant start to the year was only the beginning, as Stribling fought six more times in January alone, with only one setback, a disqualification in which he was leading until repetitive cautions for hitting on the break resulted in his removal from the ring. The aftermath of this loss was marked by a disturbance, as Stribling's father took offense and struck the referee. Nevertheless, throughout the rest of the year, Stribling continued to demonstrate his ability, fighting thirty-six times with only three losses.

As the month drifted by, Freddie had once again basked in the warm glow of success. Even as his finances and health farm remained shrouded in the shadows of uncertainty, he still possessed the allure to draw in the glittering elite. Yet as the sun set on this prosperous month, he found himself with an uncertain future, questioning if this was the pinnacle of his success or if greater glories lay ahead.

It was a moment of both triumph and misfortune, a bittersweet period. For it was the manifestation of his long-held aspiration, yet at the same time, a harbinger of his impending lamentation. A paradox of sorts, it both uplifted and crushed his spirit, a cruel reminder of the fragility of happiness. But still, he seemed to cherish it, for it was the culmination of his toil and the proof of his perseverance. Only time would tell what fate had in store for him and his treasured health farm.

And so with the sunshine and the great bursts of leaves growing on the trees—just as things grow in fast movies—I had that familiar conviction that life was beginning over again with the summer.

—F. Scott Fitzgerald, *The Great Gatsby*

As the summer began for Freddie in 1924, he was back with the army at his post in Plattsburgh, New York. He assumed a position as the physical training instructor at the Citizen's Military Training Camp, tasked as a boxing coach by Major General Bullard to mold the young soldiers into fierce fighters.[1]

With Freddie came Frankie Monroe, his protégé, a featherweight from the golden coast of California. Frankie had already made a name for himself, winning a succession of four-round bouts on the West Coast, and Freddie saw in him potential. Freddie employed the services of Frankie Monroe as his right-hand man, and his chief assistant. Frankie himself was swept away by the thrill of battle, scheduled to compete in a series of matches along the Eastern seaboard during the hazy days of summer and the crisp chill of autumn.

As a reserve officer still on active duty, Freddie oversaw the weight classes of young men at the Citizen's Military Training Camp in Plattsburgh. Each day, he presided over the boxing lessons held in the pine grove south of the historic army post, guiding the aspiring fighters through their paces. As the weeks wore on, the competitors would face off in a series of bouts, with each company conducting elimination rounds until only the strongest remained. In the final week of camp, the champions of each company would clash, vying for the coveted title of Plattsburgh Champion.

Each bout was to unfold in three rounds of two minutes each, with the potential for an additional decisive round should the judges be in disagreement. The arena would be governed by the stringent regulations of New York State Boxing, with a solitary referee keeping watch, a timekeeper resolutely ticking away the moments, and a duo of impartial judges to score the exchange of blows. The glory of the champion would be bestowed upon the victor in each weight class, along with a prize.

As Freddie dwelled in the town of Plattsburgh, his health farm remained home to some powerful boxers. Yet, he paid them no heed, leaving them to their own devices. In July, former junior lightweight champion Jack "Kid Murphy" Bernstein took refuge at Freddie's health farm to ready himself for the impending match against Jack Zivic on the twenty-third. The victorious winner was to face the world lightweight champion, Benny Leonard, in a championship bout.   Bernstein emerged victorious, winning the twelve-round decision.

As July came to an end, Freddie was consumed with a fervent desire to be rid of the health farm. He saw a glimmer of hope in the form of the National Sports Alliance and their interest in using the farm as a training ground for their pugilistic proteges and as a refuge for disabled and veteran fighters. Freddie approached the New York State Athletic Commission with a proposition for the sale, hoping to secure their agreement with the use of their funds garnered from a charity boxing match. The commission's response was one of rejection, as they declared the funds were to be deposited in a trust for the betterment of disabled boxers.

In the heat of August, Mickey Walker, who would hold titles in the welterweight and middleweight divisions, arrived at Freddie's farm. The bout that was destined for Jack Bernstein against the legendary Benny Leonard was now Mickey's to claim, a chance to prove himself against the reigning king of the lightweight division, the conqueror of Freddie himself. As the hours ticked by, the expected confrontation never came to fruition.

On the day of August twenty-third, Freddie, cruising in his automobile, chanced upon a catastrophic sight. A fire had erupted, and Freddie, a solitary figure, braved the blazing inferno that engulfed a two-story structure in New Providence. The building was consumed by its raging inferno. Without a moment's hesitation, he charged toward the door and broke it open with all his might. The scene inside was disastrous; a sea of flames and smoke consumed the room. Through the smoke and the flames, he emerged triumphant, bearing with him a trove of valuable furnishings and treasured paintings, rescued from the grasp of the raging fire. All the while, Harry Sadolf, and his family were absent, basking in the tranquil peace of the seashore, blissfully unaware of the heroism being enacted in their home.[2]

Freddie then raced to the nearest box and turned in the alarm. The New Providence fire department turned out but could only watch. The building burned to the ground, the nearest fire hydrant being a half mile away. For his effort, Freddie received severe burns and was badly cut on his face and arms by glass[3] while trying to extinguish the fire which destroyed the residence.

In the golden hues of September 1924, the plight of Freddie cast a shadow over the Long Hill Health Farm. The callous grasp of the Southern Trust and Commerce Bank, a San Diego corporation, threatened to claim his beloved lands as repayment for his mortgage's nonpayment. The sheriff listed six tracts of Freddie's prized Chatham Township properties for auction. Adjournments, a merciful reprieve, had come and gone since July until finally, Freddie procured the sum of $5,000 to save his health farm from ruin. The debt still loomed large, a formidable figure of $20,257.18[4] haunting his dreams.

Chapter XVII

The 'death car' as the newspapers called it, didn't stop; it came out of the gathering darkness, wavered tragically for a moment, and then disappeared around the next bend. Michaelis wasn't even sure of its color—he told the first policeman that it was light green. The other car, the one going toward New York, came to rest a hundred yards beyond, and its driver hurried back to where Myrtle Wilson, her life violently extinguished, knelt in the road and mingled her thick, dark blood with the dust.

Michaelis and this man reached her first but when they had torn open her shirtwaist still damp with perspiration, they saw that her left breast was swinging loose like a flap and there was no need to listen for the heart beneath. The mouth was wide open and ripped at the corners as though she had choked a little in giving up the tremendous vitality she had stored so long.

—F. Scott Fitzgerald, The Great Gatsby

I had an old press cutting in my file that was gnawing away at me for a while…a court case relating to a motoring accident that Welsh was involved in….but what stuck in my mind was the name of the plaintiff—Myrtle Wilson…Then of course it struck me where I'd heard the name Myrtle Wilson before—the woman killed in the motoring accident in the novel.[1]

—Andrew Gallimore

Amidst the bustling social scene of the Roaring Twenties, Freddie had amassed a multitude of friends, yet, despite their fame, they were of little assistance in supporting his Long Hill Health Farm. The American novelist F. Scott Fitzgerald—the living, breathing embodiment of the glamour and excitement of the Jazz Age, a phrase attributed to him—in 1923, stepped through the gates of the health farm shortly before he headed off to Europe to complete an idea he had for a novel—*The Great Gatsby*. His visit was chronicled by Alun Richards, Freddie's cousin. Born after Freddie's death, Richards was a novelist from Wales. In 1986, Richards would recount the moment he was told as a fleeting but illuminating glimpse into Fitzgerald's visit when he wrote in his memoir *Days of Absence*:

"Freddie Welsh, whose real name was Frederick Hall Thomas…emigrated to America, was commissioned in the US Army, later opened a gymnasium in New Jersey where F. Scott Fitzgerald was proud to have boxed three rounds with him."[2]

Fitzgerald found himself in the company of kindred writers captivated by the brutal ballet of fisticuffs. The literary minds, it appeared, had a penchant for pugilism's dance. A roll call of these wordsmiths reads like a gathering of the literati: Joyce Carol Oates, she of the eloquent prose; Jonathan Swift, the satirist with an ironic jab; Alexander Pope, whose couplets struck like quick jabs; and even the noble Lord Byron, a poet with the heart of a brawler. The roster continues an unending scroll of names, including Ezra Pound, the Hemingway titan, and the pugnacious Norman Mailer. The craft of crafting words, it seems, drew these souls to the ring. For in the pugilist's ritual, many writers beheld a mirror to their toil. A book akin to the fighter's bout proved a semblance of their struggle. What one sees in the ring, that climactic clash of leather and willpower reflects life.

Well before the emergence of George Plimpton and his ilk, those champions of Participatory Journalism in the 1960s, there were those who sought out sports figures to mix with. Willie Ratner, that journalist who led Madame Bey onto the path of boxing, danced his own waltz with Freddie within those roped confines. A journalism devotee enmeshed with action, Ratner scripted his conviction in flesh and blood. Freddie, embodying the essence of the prize ring, unfurled a blow, a tempest of force that etched an indelible tale above Ratner's left eye. A scar, not just of flesh but of epiphanies, a daily parable narrating the sagas of a professional pugilist's potency. Ratner, now baptized in the baptism of the ring, held the intimate cognizance of a fighter's unbridled might.

Around that juncture in 1923, Ratner's fellow journalist, Paul Gallico, a youthful scribe for the *New York Daily News*, who would go on to write many non-fiction books and novels, including *The Poseidon Adventure*, ventured to engage in fisticuffs with the colossal pugilistic sovereign, Jack Dempsey, for he believed he needed experience to write justly about boxing. Swiftly and succinctly, Dempsey ushered him down to the canvas, where young Gallico found himself draped in the velvet shroud of unconsciousness. Gallico wrote that the knockout was like an "awful explosion within the confines of my skull, followed by a bright light, a tearing sensation and then darkness."[3]

Like Fitzgerald, Ernest Hemingway brilliantly used his own experiences and experiences of others, to create his pages. Many writers are voracious readers; when they put pen to paper, it's hard to tell what's creative and what's recalled from memory, whether conscious or unconscious, as words spill onto a blank page. Hemingway said it best:

"All you have to do is write one true sentence. Write the truest sentence that you know. So finally I would write one true sentence, and then go on from there. It was easy then because there was always one true sentence that I knew or had seen or had heard someone say."[4]

In one of his greatest short stories, published in 1936, *The Short Happy Life of Francis Macomber*, Hemingway, when the protagonist is killed by a bullet to the back of the head, uses the unforgettable line "…he felt a sudden white-hot, blinding flash explode inside his head and that was all he ever felt."[5]

Hemingway, a man of brawny inclinations, took delight in the pugilistic art, stepping into the ring on occasions to dance with professionals of the ring. The sweet science weaved its way into his narratives abundantly. He famously stated, "My writing is nothing. My boxing is everything."[6] In the tale spun by George Plimpton, titled *Ring Around the Writers*, lays a recollection of Hemingway's audacious decree. The man of words was unyielding, summoning his comrade, the former titan of the boxing world, Gene Tunney, to share a ring. A presumption beyond measure, yet Hemingway's rescue came draped in Tunney's innate sense of fair play and restraint. When a

Hemingway haymaker, tinged with a tad too much earnestness considering the circumstances, came hurtling forth, Tunney retaliated with a razor-sharp right, impeccably reined in to hover but less than a fraction of an inch from the author's face. The unspoken declaration was clear.

In another curious encounter, Hemingway engaged in fisticuffs with the accomplished Canadian scribe Morley Callaghan, an adept boxer. Fitzgerald assumed the role of timekeeper, yet in a peculiar twist, he purportedly stretched the second round by an extra minute. A misstep, indeed, but within that extra span, Callaghan delivered a resounding blow that found Hemingway supine upon the canvas. With his characteristic flair for drama, Hemingway, espying Fitzgerald as the provocateur of this pugilistic tragedy, unleashed his ire. Whispers suggest that Hemingway, in later days, weaved a narrative where Fitzgerald, in a fit of impulse, elongated the round to a profane ten minutes—a notion bordering on the absurd. Callaghan, in his memoirs scripted subsequent to Fitzgerald's demise, etched the incident into the annals of literary lore. Curiously, Fitzgerald's own pen remained silent on the scuffle. Was it the shroud of shame that hushed his account or a subtler lapse of human memory, where recollections dim and alternative chronicles take root?

At the time of Fitzgerald's visit, Freddie's life lay before the eyes of all who had come to behold it. It was a tale of grandeur and opulence, splashed with colors of wealth and leisure yet tinged with the sadness of a soul yearning for more. The trappings of success were evident in every room of his mansion, every object, every breath he took. Yet, he had never truly found the meaning and purpose he so desperately sought.

In his prime, Freddie was a veritable phoenix, arising from the ashes of obscurity to bask in the radiant glow of success. He cast aside his old identity, assuming a new moniker, and reveled in the lavish lifestyle that his newfound wealth provided. He fancied himself a man of letters, surrounded by books and the trappings of intellectualism. His unrestrained pursuit of excess was causing his own empire to crumble like so much dust.

As Freddie had done with other elites, he presented to someone a gift of immense significance to him—his treasured Boxing Championship of Wales medal. The medal, gleaming with its golden luster, was not just a symbol of his athletic past but a testament to his personal life. Inscribed with the words "To our good friend; Scotty; From; Freddie & Fannie; Welsh; Xmas 1923," it was a curious gesture, one that piqued the interest of the National Library of Wales. They speculated that "Scotty" might refer to none other than the celebrated author F. Scott Fitzgerald himself. It coincided with the time he visited the health farm. However, attempts at uncovering the truth proved fruitless, and the mystery of Freddie's gift remains shrouded in the mists of time.

Inscribed medal to Scotty. Courtesy of the Chatham
Township Historical Society.

Scotty was also the moniker often bestowed upon the legendary wordsmith F. Scott Fitzgerald's daughter, Frances Scott Fitzgerald, born on October 26, 1921, by those in his inner circle. Even the likes of his comrade Ernest Hemingway, with whom he had a tumultuous relationship, referred to her as "Scotty" or "Scottie." The nickname appeared frequently in letters and compositions.[7] However, given the context of the inscription, it was more likely given to an adult.

In days past, Freddie was wont to bestow these precious engraved tokens upon men of true import. Such gifts, reminiscent of those ornate watches he presented to Senator Bill Lyons, hailing from Colorado, and to the notorious yet celebrated character, Bat Masterson himself. These were no ordinary trinkets but emblems of camaraderie, symbols of a cherished fellowship that Freddie held in the highest echelons of esteem. They were illustrious gentlemen, luminaries of their times, and Freddie, in his own way, etched their names into the annals of his own story, a tale of loyalty and admiration.

After scouring numerous biographies and articles detailing Freddie's life and times, no acquaintances of his shared the given name of Scott. It seems doubtful that Freddie enjoyed the close camaraderie of anyone named Scott other than Fitzgerald. It's worth mentioning that the paucity of information on this topic may be due to a lack of records regarding Freddie's personal affairs or that any conceivable friends named Scott were simply not of enough consequence to merit mention other than Fitzgerald.

F. Scott Fitzgerald and wife, Zelda.

In the spring season of 1924, after the sojourn to Freddie's estate, Fitzgerald and his wife, Zelda, felt the strain of their existence in Great Neck, Long Island. The burden of finances and the suffocating social scene weighed heavily upon them, leading husband and wife to make a hasty determination to flee to France and subsist on their modest means.

With a draft of *The Great Gatsby* in hand, Fitzgerald set sail for France, leaving behind the excess and chaos of their past five tumultuous years. Though some scholars, like Matthew Bruccoli, question the extent of this draft,[8] the hope was that the novel's royalties would alleviate the debt Fitzgerald owed to his publisher, Scribner's. Seeking a change in their lives, they ventured to the Old World.

They were escaping, Fitzgerald thought, "from extravagance and clamor and from all the wild extremes among which we had dwelt for five hectic years, from the tradesmen who laid for us and the nurse who bullied us and the couple who kept our house for us and knew us all too well. We were going to the Old World to find a new rhythm for our lives, with a true conviction that we had left our old selves behind forever and with a capital of just over seven thousand dollars."[9]

It was in the month of June they stumbled upon a grand residence in St. Raphael, the Villa Marie, France, with its lush gardens stretching far and wide. The couple spent their summer there, basking in its splendor. Fitzgerald penned a letter to his editor, Maxwell Perkins, with the utmost optimism, "We are idyllically settled here and the novel is going fine—it ought to be done in a month. . ."[10]

At first, Fitzgerald found himself inescapably drawn to the page. His novel, as yet incomplete, reflected the turbulent events that had come to define his existence. A storm was brewing within his marriage, and it was about to undergo a tumultuous transformation, one that would inevitably seep into the fibers of his latest novel. To finish the work in a mere month, as he had initially hoped, was a fanciful notion, as the strains of matrimony took hold and began to fray the delicate threads of his life.

A French aviator by the name of René Silvé had set his sights on the alluring and captivating Zelda. Though she had been the object of desire for many a man, Fitzgerald had grown accustomed to the attention she received. This time was different. To his surprise, Zelda had reciprocated the aviator's affections, and soon enough, the two were entangled in a tempestuous and fleeting affair.[11] The passion was brief, but its aftermath was felt in every aspect of their lives. The once-blissful union of the couple was thrown into disarray, and the progress of Fitzgerald's latest novel was thrown off course. The impact of this affair on Fitzgerald was incalculable, a wound that would never fully heal.

In the bright, glittering days of the Roaring Twenties, carefree and nonchalant affairs were met with a simple shrug of the shoulder. But not for Fitzgerald. He approached love and romance with a solemn reverence, recognizing its depth and importance in one's life. It was a matter he did not take lightly, and this was evident in the pages of his books, capturing the essence of true romance. Arthur Mizener, who wrote the first biography of Fitzgerald, *The Far Side of Paradise*, wrote in *The Atlantic*:

"Sexual matters were always deadly serious to him, a final commitment to the elaborate structure of personal sentiments he built around anyone he loved, above all around Zelda. His attitude was the attitude of Gatsby toward Daisy, who was for him, after he had taken her, as Zelda was for Fitzgerald, a kind of incarnation. 'The emotions of my youth,' he said, 'culminated in one emotion,' his feeling for

Zelda. It was the damage done to this structure of sentiments which was most disturbing in the Sllvé affair."[12]

It was the summer of 1924, a season bathed in the golden glow of possibility. Fitzgerald, with his pen as his weapon, set out to finish the work on his masterpiece, *The Great Gatsby*. Within its pages, he crafted a character inspired by the wise and whimsical wit of his dear friend Ring Lardner, a man who was friends with Freddie as well. This character, Owl Eyes, would speak Gatsby's eulogy, "The poor son of a bitch," a testament to the ill-fated dreamer who dared to love recklessly in a world where such passions were often met with bitter disappointment.

Riley V. Hampton, in comparing Larder to Dr. T. J. Eckleburg from *The Great Gatsby*, wrote, "Those eyes and what they saw, the national pastime corrupted for money, suggest the eyes of Dr. T. J. Eckleburg, of which Owl Eyes is a thematic echo, overlooking the corruption of the Valley of Ashes. As Ring Lardner was a close friend and neighbor of Scott and Zelda Fitzgerald, it seems plausible that Fitzgerald created and named his owl-eyed character at least partly as an oblique and humorous tribute to his friend. If so, the tribute is a pleasant one: the gentle, genial drunk whose integrity, in attending the funeral of the man whose liquor he has freely drunk, counterpoints Nick Carraway's, and whose capacity for wonder, at the theatrical effect of the library whose books he has 'ascertained' are 'absolutely real,' is second to Gatsby's own."[13]

The first known time someone dubbed Lardner "Owl Eyes" was during the infamous World Series of 1919, a time when the world of baseball was forever changed by the "Black Sox" game. It was there, during the excitement and drama of the competition, that a fellow sports journalist recalled Lardner's sharp wit as he teased Rollie Zeider [a former professional baseball player] over his nose.

"As Ring Lardner poked fun at Rollie Zeider's nose, Rollie countered by calling him 'Owl Eyes,' but those owl eyes, too, were seeing a lot of strange things."[14]

Ring Lardner, Owl Eyes.

"In the world of sport he was a close friend of the Welsh-American boxer Freddie Welsh," wrote Jeff Hill in *Sport and the Literary Imagination: Essays in History, Literature and Sport,* "who held the world lightweight title just before the Great War, and was on close terms with many of the country's leading baseball players. But his involvement with the Chicago White Sox, the team involved in the 'fixing' scandal of the 1919 World's Series (referred to by F. Scott Fitzgerald, another close friend, in *The Great Gatsby*) is said to have turned him away from that sport. His fame rested on his writing style, simple and expressive, depending to a great extent for its impact upon the use of popular idioms and speech rhythms...."[15]

In the golden days of American letters, Ring Lardner plied his craft with a wit and wisdom that has remained timeless. Ring Lardner, a scintillating figure in American literature, was renowned for his clever and acerbic columns on sports, the whimsical antics of matrimony, and the theatrical arts. A master of satirical prose, he elicited the admiration of literary greats such as Ernest Hemingway, Virginia Woolf, who famously proclaimed his writing to be "the best prose that has come our way,"[16] and of course, the F. Scott Fitzgerald, who held him in high esteem. A true virtuoso of the written word, entertaining and enlightening readers.

In his artistic creation, the one man who loomed largest in Fitzgerald's life was Ring Lardner, as chronicled by biographer Andrew Turnbull in his book *Scott Fitzgerald.*

"Despite their hospitality, "Turnbull wrote, "the Fitzgeralds made few friends in Great Neck where their only real intimates were the Lardners. During the year Scott was meditating *Gatsby*, and the first six months of writing it, the supreme influence in his life was "Ring." Lardner had a wondrous courtliness and consideration, though like Fitzgerald he was a practical joker of slightly sinister intent."[17]

"Fitzgerald 's friend," wrote Richard Holt, "the sports journalist and short story writer, Ring Lardner, who knew Welsh well and placed references to him in his work, taught the great novelist to see the lineaments of modernity in physical competition and in its mass consumption. The connection is as teasingly tenuous in the 'real' world as it is insistently tenable for all who would truly imagine it. The boxer [Freddie Welsh] who once read, and mixed with, the best authors may have read Fitzgerald's masterpiece before he died..."[18]

It was Lardner who convinced Fitzgerald of the beauty and tragedy of sport, particularly boxing, of the way it revealed the underlying rhythms of life—the victories and defeats that echoed in each person's soul. The sport and play of American society were masterfully depicted by authors like Ring Lardner and Fitzgerald.

It was not the first time that Lardner's pugilistic passion had caught the attention of his literary compatriot. Their conversation on the sweet science had commenced long before the pages of *The Great Gatsby* had ever graced the shelves, and Lardner's words on the subject were sure to have found a receptive audience in Fitzgerald's ear.

Boxing is a microcosm of life. It's a metaphor for the struggles we all face, and it teaches us valuable lessons about resilience, courage, and perseverance. While the outcome of any given fight may be tragic, the process of fighting itself is a noble one because it reminds us that we are all in this together and that we all have the capacity to be fighters in our own way.

"Mildly self-deprecating," Andrew Turnbull wrote, "Lardner considered himself a reporter rather than a literary man. His bailiwick was sports and popular entertainment, and he remained a little leery of the critics who were booming his work. What he gave Fitzgerald was intangible but invaluable—a fountain of wit, a cockeyed inner sense of truth, a feeling of being in cahoots with the world in general—while Fitzgerald, on his side, helped Lardner collect his first book of short stories which Scribner published."[19]

As Christian Messenger so noted in his work on the role of sport in his book *Sport and the Spirit of Play in Contemporary American Fiction*, it was Lardner and his ilk who showed that the American spirit could be understood through its games, through the stories of its players. And among these players, none stood taller than Freddie, the old friend of Lardner's.

"Certainly the legacy of sport in American fiction is that of authors such as Ring Lardner and Fitzgerald," Christian Messenger wrote, "who proved that modern American society may be imaginatively conceived and explained through its games and players. Contemporary American authors write in their wake, both in subject matter and mode of narration."[20]

Lardner and Fitzgerald forged a bond of artistic camaraderie, aiding one another in their pursuit of literary greatness, bound by a brotherhood of pen and ink. They comprehended the struggles of the writer's life all too well, and in their journeys, they found solace in each other's company, offering invaluable support as they journeyed toward their dreams.

Between October 1922 and April 1924, the two literary giants, F. Scott Fitzgerald and Ring Lardner, found themselves in the quaint and affluent town of Great Neck. With its grand estates, Great Neck was a place of opulence and refinement, a perfect backdrop for two writers of their caliber.

"It was an improbable friendship," wrote Matthew Bruccoli. "Lardner was 37, a reserved man from whom, Fitzgerald said 'an enormous dignity flowed'—a classic case of the sad wit. Fitzgerald was 26, ebullient and unpredictable. The only things they had in common were genius and alcohol. Another factor that promoted their friendship was the compatibility of their wives. Zelda Fitzgerald—who had special standards for people—did not always approve of Scott's friends, but she and the Lardner's got on splendidly. Ring conducted an elaborate mock courtship of Zelda."[21]

Freddie, with his alluring charisma, captivated the hearts and minds of the greatest writers of the time. Ring Lardner was one to recognize the potential of Freddie's story, as were many other renowned authors, such as P. G. Wodehouse, Elbert Hubbard, Felix Shay, and others, who couldn't resist the urge to put pen to paper and immortalize the enthralling tale of Freddie. He became a constant source of inspiration, appearing in many tales, both as a character and under his own name.

In the rich tapestry of reading matter, there are many instances wherein the embodiment of Freddie has been immortalized in the pages of literature. A few of the earliest allusions to him can be traced back to the musings of P.G. Wodehouse, who conjured up Freddie's image with his quill in the year 1913. Not long after, Ring Lardner added his own touches to Freddie's literary legacy in 1915.

"Well," wrote P.G. Wodehouse in his 1913 *Keeping it from Harold*, "I've made a study of it since I was a kid, so I jolly well ought to. All the fellows at our place are frightfully keen on it. One chap's got a snapshot of Freddy Welsh. At least, he says it's Freddy Welsh, but I believe it's just some ordinary fellow. Anyhow, it's jolly blurred, so it might be anyone. Pa, can't you give me a picture of yourself boxing? I could swank like anything. And you don't know how sick a chap gets of having chaps call him 'Goggles.' "[22]

F. Scott Fitzgerald and P.G. Wodehouse were forever intertwined by the presence of their shared literary agent, Paul Reynolds. There's no evidence of a strong relationship like Fitzgerald had with Lardner. However, Wodehouse wrote to his daughter Leonora about seeing Fitzgerald on the train to the city.

"I believe those stories you hear about his drinking are exaggerated," he wrote. "He seems quite normal, and is a very nice chap indeed. You would like him. The only thing is, he does go into New York with a scrubby chin, looking perfectly foul. I suppose he gets a shave when he arrives there, but it doesn't show him at his best in Great Neck. I would like to see more of him."[23]

As Wodehouse settled into the lavish lifestyle of Great Neck on Long Island in 1923, his reputation as the author of the popular post-war hit, *The Inimitable Jeeves*, only grew stronger with each triumphant performance on Broadway. The figure of Jeeves loomed large in the literary landscape, a constant presence in the pages of Wodehouse's stories.

Jeeves, the valet, with his impeccable demeanor and

unerring sense of purpose, had become the embodiment of the author's style and the embodiment of the essence of his storytelling. Over time, Jeeves evolved into a symbol of refinement, an iconic figure that was synonymous with the author's name. In the end, there was no denying that Jeeves was, without question, the most recognizable character that the author had ever created.

Lardner, writing in *The American* magazine in 1915, extolled Freddie's exceptional skill in the boxing ring, comparing the difficulty of hitting him to that of hitting a fast-moving baseball. He wrote the analogy:

"Or if it's a fast one you don't like, that's what you'll get, and even if it ain't as fast as Johnson's, you'll find that it comes past you a couple of inches higher or lower or this side or that side of where you could wallop it good. Or maybe you'll see this fadeaway that he got up himself, and it's about as easy to hit as this here Freddie Welsh."[24]

In October of 1916, Lardner published the short story *Champion* in the pages of the *Metropolitan* magazine. With a cynical gaze, he depicts the rise and fall of a sports hero, the boxer Midge Kelly, whose lack of morality and baser instincts are put on full display. The character of Freddie Welsh is woven into the fabric of this fictional tale, a testament to the power of friendship and the influence it can have on one's writing. In the story, Lardner wrote:

"You looked all right. But you aren't Freddie Welsh yet by a consid'able margin."

"I ain't scared of Freddie Welsh or none of 'em," said Midge.

"Well, we don't pay our boxers by the size of their

chests," Doc said. "I'm offerin' you this Tracy bout. Take it or leave it."[25]

In September of 1924, the Lardners, a couple comprised of Ring and his spouse, made their way to the seaside town of St. Raphael to pay a visit to the Fitzgeralds. As the days passed and memories were made, Lardner felt inclined to pen a piece for a magazine, chronicling their journey and musing on their experiences. His words, insightful and thought-provoking: "Mr. Fitzgerald is a novelist and Mrs. Fitzgerald is a novelty."[26]

In the year 1933, when Lardner was taken from the world at the age of forty-eight, Fitzgerald poured his heart out in an elegy entitled *Ring*, as a tribute to his friend's immense talent and the void he left behind. The mournful composition was published in *The New Republic*, a symbol of his sorrow and admiration for a man who had left an indelible mark on literature and the world. Lardner's departure was premature, but he left cherished memories of his wit, wisdom, and brilliance.

"At no time did I feel that I had known him enough," Fitzgerald wrote, "or that anyone knew him—it was not the feeling that there was more stuff in him and that it should come out, it was rather a qualitative difference, it was rather as though, due to some inadequacy in oneself, one had not penetrated to something unsolved, new and unsaid. That is why one wishes that Ring had written down a larger proportion of what was in his mind and heart. It would have saved him longer for us, and that is itself would be something. But I would like to know what it was, and now I will go on wishing - what did Ring want, how did he want things to be, how did he think things were?

"A great and good American is dead. Let us not obscure him by flowers but walk up and look at that fine medallion, all abraded by sorrows that perhaps we are not equipped to understand. Ring made no enemies, because he was kind, and to many millions he gave release and delight."[27]

While Fitzgerald's tumultuous life continued abroad, Freddie found himself facing new struggles at home. Freddie's world, once alight with the blazing fire of a single aspiration—his health farm—was now consumed by its rapid decline.

On the twelfth of October 1924, an unfortunate occurrence took place in the town of Summit, New Jersey, just miles from Freddie's cherished health farm, adding further turmoil to his already troubled existence.

Neal Marsiane, a young man from Parrow Street in Orange, New Jersey, piloted his sedan eastward along Springfield Avenue. With seven youthful companions seated within, the group was returning from a visit to the town of New Providence, nestled between the affluent Summit and Chatham Township. As they made their way toward the city of Newark, their journey was cut short as a second vehicle, driven by Freddie, traveling southward down Park Avenue on the wrong side of the road, collided with their sedan at the intersection of the two avenues.[28]

Amid the whirring of the engine and the rush of the wind, a young society belle, Myrtle Wilson, of Valley Road in West Orange, New Jersey,[29] rode in splendor within the sedan. In a moment's notice, the tumultuous force of the unexpected collision sent her hurtling toward the glass of the unforgiving windshield with considerable force, marring her flesh. She was transported to Overlook Hospital in Summit, where they tended to her wounds, applying four stitches to a laceration on her scalp and treating her contusions,[30] which spoke of the violence of the impact.

The fictional Myrtle Wilson, the mistress of Tom Buchanan, was the very picture of ill-fated love in *The Great Gatsby*. Her life was a tragic tango of passion and desperation, one that led to her untimely demise. Tom, a man of great wealth and status, was but a fleeting pleasure in her otherwise dull and dreary existence. It was a foolish affair, one that ultimately proved fatal for Myrtle. When Daisy, Tom's wife, and Gatsby, the enigmatic protagonist, fled a lavish soiree in Tom's motorcar, Myrtle, blinded by her infatuation and consumed by a desire to confront her lover, dashed out in front of the speeding vehicle. The car collided with her, leaving her lifeless on the roadside. In an act of chivalry, Gatsby claimed responsibility for the accident, shielding Daisy from the consequences of her recklessness.

The accident that befell Freddie was destined to inexorably link him to Fitzgerald's great masterpiece. The occurrence lay buried in the author's pages, a mystery waiting to be uncovered until it was finally revealed by Freddie's fellow countryman and biographer, Andrew Gallimore, after a slumber of nearly eight decades.

Just shy of three weeks after the accident, Freddie cruised down Springfield Avenue on the first of November 1924, his eyes fixed upon the town of Summit. As he rounded the perilous curve of Livingston Avenue in New Providence, fate intervened a second time in the form of a pole, stubbornly planted in the path of his carelessly driven car. Freddie was left with a gash on his head. He was taken to his Chatham Township home to receive medical care, where he was tended to in the aftermath of this latest occurrence on a curve in the road that had claimed several victims in the past.[31]

Early in November of 1924, Fitzgerald dispatched the fledgling draft of his masterpiece, *The Great Gatsby*, to the hallowed halls of Scribner's. Despite his efforts to perfect the work, he remained unsatisfied with the fluidity of Chapters VI and VII. Right up until the day of publication, he labored and toiled ceaselessly to refine and revise the manuscript, determined to capture the essence of his vision.

"I can't quite place Daisy's reaction,"[32] Fitzgerald wrote to his editor, Maxwell Perkins.

By winter, the Fitzgeralds had taken flight to the Eternal City of Rome. As days passed, he remained tethered to his work. Circa December 1, 1925, Fitzgerald sent the following from the Hotel des Princes.

"Dear Max:

"Your wire in your letters made me feel like a million dollars—I'm Sorry, I could make no better response than a telegram whining for money. But the long siege of the novel winded me a little and I've been slow on starting the stories on which I must live.

"I think all your criticisms are true.

(a) About the title. I'll try my best but I don't know what I can do. Maybe simply *Trimalchio* or *Gatsby*. In the former case, I don't see why the note shouldn't go on the back.

(b) Chapters VI and VII. I don't know how to fix.

(c) Gatsby's business affairs I can fix. I get your point about them.

(d) His vagueness I can repair by *making more pointed*— this doesn't sound good but wait and see. It'll make him clear.

(e) But his long narrative in chapter VIII will be difficult to split up, Zelda also thought it was a little out of key, but it is good writing and I don't think I could bear to sacrifice any of it.

(f) I have 1000 minor corrections which I will make on the proof and several more large ones which you didn't mention.

"Your criticisms were excellent and most helpful, and you picked out all my favorite spots in the book to praise as high spots. Except you didn't mention my favorite of all—the Chapter where Gatsby and Daisy meet.

"Two more things. Zelda's been reading me the cowboy book aloud to spare my mind, and I love it—tho I think he learned the American language from Ring rather than from his own ear.

"Another point—in Chapter II of my book, when Tom and Myrtle go into the bedroom while Caraway reads *Simon called Peter*—is that raw? Let me know. I think it's pretty necessary.... As ever, Scott"[33]

On January 24, 1925, Fitzgerald sent another letter to Maxwell Perkins, again, from the Hotel des Princes.

"This is a most important letter so I'm having it typed. Guard it with your life.

"1) Under a separate cover I'm sending the first part of the proof. While I agreed with the general suggestions in your first letters I differ with you in others. I want Myrtle Wilson's breast ripped off—it's exactly the thing, I think, and I don't want to chop up the good scenes by too much tinkering."[34]

He then sent a terse cable to Maxwell Perkins on the eighteenth of February 1925, transmitting his thoughts across the Atlantic with a sense of urgency, as if he were trying to convey the immediacy of his words.

"HOLD UP GALLEY FORTY FOR BIG CHANGE."[35]

The alterations made to those two chapters, in part, entailed the excision of five or six pages from the core of the altercation between Gatsby and Tom, changing the whole passage into a new form. The entire segment was rewoven with a new thread of prose,[36] and it was in Chapter VII where the fateful incident transpired as the automobile struck and snuffed out the life of Myrtle Wilson.

As the final pages of *The Great Gatsby* were being put to the test, Fitzgerald enlisted the services of Lardner to cast a critical eye over the document. His guidance, as always, was invaluable, offering insightful critiques and encouraging words as he perused the manuscript. He offered no guidance on the theme of the work. Instead, he simply stated:

"On pages 31 and 46 you spoke of the newsstand on the lower level, and the cold waiting room on the lower level of the Pennsylvania Station. There ain't any lower level at that station and I suggested substitute terms for same. On page 82, you had the guy driving his car under the elevated at Astoria, which isn't Astoria, but Long Island City.

"On page 118 you had a tide in Lake Superior and on page 209 you had the Chicago, Milwaukee & St. Paul Station. These things are trivial, but some of the critics pick on trivial errors for lack of anything else to pick on."[37]

Ring Lardner was well aware that the censuring eye of critics would seek out that one slip-up, that one blunder, to bring down an entire opus. Irrespective of whether the error was a conscious choice or malice aforethought, regardless of whether it was an allusion to another source or not, these critics would hurl down damnation upon the narrative, using it as evidence of further faults without even bothering to scrutinize it closely unlike the diligent writer who had expended his energies tirelessly in pursuit of precision.

When Fitzgerald sent a typescript to his legendary Scribner's editor Maxwell Perkins, he had galleys set from them. Unfortunately, this typescript and subsequent typescripts and carbon copies do not survive. The *Trimalchio* galleys, as they are referred to, that he made from them were sent to Fitzgerald in Rome, where he corrected and revised the work during the first two months of 1925. The author corrected the galleys in pencil but also pasted on long typed additions of text.

As James L.W. West III has noted in his edition of *Trimalchio*, the book in the original galleys was not the same novel as *The Great Gatsby* as finally published. Despite similarities, there are crucial differences. Fitzgerald conveyed or recommended additional corrections and changes to Maxwell Perkins by letter and telegram. Among other things, the author considered alternative titles, such as "Among the Ash Heaps and Millionaires" and "Gold-Hatted

Gatsby."

By spring 1925, Fitzgerald settled on "Under the Red, White and Blue." However, by the time he had communicated this to Maxwell Perkins, the book had already been published as *The Great Gatsby*, the title Perkins liked best. Fitzgerald had hesitated about the title because he said there was nothing great about Jay Gatsby and felt that the title, using a surname, might remind people of Sinclair Lewis's novel *Babbitt* [1922].

April the tenth, 1925, saw the release of a literary masterpiece, one that would capture the essence of the Jazz Age and secure its place in the annals of American literature. The novel delves into a myriad of themes. The dream, wealth, love, and class. The dream, an elusive and mythical creature, is scrutinized by the characters who relentlessly pursue it, only to find it forever out of reach. They yearn for success and happiness but are left unfulfilled disenchanted. A stark dichotomy exists between the haves and have-nots, as wealth and status not only determine one's place in society but also one's ability to form relationships. Love is shown to be complex and mercurial, swayed by social class, wealth, and personal ambition. Illusion and reality collide as the characters wade through a world of dreams and desires, oblivious to the harsh reality of their lives. The society depicted is one in decline, where morality is but a distant memory and corruption runs rampant. Desperate to achieve their goals, the characters will stop at nothing, willing to sacrifice anything for a taste of success. Overall, *The Great Gatsby* is a commentary on the social and cultural values of America in the early Twentieth Century, and the themes explored in the novel continue to resonate with readers today.

The Great Gatsby, a novel of grandiose parties and ill-fated love affairs, didn't take the world by storm at first, receiving a tepid response. In years to come, it would dazzle readers with its glittering prose and piercing commentary on the society of the time. Its author, F. Scott Fitzgerald, had crafted a work of unparalleled beauty and depth, a timeless tale that would continue to captivate generations to come.

Back in the States in December 1925, the Wilsons of West Orange, New Jersey, had taken Freddie to court. Myrtle, the striking beauty, her countenance forever marred, sought $20,000 in recompense for the injuries that had befallen her and left her permanently disfigured. Her father, William, demanded $1,000 for the wages he'd lost tending to his daughter's recovery.[38]

The trial transpired with Freddie failing to appear, resulting in a default judgment awarded against him. Freddie, forever the fighter, was not one to go down so easily. He fought to have the case reopened, claiming that the service of the summons was flawed and that the papers declaring his involvement in the legal battle were left at his health retreat in Chatham Township while he was, in fact, in the city of New York. His attorney, Howard F. Barrett, succeeded in having the case reopened. William A. Lord of Newark represented Myrtle Wilson and the other defendants, all of whom would soon seek retribution in their own right.

It was a Friday, the twenty-sixth of February in the year 1926 when Myrtle Wilson took the stand before the honorable Judge W. F. Mountain and a scrutinizing jury. In her testimony, she recounted an ill-fated ride with seven others, heading east on Springfield Avenue in Summit, New Jersey. It was then that she made the accusation that the accident was caused in the form of Freddie's recklessness. She stated that the defendant's car, careening south on Park Avenue, collided with their sedan at the crossroads. As Myrtle bore witness, Freddie's vehicle had strayed to the wrong side of the road, causing the crash.[39] Her fair features, once unblemished, now bore a cruel scar that forever marred her forehead, inflicted by the force of the impact that flung her toward the windshield, along with other injuries.

Freddie sat alertly by his counsel throughout the first day's proceedings, vigilant through the opening session as various witnesses took the stand to provide testimony for the plaintiffs. Judge W. F. Mountain then adjourned the proceedings for the day to be resumed on Monday. It was then that Freddie, unyielding and resolute, took to the stand to share his account of the events at hand. The matter was then placed in the hands of the jury, tasked with reaching a fair and just verdict.[40]

The jury delivered their verdict in favor of the Wilsons, though it proved not quite the outcome the plaintiffs sought. Myrtle Wilson, in all her suffering, was granted a sum of three hundred dollars, while her father, William, received a hundred for his trouble. The *Newark Evening News*, in its next edition, proclaimed that the once-great lightweight champion of the world had met his defeat by a decision, but it was not in the ring[41] but in the court of law.

Begin with an individual, and before you know it you find that you have created a type: begin with a type, and you find that you have created—nothing. That is because we are all queer fish, queerer behind our faces and voices than we want anyone to know or than we know ourselves.

—F. Scott Fitzgerald

The most enchanting and indelible aspect of *The Great Gatsby* resides in Fitzgerald's artistry, where he meticulously crafted a troupe of strikingly authentic characters. These aren't mere representative figments; they breathe with a pulsating vitality that feels palpably genuine. Such authenticity emanates, for in truth, it is because they were, indeed, drawn from the tapestry of existence.

F. Scott Fitzgerald seldom unveiled the inner workings of his character-crafting artistry. Yet, in the year 1923, a sliver of insight into his creative alchemy found its way to the ink-stained pages of an interview for the *Metropolitan* magazine. As he wove the tapestry of his characters for the *The Beautiful and Damned*, the words he shared were nothing short of revelatory. One could scarcely resist the temptation to believe that the same clandestine process, this deep dance of imagination, served as the linchpin of his other literary endeavors.

"I had no idea of originating an American flapper when I first began to write," Fitzgerald once told

Metropolitan magazine about *The Beautiful and Damned*." I simply took girls whom I knew very well and because they interested me as unique beings, I used them for my heroines."[1]

There's been an endless swirl of speculation surrounding the true identities of the characters in the opus magnum, *The Great Gatsby*. No one can pry the secrets from F. Scott Fitzgerald's tight-lipped soul, for he's long since departed this world. But it's not all pure fiction, as the characters are a cunning concoction of Fitzgerald's own experiences and those of the colorful individuals he encountered along the way.

The mysterious Daisy, Gatsby's elusive love interest, a woman of such allure and mystery that she could only have been fashioned from the stuff of dreams or, perhaps, from the very essence of the Jazz Age itself. Some have whispered that she was but a reflection of the author's own wife, the beguiling Zelda, whose electric energy and capricious temperament were legendary. Others insist that it was Ginevra King Pirie, a sparkling socialite and belle of Chicago's high society, who inspired the character's intoxicating beauty and captivating charm. A member of the illustrious "Big Four" debutantes, she was the muse of many a tale spun by the pen of writers.

Tom Buchanan, Daisy's husband, could have easily blended in with the pack of distinguished and affluent gentlemen that Fitzgerald had the pleasure of knowing. Perhaps he bore a resemblance to Tommy Hitchcock, a man who shared Tom's ownership of fine polo ponies and a splendid estate on the tranquil shores of Long Island. Or could it be that he resembled Ginevra's father, Charles King, the proud owner of a prestigious string of polo ponies, just like Tom? Alternatively, Ginevra's husband, hailing from the cream of Chicago's upper-class society, could also have been a parallel to Tom's lofty status.[2]

The charming and talented golfer, Jordan Baker, a dear confidant of Gatsby's once-lost love, Daisy Buchanan, is said to bear an uncanny resemblance to Edith Cummings, a golfing marvel who graced the cover of *Time* magazine, the first of her kind.

Then there's Meyer Wolfsheim, the shady underworld figure who, in the novel, tainted the 1919 World Series. Many believe that he was modeled on Arnold Rothstein—who proved to be quite the character in his own right—a Chicago gambler who was also implicated in the notorious "Black Sox" scandal of 1919.

As for Jay Gatsby himself, ask a number of Fitzgerald scholars who was the inspiration for Jay Gatsby, and you might get the same number of answers back. Arthur Mizener, the first Fitzgerald biographer, wrote that Fitzgerald's wife, Zelda, later in her life, said that a man named Max von Gerlach was the model for Gatsby. In 1923, Gerlach wrote a note to the author, which Fitzgerald's daughter, Scottie, kept. It ends with Gatsby's signature phrase, which appears forty-five times in the novel: "Enroute from the coast—Here for a few days on business—How are you and the family old sport?"[3]

Matthew Bruccoli, who was an American professor of English at the University of South Carolina, recognized as the preeminent expert on F. Scott Fitzgerald, and a scholar who had written extensively about Fitzgerald for decades, was convinced that there was more to find out about the connection between Gerlach and Gatsby. At one point, he hired a private investigator to track down more of Gerlach's history. Around the same time, another Fitzgerald scholar, Horst Kruse, was digging into the connections between Gerlach and Fitzgerald as well.[4]

As these scholars and the private detective learned more about Gerlach's life, and the more details they turned up, the less likely it seemed that Fitzgerald modeled Gatsby directly on Gerlach, who was not just a bootlegger but spent many less glamorous years as a car dealer.[5]

A St. Paul lawyer, Dan Hardy, had unearthed what he believed to be the answer to the longstanding mystery. He had stumbled upon a series of facts that he alleged pointed to Cushman Rice of Willmar, Minnesota, as the inspiration behind Jay Gatsby. Before he could make his discovery and findings public, Mr. Hardy passed away, leaving his revelations behind.

Or, could F. Scott Fitzgerald's Jay Gatsby have been a former champion boxer living in the quaint township of Chatham, New Jersey—Freddie Welsh. The proposed notion was first considered in the works by authors Richard Holt, who alluded to the connection in his 1990 book *Sport and the Working Class in Modern Britain,* and Andrew Gallimore in his 2006 book *Occupation: Prizefighter / The Freddie Welsh Story.* The idea that a man of such grandeur and mystique, such as Jay Gatsby, could have been modeled on a prizefighter is both intriguing and alluring. A concept that, like the fictional man himself, is both complex and elusive, leaving one to ponder its possibilities.

"The Americanization of Freddie," wrote Richard Holt, "and his own 'late' entry into the fray [World War I] was reported sardonically by the Welsh press. His popular support remained undiminished.

"Nevertheless, Freddie Welsh had become the focal 'American' which the localized Jim Driscoll [another boxer from Wales] could not be. Scott Fitzgerald, in 1926, caught the essence of this phenomenon, and its doomed solipsistic heroism when he created the late Victorian, James Gatz who becomes Jay Gatsby of the American century by a regimen of fanatical self-improvement through physical exercise and study. All given reality by fate..."[6]

In contemplating the curious art of molding a fictional soul from the clay of reality, one might reasonably surmise that veiling the true identity of the living person would be the prudent course to undertake. Yet, akin to a mastermind criminal subconsciously leaving behind telltale traces in the aftermath of a nefarious caper, Fitzgerald, that literary enchanter, too, left evidence strewn along the winding lanes of his prose. Among these, a conspicuous tale of an automobile mishap of no small consequence blazes like a beacon, illuminating the enigmatic dance between reality and the captivating realm of fiction.

The *Times* of London reported in 2007 that Andrew Gallimore had found an odd link between Freddie Welsh and Jay Gatsby. Not long before Fitzgerald submitted the manuscript to his publisher for *The Great Gatsby*, Freddie Welsh was involved in a car crash in Summit, New Jersey, injuring a woman, on October 12, 1924, named Myrtle Wilson. In the novel, Gatsby's old flame Daisy Buchanan was driving his car when she hit and killed a woman named

Myrtle Wilson.

Amidst the bevy of fictional figures that populated the pages of that novel, there existed a singular character whose name remained unchanged from that of a living, breathing individual—Myrtle Wilson. The only other character that comes close was Owl Eyes, the nickname given to Ring Lardner—a mutual friend of F. Scott Fitzgerald and Freddie Welsh—a well-known journalist and writer of his time. Was this a mere oversight on the part of the author or a deliberate nod to the inspiration behind the Great Gatsby himself? One can only speculate as to the true motives behind Fitzgerald's decision.

Like Gatsby, Freddie exhibited hopefulness despite the adversity he encountered; he found money could not buy your friends; and your past can be unescapable. A single dream defined his life. A dream he clung to for way too long. Though Freddie's life had not met the tragic end of Jay Gatsby when the book was published, he did follow his early demise.

Before the publication of his book on Freddie Welsh, Andrew Gallimore channeled a lengthy email to Professor Matthew Bruccoli. On August 22, 2005, Bruccoli responded:

"Dear Mr. Gallimore:

"The Myrtle Wilson/Freddie Welsh/Great Gatsby connection is intriguing and curious. But you need to make case on basis of the *Gatsby* MS [manuscript, unfortunately earlier notes and manuscripts didn't survive]. Fitzgerald wrote or rewrote *Trimalchio* on the Riviera June-September 1924. By 11 October 1924 he was in Rome waiting for galleys. I say rewrote because he brought a draft to France. Nobody knows how much of a draft or what kind of a draft. He claimed in an April 1924 letter that he had a complete draft; but I'm dubious.

"What is the evidence for Fitzgerald connection with Welsh? New fact. Fitzgerald never mentioned it in a letter...."[7]

However, it's a known fact that on February 18, 1925, Fitzgerald cabled his editor at Scribner's, Maxwell Perkins, to hold up galley forty for big changes. The changes included Chapter VII in which Myrtle Wilson is hit and killed by a car.[8]

In the wake of Andrew Gallimore's 2006 publication, a lingering intrigue arose, prompting inquisitive minds to seek the perspective of Matthew Bruccoli. The eminent scholar, known for his discerning insights into the works of the literary aristocracy, was approached for elucidation. In a display of candor, he slightly relinquished his guarded stance from the personal email, this time publicly offering his thoughts to the discerning readership. Addressing the *Times* of London, Bruccoli posited that Jay Gatsby might, perchance be a product of inspiration drawn from two distinct personalities, conjoined in the grand tapestry of Fitzgerald's visionary mind. Such revelations unveiled yet another layer of complexity, an alluring enigma that continues to shroud the myth and majesty of *The Great Gatsby*, leaving literary aficionados to ponder the beguiling leap between fact and fiction.

"Gatsby is 80 per cent Fitzgerald and 20 per cent other sources," Bruccoli stated. "The Welsh thing is interesting, but far from conclusive."[9]

"The search for Gatsby has been one that preoccupied and eluded scholars and continues to," said Bryant Mangum, a professor of English at Virginia Commonwealth University and the editor of *F. Scott Fitzgerald in Context*. "There are many, many models for Gatsby."[10]

"He's borrowing from various kinds of sources to get his story across, "says Scott Donaldson, the author of the Fitzgerald biography *Fool for Love*. "But he's really writing about himself in the book. And that's why it's so intimate and why it still resonates, I think."[11]

"To create Jay Gatsby," wrote Sarah Laskow, "though, Fitzgerald also borrowed from the lives of other men, and devotees have been trying to pin down his real-life inspirations for decades."[12]

In the opulent realm of F. Scott Fitzgerald's celebrated opus, *The Great Gatsby*, resided the enigmatic Jay Gatsby, a man adorned in the shimmering robes of wealth and grandeur. Behind those lavish parties, pulsating with life, lay an insatiable desire—to reclaim the heart of his long-lost love, the captivating Daisy Buchanan. A tale of ardor and aspiration ensues, imbued with the decadence and illusion of the Jazz Age. Similarly, in the world beyond fiction, Freddie Welsh, a man of earnest principles, was fixated upon erecting a bastion of vigor and well-being for his brethren. Albeit vastly different in pursuits, the parallels in the relentless pursuit of their yearnings cannot be denied. In the hazy complexity of existence, it is not a mere dream that holds sway but rather an indomitable ardor to triumph at any expense, and therein lies the poignant repercussions when it remains but a phantom of aspiration, drifting beyond reach. Both Gatsby and Welsh, men of mettle and fortitude, strode steadfastly, unyielding to the world's impediments, all in pursuit of their resplendent dreams.

In the world of Gatsby and Freddie, there were certain qualities that set them apart from the rest. For one, Gatsby, formerly known as James Gatz, was a man who knew the value of a name, and so he changed his to one that better suited his aspirations. Freddie, too, recognized the power of a moniker, and before one of his early fights, he transformed himself with a new name. Both men were athletes and soldiers, rising up from humble beginnings to achieve great success. And they had something else in common as well: a taste for the finer things in life. Living in extravagant homes on Long Island, both Gatsby and Freddie possessed great intellect and libraries filled with books. These were men who had made it to the top, and they knew it.

Gatsby believed that by amassing great wealth and throwing lavish parties, he could win back Daisy's affection and prove to her that he was worthy of her love. Freddie believed that by using his ring earnings to buy and renovate lavish properties and acquire friends who were famous, powerful, and well-connected, he could build his dream. Both are tragic heroes who are ultimately destroyed by their own obsession with fulfilling an all-consuming dream.

The preponderance of evidence, though circumstantial, is quite abundant. It paints a picture of Freddie Welsh as the very embodiment of Fitzgerald's creation. Inevitable parallels are found between Jay Gatsby and the real-life Freddie Welsh, their common threads binding fiction and reality ever tighter. The resemblance, unmistakable and compelling, draws forth a union between the realms of make-believe and tangible existence. Such remarkable affinities serve as the very essence of this captivating connection between these distinct yet harmonious souls.

In their shared realm of grand aspirations and opulence, they both embodied the quintessence of ambition, draped in riches and unapologetically ensnared by extravagance. Their backgrounds concealed in veils of enigma, shrouded in a tantalizing air of mystery. Idealism coursed through their veins, and a consuming fixation gripped their souls. Adrift amidst the tempestuous tides of society, they found themselves perpetually set apart, yet their magnetic charisma drew the gaze of all in their orbit.

Both were architects of their fate, hewing themselves from the granite of humble origins into beacons of success, self-made paragons of their time. Their resolve an unyielding force propelling them toward greatness. Yet, in their grandiosity lay the seeds of tragedy. The tragic hero, epitomized in their tragic stature, bore a countenance of virtue and nobility. Their virtues inspired awe, and their charm ignited passions, but beneath the facade lay the fatal flaw that would herald his undoing.

Their existence became an intricate tapestry woven of dreams and illusions, forever haunted by the echoes of a bygone era. Hearts clinging steadfast to the past, a ceaseless yearning to recapture that which had elusively slipped through their grasp. In this relentless quest, they remained oblivious to the inexorable march of time, the verity that some moments could never be captured again. The intoxicating allure of nostalgia proved a treacherous siren, inexorably guiding them toward the precipice of downfall.

In the end, both Gatsby and his real-life counterpart found themselves inexorably bound by the threads of fate, entangled in the web of their tragic destinies. Their undying aspirations and their unyielding pursuit of the unattainable reverberate in the annals of time, leaving an indelible mark on the essence of human longing. A vivid testament to the wistful paradox of the human heart, forever torn between the allure of grand illusions and the immutable grip of its own poignant fallibility.

Freddie Welsh's escapades seemed plucked from the tapestry of Fitzgerald's own imagination, embellished and delicately woven into the fabric of his novel. The extraordinary feats of Freddie demanded no such adornment to metamorphose him into the perplexing figure of Jay Gatsby. Like a Gilded Age aristocrat, Freddie Welsh possessed an innate allure, an aura of mystery, that rivaled the most captivating characters to ever grace the pages of Fitzgerald's literary domain. The parallel between the two men, so striking in its essence, unfurled like a richly adorned narrative thread, binding their lives with an uncanny resonance. In Freddie's realm, extravagance and opulent activities copied Gatsby's world of ostentation, where the line between fact and fiction blurred, and the illusion of grandeur perpetuated itself with each daring exploit. Freddie Welsh, a man with a story too grand to be confined to the pages of mere prose, had inadvertently stepped into the role of his own literary counterpart.

As the pieces of the puzzle begin to fall into place, it becomes clear that the thread connecting Freddie Welsh to Jay Gatsby is a strong one. One cannot help but conclude that it was Freddie's essence that fueled Fitzgerald's imagination, driving the development of the enigmatic and captivating character of Jay Gatsby. Freddie Welsh, if not the main inspiration for Jay Gatsby in *The Great Gatsby*, was at least one of them.

Chapter XIX

He wanted to care, and he could not care. For he had gone away and he could never go back anymore. The gates were closed, the sun was down, and there was no beauty left but the gray beauty of steel that withstands all time. Even the grief he could have borne was left behind in the country of youth, of illusion, of the richness of life, where his winter dreams had flourished.

—F. Scott Fitzgerald, *All the Sad Young Men*, 1926

The golden sun of summer in 1925 cast its fading rays upon the Long Hill Health Farm, where the days were swiftly darkening for Freddie. Despite being once renowned as a victorious champion, luminaries were failing to flock to his establishment who once basked in its glory days. As bills piled high, Freddie found himself in a desperate search for financial salvation.

"Freddie asked Jack Dempsey for a loan of $5,000 to save his farm at Summit and he refused," declared Fanny at a later date. "Everybody deserted Freddie."[1]

In a fit of desperation, he conceived a well-meaning but somewhat hair-brained scheme—to convert his health farm into a fox ranch that would entail a partnership with the prominent Pontiac Strain organization, the reigning king of the fur industry. Despite the hope that this venture would provide a financial lifeline, the reality was a bleak one. The fox ranch proved to be a fruitless endeavor, and again, his dream was crumbling.

He had embarked upon a quest, a journey of self-discovery, a search for success. He sought the secrets of vitality, the art of the ring, the grandness of golf, and the fur of the cunning fox. But each effort, each venture, ultimately proved futile in a permanent fulfillment. The health farm, the boxing camp, the boxer, the golf course, the fox breeding—all were insufficient, inadequate, and a despair that would seem to permeate every aspect of his life.

Freddie, once the epitome of vitality and virility, was now headed to becoming a shadow of his former self. The attempts to revitalize his career, his relationships, and his health were all for naught, and he was reduced to a man wracked by a sense of failure and a thirst for solace at the bottom of a bottle. It was even putting a strain on his marriage, which resulted in a separation. The gossip whispered about his downfall, and it seemed as though the once-great Freddie Welsh was destined to be remembered not for his achievements but for his decline.

As the crisp autumn winds began to blow, Freddie struggled to keep up with the demands of life. In the dreary month of November, he found himself confined within the sterile walls of a hospital in the town of Summit, New Jersey. The doctors worked to revive his ailing heart, which seemed to be plagued by a relentless series of heart attacks. His future now seemed shrouded in a haze of uncertainty.

Freddie, once a bright and hopeful young man, now found himself grappling with the harsh truth of disillusionment. The naivety of his youth had been replaced by a heavy weight of disillusion, and it seemed as though his youthful optimism was a thing of the past. Freddie, still in the prime of his life at thirty-nine years old, was haunted by the knowledge that his once bright future had been forever clouded by the realities of life.

In the year 1926, Freddie's Long Hill Health Farm fell into the clutches of foreclosure—an imminent cruel end to a once-promising venture that wrought deep agony upon the man. Freddie's health farm was to be sold in November 1926 to settle the mortgage. Freddie didn't let the farm go without a fight, even after the foreclosure had been signed.

By 1927, Freddie, somehow, was still clinging on to his health farm. With the threat of the finalization of the mortgage looming, he put up a gallant fight, even after the foreclosure had been enacted. His lawyer, Israel B. Greene, valiantly argued for an extension in the court, citing that Freddie had secured a loan of $45,000, which fell through due to a legal tussle. Besides, a wicked snowstorm had prevented prospective buyers from exploring the property. Mr. Greene implored the court on Freddie's behalf, informing them of a syndicate that had offered to help pay the mortgage. To top it all, Freddie had turned down offers of $35,000 and $50,000, deeming them unfit and a guise to capitalize on his money troubles, despite the fact he had been willing to sell it for $10,000 almost five years earlier. Vice Chancellor Backes reopened the case, granting Freddie a 30-day extension, valid till April 1, 1927.

Freddie's prospects were dimming as he found himself in dire need of a cash infusion to secure the future of his beloved health farm. In a stroke of luck, William C. Armstrong of Chatham Township emerged as a potential benefactor, ready to offer the necessary financial muscle.

But tragedy struck before the loan could materialize, as Armstrong met his untimely demise in a fatal automobile accident.

After death had taken Armstrong, who had promised to furnish the financial strength, adversity seemed about to deliver the knockout blow. It appeared as if destiny had conspired against Freddie as adversity reared its ugly head. However, a silver lining emerged in the form of Albert Birkmaier and a consortium of eight Newark entrepreneurs, who stepped in to salvage the situation. Another Chancery edict provided a brief respite, granting Freddie, again, a reprieve of thirty days to secure the much-needed funds.

The promises of the Newark syndicate evaporated, leaving Freddie with nothing but dashed hopes and a litigious mind. Fueled by resentment and seeking justice, he brought a suit against those nine businessmen before the Supreme Court of Newark, seeking a hefty sum of $150,000 as compensation for their deceit. For the foreclosure on the health farm, the court ruled in Freddie's favor, setting aside the sale and granting him until April 29, 1927, to, once again, come up with the money to settle his debt. However, the sum of money he sought from the Newark syndicate remained pending litigation. Freddie, despite his best efforts, could not secure the needed funds. The once-mighty, wide-reaching health farm was destined forever to be lost to him.

In the days of May 1927, fate dealt a final, merciless blow—the health farm was seized by the ruthless grasp of foreclosure, a victim to the unyielding demands of the mortgage. In a cruel twist, it was George T. Brown—once a friend to Freddie in the untroubled days of his prosperity—who now held the reins of power, master of the situation in this, the hour of his most dire need. Brown took all properties tied to the debt.

The *Oakland Tribune* wrote:

"Summit, N. J., May 11.—Freddie Welsh's health farm near here has slipped through his fingers. The plant he valued at $200,000, bought with money he earned as lightweight champion of the world, went to satisfy a mortgage which was foreclosed by one of his friends of better days. All of Welsh's priceless treasures, his Elbert Hubbard books in the original manuscript, his bronzes and ring trophies, went in the sale."[2]

The precious contents, exquisite signed first-edition books, priceless treasures, his Elbert Hubbard books in the original manuscript, his bronzes and ring trophies, and luxurious trappings, all adorned with Freddie's signature touch, were shamelessly consumed by the gaping jaws of the court's relentless pursuit. The lavishness he had bestowed upon the house with such great expense was now reduced to a bitter memory, as all that remained for him were mere crumbs of what he once possessed. Despite multiple attempts at prolongation, the court inevitably seized it all. Freddie had forfeited all that he held dear; his entire world had been shattered, and there was no turning back. It was now lost in the sea of dreams.

It had been the culmination of his aspiration, a beacon of his hopes. It was the embodiment of his fantasy but would also be the root of his lamentations. A paradox of sorts, a mingling of elation and sorrow. It was the realization of his dream and the source of his despair.

Chapter XX

It is in the thirties that we want friends. In the forties, we know they won't save us any more than love did.

—F. Scott Fitzgerald, *The Notebooks of F. Scott Fitzgerald*

Let us learn to show our friendship for a man when he is alive and not after he is dead.

—F. Scott Fitzgerald, *The Great Gatsby*

First you take a drink, then the drink takes a drink, then the drink takes you.

—F. Scott Fitzgerald

Freddie's life careened out of control, spiraling down a treacherous path that few dare to tread. A place devoid of light, where the essence of his being was in peril. Stripped of his titles, adulation, and wealth, and with a once-vibrant social circle having abandoned him, leaving him to fend for himself. The unimaginable occurred for the health-conscious man as he resorted to heavy drinking and constant fretting over his dwindling finances. His physical state was deteriorating rapidly; the once-chiseled features of his face now bore the unmistakable marks of brawls fought outside the ring, the scars of a life wildly out of control. Freddie's fate seemed doomed, a tragic end to a once-promising life.

It was June of 1927 when Joe Williams, a writer of

sport, laid his eyes upon Freddie as he traveled uptown concealed within the Seventh Avenue subway's belly. In his column, Joe set forth a description of what he beheld. The man he spied, once a luminary, world's lightweight champion, and victor of the boxing world, was now a specter of his former self. Unrecognizable was he to those who once held him in esteem. A shadow of his once-glorious self, adrift in the cavernous underworld of the city.

"There wasn't anything about the exterior aspects of the erstwhile prontyprid [sic] Pride to indicate he was running around with the Morgans or the Guggenheims," Williams wrote in the *Pittsburgh Press Sun.*

"A slightly dented beak in that eerie far-look you see in the eyes of fighting men who have been through the fist fire of grueling struggles stamped him unmistakably as a withered cauliflower.

"Welsh was before the big dough era in the ring. He made money but not big money. The Leonards and Tendlers had greater success at the turnstiles—and been blessed of more frugal natures they aren't riding in the subways these days."[1]

It was in the month of July that the streets of the West Forty-seventh Street station were alight with the reckless energy of a free-for-all fight. It was there that a lone patrolman, George Meyers, dared to step in and put an end to the chaos. Though other fighters managed to slip away into the murky abyss of the city's teeming underworld, Meyers apprehended two of the brawlers, determined to bring them to justice.

One of the men, who claimed to go by the name

Edward Delaney, was twenty-four years of age and hailed from 410 West Fiftieth Street. The other man said he was Freddie Welsh, a former lightweight boxing champion. But for the police blotter, he gave his name as forty-one-year-old Frederick Thomas, a boxing instructor at 333 West Thirty-fifth Street. Only the timely intervention of the patrolman had saved Freddie from an even greater drubbing. The two men were locked up, left to the confines of their cell.

On July 17, 1927, Freddie found himself standing before a magistrate of New York City, sporting a most unseemly black eye and bruises that bespoke of fisticuffs, charged with disorderly conduct. Freddie ventured to explain away the unsightly marks to the magistrate that he had just been in a friendly battle with a friend, calling it a "little dancing matter."[2] A quarrel that had escalated into a bitter brawl. The magistrate deemed it nothing more than a friendly tussle and dropped the charges against both men.

Later in July, amid the gleaming edifices that scraped the New York skyline, there stood the Hotel Sidney, nestled on West Sixty-fifth Street, where Freddie sought refuge. Tucked away in its squalid confines, he sought solace from the cruel world that had dealt him a merciless blow. A few friends came to pay their respects, pitying his pitiable state, lamenting the shattering of his once-impenetrable spirit. And then, as the sun set on a summer's day, the once-great pugilist, Freddie Welsh, in the forty-first year of his life, took to the ring for the final time—not to battle a fierce foe, but to face his own internal torment that had long besieged him. The world he had known was already slipping from his grasp.

On July 29, 1927, Freddie was in a dimly lit quarter

of the Sidney Hotel where he had been staying. A sorry end had come for one who had once lived a life of grandeur. The maid who stumbled upon the scene was met with an unseemly sight of the body of Freddie Welsh, once a champion pugilist, now a forgotten man, his attire a garish display of floral-patterned pajamas and a robe,[3] the very symbol of his fallen status, a far cry from the glitz and glamour of his heyday.

His final moments were marked by an eerie stillness as he lay slumped over a writing desk in a state of repose. The wretched soul had been felled by the hand of fate while seated at his desk, an apparent heart attack being the culprit. And yet, even in death, his hand, a hand that once shot through space to his opponents' jowls, outstretched seemed to reach out for something beyond his mortal self, something that he could only see: Freddie's sole companion in death, a copy of *Elbert Hubbard of East Aurora* by Felix Shay that lay on his bed. The well-thumbed book was opened to the page that had the phrase:

"Get your happiness out of your work, or you will never know what happiness is."[4]

A physician, beckoned by the hotel staff, scanned the still form sprawled out, and a cursory diagnosis was made. The physician took in the scene, ascertaining the likely perpetrator of the demise. He attributed the fatal blow to a weak heart, which had succumbed to its own frailty.

Freddie's once beloved wife, estranged from the prizefighter, labored as a maid in the neighboring establishment known as the Hotel St. Paul. A few minutes after the discovery of her husband's death,[5] she was summoned to the scene. The bitter tears flowed as she railed and let loose a flurry of verbal attacks upon the pugilistic companions who had abandoned him. A tempestuous storm, lashing out with all the pent-up frustration and pain of a life half-lived.

In a voice dulled by defeat, Fanny spoke of the pitiless exodus of his wealth. Her words rang out, each syllable a piercing shard of reality. His funds had dwindled, disappearing with the delicate steps of time.[6] The health farm he once possessed had been cruelly surrendered, now a phantom of his past. Even his prized championship belt, once held high as a symbol of his glory, was pawned for a paltry sum of $100. Desperate, he had scoured the streets in search of labor, but his appeals to former acquaintances of the prize ring, their hearts hardened to his plight, ears deaf to his pleas. Just the day before, a letter from William Muldoon, chairman of the Boxing Commission, brought him no solace—for even he had coldly informed him that he could find no work for him.[7] [8] [9]

"This is a hard-boiled age," Fanny said, "When you're up, your way up, but when you're down, you're sure down. Freddie knew them all when he was on top, but none of them knew him when he was down and out."[10]

The doctors had decreed that his demise was wrought by the insidious grip of heart disease. But his estranged spouse, from whom he had been distanced for a few years, differed.

"It was his heart that killed him, all right." Fanny stated. "It was broken. When Freddie had money, any friend could get it from him. When he was strapped, they didn't know him. He died without a cent to his name. He recently hocked two of his belts valued at $1000."[11]

"They didn't even invite him to the big fights, Freddie, who was a champion and fought the best of them in his day."[12]

Fanny, in her melancholic reverie, declared that his passing was a consequence of those "fickle fared-weathered friendships,"[13] a sentiment that found favor with the press. They plastered headlines across the pages of their papers, lamenting his passing with such headers as "Freddie Welsh Abandoned by Friends; Poor at Death."[14] The bonds of loyalty are frail, and the vagaries of fortune determine the fate of a man; Freddie fell victim to the caprices of fate, a casualty to the superficiality of those who called themselves his companions.

"Only last week," Fanny continued while grimly drying her eyes, "Jack Dempsey, whom Freddie defended when he was called a slacker, was in town, and he wouldn't even come to see Freddie. Freddie was sick, and he wrote Dempsey a letter asking Jack to just stop in and say hello. Freddie never even got an answer to that letter."[15]

Though their time apart was fraught with tension, Freddie and his wife remained bound in matrimony for twenty-two years. She stated they were "still the best of friends."[16] Their union bore a pair of two sprightly children. Young Betty, at the tender age of thirteen, was on the cusp of adolescence, while Freddie Jr., aged eleven, was still basking in the innocence of childhood. The children, at the time of Freddie's demise, were indulging in a brief respite in the surroundings of Hope Farm in Verbank, New York.

With his final breaths, Freddie remained embroiled in a legal tangle, still a plaintiff in a towering $150,000 damage suit seeking to reclaim a portion of his dwindling wealth. He had clung onto the hope of redemption, still within the clutches of the court in Newark. His pockets were barren, his accounts long since depleted, yet he persisted in his pursuit of justice. He refused to be defeated, even in death.

Freddie's brother, Stanley, would not let the matter rest until an autopsy was carried out. As per his insistence, it was granted. Stanley said that in justice to the family, he desired the newspapers to say that Freddie did not die in poverty. He had suffered reverses and his sensitive nature impelled him to feel that he had lost the esteem of many who had been glad to greet him in the days of prosperity, but he was not broke, according to him.

A most peculiar claim he made was that Freddie was not languishing in abject poverty at the time of his passing in his final hours, not at all. To the contrary, Stanley insisted that the deceased possessed a considerable fortune—a whopping $130,000 worth of real estate, to be precise. In part, this consisted of a plot of land in Vernon, California, which Stanley espoused. Freddie declined a hefty offer of $83,000 a mere three weeks prior to his untimely demise. He even held real estate on opulent Long Island, worth $45,000.

"Freddie owned property in California," Stanley said, "for which he recently refused $83,000 and has a substantial equity in property worth $45,000 at Bayside, Queens."[17]

"Freddie's one great ambition," said his brother,

"was to make his family independent, and he did that well. I would like to do everything in my power to change the impression that he died poor."[18]

He added that Freddie was the fortunate inheritor of a trust fund bestowed upon him by the grace of his mother's will. Its overflowing yield endowed him with prosperity befitting the most opulent of lifestyles, or so he claimed. The significant trust fund existed tucked away in the Summit Trust Company of Summit, New Jersey. Not only that, but his relatives in Wales were of considerable means and owed much of their affluence to his generosity. If the need arose, they would have been there for him. Such was the discordance of fortune and despair that accompanied Freddie in life and death. He contended Freddie was still a man of means, and Stanley made it his duty to see that the world knew it.

Not a sliver of evidence arose to corroborate such statements. Freddie's estranged wife, Fanny, had already begged to differ from his brother and that his earthly departure was marked by a lamentable absence of monetary means. It was an odd conclusion to a tale shrouded in pecuniary mysteries.[19]

In the curious nature of society, the once revered and celebrated Freddie, in his final days, found himself relegated to the fringes of society, discarded like yesterday's news. Now that he had passed on to that great beyond, the same people who had shunned him were tripping over themselves to sing his praises and shower him with adulation. It was a familiar tale, one that speaks of the untrustworthiness of human nature.

Though he did not seek the counsel of sports journalists in his darkest hours, they were quick to extol his virtues on the grand stage of print. With each article penned in his honor, Freddie was lifted higher still until his name shone again in the limelight. It may have again been fleeting, but at that moment, Freddie was the undisputed champion of his own story.

Ed Van Every, who penned articles about Freddie during his fighting career, wrote:

"Those who saw the passing of his crown to Benny Leonard must find it hard to believe that so brave a heart could break even under misfortune."[20]

"I think the finest thing that should go down to the credit of Freddie Welsh in the fistic history of this country," said Joe Humphries, who managed Freddie in a few of his fights, "is the fact that Captain Freddie Welsh, though of English birth, was an American through and through once he had become a citizen of this land. When the World War broke out, he was one of the first to enlist. He was commended for his work in the training camps and earned other ranking previous to his appointment as captain."[21]

"Broadway the invincible," wrote another journalist Arthur Mefford, "the champion double-crosser of all time, which no man ever licked and which no man ever will, erased another name yesterday from the roster of celebrities who helped build up its reputation....died of a broken heart. Freddie Welsh has been dying on his feet...because the friends he aided when he was rich wouldn't look after him when he was poor."[22]

Hype Iago, the renowned chronicler of sporting feats,

possessed a keen understanding of the woes and triumphs that befell Freddie, a man whom he knew all too well. In his eloquent elegy just one day after his death, he painted a vivid portrait of a soul in turmoil, a man beset by challenges both in and out of the ring.

"Freddie Welsh never grew up," Iago wrote. "One of the finest characters boxing ever produced, he just couldn't get down to the importance of taking life seriously. He played hooky from responsibility right up to the closing days of his eventful career. It is with a feeling of the deepest sorrow that I find myself writing of the death of a man who didn't have an enemy in all this wide world.

"Men worthwhile like Freddie Welsh for his fairness, his absolute honesty, his gentle character, his gloriously boyish attitude toward life.

"He had one big dream in life after the loss of his lightweight title. That was to create the most celebrated health farm in the world.

"He and Elbert Hubbard planned this farm. Long before Welsh ever became champion he and the bard of Aurora had worked out the plans for a somewhat different resort where the rich and the poor could seek life's real treasure—health.

"Hubbard admired Welsh greatly. In the boxer's splendid library are many valuable first copies of Hubbards best known works. One is a bound volume containing little scraps on which Hubbard potted down bright sayings as they flashed across his fertile brain.

"Little cards, cuffs, a menu card, Pullman slips, pieces of maps, every imaginable kind of makeshift note paper he used to record the thoughts as they came to him. All these he compiled in a carefully bound book and gave to the boxer. This book was one of the many treasures.

"Then, too, Hubbard had his workers at Aurora fashion into great leather-bound scrapbooks in which Welsh pasted all these newspaper stories of his career, from the beginning to the end. There is one story—the saddest in his term on earth which he never will paste up. Even this little expression of my appreciation will never find its way into the great books he so treasured.

"There isn't any question that Freddie Welsh's death was brought about by his intense grief of losing his health farm. One of his supposed friends, a real estate shark, tricked him so that the place was sold over his head, even as he was making a desperate effort to rally his friends around him to satisfy a mortgage claim. Only two weeks ago he told me that Mayor Frank Hague and some of his New Jersey friends were about to make it possible for him to reclaim his beautiful place at Summit.

"Shortly before that, he had got the promise of another friend to come to the rescue. He was to give Freddie $40,000 in cash to save his place. On the morning of Welsh was to call on him, this friend dropped dead of heart disease in his office. That is only a sample of the way things were breaking for this fine fellow of late. He died dead broke. When he had it, he tossed money into the four winds. There never was such a thing as tomorrow in Freddie Welsh's life. He lived as it came. When money rolled in, he rode the crest of the wave like king. Laughing morning, noon, and night, I can't recall his ever so much as frowning. He heard the finest nature of any man I've ever met, in or out of boxing."[23]

A singular periodical expressed the situation with piercing brevity, proclaiming, "Now that he's dead, Freddie Welsh will no longer be forgotten."[24]

Abandoned by the indifferent world in the dwindling moments of his existence, he was, without question, certainly not lost in the obscurity of his passing. Freddie's old-time friend Humbert Fugazy, with whom Freddie had shared simpler days before he acquired his opulence and repute, assumed the task of arranging his final farewell.

Young Griffo, a friend of Freddie in their balmy lightweight fistic careers, who had triumphed as the inaugural Australian victor of a global championship, found himself lingering hesitantly on the threshold of Devlin's somber funeral parlor, gripped by a paralyzing apprehension that restrained his entry. Tears welled unapologetically in his expressive eyes, evoking a poignant display of vulnerability. A discerning observer amidst the hushed ambiance of mourning, Edward Devlin, the astute custodian of the departed and boxing enthusiast, swiftly discerned the distraught figure before him, for their paths had crossed in a past of consequence.

"Go around to the Boyertown Chapel this afternoon, Griff," said Devlin, "he'll be laid out there."[25]

Within the annals of the United States Army, Freddie was adorned with the moniker of Captain Fredrick Hall Thomas, a title of prestige that was accompanied by a pristine military record. In his final send-off, they decorated Freddie's form in his army uniform, bearing the regal insignia of a captain. His dignified frame was then presented in a solemn chamber, residing within Devlin's Boyertown

Chapel, located at 671 Eighth Avenue.[26]

Fanny, the estranged wife, adorned the bier with his coveted Lonsdale and lightweight championship belts, a poignant reminder of the glory he had achieved and the legacy he left behind. Among a sea of mourners, she remained one of the few who had known him not only as a world champion but stood steadfastly loyal to him in his final hours. The world knew him as a champion, but it was only those few who truly knew the man behind the titles.

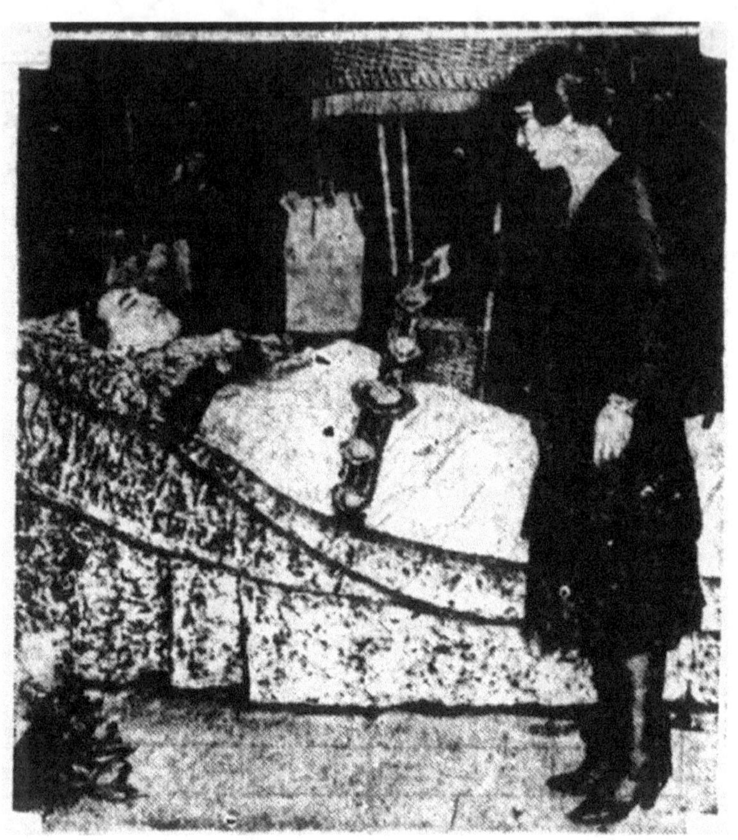

Fanny mourns Freddie, placing his championship belt on
him.

A profusion of illustrious guests graced the solemn
occasion, including actors, athletes, and even statesmen and
beyond, amassed to pay their respects, their numbers ranging
from 1,500 to, as some would have it, 5,000.

Joe Lynch, former conqueror of the pugilistic realm,
sought solace in revisiting Freddie, his dear comrade, one
final time. Amidst a sea of indifferent faces, he stood as one
of the precious few who had graced the threshold of

Freddie's Sidney Hotel room in the twilight hours preceding his eternal departure. The news of Freddie's untimely demise had arrived like an unanticipated uppercut, inflicting a staggering blow upon Joe's unsuspecting senses. The stark reality of mortality's cruel embrace, surreptitiously unveiled through the printed word, had left him momentarily breathless, awash in a cascade of disbelief.

"I met Freddie only last week," said Lynch, "and he told me he was getting along fine. If I had known he was in need of money he could have had it from me."[27]

Though Fanny had professed that Freddie had ventured to implore Jack Dempsey for a monetary favor, it seemed that his pride stood as an insurmountable barrier, preventing him from extending his pleas any further. He never asked Joe Lynch for help.

A modest and scarcely renowned assemblage of pugilists hailing from the metropolis' famous pugilistic sanctuary, Lou Stillman's gymnasium, likewise made an appearance to pay their respects to Freddie, who now lay motionless in his satin-draped casket. These palookas, largely unrecognized in the realm of pugilism, were men of meager stature, bearing the telltale marks of their arduous battles—cauliflower ears and contorted noses—while clutching their boxing attire firmly beneath their powerful arms, symbolizing their identity and purpose.

As for Jack Dempsey, who was in California and had been accused by Fanny of neglecting Freddie when he sought a visit in his sickroom, only dispatched a message of condolence. Amidst the throng of lavish bouquets, one could not help but notice the grandiose wreath bestowed by Jack

Dempsey himself that stood out like a beacon in the midst of a dark night. But alongside this token of affection was an unmistakable void, a conspicuous absence of the physical form of the former world heavyweight champion. A simple card inscribed "good-by, Freddie,"[28] accompanied the wreath, which served as a final farewell from the missing mourner.

The dissolution of their bond, once so fiercely held, remained shrouded in mystery. None could say what poison had seeped into the veins of their friendship or discern the precise moment when their bond had crumbled, rendering it a meager shadow of its former splendor. Or was it merely a mirage? For all the talk and fervent speculations, the truth remained elusive. Such is the mysterious nature of life that even in death, we are left with mysteries that may never be solved.

The swollen crowd continued to flock into the chapel to catch a glimpse of the body lying there. A continuous stream of visitors graced the chamber, bidding farewell to the beloved Freddie Welsh. Not a single prominent figure from the illustrious nocturnal life of New York City was absent, for this was a moment of profound significance—a time to pay last respects to a man who had touched the hearts of so many. It continued until a quarter past one that afternoon when they shut the casket for good.

Where the mournful hymns ricocheted through the hallowed halls, Dan McKettrick stood as the conductor of the final symphony for the departed. He and Harry Pollock had wielded the reins of Freddie, but now they were but mere memories in the vast expanse of time. McKettrick shouldered the burden of the moment, presiding over the solemn service. And as the last notes of the requiem faded away, all were bidding farewell to the life of Freddie.

He received a military funeral led by Major Row of Governor's Island due to his service during the First World War. The military men held him in high esteem, for an entourage of eight privates and Corporal Laverne Jackson, hailing from the 16th United States Infantry stationed at Fort Jay,[29] stood with reverent respect as the casket of this honorable soldier was conveyed and settled within the solemn hearse. A collective of boxing champions, including Abe Attell, Benny Leonard, Johnny Dundee, Mickey Walker, Mike McTigue, and Jack Britton, served as his pallbearers.

With a ceremonial entourage of soldiers, Freddie was solemnly shepherded to his final destination, the Fresh Pond Crematory and Columbarium at Middle Village, Queens County, New York, where he would be returned to ashes.

Freddie's existence unfolded akin to a novel spun upon life's grand stage. He ascended, with arduous determination, from the murky depths of obscurity, transcending the barriers of mediocrity until he found himself basking in the golden glow of triumph, only to be cast back into the shadows from which he had emerged. In his onerous odyssey, he discerned the disheartening truth, for it appeared that the company of people was fleeting, evaporating into naught but mere apparitions when one's fortunes dwindled. Dreams, those ethereal illusions, captivated and deluded, carrying within their hallowed whispers the seeds of ruin. Life, with its grand promises and beguiling allure, revealed itself to be a tempestuous sea of disillusionment, teeming with treacherous currents that gnawed at the soul.

As the ink of remembrance dried on the yellowed pages of history, it was a truth universally acknowledged that the concluding chapter of Freddie's existence could never be amended. The narrative of his life, once set in motion, possessed an unyielding finality that defied the whims of revision. No amount of fervent longing or wistful yearning could alter the inexorable course of his destiny. Like the fading echoes of a forgotten phrase, the chapters of his tale unfolded with an immutable life of confliction, their prose etched upon the annals of time, forever preserving the reverberations of his transient existence and his extraordinary gift for hope. It was a bitter realization, drenched in the melancholy hues of regret, for all who bore witness to the irrevocable conclusion of Freddie's story.

Epilogue

I went over and looked at that huge incoherent failure of a house once more.

—F. Scott Fitzgerald, The Great Gatsby

In that curious incident, when existence mirrors art, one finds oneself captivated. As if plucked from the pages of a Fitzgeraldian tale, reality, like a masterful stroke of the author's pen, the ordinary transforms into the extraordinary, blurring the boundaries of what is real and what is a splendid fabrication of the mind. It is in these moments, when life surrenders to the intoxicating allure of art, that the fragile fabric of our existence gains a shimmering sheen, evoking a sense of wonder that resonates deeply within the human soul.

The mansion, that grandiose spectacle of the locale, had drawn innumerable luminaries over the years not for its splendor but for the singular, celebrated resident within—Freddie. Yet now, it remained with but a meager pair of inhabitants, a stark contrast to its golden days. Over its three-plus decades of existence, it had shed all of its lords and masters, save for the present owner, whom it would choose to spare.

Even in the throes of death, the elusive tendrils of the Long Hill Health Farm reached out to ensnare Freddie like a desperate lover. It was an autumn day on the thirteenth of October in the year 1927 when the Long Hill Health Farm breathed its last. Once a magnificent spectacle that drew the envy of the surrounding region, it was now consumed by the wrath of fire that ravaged the grandiose mansion perched high atop the hill.

Reports revealed that the flames had originated from one of the fireplaces that had warmed the mansion's hearth for many a cold night. The fire erupted, its feral flames embracing the night shortly before one AM, ablaze with unwavering defiance, while the relentless deluge of rain sought in vain to quell its insatiable appetite. The mansion stood unyielding, spurning the gallant efforts of its would-be rescuers. From Chatham Township and New Providence, the valiant firefighting forces arrived, summoned by the urgency of the hour. Their noble endeavor was thwarted despite the rain, shackled by the cruel scarcity of the life-giving liquid from hydrants. Forced into an agonizing impasse, they became mere spectators, helplessly consigned to bear witness as the inferno consumed its coveted prize, relinquishing its sovereignty only when the clock struck three and all was lost.[1]

The flames had lashed out like a beast, licking up everything in its path, consuming the heart of the mansion. But in the wake of this tragedy, a strange and desperate affair had ensued. For what the flames couldn't take, people, like vultures to flesh, flocked to the scene, feverishly hauling off the remnants that weren't overly charred, hoarding them away for themselves. It was a pitiful sight, yet in a way, it seemed fitting. For in this age of excess and indulgence, what was left for those who had scant little received the scraps that fell from the master's table. A tale of despair and dishonesty had befallen the once-great estate.

"I remember when it caught fire," a neighbor, Mrs.

Clingen, said, "my father went to help pull out the furniture and give the firemen a hand with the water buckets."

"In those days when people saw smoke," Mrs. Clingen continued, "for some reason, they took advantage of the situation."[2]

What remained after the flames had ravaged and the scavengers had pillaged were the charred remnants of what once adorned Freddie's mansion. Amidst the ashen ruins lay the scorched vestiges of his treasured belongings. The inferno had raged with such fervor that it had left only smoldering ruins in its wake. At the time of the blaze, two hapless souls had the misfortune of being present: George T. Brown, the ruthless money lender who had seized the property, and his better half. By some miracle, the pair escaped unscathed from the blazing inferno.

As the grand mansion crumbled into oblivion, so too did Freddie's essence, his worldly treasures, and that elusive dream dissipating into the abyss. The fabric of existence, indifferent to his demise, persisted unabated, relentlessly swept by the tides of time, ever receding into the depths of the past, forever destined to be inscribed upon its timeless pages.

Bibliography

1999. *Christie's Lot 233 / Sale 8299. Christie's Auction. .* November 30. Accessed 2016. http://www.christies.com.

St. Louis Post Dispatch. 1921. "Leonard May Box Welsh for Title in Rickard Arena." April 21: 19.

(Ginger), Roland Hulme. 2022. *What can F. Scott Fitzgerald teach us about writing?* August 26. Accessed October 30, 2023. https://www.hiddengemsbooks.com/what-f-scott-fitzgerald-teaches-about-writing/.

Akron Evening Times. 1918. "Freddie Welsh, Once Champ Boxer, Now Buck Private." Setember 25: 10.

Altoona Tribune. 1923. "Private John Coolidge." August 25.

Andrew Turnbull, ed. 1966. *The Letters of F. Scott Fitzgerald.* Laurel: Dell Publishing Co., Inc.

—. 1963. *The Letters of F. Scott Fitzgerald.* New York: Scribner.

Asbury Park Evening Press. 1926. "Freddie Welsh Sued." February 27: 2.

Asbury Park Press. 1927. "Group to Lift Welsh Health Farm Mortgage." March 31: 8.

Augusta Chronicle. 1924. January.

Benson, Peter. 2006. *Battling Siki: A Tale of Ring Fixes, Race, and Murder in the 1920s.* Fayetteville: University of Arkansas Press.

Bernardsville News. 1923. "Boxing Exhibit Draws Crowded House." June 21: 3.

Bernardsville News. 1924. "Freddie Welsh in Auto Accident." November 6: 5.

Bernardsville News. 1924. "Heavyweight Champion Planned Cycling Career." January 3.

Berry, John. 2020. "During the Roaring 20s, Walter Hagen was a sporting icon in post World War I America." *Lake County Record Bee*, May 9.

Bonhams. 2021. *A FREDDIE WELSH LIGHTWEIGHT CHAMPIONSHIP PRESENTATION WATCH.* Accessed December 10, 2021. https://www.bonhams.com/auctions/27079/lot/122/?category=list.

Borders Cities Star. 1925. "Former Champ Takes Up Foxes." July 18: 3.

Borrelli, Christopher. 2013. "Revisiting Ginevra King, the Lake Forest woman who inspired 'Gatsby'." *Chicago Tribune*, May 7.

Brockway, Anthony. 2007. *Babyon Wales.* January 16.

Brooklyn Daily Eagle. 1927. "Freddie Welsh, Idol of Boxing, Dies in Solitude." July 29: 2A.

Brooklyn Daily Eagle. 1927. "Freddie Welsh, so He Says, Arrested in Street Battle." July 16: 2.

Brooklyn Daily Eagle. 1923. "Navy Boxers Getting Ready for Finals." December 16.

Brooklyn Daily Eagle. 1921. "News of the Fights and Fihters." December 30: 2 A.

Brooklyn Daily Eagle. 1917. "Welsh Says a Champion Should Defend Title Once a Year." May 13: 2.

Brooklyn Daily Eagle. . 923. "Young Stribling Wheels 'the folks'." December 29: 11.

Brown, Warren W. 1921. "Cyclone Bill Lyons Grants

Interview." *San Francisco Call and Post*, March 11:
18.

Bruccoli, Matthew. 2005. *Email: Matthew Bruccoli to
Andrew Gallimore.* South Carolina University,
August 22.

Bruccoli, Matthew J. 1976. *A Literary Friendship - The
New York Times on the Web.* November 7.
Accessed September 24, 2022.
https://archive.nytimes.com/www.nytimes.com/boo
ks/00/12/24/specials/fitzgerald-
lardner.html?source=post_page------------------------
--
&fbclid=IwAR0AX4V5g2rDHPydECwYTuUxi2y
PAR_GWo4caVayNCicKLzyF85XcktlkkA.

Bruccoli, Matthew Joseph. 2002. *Some Sort of Epic
Grandeur: The Life of F. Scott Fitzgerald (2nd rev.
ed.).* Columbiia: University of South Carolina Press.

Burlington Free Press. 1927. "Freddie Welsh Dies in
Poverty." July 29: 12.

Burlngton Free Press. 1923. "Freddie Welsh, Officer."
August 1: 13.

Callaghan, M. G. 1923. "Kayo Would Not Disturb Her,
Say's Stribling's Ma." *Brooklyn Daily Eagle*,
December 30: 14 A.

Capital Times from Madison, Wisconsin. 1921. April 22:
10.

Carpentier, Georges. 1920. "What Georges and "Bat" had
to Say To-day." *Syracuse Journal.*

Casey, Mike. 2011. *Fast Freddie: Why Welsh Was a
Wonder. East Side Boxing. News Archives.* August
11. Accessed March 5, 2023.

https://www.boxing247.com/weblog/archives/1344
69.

Casper Sunday Morning. 1923. ""Wild Jno." Here to Do
Best He Can." June 10: 1.

Chatham Pres. 1924. "Welsh Teaching Boxing at
Plattsburg Camp." July 19.

Chatham Press. 1917. "A Rest and Training Resort on
Long Hill. Chatham Press. May 12, 1917." May 12.

Chatham Press. 1920. "Carpentier to Train in Chatham."
September 18: 4.

Chatham Press. 1920. "Feddie Welsh to Re-Enter the
Ring." May 8: 8.

Chatham Press. 1927. "Fire Destroys Health Farm."
October 15: 1.

Chatham Press. 1918. "Freddie Welsh an Excellent Host."
June 8: 9.

Chatham Press. 1920. "Freddie Welsh Coming Home."
February 21: 8.

Chatham Press. 1927. "Freddie Welsh Gets a Respite."
April 2.

Chatham Press. 1924. "Payment Made on Mortgage,
Adjourn Sale on Welsh Farm." September 20: 1.

Chatham Press. 1917. "Registration on Tuesday." June 2:
8.

Chatham Press. 1922. "Sheriff's Sale." February 11: 7.

Chatham Press. 1918. "Welsh Health Farm Incorporated."
November 9: 1.

Chicago Daily Tribune. 1924. "Freddie Welsh is Burned
Helping to Put out Fire." August 24: 5.

Constitution. 1927. "Fighters, 'Palookas' Pay Tribute to
Fallen Champion." July 30: 10.

Corbett, James J. 1921. "Welsh's Comeback Would be Contrary to History." *Fort Wayne News And Sentinel*, January 10: 12.

Courier News. 1921. "Bob Martin Is Training at Summit Farm." June 28: 13.

Courier News. 1924. "Freddie Welsh, Former Boxer, Fights Fire in New Providence." August 25: 13.

Courier News. 1918. "Freddie Welsh Offers Farm to Uncle Sam." August 17.

Courier News. 1926. "Latzo Training for Harmon Bout." June 15: 17.

Crose, Sean. 2022. *Hemingway, Fitzgerald & The Round That Went On Too Long.* December 22. Accessed November 11, 2023. https://www.thefightcity.com/hemingway-fitzgerald-and-the-round-that-went-on-too-long/.

Daily News. 1927. "Freddie Welsh Gets Military Funeral Today." July 30: 21.

Dalton, Rodney G. n.d. *The Story of Captain Davis Dalton.* Accessed December 9, 2022. https://www.daltondatabank.org/Chronicles/Davis_Dalton.htm. .

Daniel, Daniel M. 1950. *The Mike Jacobs Story.* Ring Book Shop.

Davies, Sean. 2002. *Freddie Welsh.* April 11. Accessed May 4, 2023. http://news.bbc.co.uk/sport2/hi/boxing/1901425.stm . .

Day. 1914. "Ritchie Loses His Title to Welsh in 20-Round Go." July 8: 9.

Dean, Alison. 2021. "My Boxing is Everything: On Trying

to Punch Like Ernest Hemingway." *Literary Hub*, May 6.

Detroit Free Press. 1919. "Freddie Welsh let Go by Court." October 22.

Donaldson, Scott. 1983. *Fool for Love: F. Scott Fitzgerald.* New York: Congdon & Weed.

Dougher, Louis A. 1919. "Looking 'Em Over." *Washington Times*, March 19: 16.

Duffy, Edward P. 1923. "Stribling is Fit for Rosenberg." *Sun And Globe*, December 31: 11.

2023. *Ernest M. Hemingway.* Accessed August 7, 2023. https://www.poetryfoundation.org/poets/ernest-m-hemingway.

Evening News. 1920. "Carpentier Returns Today from France." September 13.

Evening News, Wilkes-Barre. 1927. "Wife Mourns Freddie Welsh." August 2: 13.

Evening Report. 1920. "Freddie Walsh [sic] Says That He Will Be Back." March 6: 5.

Evening Telegram—New York. 1920. "Carpentier is Here to Fight." September.

Every Evening—Wilmington, Delaware. 1927. "Freddy Welsh Shunned by All He Aided Says His Wife." July 29: 18.

Every, Ed Van. 1927. "Welsh, Former Champion, Who Died of Broken Heart, One of Game's Best Boxers." *St. Louis Post-Dispatch*, July 29: 15.

Farrell, Henry L. 1921. "Training for the Fight." *Daily Republican*, July 1: 5.

—. 1921. "Dempsey Resting on Jersey Farm." *Freeport Journal-Standard*, April 28.

—. 1921. "Kearns Says Dempsey is Only "Playing Around" in Jersey." *Norwalk Hour*, April 29: 19.

—. 1920. "Welsh Will Have Chance at Title." *Trenton Evening Times*, January 29: 21.

Fernald, Gus. n.d. "Interview by Historical Society of Chatham Township."

Fitzgerald, F. Scott. 1963. *F. Scott Fitzgerald to Maxwell Perkins, June 26, 1921, in The Letters of F. Scott Fitzgerald.* Edited by Andrew Turnbull. New York: Scribner.

—. 1980. *Letter to Ring Lardner, April 10, 1924. In Correspondence of F. Scott Fitzgerald.* Edited by Matthew J. Bruccoli. Vol. 1. Columbia: University of South Carolina Press.

—. 1920. *Myra Meets His Family. In Flappers and Philosophers.* New York: Charles Scribner's Sons.

—. 2015. *The Beautiful And Damned.* New York: Signet.

—. 1945. *The King of the Jews. In The Crack-Up.* Edited by Edmund Wilson. New York: New Directions.

—. 1978. *The notebooks of F. Scott Fitzgerald.* Edited by Matthew Bruccoli. New York: Harcourt Brace Jovanovich.

Fitzgerald, Francis Scott. 1963. *The Letters of F. Scott Fitzgerald.* New York: Dell Publishing Co., Inc.

Floto, Otto. 1917. "A Letter From Sal." *San Francisco Call and Post*, November 27: 13.

Fort Wayne Journal Gazette. 1920. "It's a Bear." October 31: 9.

1917. "Freddie Welsh Tries Hand at Building Men." August 20: 4.

Gallimore, Andrew. 2005. *Email: Andrew Gallimore to*

Matthew Bruccoli. South Carolina University, August N/A.

—. 2006. *Occupation: Prizefighter / The Freddie Welsh Story*. Lancashire, United Kingdom: Revival Books Ltd .

Gerald, J. V. Fitz. 1918. "The Round-Up. Washington Post." *Washington Post*, November 9: 8.

Gerbasi, Thomas M. 2000. *Ring Ramblings: Tales of a Cyber Journalist*. San Jose: Writer's Club Press.

Gertz, Steven J. 2009. "Ernest Hemingway: Down For The Count." *Fine Books & Collections*, September.

Gettysburg Times. May 7, 1921. 1921. "About the Big Fight." May 7: 4.

Gravy. 1918. "Sportography." *El Paso Herald*, March 5: 9.

Gustkey, Earl. 1995. "This Champion Was a Real Bum." *New York Times*, June 25.

Hampton, Riley V. 1976. ""Owl Eyes in The Great Gatsby."." In *American Literature 48, no. 2*, 229. Durham: Duke University Press.

Handshaker, John. 1923. "Conscientious Worker Is Always Conscientious, As With Wild Jno Reilly!" *Casper Sunday Morning Tribune*, June 17: 4.

Harris, Gareth. 2004. *Freddie Welsh: World Champion Lightweight Boxer, Pontypridd Legend. Pontypridd*. Pontypridd: Coalopolis Publishing.

Harrisburg Telegraph. 1927. "Freddie Welsh Did Not Die Poor, His Brother Tells." August 1: 16.

Heller, Peter. 1994. *In this Corner…!* New York: Da Capo Press.

Hemingway, Ernest. 1953. *The Hemingway Reader*. New York: Charles Scribner's Sons.

Hill, Jeffrey. 2006. *Sport and the Literary Imagination: Essays in History, Literature and Sport.* Bern: Peter Lang AG International Academic Publishers.

Holt, Richard. 1990. *Sport and the Working Class in Modern Britain.* Manchester: Manchester University Press.

Honolulu Advertiser. 1927. "Sport Flashes." August 11: 9.

Honolulu Advertiser. 1922. "They're All the Same!" April 28: 4.

Hoosevelt, Theodore. 2020. *jack Dempsey Vs. Jess Willard 1919: The Most Brutal Fight In History.* March 14. Accessed January 27, 2022. https://historythings.com/jack-dempsey-vs-jess-willard-1919-brutal-fight-history/.

Hubbard, Elbert & Alice. 1915. *In Memorandum.* East Aurora: The Royrofters.

Hubbard, Elbert. 1914. "AJourney of Afirmation." *FRA*, September.

—. 1914. *The Fra*, October: xxxi.

Hudson Dispatch. 1971. "New York Governor Forced Fight to JC." July 2.

Huffington Post. 2013. "7 Life Lessons From 'The Great Gatsby'." September 24.

Iago, Hype. 1927. "Freddie Welsh, Ex-Champion Had Faith in Fellowships of Man." *Evening News, Wilkes-Barre*, July 30: 9.

2014. *Jack Dempsey vs. Luis Angel Firpo.* October 17. Accessed Februry 6, 2022. http://boxrec.com/media/index.php/Jack_Dempsey_vs._Luis_Angel_Firpo.

Johnson, Raymond. 1942. "Lew Jenkins Tossed Away

Chance To Be Wealthy." *Nashville Tennessean*, February 25: 10.

Kahn, Roger. 1999. *A Flame of Pure Fire: Jack Dempsey and the Roaring '20.* New York: Harcourt Brace & Company.

Lake Haptcong Breeze. 1920. "Freddie Welsh, Former Lightweight Champion of the World, Acts in the Movies with Hudson Maxim." August 14: 5.

Lardner, Ring. 1986. *he Best Short Stories of Ring Lardner.* London: Pan Books.

Laskow, Sarah. 2013. *Will the Real Great Gatsby Please Stand Up?* May 6. Accessed December 19, 2021. https://www.smithsonianmag.com/arts-culture/will-the-real-great-gatsby-please-stand-up-53360554/.

Lawrence, Jack. 1929. "Richard, Bom During Raid on James Boys, Lived Exciting Life." *Syracuse Journal*, January 8.

Leonard, Benny. 1921. "My Hardest Ring Battle." *Pittsburgh Times*, December 20.

Lewiston Daily Sun. 1927. "Health Farm Destroyed by Fire in New Jersey." October 12: 13.

Lieb, Frederick G. 1949. *The Story of the World Series: An Informal History.* New York: Putnum.

Lincoln Evening Journal. August 25, 1923. p. 7. 1923. "President Coolidge's Son Keeping in Trim in Training Camp with Freddie Welsh's Aid." August 25: 7.

Los Angeles Herald. 1915. "Boxing Alright for Freddie, Not for Son." August 12: 13.

Los Angeles Times. 1924. "Champion Burned Ex-lightweight." August 24: 12.

Los Angeles Times. 1927. "Freddie Welsh Honored." July 31.

Los Angeles Times. 1924. "Freddie Welsh is Chosen Instructor." July 1: 2.

Madison Eagle. 1920. "Freddie Welsh's Bear Dies at Famous Health Fam." July 23: 2.

Madison Eagle. 1925. "H. F. Barrett Represents Freddie Welsh in Suit." December 25: 7.

Madison Eagle. 1918. "Hudson Maxim Endorses Gov't Aero-plane Program at Welsh's Barbecue." June 7.

Malvern, Jack. 2007. "Old Sport, it Turns Out Gatsby was a prizefighting Welshman." *The London Times,* January 13.

Mangum, Bryant. 2017. *An Affair of Youth.* June 9. Accessed October 30, 2023. https://broadstreet.medium.com/an-affair-of-youth-3f699ead9f0a.

Matthew J. Bruccoli, ed.,. 1965. *Selected Letters of Ring Lardner.* New York: Charles Scribner's Sons.

Matthew J. Bruccoli, Editor. 1980. *Fitzgerald, F. Scott, and Zelda Fitzgerald. Correspondence of F. Scott Fitzgerald.* Random House.

McCrum, Robert. 2013. *Wodehouse and Fitzgerald – emblems of a lost age.* January 3. Accessed February 10, 2023. https://www.theguardian.com/books/booksblog/2013/jan/07/wodehouse-fitzgerald-lost-age. .

McGann, Sparrow. 1921. "Dempsey Not Training but Will Start Monday in Atlantic City Camp." *Great Falls Tribune Sun,* May 1: 12.

Mefford, Arthur. 1927. "Death Kayos Freddie Welsh: Ex

Champ Worn Out By Low Punches on Broadway." *Daily News*, July 29: 9.

Messenger, Christian. 1983. *Sport and the Spirit of Play in American Fiction.* New York: Columbia University Press.

2013. *Michael Struss Jacobs.* Accessed February 5, 2022. https://www.jewishvirtuallibrary.org/jsource/judaica /ejud_0002_0011_0_09907.html.

Milwaukee Journal. 1927. "Freddie Welsh Losses Summit Health Farm." ayy 3: 24.

Milwaukee Sentinel. 1917. "Freddie Welsh Tries Hand at Building Men." August 20.

Minneapolis Daily Star. 1923. "Jack Plays Santa to Birds." December 24: 9.

Mizener, Arthur. 1951. "F. Scott Fitzgerald: A Biography. The Atlantic. February 1951. ." *The Atlantic*, February.

Moving Picture World. 1921. "Pathe Gets Exclusive Rights to to Picture of Dempsey in Training." May 14: 180.

Murphy, Joe. 1913. "Fifty Rounds of Boxing--Wow!!" *San Francisco Call*, March 20: 9.

Murry R. Nelson, ed. 2009. *Encyclopedia of Sports in America: A History from Foot Races to Extreme Sports.* Westport: Greenwood Publishing Group.

New Castle News. 1918. "Feddie Welsh Will Help Wounded Soldiers." December 20: 20.

New Castle News. 1927. "Former Friends View Remains of Ex-champion." July 30: 14.

New Castle News. 1919. "Joe Chip Doesn't Know His Captain is Ex-Champion Boxer Freddie Welsh." January 28: 14.

New Castle News. 1921. "Two Knockouts for Fred Welsh." May 6: 23.

New Castle News. 1919. "Welsh Promoted to Captancy in U. S. Army." March 10: 12.

New York Evening Post. 1926. "Freddie Welsh is Sued." February 27: 2.

New York Times. 1921. "Arena is Largest Ever Constructed." June 26.

New York Times. 1920. "Carpentier Feted at I.S.C. Luncheon." September 15.

New York Times. 1920. "Carpentier Knocks Levinsky Out in the Fourth Round." October.

New York Times. 1921. "Champion Engages Two More Trainers." May 5.

New York Times. 1927. "Freddie Welsh Dies Jobless and Alone." July 29.

New York Times. 1917. "Freddie Welsh, Farmer." August 12.

New York Times. 1922. "Real Estate." September 15: 35.

New York Times. 1923. "Sailors to Engage in Finale Workouts." December 14.

New York Times. 1923. "Vincenti Plans Rest." December 16: 10.

New York Times. March. 1915. "Philadelphia Bouts Made Ring History." March 21: 3.

Newark Evening News. 1926. "Car Victim Starts Suit against Freddie Welsh." February 27: 7.

Newsroom, WCT. 2006. "The Man Who Was Gatsby?" *West Central Tribune*, July 12.

Niagara Falls Gazette. 1921. "Dempsey's Weakness Affection for Kids." June 1: 12.

Oakland Tribune. 1927. "Freddie Welsh Loses $200,000 Estate in Sale." May 11.

Oakland Tribune. 1920. "Freddie Welsh Stops an Unknown Boxer." December 29: 16.

Oakland Tribune. 1921. "Freddie Welsh Wins Decision over Forbes." August 18: 17.

Ogden Standard-Examiner. 1922. "Britton Is a 'Goner,' So, Welsh Believes." March 1: 11.

Ortiz, Martin Hill. 2022. *Champion by Ring Lardner.* Accessed December 5, 2022. http://martinhillortiz.blogspot.com/.

Ozanich, David. 2012. *The Great Gatsby's Gold Coast.* October 1. Accessed July 1, 2022. https://www.bbc.com/travel/article/20120926-the-great-gatsbys-gold-coast.

Pantagraph. 1918. "Prof. Freddie Welsh. Pantagraph. January 2, 1918. p. 5." January 2: 5.

Pantalone, Gene. 2016. *Madame Bey's: Home to Boxing Legends.* Bloomington: Archway Publishing.

Pearson, Ray. 1922. "Freddie Welsh Fails in Effort to Come Back." *Argus Leader*, April 15.

Perry, Lawrence. 1923. "Walter Hagen is Practical." *Richmond Item*, April 14: 5.

Philadelphia Inquirer. 1923. "First Northern Fight for Stribling." December 31: 10.

Pietrusza, David. 2011. *Rothstein: The Life, Times, and Murder of the Criminal Genius Who Fixed the 1919 World Series.* New York: Basic Books.

—. 2003. *Rothstein: The Life, Times, and Murder of the Criminal Genius Who Fixed the 1919 World Series.* New York: Carroll & Graf Publishers.

Pilgrim, John. 1925. "Watching the Parade." *Hamilton Daily News*, February 3: 6.

Pittsburgh Daily Post. 1919. "Freddie Welsh Charged with Satisfying Hunger on Ex-Manager's Ear." October 15: 4.

Play, Fair. 1923. "Gorgia Flash Busy Training in New Jersey." *Times Herald*, December 29: 13.

1920. "Press Photo. Summit, New Jersey."

Press, Associated. 1921. "Freddie Welsh Comes Back." *Harrisburg Telegraph*, May 4: 13.

—. 1969. "Walter Hagen Dies." *Nashua Telegraph*, October 6: 16.

—. 1925. "Sports Briefs." *Niagara Falls Gazette*, November 24: 23.

—. 1980. "Scribe Willie Ratner; Plimpton of His Time." *Sunday Register*, April 6: A4.

Ratner, Willie. 1969. "Ehsan's Training Camp on the Ropes." *Newark Evening News*, April 23.

—. 1942. "Punching the Bag." *Newark Evening News*, January.

Reading News-Times. 1918. "Freddie Welsh Booster for Boxing in Jersey." February 19: 8.

Richards, Alun. 1986. *Days of Absence.* London: Michael Joseph.

Richards, Alun. 2009. "Days of Absence." In *Dai Country*, by Dai Smith, 51. Cardigan: Parthian.

Riley, Martin Robson, and Martin Robson Riley email. 2021. *[LLGC Cymraeg] Freddie Welsh inscribe medal.* May 24.

Roberts, Randy. 2003. *Jack Dempsey: The Manassa Mauler.* Chicago: University of Illinois Press, .

Robertson, Stewart. 1938. "She Puts'em in the Pink." *The Family Circle*, October 7.

Ron Rapoport, Ed. 2017. *The Lost Journalism of Ring Lardner*. Edited by Ron Rapoport. Lincoln: University of Nebraska Press.

Ron Rapoport, editor. 2008. *The Portable Ring Lardner*. Penguin Classics.

Rosenblatt, Josh. 2019. "Why Are Writers Drawn to Boxing?" *Literary Hub*, March 14.

Runyon, Damon. 1921. "Dempsey's Green Suit Raises Ire of Pet Monk." *Mercer Sun-Star*, April 20: 7.

Ruse, Leslie. 2017. *Morristown presentation all about inventor Maxim*. March 22. Accessed January 13, 2022. https://www.dailyrecord.com/story/news/local/2017/03/22/morristown-presentation-inventor-maxim/99485958/.

Salazar, Marion T. 1918. "Freddie Welsh Wearing Overalls and Doing His Bit for Uncle Sam." *San Francisco Call and and Post*, June 25: 12.

San Antonio Evening News. 1921. "With the Pugs." July 11: 6.

San Francisco Call and Post. 1922. "'Wild Bill' Lyons, Famous Timekeeper and Pal of Jack Dempsey, Arrives for Visit." November 1.

San Francisco Call and Post. 1917. "Freddie Welsh Buys a Health Farm, But He Won't Quit Ring." April 4: 14.

San Francisco Call. 1911. "Champion Goes Under the Knife, but Rallies." November 30: 13.

Saratogian. 1924. "The Editor's Chair." July 5: 9.

Scranton Republican. 1921. "Dempsey Arrives in New

York City." April 15: 20.

Scranton Republican. 1921. "Dempsey Picks Out Training Quaters." April 20: 16.

Shapiro, Michael. 1978. "Focus." *Courier-News*, August 5.

Shay, Felix. circa 1917. *A Little Journey to the Fred Welsh Health Farm.* n/a: n/a.

Siki, Battling. 1922. *Siki, Battling. Battling Siki's Autobiography, as told to Milton Bronner. Bellingham, WA: .* Bellingham, WA: Belligham American.

Snyder, Dean. 1920. "Back to Fight." *Arizona Public Sun*, September 26: 3.

Sorg, Jeff. 1980. "Pro-Boxers Jogged Chatham Streets in the 1920's." *Chatham Township Independent*, October 8.

Springfield Missouri Republican. 1921. "Freddie Welsh Greeting Dempsey Who Is Peparing for Carpentier Battle." May 17: 7.

St. Louis Post-Dispatch. 1921. "Champion Takes Chances Posing for Cameramen." April 22: 29.

Stern, Bill. 2006. ". Freddie Welsh Documentary (Boxing Legend) film. Torpedo for BBC Wales, Presented by Trevor Fishlock."

Sugar, Bert Randolph. 1984. *The 100 Greatest Boxers of All Time.* New York: Bonanza Books.

Summit Herald. 1923. February 16: 10.

Summit Herald. 1921. "American Legion a Great Success-- 100 Attend." May 5: 7.

Summit Herald. 1918. "Arthur W. Prevost." September 27: 16.

Summit Herald. 1919. "Capt. Freddie Welsh Held."

October 17: 8.

Summit Herald. 1920. "Fireman's Carnival." June 25: 1.

Summit Herald. 1920. "Freddie Welsh Back in the Ring Game." April 30: 3.

Summit Herald. 1920. "Future Heavy Welght "Champ" Born Here." September 3: 2.

Summit Herald. 1918. "Motor Carn Burns." May 3: 1.

Summit Herald. 1917. "Notes of the City." June 22: 5.

Summit Herald. 1918. "Notes of the City." August 30: 9.

Summit Herald. 1918. "Notes of the City." September 27: 16.

Summit Herald. 1917. "Notes of the City." November 2: 10.

Summit Herald. 1947. "Remember When?" October 16: 6.

Sun And Globe. 1923. "10 Dempsey to Train at Summit, N. J." December 15.

Sun and New York Herald. 1920. "French Boxing Champ and His Bride." March 18: 10.

Sun. 1917. "Beaten Boxer Insists He Is Still Champion." May 29: 18.

Sunday Oregonian. November 5, 1916. p. 6. 1916. "The Odd Contrast of the Fighter and the Dancer." November 5: 6.

Sussman, Jeffrey. 2020. *Big Apple Gangsters: The Rise and Decline of the Mob in New York.* Lanham: Rowman & Littlefield.

Syracuse Journal. 1929. "Rickards Were Poor When Tex Was a Kid Back in Kansas City." January 9.

Tad. 1919. "Freddie Welsh Is There." *Washington Times,* June 30: 12.

—. 1922. "Welsh Trains Kansas for Leonard Bout."

Washington Times, January 31.

The Lord Is Passing by. 1915. "A Vegetarian." January: 31.

n.d. "Theme Of Boxing in The Great Gatsby." *Bartleby Research.* Accessed March 23, 2023. https://www.bartleby.com/essay/Theme-Of-Boxing-In-The-Great-Gatsby-PCATMXZWP6.

Thompson, Neal. 2013. *A Curious Man: The Strange and Brilliant Life of Robert "Believe It or Not!" Ripley.* New York: Three Rivers Press.

Time. 1927. "Sport: Death of Welsh." August 8.

Times-Leader. 1927. "Freddie Welsh Abandoned by Friends; Poor at Death." July 29: 23.

Troy Times. 1921. "Chronology of Dempsey-Carpentier Bout." July 2: 9.

Troy Times. 1924. "Tendler Still Under Suspension." July 30: 6.

Tucumcari News. circa 1918. "Freddie Welsh in Uniform. Tucumcari News. circa 1918."

Turnbull, Andrew. 1962. *Scott Fitzgerald.* New York: Charles Scribner's Sons.

Underwood, George B. 1921. "Dempsey Set for Campaign of Training." *Boston Post Sun*, April 24: 11.

—. 1923. "Decision Likely in Jersey Soon." *Evening Telegram—New York*, January 30: 10.

UPI. 2007. "Author Says Welsh Boxer Model for Gatsby." January 14.

Variety. 1927. "Freddie Welsh Died of a Broken Heart." August 3: 32-B.

Vreeland, W. C. 1923. "College Lad, Just 19, Hopes to Win the Heavyweight Title before He Gives up the Ring for a Career." *Brooklyn Daily Eagle*, December 30:

14 A.

Washington Herald. 1922. "Fight Notes." February 20: 9.

Washington Post. 1919. "Jack Dempsey Will Be Star of Boxing Bill for Soldiers." March 1: 10.

Washington Times. 1918. "Freddie Welsh Now Lieutenant M. R. C." November 5.

Washington Times. 1919. "Walter Reed's Wounded Will See Jack Dempsey." February 17: 11.

Welsh, Freddie. 1923. "Former Champ Knocks Out Rugged Foe in Professional Fight." *Star Tribune Sun*, February 25: 4.

—. 1923. "Former Champion Becomes Physical Culture Instructor." *Star Tribune Sun*, March 4: 4.

—. 1923. "Life of Former Lightweight Ring Champion Full of Disappointments." *Star Tribune Sun*, February 18: 4.

Williams, Joe. 1927. "As Joe Williams Sees It." *Pittsburgh Press Sun*, June 12: 6.

Willis J. Abbot, Silas Bent, Mosses Koenigsberg. 1928. "Mr. Mosses Koenigsberg." *The Press*, January 21: 8.

Winnipeg Tribune. 1923. "Easiest Fight too Win, Leonard's Hardest." October 26: 18.

Wodehouse, P.G. 1913. "Keeping it from Harold." *The Strand*, December 1.

Worthpoint. 2021. *HOME > WORTHOPEDIA®.* Accessed December 10, 2021. https://www.worthpoint.com/worthopedia/1916-freddie-welsh-lightweight-1697327950.

Yonkers Statesman. 1924. "Bernstein Primed for Zivic Battle." July 21: 10.

Endnotes

Chapter I

[1] Freddie Welsh, "Life of Former Lightweight Ring Champion Full of Disappointments," *Star Tribune Sun*, February 18, 1923, 4.
[2] Elbert & Alice Hubbard, *In Memorandum*, (East Aurora: The Roycrofters, 1915), 350.
[3] Felix Shay, *A Little Journey to the Fred Welsh Health Farm*, Circa 1917, 6.
[4] Joe Murphy, "Fifty Rounds of Boxing—Wow!!," *San Francisco Call*, March 20, 1913, 9.
[5] "Prof. Freddie Welsh," *Pantagraph*, January 2, 1918, 5.
[6] Elbert Hubbard, *The Fra*, October 1914, xxxi.
[7] Felix Shay, *A Little Journey*, 1.
[8] "News of the Fights and Fighters," *Brooklyn Daily Eagle*, December 30, 1921, 2A.

Chapter II

[1] Gareth Harris, *Freddie Welsh: World Champion Lightweight Boxer, Pontypridd Legend*, (Pontypridd: Coalopolis Publishing, 2004), 2.
[2] Freddie Welsh, "Life of Former Lightweight Ring Champion Full of Disappointments," *Star Tribune Sun*, February 18, 1923, 4.
[3] Welsh, "Life of Former Lightweight Ring Champion," 4.
[4] Welsh, "Life of Former Lightweight Ring Champion," 4.
[5] Welsh, "Life of Former Lightweight Ring Champion," 4.
[6] Welsh, "Life of Former Lightweight Ring Champion," 4.
[7] Welsh, "Life of Former Lightweight Ring Champion," 4.
[8] Welsh, "Life of Former Lightweight Ring Champion," 4.
[9] Welsh, "Life of Former Lightweight Ring Champion," 4.
[10] Welsh, "Life of Former Lightweight Ring Champion," 4.
[11] Gravy, "Sportography," *El Paso Herald*," March 5, 1918, 9.
[12] Welsh, "Life of Former Lightweight Ring Champion," 4.
[13] Welsh, "Life of Former Lightweight Ring Champion," 4.
[14] Welsh, "Life of Former Lightweight Ring Champion," 4.
[15] Welsh, "Former Champ Knocks Out Rugged Foe," 4.
[16] Welsh, "Life of Former Lightweight Ring Champion," 4.

[17] Welsh, "Former Champ Knocks Out Rugged Foe," 4.
[18] Welsh, "Former Champ Knocks Out Rugged Foe," 4.
[19] Welsh, "Former Champ Knocks Out Rugged Foe," 4.
[20] Welsh, "Former Champ Knocks Out Rugged Foe," 4.
[21] Welsh, "Former Champ Knocks Out Rugged Foe," 4.
[22] Welsh, "Former Champ Knocks Out Rugged Foe," 4.
[23] Welsh, "Former Champ Knocks Out Rugged Foe," 4.
[24] Welsh, "Former Champ Knocks Out Rugged Foe," 4.
[25] Welsh, "Former Champ Knocks Out Rugged Foe," 4.
[26] Welsh, "Former Champ Knocks Out Rugged Foe," 4.
[27] Welsh, "Former Champ Knocks Out Rugged Foe," 4.
[28] Welsh, "Former Champ Knocks Out Rugged Foe," 4.

Chapter III

[1] Freddie Welsh, "Former Champ Knocks Out Rugged Foe in Professional Fight," *Star Tribune Sun*, February 25, 1923, 4.
[2] Welsh, "Former Champ Knocks Out Rugged Foe," 4.
[3] Welsh, "Former Champ Knocks Out Rugged Foe," 4.
[4] Freddie Welsh, "Former Champion Becomes Physical Culture Instructor," *Star Tribune Sun*, March 4, 1923, 4.
[5] Gravy, "Sportography," *El Paso Herald*," March 5, 1918, 9.
[6] Freddie Welsh, "Former Champion Becomes Physical Culture Instructor," 4.
[7] Welsh, "Former Champion Becomes Physical Culture Instructor," 4.
[8] Welsh, "Former Champion Becomes Physical Culture Instructor," 4.
[9] Rodney G. Dalton, "The Story of Captain Davis Dalton," 2022, https://www.daltondatabank.org/Chronicles/Davis_Dalton.htm.
[10] Welsh, "Former Champion Becomes Physical Culture Instructor," 4.
[11] Welsh, "Former Champion Becomes Physical Culture Instructor," 4.
[12] Welsh, "Former Champion Becomes Physical Culture Instructor," 4.
[13] Welsh, "Former Champion Becomes Physical Culture Instructor," 4.
[14] Mike Casey, "Fast Freddie: Why Welsh Was a Wonder. East Side Boxing. News Archives," August 11, 2011, https://www.boxing247.com/weblog/archives/134469.
[15] Casey, "Fast Freddie."
[16] "Freddie Welsh in Uniform," *Tucumcari News*, circa 1918.
[17] Sean Davies, "Freddie Welsh," April 11, 2002, http://news.bbc.co.uk/sport2/hi/boxing/1901425.stm.
[18] "A Vegetarian," *The Lord Is Passing by*, January 1915, 31.

19 "Champion Goes Under the Knife, but Rallies," San Francisco Call, November 30, 1911, 13.
20 "Champion Goes Under the Knife," 13.
21 "Champion Goes Under the Knife," 13.

Chapter IV

1 Matthew Joseph Bruccoli, *Some Sort of Epic Grandeur: The Life of F. Scott Fitzgerald (2nd rev. ed.)*, (Columbia: University of South Carolina Press, 2002), 213-214.
2 David Pietrusza, *Rothstein: The Life, Times, and Murder of the Criminal Genius Who Fixed the 1919 World Series*, (New York: Basic Books, 2011), 268.
3 Jack Malvern. Old Sport, it Turns Out Gatsby was a prizefighting Welshman. *The London Times*. January 13, 2007.
4 Pietrusza, *Rothstein: The Life, Times*, 424.
5 Peter Heller, *In this Corner...!*, (New York: Da Capo Press, 1994), 26.
6 Bert Randolph Sugar, *The 100 Greatest Boxers of All Time*, (New York: Bonanza Books, 1984), 119.
7 Ed Van Every, "Welsh, Former Champion, Who Died of Broken Heart, One of Game's Best Boxers," *St. Louis Post-Dispatch*, July 29, 1927, 15.
8 Jeffrey Sussman, *Big Apple Gangsters: The Rise and Decline of the Mob in New York*, (Lanham: Rowman & Littlefield, 2020).
9 Pietrusza, *Rothstein: The Life, Times*, 235.
10 Ron Rapoport, Ed., *The Lost Journalism of Ring Lardner*. (Lincoln: University of Nebraska Press, 2017), 265.
11 Pietrusza, *Rothstein: The Life, Times*, 242.
12 Mike Casey, "Fast Freddie: Why Welsh Was a Wonder. East Side Boxing. News Archives," August 11, 2011, https://www.boxing247.com/weblog/archives/134469.
13 Ritchie Loses His Title to Welsh in 20-Round Go. *Day*. July 8, 1914. p. 9.
14 Heller, *In this Corner...!*, 27-28.
15 Heller, *In this Corner...!*, 27-28.
16 Bill Stern. Freddie Welsh Documentary (Boxing Legend) film. Torpedo for BBC Wales, Presented by Trevor Fishlock. 2006.
17 Andrew Gallimore, Email, Andrew Gallimore to Matthew Bruccoli, South Carolina University, August, 2005.
18 Louis A. Dougher, "Looking 'Em Over," *Washington Times*, March

19, 1919, 16.

[19] Dougher, "Looking 'Em Over," 16.

[20] Andrew Gallimore, Email, Andrew Gallimore to Matthew Bruccoli, South Carolina University, August, 2005.

[21] "The Odd Contrast of the Fighter and the Dancer," *Sunday Oregonian*, November 5, 1916, 6.

[22] Freddie Welsh, "Former Champion Becomes Physical Culture Instructor," 4.

[23] "Boxing Alright for Freddie, Not for Son," *Los Angeles Herald*, August 12, 1915, 13.

[24] Freddie Welsh, "Former Champion Becomes Physical Culture Instructor," 4.

Chapter V

[1] "Philadelphia Bouts Made Ring History," *New York Times*," March 21, 1915, 3.

[2] Shay, *A Little Journey*, Circa 1917, 9.

[3] "Freddie Welsh, Boxer, Buys $60,000 Estate for Home and Training Farm," *New York Herald*, March 26, 1917.

[4] Otto Floto, "A Letter from Sal," *San Francisco Call and Post*," November 27, 1917, 13.

[5] "Freddie Welsh Buys a Health Farm, But He Won't Quit Ring," *San Francisco Call and Post*, April 4, 1917, 14.

Chapter VI

[1] Willis J. Abbot, Silas Bent, Mosses Koenigsberg, *The Press*, January 21, 1928, 8.

[2] "Easiest Fight to Win, Leonard's Hardest," *Winnipeg Tribune*, October 26, 1923, 18.

[3] Benny Leonard, "My Hardest Ring Battle," *Pittsburgh Times*, December 20, 1921.

[4] "Easiest Fight to Win," 18.

[5] "Easiest Fight to Win," 18.

[6] Leonard, "My Hardest Ring Battle."

[7] "Easiest Fight to Win," 18.

[8] "Easiest Fight to Win," 18.

[9] Leonard, "My Hardest Ring Battle."

[10] "Easiest Fight to Win," 18.

---

[11] Leonard, "My Hardest Ring Battle."

[12] Leonard, "My Hardest Ring Battle."

[13] Leonard, "My Hardest Ring Battle."

[14] Van Every, "Welsh, Former Champion," 15.

[15] Leonard, "My Hardest Ring Battle."

[16] Leonard, "My Hardest Ring Battle."

[17] "Beaten Boxer Insists He Is Still Champion," *Sun*," May 29, 1917, 18.

[18] "Sorry for Welsh," *Sun*, May 29, 1917, 18.

Chapter VII

[1] Otto Floto, "A Letter From Sal," *San Francisco Call*, November 27, 1917, 13.

[2] Shay, *A Little Journey*, Circa 1917, 11.

[3] Shay, *A Little Journey*, Circa 1917, 7.

[4] Andrew Gallimore, *Occupation: Prizefighter: Freddie Welsh's Quest for the World Championship*, (Lancashire: Revival Books Ltd, 2006), 309.

[5] "Christie's Lot 233 / Sale 8299," *Christie's Auction.* November 30, 1999. http://www.christies.com.

[6] Shay, *A Little Journey*, Circa 1917, 11.

[7] Shay, *A Little Journey*, Circa 1917, 13-14.

[8] Shay, *A Little Journey*, Circa 1917, 15.

[9] Shay, *A Little Journey*, Circa 1917, 15.

Chapter VIII

[1] Shay, *A Little Journey*, Circa 1917, 17, 19, 21, 23.

[2] "Notes of the City," *Summit Herald*, November 2, 1917, 10.

[3] Leslie Ruse, "Morristown presentation all about inventor Maxim," *Daily Record*, March 22, 2017, https://www.dailyrecord.com/story/news/local/2017/03/22/morristown-presentation-inventor-maxim/99485958/.

[4] "Freddie Welsh an Excellent Host," *Chatham Press*, June 8, 1918, 9.

[5] "Hudson Maxim Endorses Gov't Aero-plane Program at Welsh's Barbecue," *Madison Eagle*, June 7, 1918, 13.

[6] "Freddie Welsh an Excellent Host," 9.

[7] "Freddie Welsh an Excellent Host," 9.

[8] Marion T. Salazar, "Freddie Welsh Wearing Overalls and Doing His

Bit for Uncle Sam," *San Francisco Call and Post*, June 25, 1918, 12.

Chapter IX

[1] "Welsh Health Farm Incorporated," *Chatham Press*, November 9, 1918, 1.

[2] "Freddie Welsh, Once Champ Boxer, Now Buck Private," *Akron Evening Times*, September 25, 1918, 10.

[3] Hype Iago, "Freddie Welsh, Ex-Champion Had Faith in Fellowships of Man," *Evening News, Wilkes-Barre*, July 30, 1927, 9.

[4] J. V. Fitz Gerald, "The Round-Up," *Washington Post*, November 9, 1918, 8.

[5] "Joe Chip Doesn't Know His Captain is Ex-Champion Boxer Freddie Welsh," *New Castle News*, January 28, 1919, 14.

[6] "Walter Reed's Wounded Will See Jack Dempsey," *Washington Times*, February 17, 1919, 11.

[7] Tad. Freddie Welsh Is There. *Washington Times*. June 30, 1919, 12.

[8] Theodore Hoosevelt, "Jack Dempsey Vs. Jess Willard 1919: The Most Brutal Fight In History," March 14, 2020. https://historythings.com/jack-dempsey-vs-jess-willard-1919-brutal-fight-history/.

[9] "Freddie Welsh Back in the Ring Game," *Summit Herald*, April 30, 1920, 3.

[10] "Freddie Welsh Charged with Satisfying Hunger on Ex-Manager's Ear," *Pittsburgh Daily Post*, October 15, 1919, 4.

[11] "Freddie Welsh let Go by Court," *Detroit Free Press*, October 22, 1919.

Chapter X

[1] "Freddie Walsh [sic] Says That He Will Be Back," *Evening Report*, March 6, 1920, 5.

[2] "It's a Bear," *Fort Wayne Journal Gazette*, October 31, 1920, 9.

[3] "Freddie Welsh, Former Lightweight Champion of the World, Acts in the Movies with Hudson Maxim," *Lake Hopatcong Breeze*, August 14, 1920, 5.

[4] John Pilgrim, "Watching the Parade," *Hamilton Daily News*, February 3, 1925, 6.

[5] Pilgrim, "Watching the Parade," 6.

6 "Carpentier Feted at I.S.C. Luncheon," *New York Times*, September 15, 1920.

7 "Carpentier is Here to Fight," *Evening Telegram—New York*, September 1920.

8 "Carpentier to Train in Chatham," *Chatham Press*, September 18, 1920, 4.

9 "Carpentier Feted at I.S.C. Luncheon,"

10 "Georges Carpentier. What Georges and "Bat" had to Say To-day," *Syracuse Journal*, 1920.

11 "Freddie Welsh Stops an Unknown Boxer," *Oakland Tribune*, December 29, 1920, 16.

12 James J. Corbett, "Welsh's Comeback Would be Contrary to History," *Fort Wayne News and Sentinel* , January 10, 1921, 12.

Chapter XI

1 Roger Kahn, *A Flame of Pure Fire: Jack Dempsey and the Roaring '20s*, (New York: Harcourt Brace & Company, 1999), 237.

2 "Chronology of Dempsey-Carpentier Bout," *Troy Times*, July 2, 1921, 9.

3 "1916 FREDDIE WELSH LIGHTWEIGHT CHAMPION POCKET WATCH," 2021, https://www.worthpoint.com/worthopedia/1916-freddie-welsh-lightweight-1697327950.

4 Warren W. Brown, "Cyclone Bill Lyons Grants Interview," *San Francisco Call and Post*, March 11, 1921, 18.

5 Damon Runyon, "Dempsey's Green Suit Raises Ire of Pet Monk," *Mercer Sun-Star*, April 20, 1921, 7.

6 "'Wild Jno.' Here to Do Best He Can," Casper *Sunday Morning*, June 10, 1923, 1.

7 John Handshaker, "Conscientious Worker Is Always Conscientious, As With Wild Jno Reilly!," *Casper Sunday Morning Tribune*, June 17, 1923, 4.

8 Runyon, "Dempsey's Green Suit," 7.

9 Runyon, "Dempsey's Green Suit," 7.

10 Runyon, "Dempsey's Green Suit," 7.

11 Runyon, "Dempsey's Green Suit," 7.

12 George B. Underwood, "Dempsey Set for Campaign of Training," *Boston Post Sun*, April 24, 1921, 11.

13 Underwood, "Dempsey Set," 11.

14 "Champion Takes Chances Posing for Cameramen," *St. Louis Post-*

Dispatch, April 22, 1921, 29.

[15] "Freddie Welsh Greeting Dempsey Who Is Preparing for Carpentier Battle," *Springfield Missouri Republican*, May 17, 1921, 7.

[16] Underwood, "Dempsey Set," 11.

[17] Underwood, "Dempsey Set," 11.

[18] Underwood, "Dempsey Set," 11.

[19] Underwood, "Dempsey Set," 11.

[20] Henry L. Farrell, "Dempsey Having Fine Time Over in New Jersey," *Freeport Journal-Standard*, April 28, 1921, 10.

[21] Underwood, "Dempsey Set," 11.

[22] Underwood, "Dempsey Set," 11.

[23] Underwood, "Dempsey Set," 11.

[24] Underwood, "Dempsey Set," 11.

[25] Underwood, "Dempsey Set," 11.

[26] Underwood, "Dempsey Set," 11.

[27] "Leonard May Box Welsh for Title in Rickard Arena," *St. Louis Post Dispatch*, April 26, 1921, 19.

[28] Henry L. Farrell, "Welsh Will Have Chance at Title, *Trenton Evening Times*, January 29, 1920, 21.

[29] Henry L. Farrell, "Dempsey Resting on Jersey Farm," *Freeport Journal-Standard*, April 28.

[30] Farrell, "Dempsey Having Fine Time," 10.

[31] Henry L. Farrell, "Kearns Says Dempsey is Only 'Playing Around' in Jersey," *Norwalk Hour*, April 29, 1921, 19.

[32] Farrell, "Kearns Says Dempsey," 19.

[33] Farrell, "Kearns Says Dempsey," 19.

[34] Farrell, "Kearns Says Dempsey," 19.

[35] Sparrow McGann, "Dempsey Not Training but Will Start Monday in Atlantic City Camp," *Great Falls Tribune Sun*, May 1, 1921, 12.

[36] "Latzo Training for Harmon Bout," *Courier News*, June 15, 1926, 17.

[37] "About the Big Fight," *Gettysburg Times*, May 7, 1921, 4.

[38] Henry L. Farrell, "Training for the Fight," *Daily Republican*, July 1, 1921, 5.

[39] "About the Big Fight," 4.

[40] Randy Roberts, *Jack Dempsey: The Manassa Mauler*, (*Chicago*: University of Illinois Press, 2003), 120.

Chapter XII

[1] David Ozanich, "The Great Gatsby's Gold Coast: BBC," October 1, 2012. https://www.bbc.com/travel/article/20120926-the-great-gatsbys-gold-coast.

[2] "Britton Is a 'Goner,' So, Welsh Believes, *Ogden Standard-Examiner*, March 1, 1922, 11.

Chapter XIII

[1] Ray Pearson, "Freddie Welsh Fails in Effort to Come Back, *Argus Leader*, April 22, 1922.

[2] "They're All the Same!," *Honolulu Advertiser*, April 28, 1922, 4.

[3] "They're All the Same!," 4.

[4] "Real Estate," *New York Times*, September 15, 1922, 35.

Chapter XIV

[1] Andrew Turnbull, ed. *The Letters of F. Scott Fitzgerald.* (New York: Scribner, 1963), 221-222.

[2] George B. Underwood, "Decision Likely in Jersey Soon," *Evening Telegram—New York*, January 30, 1923, 10.

[3] Lawrence Perry, "Walter Hagen is Practical," *Richmond Item*, April 14, 1923, 5.

[4] John Berry, "During the Roaring 20s, Walter Hagen Was a Sporting Icon in Post World War I America," *Lake County Record Bee,* May 9, 2020.

[5] Associated Press, "Walter Hagen Dies," *Nashua Telegraph*, October 6, 1969, 16.

[6] Willie Ratner, "Punching the Bag," *Newark Evening News,* January 1942.

[7] "President Coolidge's Son Keeping in Trim in Training Camp with Freddie Welsh's Aid," *Lincoln Evening Journal*, August 25, 1923, 7.

[8] Peter Benson, Battling Siki: *A Tale of Ring Fixes, Race, and Murder in the 1920s*, (Fayetteville: University of Arkansas Press, 2006), inside dust jacket.

[9] Thomas M. Gerbasi, *Ring Ramblings: Tales of a Cyber Journalist,*

(San Jose: Writer's Club Press.
2000), 185.
[10] Michael Shapiro, "Focus," *Courier-News*, August 5, 1978.
[11] Willie Ratner, "Ehsan's Training Camp on the Ropes," *Newark Evening News*, April 23, 1969.
[12] Willie Ratner, "Ehsan's Training Camp on the Ropes,".
[13] Willie Ratner, "Ehsan's Training Camp on the Ropes,".
[14] The story of Madame Bey is documented in the book *Madame Bey's: Home to Boxing Legends*.

Chapter XV

[1] "Sailors to Engage in Finale Workouts," *New York Times*, December 14, 1923.
[2] M. G. Callaghan, "Kayo Would Not Disturb Her, Say's Stribling's Ma," *Brooklyn Daily Eagle*, December 30, 1923, 14 A.
[3] Callaghan, "Kayo Would Not Disturb Her," 14 A.
[4] Callaghan, "Kayo Would Not Disturb Her," 14 A.
[5] Callaghan, "Kayo Would Not Disturb Her," 14 A.

Chapter XVI

[1] "Freddie Welsh is Chosen Instructor," *Los Angeles Times*, July 1, 1924, 2.
[2] "Freddie Welsh, Former Boxer, Fights Fire in New Providence," *Courier News*, August 25, 1924, 13.
[3] "Champion Burned Ex-lightweight," *Los Angeles Times*, August 24, 1924, 12.
[4] Payment Made on Mortgage, Adjourn Sale on Welsh Farm. *Chatham Press.* September 20, 1924, p. 1.

Chapter XVII

[1] Andrew Gallimore, Email, Andrew Gallimore to Matthew Bruccoli, South Carolina University, August, 2005.
[2] Alun Richards, *Days of Absence*, (London: Michael Joseph, 1986), 32.
[3] Josh Rosenblatt, "Why Are Writers Drawn to Boxing?," *Literary Hub*, March 14, 2019.

[4] "Ernest M. Hemingway," 2023.
https://www.poetryfoundation.org/poets/ernest-m-hemingway.

[5] Ernest Hemingway, *The Hemingway Reader*, (New York: Charles Scribner's Sons, 1953), 571.

[6] Sean Crose, "Hemingway, Fitzgerald & The Round That Went On Too Long," *The Fight City*, December 22, 2022, https://www.thefightcity.com/hemingway-fitzgerald-and-the-round-that-went-on-too-long/.

[7] Matthew J. Bruccoli, Edited by. Fitzgerald, F. Scott, and Zelda Fitzgerald. Correspondence of F. Scott Fitzgerald. Random House, 1980.

[8] Matthew Bruccoli, Email, Matthew Bruccoli to Andrew Gallimore, South Carolina University, August 22, 2005.

[9] Arthur Mizener, "F. Scott Fitzgerald: A Biography," *The Atlantic*, February 1951, 72.

[10] Mizener, "F. Scott Fitzgerald: A Biography." 72.

[11] Mizener, "F. Scott Fitzgerald: A Biography." 72-73.

[12] Mizener, "F. Scott Fitzgerald: A Biography." 72-73

[13] Riley V. Hampton, "Owl Eyes in The Great Gatsby," *American Literature*, Vol. 48, No. (Durham: Duke University Press, 1976), 229.

[14] Frederick G. Lieb, *The Story of the World Series: An Informal History* (New York: Putnam, 1949), 137.

[15] Jeffrey Hill, *Sport and the Literary Imagination: Essays in History, Literature and Sport*, (Bern: Peter Lang AG International Academic Publishers, 2006), 136.

[16] Robert McCrum, "Wodehouse and Fitzgerald – emblems of a lost age," January 3, 2013. https://www.theguardian.com/books/booksblog/2013/jan/07/wodehouse-fitzgerald-lost-age.

[17] Andrew Turnbull, *Scott Fitzgerald*, (New York: Charles Scribner's Sons, 1962), 127.

[18] Richard Holt, *Sport and the Working Class in Modern Britain*, (Manchester: Manchester University Press, 1990), 215-216.

[19] Turnbull, *Scott Fitzgerald*, 128.

[20] Christian Messenger. *Sport and the Spirit of Play in American Fiction*. (New York, Columbia University Press, 1983).

[21] Matthew J. Bruccoli, "A Literary Friendship," November 7, 1976, https://archive.nytimes.com/www.nytimes.com/books/00/12/24/specials/fitzgerald-lardner.html?source=post_page--------------------------&fbclid=IwAR0AX4V5g2rDHPydECwYTuUxi2yPAR_GWo4caVay NCicKLzyF85XcktlkkA. A Literary Friendship.

[22] P.G. Wodehouse. Keeping it from Harold. *The Strand*. December 1, 1913.

[23] Robert McCrum, "Wodehouse and Fitzgerald – emblems of a lost age," January 3, 2013. https://www.theguardian.com/books/booksblog/2013/jan/07/wodehouse-fitzgerald-lost-age.

[24] Ron Rapoport, Ed., *The Lost Journalism oof Ring Lardner*. (Lincoln: University of Nebraska Press, 2017).

[25] Ring Lardner, *The Best Short Stories of Ring Lardner*, (London: Pan Books, 1986), 113.

[26] Bruccoli, "A Literary Friendship."

[27] Bruccoli, "A Literary Friendship."

[28] "Car Victim Starts Suit against Freddie Welsh," *Newark Evening News*, February 27, 1926, 7.

[29] "Car Victim Starts Suit against Freddie Welsh," 7.

[30] "H. F. Barrett Represents Freddie Welsh in Suit," *Madison Eagle*, December 25, 1925, 7.

[31] "Freddie Welsh in Auto Accident," *Bernardsville News*, November 6, 1924, 5.

[32] Mizener, "F. Scott Fitzgerald: A Biography." 73.

[33] Andrew Turnbull, ed. *The Letters of F. Scott Fitzgerald*. (New York: Scribner, 1963), 195-196.

[34] Turnbull, ed. *The Letters of F. Scott Fitzgerald*, 195-196.

[35] Mizener, "F. Scott Fitzgerald: A Biography." 73.

[36] Mizener, "F. Scott Fitzgerald: A Biography." 73.

[37] Bruccoli, "A Literary Friendship."

[38] "H. F. Barrett Represents Freddie Welsh in Suit," 7.

[39] "Car Victim Starts Suit against Freddie Welsh," 7.

[40] "Freddie Welsh Sued," *Asbury Park Evening Press*, February 27, 1926, 2.

[41] Gallimore, *Occupation: Prizefighter*, 337.

Chapter XVIII

[1] (Ginger), Roland Hulme, "What can F. Scott Fitzgerald teach us about writing?," August 26 2022, https://www.hiddengemsbooks.com/what-f-scott-fitzgerald-teaches-about-writing/.

[2] Sarah Laskow, "Will the Real Great Gatsby Please Stand Up?," May 6, 2013. https://www.smithsonianmag.com/arts-culture/will-the-real-great-gatsby-please-stand-up-53360554.

[3] Laskow, "Will the Real Great Gatsby Please Stand Up?."

[4] Laskow, "Will the Real Great Gatsby Please Stand Up?."

[5] Laskow, "Will the Real Great Gatsby Please Stand Up?."

[6] Richard Holt, *Sport and the Working Class in Modern Britain*, (Manchester: Manchester University Press, 1990), 215-216.

[7] Matthew Bruccoli, Email, Matthew Bruccoli to Andrew Gallimore, South Carolina University, August 22, 2005.

[8] Mizener, "F. Scott Fitzgerald: A Biography." 73.

[9] UPI, "Author Says Welsh Boxer Model for Gatsby," January, 14, 2007.

[10] Laskow, "Will the Real Great Gatsby Please Stand Up?."

[11] Laskow, "Will the Real Great Gatsby Please Stand Up?."

[12] Laskow, "Will the Real Great Gatsby Please Stand Up?."

Chapter XIX

[1] "Freddie Welsh Died of a Broken Heart, *Variety*, August 3, 1927, 32-B.

[2] "Freddie Welsh Loses $200,000 Estate in Sale," *Oakland Tribune*, May 11, 1927.

Chapter XX

[1] Joe Williams, "As Joe Williams Sees It," *Pittsburgh Press Sun*, June 12, 1927, 6.

[2] "Freddie Welsh Abandoned by Friends; Poor at Death," *Times-Leader*, July 29, 1927, 23.

[3] "Freddie Welsh Dies in Poverty," *Burlington Free Press*, July 29, 1927, 12.

[4] "Freddie Welsh Dies in Poverty," 12.

[5] "Freddy Welsh Shunned by All He Aided Says His Wife," *Every Evening—Wilmington, Delaware*, July 29, 1927, 18.

[6] "Freddy Welsh Shunned," 18.

[7] "Sport: Death of Welsh," *Time*, August 8, 1927.

[8] "Freddie Welsh Dies Jobless and Alone," *New York Times*, July 29, 1927.

[9] "Freddie Welsh, Idol of Boxing, Dies in Solitude," *Brooklyn Daily Eagle*, July 29, 1927, 2A.

[10] "Freddy Welsh Shunned," 18.

[11] "Freddie Welsh Dies in Poverty," 12.

[12] "Freddy Welsh Shunned," 18.
[13] "Freddie Welsh Abandoned," 23.
[14] "Freddie Welsh Abandoned," 23.
[15] "Freddie Welsh Abandoned," 23.
[16] "Freddie Welsh Dies in Poverty," 12.
[17] "Former Friends View Remains of Ex-champion," *New Castle News*, July 30, 1927, 14.
[18] "Freddie Welsh Did Not Die Poor, His Brother Tells," *Harrisburg Telegraph*, August 1, 1927, 16.
[19] "Freddie Welsh Did Not Die Poor," 16.
[20] Van Every, "Welsh, Former Champion," 15.
[21] Van Every, "Welsh, Former Champion," 15.
[22] Arthur Mefford, "Death Kayos Freddie Welsh: Ex Champ Worn Out By Low Punches on Broadway," *Daily News*, July 29, 1927, 9.
[23] Hype Iago, "Freddie Welsh, Ex-Champion Had Faith in Fellowships of Man," *Evening News, Wilkes-Barre*, July 30, 1927, 9.
[24] "Fighters, 'Palookas' Pay Tribute to Fallen Champion," *Constitution*, July 30, 1927, 10.
[25] "Fighters, 'Palookas'," 10.
[26] "Freddie Welsh Gets Military Funeral Today," *Daily News*, July 30, 1927, 21.
[27] "Former Friends View Remains of Ex-champion," 14.
[28] "Freddie Welsh Honored," *Los Angeles Times*, July 31, 1927.
[29] "Freddie Welsh Gets Military Funeral Today," 21.

Epilogue

[1] "Remember When?," *Summit Herald*, October 16, 1947, 6.
[2] Jeff Sorg, "Pro-Boxers Jogged Chatham Streets in the 1920's," *Chatham Township Independent*, October 8, 1980.

www.ingramcontent.com/pod-product-compliance
Lightning Source LLC
Chambersburg PA
CBHW070404310726

48977CB00003B/553